WHO COULD BE MAN ENOUGH FOR
MARIANNE OLIVER?
WHO COULD COMPETE WITH HER BRILLIANCE
AND BEAUTY?

THREE MEN WOULD TRY . . .

TOBY HANSFORD

He turned his back on his powerful family to make Marianne his own. But even he couldn't protect her from the wrath of his parents' revenge. . . .

GREGORY WINDHAM

Financial wizard and notorious ladies' man, his empire spanned the globe. Only a woman like Marianne could challenge him in the bedroom and the boardroom. . . .

BRADFORD YOUNG

His Ivy League charm and loyal friendship masked a passionate heart. Marianne thought she knew her darling Brad so well – until she had to face the real man. . . .

CHINA SILK

Gripping drama . . . great entertainment

FLORENCE HURD

CHINA SILK

Futura

A Futura Book

First published in the United States of America
in 1986 by Ballantine Books, a division of
Random House, Inc., New York

This edition published in Great Britain in 1988 by
Futura Publications, a Division of
Macdonald & Co (Publishers) Ltd
London & Sydney

ISBN 0 7088 3609 7

Reproduced, printed and bound in Great Britain by
Hazell Watson & Viney Limited
Member of BPCC plc
Aylesbury Bucks

Futura Publications
A Division of
Macdonald & Co (Publishers) Ltd
Greater London House
Hampstead Road
London NW1 7QX
A member of Maxwell Pergamon Publishing Corporation plc

PROLOGUE

"**W**HAT IS IT?" WHISPERED THE CAUTIOUS VOICE.

"Hors d'oeuvres. You can't have been in China very long if you've never had *léng pán*."

"They've disguised it."

"But how beautifully served!"

The diners were speculating over a platter of cold meats, shredded vegetables, and minced quail eggs arranged in the form of a large colorfully winged butterfly.

"This restaurant is such a lovely place. Don't you agree, Marianne?"

"Yes—yes, I do."

To Marianne, the unusual dining pavilion gave the illusion of floating on water. One of the many teahouses scattered about the gardens of Liewan Lake, it nevertheless seemed isolated, unconnected to anything as ordinary as a restaurant, even a dining establishment as illustrious as the Ban Xi. Eating houses in China, even those serving world-class food, were often austere. To the natives, edifying cuisine, not decor, was the main purpose of a restaurant. But the Cantonese, unique in

1

many ways, prided themselves in presenting their diners with exotic surroundings both indoors and out, often setting their *fànguǎrs* among rustling bamboo groves, giant, junglelike ferns, flowering vines, and feathery palms, interspersed here and there by little pagodas with up-swept eaves.

Such was the Ban Xi. A wonderful place to let go and relax. What more could anyone ask than a beautiful setting, good company, delicious food, and a nonstop flow of *mao tai*, the crystal-clear Chinese liquor that exploded like dynamite on the unsuspecting palate, turning grumpies into happies in just a few sips?

But Marianne couldn't relax. Nerves that had tied themselves into knots refused to become undone. The *mao tai* warmed her cheeks and gave her a mild buzz, but it did nothing to ease the tight muscles at the back of her neck or the ache behind her eyes.

Her gaze went past the assembled guests to the scene outside the sliding glass doors where the black, watery surface reflected the glow of colored lanterns. Strung along a narrow causeway and across a wooden bridge, they rimmed the still lake, festooning lichee, camphor, and persimmon trees. The Cantonese night was soft, languorous, the kind of tropical night that should tranquilize the troubled mind. But though she tried, Marianne could not curb her inner anxiety. Her thoughts kept racing from one supposition to the next, reviewing events, scrutinizing casual remarks and conversations for a clue she might have missed.

Who was working to destroy what she had so painstakingly planned to accomplish here in China?

It hurt. It hurt to think that people you trusted . . .

Suddenly a chair scraped, jarring Marianne to attention.

"Quiet! Quiet!" A handsome, lean-jawed man in his mid-forties rose to his feet, tapping for order with his chopsticks. "Let's have a little quiet, please."

The people seated at the round table paused in their chatter.

"I want to propose a toast." He raised his glass. "To our guest of honor, Madam President of Casey Corporation, a beautiful and brilliant lady, the best thing that ever happened to that outfit—take my word for it. Wait! I'm not done! *Please!* To a gal who's an unqualified ten and a real winner, who means much to me and to all of us. Happy birthday, Marianne Oliver!''

The salute was taken up with enthusiasm as glasses clinked.

"Cheers!"

"I'll drink to that!"

"To Marianne!"

"Gambei! Gambei!" Mr. Lu and his two Chinese colleagues shouted, draining the fiery *mao tai* in one draft, twirling their empty glasses over their heads.

Laughter and a round of hearty applause.

Marianne, in a peacock-blue silk molded and draped to her slim figure, precious white jade at her throat and ears, mouthed a thank-you, smiling at the eleven guests gathered to celebrate her thirty-sixth birthday.

She tried to make the smile sincere. Only she knew it was forced. A fake. Lips curved up over white teeth, a pleasant glint to the eye. Adversity had taught her that. Smile. Grin that phony grin even though you hate it. "Thank you," she murmured again.

Who? Who in this circle of cheering well-wishers was willing to discredit her and possibly destroy her career? She couldn't be sure. Strong suspicions, but no certainties. Someone not only was leaking vital Casey information to the Chinese with whom she was negotiating but was also slandering her as an ineffectual if not untrustworthy trading partner. Who was here at the Ban Xi exuberantly trumpeting happy birthday while secretly working to cut the ground from under her feet?

Who? Not the three Chinese. They were strangers, pragmatic businessmen who bore her no ill will.

She looked around the table at the flushed faces, the sober ones. Could she be wrong? These past three weeks had been grueling ones; she could simply be suffering from nerve-racking stress. Stress made you irrational, suspicious, paranoid. Yet in this business dirty tricks were part of the game. It was who got there first with the most that counted. And what of the people here tonight who weren't directly connected to Casey, the people with whom she had personal relationships? In the heat of anger even a trusted friendship could change to animosity and betrayal.

Was she dramatizing?

Her eyes ticked her guests off again: her lover, the host of this elaborate Chinese banquet, his warm looks sending messages of intimacy; her dear, longtime college friend, raising his glass once more in silent tribute; her mother, nodding in approval; her loyal and dedicated secretary; her silk expert and his little wife, beaming at her; and her ex-in-laws, enemies years ago, but since regretful and wanting to make up for past unkindnesses. Not everyone at this gala affair tonight might be a one-hundred-percent-for-Marianne booster, but wasn't it a little extreme to imagine a Judas among them?

There was a sudden burst of applause and cries of "Hear! Hear!"

The red-jacketed waitresses had brought in three large platters of what appeared to be dumplings.

"Bake 'n' serve rolls," someone joked.

"We have those in the States. It just looks different here. It's *dim sum*."

"It means 'to touch the heart,' " Mr. Lu offered.

How poetic, Marianne thought, "to touch the heart." Assuming everyone has a heart to touch. Do I still have one? Or has ambition taken me beyond feeling—as my friend accused the other day? I've had to learn how to put up a cool front, but it doesn't mean that I can't hurt like hell behind it. It doesn't mean that I'm never lonely or afraid or that I'm incapable of giving and receiving love.

She had come to China so confident, so sure of success. Deplaning in a muggy April Cantonese afternoon weeks ago, driving down the gray-green tree-lined streets thronged with pedestrians and bicycles, past little doll-like schoolchildren in crocodile queues, remarking on the squatting peasants bargaining over cabbages and fish, she had been certain her personal life was under control, sure that the raw silk contract she wanted would—after patient negotiation—be hers. It was the same confidence that had taken her up the managerial ladder to the presidency of Casey and, she hoped, would take her even higher, to the boardroom of Casey's giant holding company, Billings.

But something had gone wrong. She had not anticipated reopening the scarred-over wound of an old bitterness toward her mother, nor had she expected the explosive confrontation with her daughter, the painful, accusatory anger of her best friend, or her sudden doubt about the man she loved. The thought of possible failure with the Chinese had never occurred to her. Now the deal that had seemed close enough to grasp was inexplicably slipping away. The once-friendly Chinese had turned strangely chilly and aloof, hinting at Casey's insolvency, quoting figures they could have learned only from a Casey insider.

Who? How were the Chinese getting their information? She wasn't sure; she didn't know.

There was still a chance to turn the Chinese around— slim, but a chance. She'd work it out somehow. She'd have to. She had gone through worse battles and had come out victorious. And this time . . .

"Speech," a ring of lit-up, half-tipsy faces and wildly clapping hands demanded. "Speech!"

"Stand up, Marianne, and give us a speech!"

"Tell it like it is!"

"Yes, yes!"

"C'mon, don't be bashful!"

Marianne rose slowly, her smile in place. "Thank you, thank you. This reminds me of testimonial dinners we have at home. Only the food and the surroundings and the guests . . ." she said, bowing to the Chinese, "are far superior. First of all, I want to thank our host for this honor. His generosity"—she touched the jade at her throat, a perfectly matched string, its luster testifying to its worth—"as we all know, is legend. And the rest of you who have been kind enough to bring gifts." She motioned to the little heap of cards and beribboned packages on a side table which she hadn't opened yet. "You have no idea how much I appreciate your warm wishes. I thank you all from the bottom of my heart."

When Marianne sat down, the heat of the *mao tai* stinging her cheeks, she had a sudden eerie feeling. Perhaps it was the liquor, but she had the sensation that she was looking at the whole scene from an objective distance: the round table with its crimson cloth, the lacquered chopsticks, the scoop-shaped soup spoons, the porcelain rice bowls, the colored glass windows on the far wall throwing shards of white and green light on the tiled floor. In her mind's eye she saw herself, Marianne Oliver, a slim young woman in blue silk, with light brown hair, cut and styled to bring out its natural wave, a straight nose, and gray-blue eyes, sitting among a group of people in a floating pavilion that looked out on a dark, exotic landscape.

And then her inner sight seemed to shift to another plane where everything suddenly became familiar, background voices chattering in a foreign tongue, the distant plunk of an *er hu*, the pungent odor of spices, of ginger and soy. The brush painting on the wall, a misty river scene with a cormorant bending its beak to the shadowy water, the carved, lacquered screen in the corner somehow seemed impressed on a dark fold of her brain. It was a strange sensation, an elusive feeling of déjà vu. She had been here before, or somewhere similar, and something was about to happen; some distant, approaching storm was about to break.

Don't be ridiculous, she told herself. She didn't believe in such superstitious nonsense. She had come to China to negotiate a contract. There were hitches, and her nerves were edgy. And she had certainly seen enough Chinese paintings to make cormorants and misty mountains familiar. Why the feelings of déjà vu?

But later she would understand how the mind can distort memory—how the child can retain infantile impressions without a knowledge of their source. And she would come to see how her quest for China silk—the rich, glamorous fabric reeled from the cocoon of the drab moth, its creation a secret held closely by Chinese emperors for centuries, fought over and died for since ancient times and now proving elusive of her own grasp—would serve as a catalyst not only for her career but for making a final peace with her past.

CHAPTER I

Marianne Oliver was born in Canton, China.

When she was six months old, Mao Zedong entered Peking at the tail end of his Liberation Army and changed the course of history for one-fourth of the world's population. After the mad rout of the "foreign devils" in Shanghai and its subsequent fall in May of '49, it was a foregone conclusion that Canton would be next. Marianne's parents, William and Sarah Oliver, teachers at the old Lingnam University (now Zhong Shan) did not panic. The Chinese had a traditional respect for scholars, and the Olivers were much revered for their academic dedication. Both had been born in China, William Oliver of a father whose small inheritance had allowed him to establish his family in Shanghai, where he pursued his study of Chinese literature, Sarah of people who taught at the Shanghai American School. Though educated in, and declared citizens of, the United States, William and Sarah considered China their real home.

Even when tales radiating out from the north told of flight, internment, and execution, the Olivers refused to be alarmed. Nevertheless, when urged by their physician and close friend, Dr. Chen, to send their infant daughter to safety, the Olivers finally agreed. They were certain that the upheaval would soon quiet down. Once the new government was established they would be able to bring Marianne back to Canton. Future events proved them wrong on both counts.

But in the meanwhile Marianne, wrapped in a bright, quilted blanket and wearing an inexpertly crocheted pink bonnet on her small head, was carried aboard a steamer standing by at Huangpu in the Pearl River. The Hallisters, her temporary guardians and missionary friends of the Olivers, would deliver Marianne halfway across the world to Passaic, New Jersey, into the care of Robert and Emma Parker, cousins of William's.

Marianne, of course, remembered nothing of these historic events or her flight from Canton. A spotty account was given to her later by the Parkers, who, in turn, had it told to them by missionaries. But Marianne herself had no conscious memory of the typhoon that nearly swamped their ship as it crossed the Pacific, the humid passage by way of the Panama Canal, or the dusty train ride from New Orleans. Nor could she recall the Parkers' astonishment as they accepted the bundle delivered into their arms. Emma, looking down at the trusting face under its pink bonnet, now soiled and unraveling, was less than thrilled with this unasked-for gift, while Robert exclaimed in an awed voice, "A baby!"

Marianne's earliest recollection was of being cradled and rocked in warm arms, the rocker squeaking in rhythm to the vibrant tone of a low, sweet voice.

Sleep, baby, sleep.
Thy father watches the sheep.
Thy mother is shaking the dreamland tree
And down falls a little dream on thee.

Years later, when asked, Emma said she couldn't for the life of her place that lullaby. "Must have got it from a book," she claimed.

*   *   *

Most of what Emma knew about infants came from a book, for like Marianne, she, too, had been foisted on childless relatives—two middle-aged spinster sisters, Betsy and Violet—whose staunch Methodism left no choice but to accept their new responsibility as God's will, though they might wish God had willed otherwise. Living on a meager annuity left by their father, the Burnham sisters considered the arrival of Emma, one more mouth to feed, a rather stringent test of their devotion to the Almighty.

Emma, unlike her aunts, did not believe Marianne's arrival was a sign of God's will. It was an imposition thrust upon her by two strangers who resided half a world away. She resented Marianne's intrusion. The tidy house was hers, Robert, warts and all, was hers, and she didn't want to share them!

If only Robert wasn't so *taken* with Marianne, she thought, I could tolerate the child a great deal more. But whenever he held Marianne in his arms, his face glowed the way it hadn't done for *her* since their courtship bird-watching days when she had spotted a rare limpkin. She was jealous, plain jealous.

She hid it, of course. One, because she still had enough of the aunts' Ten Commandments ground into her to feel that envy, especially of a baby, was a sin. Two, because she wanted to please Robert, even if it meant playing Mom to this newcomer.

It was a role that did not come easily to Emma. Her snapping voice, the brusqueness, tempered now and then with sympathy, was confusing to the child.

"Bad girl!" scolded Emma as four-year-old Marianne inadvertently knocked over a bowl of eggs on Emma's newly waxed kitchen floor. "See what you've done! Six eggs wasted, my floor ruined. Do you know what eggs cost? Well, do you? Why do you have to be so clumsy? Don't just stand there. *Say* something."

Marianne, her eyes slowly filling with tears, gazed up at Emma. Mute, helpless, begging to be forgiven.

The flush died on Emma's cheeks. "All right," she

sighed. "I suppose it can't be helped. Here, now, don't cry. What are all those tears for? Aunt Emma has a cookie for you. A nice chocolate cookie. Take it." A quick hug, a kiss on the top of the head. "There, now we've made up. Give Aunt Em a kiss."

But if Emma was unpredictable, blowing hot and cold, Robert was a constant. Marianne's presence gave him pleasure. During Marianne's infancy Robert brought home stacks of books from the library on child rearing. He had taught Emma how to diaper the baby, how to make her formula, when and how to feed her. In the evenings and on weekends Robert had taken over these tasks himself. He had loved the wee fist that clung to his thumb, the little smile that quirked her rosebud mouth, the gray eyes that looked up at him so trustingly.

When Marianne was old enough Robert would take her on long walks, pointing out the birds, the trees and flowers, naming them for her, answering her childish questions as soberly as he would a grown person's. Marianne loved those outdoor excursions, her hand in Uncle Bob's big paw, his long, thin face looking down at her with affectionate patience.

Unlike other parental adults, Robert did not think it necessary to banish Marianne from the room when he and Emma discussed their problems or those of their neighbors. "No secrets from our little friend," he'd say. They spoke freely in her presence. The realities of the world outside were matters Robert felt Marianne had a right to hear about and, if she wished, to comment upon.

Bob, honest to the point of painfulness, never pretended to Marianne that he and Emma were her real parents. They were always Aunt Em and Uncle Bob. As soon as Marianne was able to understand—or Bob thought she was able—he explained that her own father and mother were in China and assured her that in time they would come for her. To Marianne this amazing revelation became a source of wonder mingled with suspense. She would lie awake at night trying to imagine what her mother and father looked like. She had no pictures, only Uncle Bob's rather hazy description of her father, a tall man with a shock of brown hair, and her mother, fair with a dimpled smile that displayed beautiful white teeth.

At school, Marianne looked up Canton on the map of China in her geography book, a black, meaningless dot on a pink, green, and yellow patchwork of oddly named provinces. She studied the photograph of a Chinese family on the opposite page, mother and father, a boy and a girl, with their dark almond-shaped eyes, the pitch-black hair. They were nothing like her or the parents she had created in her daydreams. Her mother and father became very real to her. Any day, she imagined, she'd be getting a letter from them saying they were leaving Canton, heading for New Jersey. "We can hardly wait to see you, and how you've grown," they would write. "Going into the third grade already! And the best reader in your class!"

Or maybe they would make their arrival a surprise, appearing on the doorstep one late afternoon with a blaze of golden sun behind them, Papa tall and Mama smiling. How many times she went through that meeting, her inventive mind embellishing it with kisses and hugs and everybody crying because they were so happy. In her fantasy she had the Olivers deciding to remain in New Jersey, setting up housekeeping with the Parkers, the five of them under the same roof, one big family, living happily ever after.

There were long stretches when she did not think about them at all. At other times they would invade her dreams and she would find herself running to meet them. Waking, her anticipation sharpened by the dream, she would think that surely today, tomorrow, the day after at the latest, the longed-for letter would arrive.

As the years went by and Marianne grew older her expectations dwindled. She longed to hear from them, a few sentences, a note, a card on her birthday or at Christmas. She wanted Sarah and William to acknowledge her existence, to break the silent denial.

One evening shortly after Marianne's twelfth birthday, Robert came home from work, got into his slippers, and, sinking down into his favorite chair with the mail,

said, "Ah, here's something from the Hallisters. They're
the folks who brought you over from China," he added,
glancing at Marianne over his reading glasses.

She pulled up a velour footstool and sat at his feet,
her arms prickling with excitement. " 'Course I know
the Hallisters. What do they say? Oh, read it, read it!"

"I never said anything because I didn't want you to
get your hopes up, but for some time I've been writing
to churches and missionaries trying to locate them." He
tore the envelope open. "I thought they might have
some news of your mummy and daddy."

She clasped her knees tightly. "Hurry! Please, hurry,
Uncle Bob."

He shook a thin page of cheap stationery out and,
readjusting his glasses, read:

Dear Mr. Parker:

We are sorry we could not have answered your letter
sooner. Information from China is almost impossible
to obtain since Mao has shut the country down.
We have so many friends who are still there about
whom we are concerned. We've written time and again
but have heard nothing. We did come across one small,
rather garbled report from a Reverend Hardy who
claims the Olivers are still in Canton, but we have
no way of affirming this.

Hoping you and your dear wife are well. Our best
to Marianne. I wish we could do more for her.
We appreciate how anxious she must be. We pray
daily for the safety of those we left behind.

Your servants in God,
John and Esther Hallister

Marianne's disappointment was so keen she couldn't
speak. Tears hung on her lashes. Her small face seemed
to have shrunk. Robert leaned over and kissed her cheek.
"We mustn't give up hope, Sis."

"Yes, Uncle Bob," she replied obediently.

He watched with compassion as she slowly left the room to go up and wash for dinner.

A few minutes later as Marianne descended the stairs, she overheard Emma speaking to Robert. "You should have told her they died."

"I know. The lie would have been a kindness. But they may be able to get some word to her yet."

"I doubt it. By this time they've probably forgotten all about her."

"No!" Marianne cried, stumbling on the last step, rushing into the living room. "No! They haven't! They haven't forgotten me! I don't believe it. I won't!"

"There now, love," Robert soothed as she burst into a storm of sobs. He took her in his arms. "Of course they haven't forgotten. Take my handkerchief. That's a good girl. Now blow."

Emma left the room in silence."

Marianne wiped her nose and her eyes. "The Hallisters said China was shut down, didn't they, Uncle Bob?" she cried. My mom and dad could have written scads of letters that never got here."

"That's very possible, Sis."

"I'm still their little girl, aren't I, Uncle Bob?" she asked, looking up at him with anxious eyes.

"Of course you are."

Marianne went on waiting, writing to her parents' last address in Canton pages of carefully composed script which, once mailed, seemed to drop into some cosmic dead-letter box. Maybe Aunt Emma is right, she began to think. Maybe her folks had forgotten all about her.

Her disillusionment, though it ran deep, was tempered by Bob's continuing reassurance and by Emma's periodic, inexplicable bursts of affection. Emma, when she chose, could be a surprisingly fierce champion.

One episode stood out in Marianne's mind. She had come home weeping because two girls from her class, having discovered she had been born in China, teased her by singing, "Chinaman, chink, where's your pigtail, fink?" Marianne, fighting mad, had slapped and punched one of the girls. The pair had then ganged up on her, throwing her to the ground and tearing her new sweater. To add to her humiliation, a group of children stopped to watch the fight, a ring of scuffed shoes and knobby knees, laughing down at her.

When Emma heard this her face turned a blotched red. "What's their names? I want to know their names and where they live!" she demanded, thrusting her arms into her coat and ramming on her hat. "You're every bit as good, if not better than those brats. I'm going to see they get the whipping they deserve. And they'll pay for your sweater or I'm not Emma Parker."

"Oh, Aunt Em!" Marianne impulsively threw her arms about Emma.

"Let go, Marianne. I haven't got time for that now."

It was this contradictory behavior that Marianne found hard to deal with. Often on her walks with Uncle Bob she would complain. "Why does Aunt Em love me one minute, then hate me the next?"

"She doesn't hate you, darling. You mustn't mind her moods. She's had a hard life."

Still Marianne kept trying. She wanted Aunt Em to love her but couldn't seem to find the right formula. With Uncle Bob it was easy. It took so little to make him smile, to have him pat her on the head, say, "That's my Marianne." When she brought her school report home with all As, except for math, which was A+, he beamed. "Not many girls do well in math. Sis, you're a whiz."

In junior high, Marianne became very competitive, head of the debating team, winner of the city-wide spelling bee, the top of her class as a freshman in Beaufort High. She went out for girls' hockey, played the cornet in the school band, and yet had no close friends. Even as a child she wasn't encouraged to bring her classmates home. "Go out in the yard to play," Emma would instruct, though it might be ten above. Or "I just finished scrubbing the bathroom. Maybe Ida's mother won't mind if you go over there." Or "Jenny left mud marks on my rug. Can't you go to *her* house?" Marianne was too embarrassed to keep going to *her* house when she couldn't invite back.

She grew into a lovely girl, tall, willowy, her gray eyes with their flecked irises set under winged brows a shade darker than her light brown hair. Her popularity with boys was hamstrung by two things: Emma's horror stories of girls who had let boys "take liberties"—a hand on the breast was the sure road to rape and/or pregnancy—and Uncle Bob's strict rules. In by ten-thirty on school nights, by eleven on weekends. Impossible! A movie didn't let out until ten!

Marianne cried, begged, stormed. For the first time in her life she actually hated Robert. But he was adamant. "You were entrusted to our care and if we're strict it's for your own good."

"You know what boys want, especially at this age, Marianne," Emma said. "Wait until you're older and you find the right young man. A decent person with a good future."

Who cared about decent? She wanted to tell Mick Farrell it was okay to French kiss her, not pull away, that it was okay to squeeze her tight, to maybe feel her breast. She wanted to be held, to be stroked. Marianne wanted to experience those forbidden things her girlfriends giggled and sighed about.

In her senior year Marianne, encouraged by Uncle Bob, applied for scholarships at several universities. "I'd gladly foot the whole bill if I could afford it, Sis. I'll help you all I can, pocket money and books or whatever. You've got too good a mind to stop now."

Six months before graduation Marianne won her scholarship to Cornell University. There, with an impetuosity that surprised even her, she had her first love affair and met, among others, Bradford Young, a tall, skinny redhead who soon became her closest friend.

"You know," she was fond of telling Brad long after they both had left the university, "Cornell was the turning point of my life."

"Mine, too," he would concur, though he had never had the courage to tell her that his turning point was meeting her.

CHAPTER II

THEY HAD BEEN SO YOUNG THEN, MARIANNE BARELY NINE-
teen, Brad four months older, both into their second
year at Cornell. She sat across from him in Math 3066,
legs crossed, her lovely profile tilted. Wearing blue jeans
and an orange T-shirt, her long, silky corn tassel hair
tied back with a black ribbon, she seemed by far the
prettiest girl he had seen on campus. When she turned
and caught him staring she smiled, a quick impish grin
that made her gray eyes dance. That's all it took. Brad
had known even then that something momentous had
happened to him.

They fell into the habit of meeting two or three times a
week at Willard Straight's. Brad found talking to Marianne pleasurable as long as he kept the conversation
on a friendly plane. It was when he tried to make
faint moves toward a man/woman relationship—how's
about dinner, a movie, a little dancing?—that she became somewhat distant. She and her jock boyfriend Sam
were always doing something in the evening. Sam this
and Sam that. Brad didn't want to hear about Sam. He

17

had seen them together once, walking across campus. Just the back of Sam; athletic, broad shoulders, blond hair, a real fraternity jock.

So he talked about math, about Oriental Religion and Philosophy, a course they had both taken from the same professor but at different times. He was surprised to learn that Marianne had been born in China, that her father and mother were still there.

"Have they tried to get out?"

"No," she said, turning her head for a brief moment. "I don't think they want to."

"What about letters?"

"I've written, they've never answered. They sent me to Uncle Bob's and Aunt Em's when I was a baby—and not a word since."

"It's been pretty turbulent over there with Mao's Great Leap Forward," he said carefully.

"Oh, I think they're still alive," she said quickly. "The missionaries who brought me over heard just last summer from friends that the Olivers were thought to be living in Fonshan—that's close to Canton." It had been the second letter the Hallisters had written to Uncle Bob and it had devastated Marianne more than the first.

"Mail being what it is, Marianne . . ."

"The Hallisters get letters."

"And that bothers you? It must."

"Not too much." She gave him a trembly smile. "What about your folks?" she asked, eager to change the subject.

"There isn't a whole lot to say." He spoke of his father's addiction to horse racing, making a little joke of it, his mother's penchant for a little now-and-then klepto-mania. "She's really a dear. Eccentric, not dotty, as the English would say." He talked about his favorite sister, Ginny, who had married a Madison Avenue ad man, "a very nice guy," and who would be getting her BA from NYU in the spring.

In a surprisingly short time they became good friends, confiding in each other, telling each other little incidents of their childhood, painful and amusing episodes they had never really talked about with anyone else. Marianne opened up on the subject of her parents, confessing that she still felt hurt at their long silence. They discussed future plans. Brad was thinking of switching from math to physics. Marianne, even if she did get married (to Sam, she implied), planned to go on for her MBA. "Uncle Bob thinks I'd make a super business executive. I'm not so sure about the super or even the executive bit. There aren't many women at the top, you know. But I'd like to get involved in some kind of manager-type job, one that isn't routine."

They were sitting over mugs of coffee at Straight's when Marianne said, "You know, Brad, I always wanted a brother." She reached over and squeezed his big freckled hand. "I'm not going to embarrass you by making a sentimental speech. But as far as I'm concerned, you're it."

Brad felt both elated and dismayed.

He had inherited his mother's red hair and his father's bony frame. And his charming smile. Without it he would have been just another homely kid, the kind girls would pass over after a first glance. In college, he'd had his share of meaningless fumbles in bed. But with one or two exceptions—hardly notable—he'd forgotten the names and faces of these girls. Marianne he would never forget. "What happens if I fall for you?" he said. "I mean, like in love."

"Oh, Brad, you're kidding. You won't." The gray eyes looked at him earnestly. "You *are* kidding. It would ruin everything, because I don't think—I mean, I couldn't—not in that way. You aren't . . . ?"

"No."

What was he supposed to say? I love you and I don't give a damn about being your brother? But he was afraid that would be goodbye, that what he had now—and treasured—would be lost.

And, of course, there was Sam.

It was after they had returned from spring vacation and Marianne was absent from class twice in a row that he called her. Her roommate said she was ill and wasn't seeing anyone.

Nevertheless, Brad, armed with a few branches of lilac blossoms he had plucked from someone's back yard and wrapped in a newspaper, went out to the apartment on Turkey Hill Road where she lived with three other girls.

One of her roommates, a tall, thin grad student whose name—Elsie Dobbs—and pedigree—top drawer Rochester—Marianne had mentioned several times, opened the door. Elsie glared at him.

"I'm Brad," he said. "I'd like to see Marianne."

"You can't. She's . . ."

"Who is it?" Marianne called.

"It's me." Brad stepped into a living room so small he had the inclination to duck his head and pull in his arms.

The roommate shrugged, picked up her books, and left, slamming the door behind her.

Brad found Marianne in bed. She was propped up on the pillows wearing an old, ragged yellow sweater over her nightgown. Her eyes were red-rimmed and puffy.

"Hello, Brad," she said tonelessly.

"Got a cold?" he asked cheerfully, sitting on the opposite twin bed. He held the wrapped lilacs out. "Something for you."

She bent her head and inhaled, then looked up at Brad, the gray eyes clouding with tears. "Thank you. That's sweet. The lilacs, I mean." A tear spilled over. She wiped it away with the back of her hand. "I haven't got a cold," she confessed.

"What's wrong?" he ventured tentatively.

She shook her head. "It's—it's Sam. He . . ." She sniffed loudly and reached for a Kleenex. "He's engaged."

Brad suppressed a smile. It wasn't funny. Marianne was hurting. Poor kid. "But I thought . . ."

"So did I. I thought we were in love. He told me so. And I let him . . . He was the first one. I mean I went to bed with him. Can you believe I was a virgin? I never even went partway, but Sam . . . He had such beautiful manners and knew how to treat a girl to make her feel special, and he talked as if we had some kind of future together. God, I must be the biggest chump in the world." A fresh batch of tears trickled down her cheeks.

"You're not a chump, Marianne. Do you think you're the first person who's been taken in by a lot of bull? What happened?"

She blew her nose. "Seems like he's had this other girl all along. She's at Sarah Lawrence. His family and hers have known each other for ages and she . . ." Marianne bit her lip. "He says he still loves me. But Clarissa—that's her name, wouldn't you know?—Clarissa will make the kind of wife he needs to further his career. She's got all these important connections. Her uncle is a senator—and who am I? Plain Marianne from Passaic whose Aunt Em fries the best jelly doughnuts on Grover Street." She covered her face and began to sob.

He went and sat beside her, taking her in his arms. He patted her head, feeling the shape of it beneath the silky hair. "You're the most beautiful girl I've ever met. Don't call yourself plain or put yourself down."

Looking up at him, she pushed a damp strand of hair from her forehead. "I can handle a lot of things. Not having money or nice clothes, tough going in class, even a B grade, but when people I love turn their backs on me, I guess I freak out. That's stupid, isn't it? Trying to analyze myself with a lot of psychobabble."

"No one likes being ditched, Marianne. But I still love you."

He wanted to kiss her, was on the verge when she threw her arms around him. "Oh, Brad, what would I do without you?"

He unwound her arms. "Tell you what. Get dressed. I'll wait. You remember Toby?" He had casually introduced his friend, Toby, to Marianne early on in their friendship. "Well, Toby and his girlfriend Sabrina and I are going to a basketball game tonight and you're coming with us. Don't shake your head. I won't take no for an answer."

If Brad had known that Toby and Sabrina had had one of their cat-and-dog fights that day and that Toby would

show up without her, if he had guessed that Marianne,
who swore on the way over that she was down on men
for the rest of her life, would shortly change her mind,
he never would have brought the two together. But they
met. And the rest seemed to follow a preordained destiny.

Marianne's first impression of Toby, she admitted to
Brad, was that he appeared to be a darker version of
Sam: handsome, self-confident, and definitely not in the
penny-pinching class. Toby handled money with the kind
of casual indifference habitual to people who never had
to debate whether they should choose the $5.95 liver
and onions on the menu or the $6.95 chopped steak. To
Marianne, Toby's yellow cashmere and Gucci loafers
spelled rich. Was he?

Well, yes, Brad had to concede. Afraid that Marianne
might be a little more interested in Toby than she seemed,
he wanted to add a few uncomplimentary, if not damning, remarks about his friend, but he couldn't. Not with
a clear conscience. He liked Toby. They had been good
friends for years. Toby was a warm human being, intelligent, amusing, and generous to an embarrassing fault.
When Brad's father had died and Brad was thinking
of quitting college Toby had tried to lend him money,
a loan which Brad refused because he knew Toby would
never accept repayment. And Brad would always remember how a year earlier Toby had bailed him out of
jail, coming down at two in the morning, a one-man
rescue team, shaking his head, grinning, because he
never expected good old Brad to become involved, even
peripherally, in a drunken brawl. He had called Toby
because he knew Toby would come through. He was
that kind of guy.

How Toby got that way was a mystery to anyone who
knew his parents, Ed and Dorothy Hansford. Edward
had inherited millions from his father, James Hansford II, who had been left *his* money by Hansford I,
a sea captain who was believed to have engaged in
illicit rum running during Prohibition. The truth was
less romantic. Captain Hansford had made his bundle by

buying up slum tenements which he knew—by way of inside tips—were to be cleared for highway construction. Toby's father inherited this fat legacy and had parlayed it into a tidy fortune through real estate deals. He was a stiff man, formal, not given to small talk or pleasantries, his handsome dark looks unnoticed because of his wooden expression. He rarely smiled.

Dorothy was a second cousin, a girl who had nothing to commend her but a pretty face, impeccable manners, and an elegant taste for clothes. As Mrs. Hansford she developed a snobbery that parted her from her former friends and endeared her to her new ones, who loved to gossip about the nouveau riche over lunch at the Russian Tea Room. Brad often felt that she had a large ice cube where her heart should have been. But this was not strictly true. In her own cool way she loved her husband. She was fond of the children, too—but at a distance. Dorothy's main ambition was that Toby and Hazel should both make "suitable marriages." She was pleased when on a visit to England Hazel caught the eye of a young man who was the great-nephew of a duke. For Toby she had picked Sabrina Donaldson, the daughter of one of her Russian Tea Room cronies, an auburn-haired beauty, moneyed, with a pedigree that went back (so the family claimed) to Peter Stuyvesant.

Sabrina had a reputation for bed-hopping bordering on nymphomania, a not-too-well-kept secret about which the Hansfords obviously knew nothing. A spoiled, vivacious girl, she had seduced Bradford the summer he was seventeen while he was staying at the Hansfords.

He had never told Toby about it. He was too ashamed.

CHAPTER III

MARIANNE SAID SHE WASN'T READY TO GET INVOLVED with another man so soon after Sam. Whenever she thought of their last meeting she turned sick with hurt and rage. He had not only shafted her with the news about his engagement—and with such aplomb, no apology, no "sorry, dear"—but he had also had the arrogance to assume they would go on as before.

Why had she thought herself so madly in love with Sam in the first place? What had she seen in that muscle-bound, self-important, blond nobody to allow him to lead her so docilely to bed?

Well—not so docilely, she remembered.

Leaving Passaic and coming up to Cornell had been like entering Wonderland. Situated on the crest of a hill overlooking Cayuga Lake, with deep gorges cut by streams and waterfalls, the University was an antipode away from Beaufort High and its utilitarian cement environs. At Cornell she was offered so many choices it made her head swim. Interesting courses to take, new people to meet, absorbing things to do. Above all she felt the exhilaration of being on her own. She was free. No need to keep her dresser drawers on alert for inspection or to guard against dirty fingerprints on doorknobs or light switches. She didn't have Aunt Em glaring at her because she came home with her lipstick smeared and Uncle Bob giving her a lecture each time she was ten minutes late. All of Marianne's roommates were on the Pill and having torrid romances with perfectly wonderful men.

Marianne couldn't help but feel that until now she had been a ward under house arrest and that suddenly by some stroke of good fortune she had been released from protective custody. Liberated, she nevertheless had been aware of her inexperience.

She had been ashamed to confess she was still a virgin. But Sam had fixed all that. She had met him at a freshman dance and he had been the first man to take her out, wining and dining her in a style that no high school kid back home could have measured up to. He had sent her potted marguerites, called her "love," oozed masculinity. And she had all these vague yearnings, a need to love and be loved, to give herself in passion to a real man.

Sam's attentiveness, it proved, had been an act. Sam loved only Sam. She had been nothing to him but an easy lay.

But Toby was another matter.

She dated him the first Saturday night after they had met. They went dancing and when he left her that night he kissed her softly on the cheek, then tentatively on the lips.

He called her again. While she was busy studying for finals and couldn't see him. "I have to make grades if I want to keep my scholarship," she explained. Toby finished his exams before she had taken her last one and left a note on her door saying he was going to Europe with his folks and would keep in touch.

No Europe for Marianne. Not even a vacation. Instead, after a few days with the Parkers in Passaic, she took the bus up to Old Orchard, Maine, where she had

worked the summer before as a desk clerk in one of
those old, rambling, gingerbreaded hotels built at the turn
of the century, a wooden structure with Victorian cupo-
las and a widow's walk. Marianne had a tiny gable room
under the eaves that heated up like a furnace on the first
hot day and stayed that way most of the summer. But
her job provided room and board and she was able to
save nearly all of her salary. She was often lonely.
Socializing with the guests was not encouraged, and
Marianne found little in common with the other help.
She kept busy during her off hours, hiking on the beach,
reading, writing letters. She thought about Toby a lot.
He hadn't written as he had promised, and she wondered if he'd forgotten about her. She had been right,
she told herself, to be cautious with that one. Yet she
couldn't keep her mind away from him, the dimple at
the corner of his mouth, the way he laughed, the way he
listened as if he were really interested when she talked.

Brad, who worked in a print shop in Buffalo during
his summers, drove up to visit one weekend. When
Marianne saw him she almost cried. She was that happy
to see a familiar face, that hungry for a friend to talk to.
Before he left she asked him if he had heard from his
best friend.

"No, but Toby's a lousy letter writer. I won't hear
until the end of the summer when he gets back."

So Marianne was astounded one Sunday afternoon
when the bellboy announced, "There's a Toby Hansford
looking for you."

She didn't even have time to comb her hair or put on
lipstick because Toby had followed the bellboy out.

"Hello, Marianne."

"I thought . . ." She felt her face getting hot. He
looked fit. Handsome. Strong, tanned legs—the dark
hair bleached by the sun—in white Bermuda shorts, his
chest straining at a navy blue golf shirt. Play it cool,
Marianne. She gave him an uncertain smile. "I—I thought
you were in Europe."

"I was. Hated it. Boring. I would have come back
sooner. I missed you, Marianne."

She swallowed. He was gazing at her with a tender look in his dark eyes. She lowered her own. "Yes—well, I wondered why you didn't write. Brad said you weren't very good about letters, and . . ."

"Marianne—did you hear me?"

She stared at his tennis shoes, white, neatly laced. There was a grass stain along the side of the right one.

"I couldn't get you out of my head. All through that damn flight home I felt like pushing the plane. It couldn't go fast enough. Marianne—are you listening? Look at me."

"Toby . . ." She lifted her eyes, everything she felt reflected in them: fear, caution, a deep yearning to believe him. "Toby, I . . ."

He pulled her into his arms and kissed her hard and possessively. It was even better than the kiss she had dreamed about.

They were walking hand in hand on the beach. A full moon flooded the night with ivory light glinting off the waves as they crashed, sending curling ripples of froth at their feet. Marianne knew the names of the stars and she pointed them out to Toby: Ursa Major, Ursa Minor, Sagittarius. He told her about Venice and Paris, about his sister whose wedding he and his parents had attended in Leeds.

"You know, I looked at Hazel and Dennis, their faces all lit up, and I thought—by God, they're in love. And then I thought of you. I know it sounds crazy, but, Marianne . . ." He paused, turning to her. "It's true."

He pulled her to him and, holding her close, kissed her, his wide, sensuous mouth firm and warm. Crushed against his ribs she could feel his heart racing, her own heartbeat throbbing in her ears.

Toby's hand rode down her back, pressing her against his erection. She felt heat between her legs and unconsciously leaned into him, bunching the back of his shirt in tight fists.

"Don't . . ." he groaned, pushing her away, taking

hold of her wrists. His arms were trembling like Marianne's knees.

She did not speak. Everything was mixed up. The
moonlight, the sea, Toby, herself. She had never felt
this way before. She was afraid to put a name to it, to
call it desire or love.

"Marianne?" He lifted her chin with a finger. "I'm not
here to lay you. But to tell you—I don't know how to
say it, damn! I love you, Marianne. I know we've only
seen each other three times, four, and it may sound like
I'm putting you on. But I'm not. I do love you, Marianne."

He let go of her wrists and she came into his arms
again, the slow, beautiful kiss on her lips once more.

He had registered at the Sea Shore Inn. When they
got back Marianne did not climb the stairs to her attic
room but slipped inside Toby's.

Toby began kissing her again, little kisses over her
face and forehead, his tongue sipping, licking, teasing
her earlobe. He kissed her throat, then lowered his head
and pressed his lips to her breast. She could feel his hot
breath through the cloth of her gingham shirt, the nylon
bra. She unbuttoned her shirt and then unhooked her
bra, amazed at her audacity, for it was Sam who had
always made the moves while she remained passive. But
now she wanted Toby to touch her naked breasts, she
wanted his mouth on her skin.

"Marianne . . ."

In the moonlight pouring in through the gauze-curtained
window her breasts had taken on a pearly sheen. He
kissed each one tenderly, then withdrew. She caressed
his face, her fingers lingering on his mouth.

He buried his head in her breasts. "Marianne, you
can't . . ."

He was trying to restrain himself and she loved him
for it. He didn't want to rush her. Had Brad told him
about her fiasco with Sam, that she had very little
experience?

But she forgot Brad as Toby began to kiss her breasts
again. When he took a nipple in his mouth, his tongue
swirling and licking, his lips gently sucking, a moan rose

in her throat. Her hands went to his shirt, trying to pull it up, and in her struggle they both fell back on the bed. His erection felt hard against her hip.

"Marianne . . ." He tried to rise but got tangled up in her legs.

"Marianne, I didn't bring anything. We can't—you might . . ."

Tears burned in her eyes. He'd told her the truth. He hadn't come to Old Orchard to get her into bed. He had come to see her, to tell her he loved her. Tears burned her eyes. She wound her arms about his neck.

"Toby, Toby, it's all right." She wanted him with a sudden surge of desire she couldn't explain. She had never felt this way with Sam.

With a slow, beautiful deliberateness he finished undressing her, kissing breasts, belly, the patch of pubic hair, her thighs, her sandy toes.

Naked together in bed they lay clasped in each others arms, kissing and murmuring until their voices were stilled by a rising tide of excitement which bound them into a moving, heaving, panting rhythm. Marianne's mind let go, obliterated Sabrina, Brad, Sam, Aunt Em's dark warnings. Only Toby was real, these moments, this pure, wonderful pleasure.

Afterward, sweat-soaked, her hair loose from its ponytail, Marianne lay in the circle of Toby's arms, smiling. She was happy. It had to be love.

In the fall of 1969 when they returned to campus they were already an inseparable twosome. It was a troubling year, with the Vietnam War heating up, Muhammad Ali refusing to be drafted, Nixon promising to get the Americans out of Southeast Asia with honor, and student demonstrations on campuses across the country. But aside from noting these events, little of the turmoil seemed to affect Toby or Marianne. Those were the happy days, the golden hours of autumn with the trees shedding their leaves, the smell of wood smoke, the purple twilights, the first snow, a pristine white under the ragged tracery of black branches. They studied hard, made love whenever privacy permitted, played whenever time allowed.

Brad, sometimes with a date, more often without, would occasionally join them for a movie, a football game, a walk along country lanes. Brad was the first to know about Toby and Marianne's engagement. Toby hadn't told his parents yet. He was taking Marianne home with him for the spring break to meet them.

Marianne, without having to be told, knew it would be an ordeal. Brad's terse rundown of the Hansfords when she had asked about them a year before remained stuck in her memory. Toby had been kinder.

"Mother's not too bad when you get to know her. She'll seem a little chilly, and Dad's the same way, but don't let it throw you. They'll love you, I know."

"Is that wishful thinking, Toby?"

"No," he said, hugging her, "it's a fact."

The house was larger and even more beautiful than Marianne had anticipated, its red brick faded to a mellow umber, the white pillars rimming the portico tall and substantial like columns upholding a Greek temple. Hedges were neatly clipped, the trees pruned to vase-shaped precision, the lawns primly manicured, not a fallen leaf or broken twig or scrap of paper to mar the Hansford acres that rolled down to the water's edge.

The inside was just as tidily sterile. Done in pale ivories and beiges, with deep-pile carpets sinking underfoot and marble fireplaces.

The Hansfords themselves weren't bad. They were terrible. They did not love her as Toby had promised. They did not even come close to liking her. While Ed Hansford kept tight-lipped and monosyllabic, his disapproval as loud as a scream, Dorothy was volubly snide.

"I understand you're from Jersey," Dorothy sniffed in a tone that placed Passaic somewhere between the slums of Bombay and those of the Bronx.

They were having a formal, candlelit dinner served by the houseman, whose varicose nose and minted whiskey breath were at odds with his starchy manner.

"Perhaps you know the Heberts?" Dorothy challenged,

watching Marianne's choice of cutlery as the course
changed from *potage parmentier* to *coquilles St. Jacques.*
"He's with DuPont."

"I'm afraid not," Marianne replied politely, looking
youthful and vulnerable in soft blue crepe.

"The Peter Grays, then?" Dorothy probed. "They
have a home in Princeton."

"Mother," Toby interposed, "Princeton and Passaic
are not exactly next door to each other."

"Oh, aren't they?"

It suddenly occurred to Marianne that perhaps Dorothy Hansford was not very bright. Yet she and her
husband seemed so formidable. Marianne looked across
at Toby, and his smile, the warmth in his eyes, gave her
comfort.

As the meal progressed Dorothy continued to domi-
nate the conversation.

Marianne couldn't understand why Toby had ever imagined his parents would accept her. Didn't he see how
they were trying to humiliate her?

For a few terrible moments her anger rose against
Toby. But when she met his eyes she saw that he wasn't
listening to his mother; his attention, his ears and his
eyes, all of him was focused on her. His concentrated
gaze told her how much he loved her. She flashed him a
bright smile. To hell with the Hansfords. They were his
parents only through some freak biological accident.
Toby had probably inherited his genes from that rum-
running grandfather he had told her about. He couldn't
possibly belong to these two.

"Oh, by the way, Toby"—Dorothy touched his hand
deliberately, as if to distract him from Marianne—"I
bumped into Sabrina last week. Stunning, as usual. She
does have that glorious auburn hair. She asked after
you, Toby. Wanted to know why you hadn't called. You
must. She's such a darling," she purred.

Marianne had met Sabrina. She had come up to Ithaca
one Saturday, moving in on Toby like a bitch in heat.
Toby had set her straight and they had had a fight that
could be heard clear up to Forest Home Drive.

By the afternoon of the second day Marianne's composure had needled Dorothy to frustrated rage. She finally took Toby aside and asked him to please leave with Marianne and not bring her back. It was then that Toby told her they planned to marry.

Dorothy did not faint or dissolve into hysterics, but she wept, her tears punctuating a timeworn reproach. "After all I've done for you, this is my reward. Who is she? Nobody, a girl from Passaic, a zero, a fortune hunter. I tell you, she doesn't love you, she just wants your money." And the *coup de grace,* "What will my friends think?" Ed, less verbose, showed his displeasure in a series of grunts. He did not go as far as to play the heavy parent, warning Toby that he'd be cut off without a dime if he married Marianne, but he hinted in a very pointed manner that things would be "tough" if he did.

CHAPTER IV

MARIANNE AND TOBY WERE MARRIED BY A JUSTICE OF the peace in Passaic with Uncle Bob, Aunt Em, and Brad as witnesses. Returning to Ithaca, the newlyweds rented an off-campus apartment and continued with their schooling, Marianne on her scholarship, Toby borrowing against a trust he would receive on his twenty-fifth birthday.

The apartment was furnished in depressing castoffs, but Marianne added a few touches that made it seem less like a Goodwill showroom and more like a cozy nest for a couple of clever but poor students. She replaced the worn leather sofa that came with the apartment with a green brocade one that she had bought at a garage sale for twenty dollars. Bright, oversized posters of exotic birds went up on the walls they had painted a fresh white; plants, ferns, acanthus, and vines grown from sweet potatoes hung from the ceiling.

Marianne worked out a budget and held Toby to it. He grumbled a little but finally agreed that she was the businesswoman and he was the impractical "mad" scientist. Nevertheless, they had their first quarrel over money. When an aunt of Toby's sent them a thousand-dollar wedding check, Toby went out and bought a motorcycle.

Marianne, speechless with astonishment, could only stare at him when he announced his purchase.

"Don't look at me like that. It's a good buy and it makes sense. The two of us have different schedules. You have an eight o'clock and I don't have to be in class until ten. A motorbike is cheaper than buying another car."

"What about a plain old-fashioned pedal bicycle?" she asked sarcastically. "Or walking?"

"Marianne," he continued impatiently, "it's really very practical. With a sidecar I could even do the shopping or go to the Laundromat on Saturdays. You ought to try it, Marianne. It's fun."

"I'm not going to ride that thing. Don't you realize we could have used the money to buy a decent bed, a chest of drawers, a bookcase instead of those crappy orange crates we have now? I would think you'd consult me. At least. But oh, no, that check was burning a hole—"

"Shit! Okay! I'll take the damned thing back," he yelled.

"Toby . . ." Marianne began, trying a calmer, more conciliatory tone. She had never seen him so angry, and it upset her. "This was supposed to be a joint venture. We agreed to talk things over before—"

"To hell with it!" he shouted, and he stormed out of the house.

That night they went to sleep, each clinging to his own edge of the bed—clinging because the mattress sagged in the middle. Their mutual anger had been so devastating they couldn't bear to look at one another, let alone touch. Marianne had thought of sleeping on the sofa but changed her mind. She'd be damned if she was going to be the one to give up her bed. Let *him* sleep on the sofa.

They woke up in the middle of the night in each other's arms.

She loved being married. It was tough at times, and

she knew Toby was hurt by his parents' silence, but she refused to let anything cast a shadow over their life together. She loved coming home to their little apartment, shabby as it was, to see Toby's shoes lined up on the floor of the closet, his baseball hat on the hook on the back of the bathroom door, his bike gloves thrown carelessly on the bed. Or sometimes she would come home and find him in the kitchen, beer in hand, a bleached flour sack tied around his waist, presiding over two or three burbling pots on the stove, often with Brad supervising.

She thought being a married student was having the best of two worlds. She found her senior year interesting and challenging and was planning to study for her Certified Public Accountant exam the next summer and then go on to graduate school for the MBA in the fall. Toby had already applied for admission to the Scripps Institute of Oceanography on the West Coast. If they accepted him, Marianne could pursue her own studies at the nearby University of California at San Diego.

Brad had plans, too. He was going into teaching—physics. "Professor Bradford Young," Marianne said with mock thoughtfulness. "Has a nice ring to it."

"I'm also learning how to speak Chinese. It's a tricky language, intriguing. Getting your tongue and the pitch of your voice in the right place is the big problem. But I'm making progress."

"Good. Maybe when you reach a point past 'hello' and 'how much?' you can wangle your way behind the Bamboo Curtain and see if I still have a father and mother."

"Do I catch a note of sarcasm?"

"God forbid! Why should I be sarcastic? On second thought, maybe you'd better forget it. Ma and Pa Oliver probably would feel embarrassed if you reminded them they had a daughter."

"Marianne, I can't believe you're still on that kick. What is it with you?"

"It's not a kick. You wouldn't understand. You've

got a mother. Parents. Whatever she is, she loves
you."

"Listen, Marianne," Brad said, "you think Toby's
had the best of mothers?"

"Maybe not. But *he* feels she cares, and that's what's
important."

"Bullshit."

"Bullshit, it's true."

Marianne and Toby had been married ten months, two
weeks, and three days when Marianne found she was
pregnant. There had been no plans for a baby. In fact,
they had decided not to have children until they had
finished their education. Oddly enough, Marianne was
not dismayed. She secretly wondered if her "forgetting"
to get to the drugstore for a fresh round of pills was a
subconscious wish for motherhood.

Toby, hearing the news, was speechless, his eyes
searching for some kind of clue from Marianne's expression. But when he saw the worried yet hopeful look she
gave him, he broke into a grin.

"Great! It'll be a belated graduation present from both
of us to each other."

"But what about Scripps and our plans to go to the
West Coast?"

"We'll postpone it for a year. I haven't heard from
Scripps anyway. In the meanwhile, I can take more
courses here and you can start on your MBA. We're
going to have one educated baby."

Karen Marie Hansford was born with blue eyes, a full
head of downy hair, and a sweet, pouty mouth that
brought tears to Marianne's eyes. She couldn't believe
that this child, this baby, this human creature was hers.

Toby, unwrapping her cocoon blanket and gazing at
her with a startled look on his face, said, "Who d'you
think she looks like?"

"No one," Marianne said. "She's too little."

"No," he said decidedly, "I think she takes after
me."

The baby's face suddenly contorted and turned crimson. She began to howl, and Toby quickly handed her back, grinning sheepishly.

"I've called my parents," he said. "I thought they ought to know." He watched Marianne intently, awaiting her response.

Marianne put the baby to a full breast. "What did they say?" she asked sharply. "Don't tell me, let me guess. It's not yours."

"No. Nothing like that. In fact, Mother said she would like to see her granddaughter."

"Doesn't sound like her. Sure you're not making it up?"

"No. She said, 'How nice. A little girl. I'd love to see her.' "

"Just like that?"

"Marianne, give her a chance."

"I have," she snapped. "We've been married a year and a half. Not a word. They didn't even come to your graduation. It's not me I care about as much as you."

Toby had hidden his hurt at his parents' absence from graduation by getting very drunk that night, so drunk Marianne had had to put him to bed. She had felt terrible about it at the time, blaming herself for causing the rift.

"Mother's had a falling out with Hazel. She's feeling the pinch. I think she and Father are lonely."

"Would you like them to see Karen?"

"Well—yes. But if you say no, I can put them off."

"I'm not wild about the idea." She studied his face. His eyes seemed to be pleading with her. "But sure, okay," she said gently.

Why not? It was their grandchild, wasn't it? What did it matter now if the Hansfords looked down their noses at her? She, Marianne, had borne a beautiful child who would have a loving mother and a doting father. They would be a close-knit threesome. A family.

Toby planted a kiss on her cheek, another on the top of the baby's little scalp. "You're a sweetheart. I knew you'd say yes."

*   *   *

The Hansfords arrived ten days later, putting up at the Statler Inn. They were aghast when they saw the apartment.

"We must get you better housing," Dorothy announced immediately.

Marianne made no comment.

"She's sweet," Dorothy conceded, holding her grand-daughter gingerly. Then as the baby's hand clutched her finger a tearful smile broke out on her face.

The smile thawed Marianne. Anyone who smiled at her child couldn't be all bad.

"She has the Hansford nose, doesn't she, Ed?"

Ed grunted, relaxing his features momentarily to peek-a-boo at Karen drowsing like a pink-cheeked cherub in Dorothy's arms.

They received a thousand-dollar gift for "baby Karen" from the Hansfords, which went immediately into the bank. An offer of a substantial monthly allowance, how-ever, was politely but firmly refused, though it wasn't easy. Marianne had given up her classes and with it her scholarship, and they were relying on Toby's trust income and his job as a biology lab assistant to carry them. Marianne still planned to finish her education but for now thought she ought to wait until Karen reached nursery school age. She didn't mind. She liked the role of mother and wife. She was even learning to cook.

One late afternoon she was putting Karen down for her nap when there was a knock on the door. It was too early for Toby, and Brad always called out before he came in.

With the baby's wobbly head nestled under her chin, Marianne went to the door. Two policemen were stand-ing there. At the sight of them she immediately thought of the plastic bag of marijuana belonging to Chuck, a friend of Toby's. Chuck, who had dropped by the previ-ous evening for a smoke and a chat, had forgotten to take it with him when he left. Where had she put it? Was it still in plain view on the coffee table?

"Mrs. Hansford?"

"Yes?"

"May we come in?"

She held onto the doorknob with her free hand. Should she ask to see a warrant? Only yesterday there had been a raid on an apartment across the street and she had watched as three boys and a girl had been led away in handcuffs.

"What's this about?" she asked. Karen's breath was warm on her neck.

"I think it would be better if we could come inside." Only one of them spoke. The other stood behind, his eyes sliding away from Marianne's direct gaze.

"Please, Mrs. Hansford."

"What's this all about?" she repeated, a note of hysteria creeping into her voice.

"There's been an accident. Your husband . . ."

Marianne sat down. Karen had begun to make noises. She was wet.

"Bad?" she heard herself ask through lips suddenly gone dry. It was the motorcycle, that damned bike! Only a few days earlier she had read highway accident statistics showing that motorcycles . . .

"Very bad. He was struck by an auto while making a left turn."

"Oh, God!" Marianne suddenly jumped up, still clutching Karen, who began to cry. "Where is he? Where did they take him? What hospital? I'll get my coat. . . ."

"I'm sorry, Mrs. Hansford," the policeman said soberly. "He was killed instantly."

Did she scream? Cry? Faint? She must have done something—blacked out, probably, because she couldn't remember. She couldn't remember whether she called Brad or the police had. All she could recall was holding Karen tightly, holding on to her as if she were the only solid grip on the brink of an abyss and if Marianne let go she'd go down into howling darkness.

She was still holding Karen, whose screams of hunger and discomfort she did not hear, when Brad came through the door and took her and the baby, both sobbing, into his arms.

*   *   *

Dead at the scene. It had happened so suddenly. One moment Marianne was a happy wife and mother, the next a widow. Her loss was so stunning she couldn't believe it was Toby in that coffin, Toby about to be lowered into the ground.

"It all seems so unreal," she said to Dorothy. They were driving to the cemetery—the Hansfords, Hazel, hastily summoned from Leeds, and Marianne—in a black limousine.

Dorothy turned icy blue eyes on Marianne. "I don't want to talk about it. Not with you. If Toby hadn't married you he'd still be alive."

"Mother!" Hazel exclaimed. "How could you? And at a time like this . . ."

"Hazel," Ed Hansford cut in sharply, "leave your mother be."

"Yes," Marianne said in a voice that trembled on the edge of bitter sarcasm, "let her talk."

Marianne had not looked to Dorothy for any great show of warmth. She had not expected this cold, shallow woman to throw her arms around her bereaved daughter-in-law and weep together with her. But this . . . how could Dorothy be so cruel?

"I have plenty to say." Dorothy's thin lips had a wry twist to them. "You lured a fine, decent boy into marriage—I don't know how you did it. If he had married a well-bred, socially acceptable girl instead of a tramp . . ."

"Mother!" Hazel exploded. "Will you shut up? I mean it, shut up!"

"Hazel, you are not to talk to your mother that way. I won't have it!" Ed Hansford warned.

"Then tell her to be quiet."

Dorothy leaned across Ed, who was sitting between them. "I will do no such thing!"

The ride to the cemetery was finished in strained silence.

*   *   *

Marianne sat in the Hansfords' cold Long Island living room watching Dorothy, composed and dignified, dressed in de la Renta black velvet, standing next to stolid Ed, receiving friends and relatives who had come to pay their respects. A feeling of sick, impotent anger came and went. Dorothy's attack in the limousine had been inexcusable. I'm her scapegoat, Marianne thought, her whipping boy. I've provided her with the opportunity to ease her pain and her rage. Marianne, Miss Nobody from Nowhere.

To Marianne the entire funeral was a travesty, a show. The fleet of sleek, chauffeured limousines, the wreaths of white orchids, white roses, and mums, the silver-handled casket, the nasal-toned Episcopalian minister all seemed staged, an ostentatious production. And now this catered buffet for "family and close friends," a prodigious display of food she found nauseating. The only thing she had asked for was a cup of tea, though her chilled hands, wrapped around it, were unable to gather much warmth.

Her eyes searched the room for the Parkers: Uncle Bob in a corner, pinned down by a little man with a goatee who kept shaking his finger as he talked, Aunt Em in her black "best coat" with a fox collar and the usual felt hat with its drooping cluster of fake cherries, refusing to be intimidated by her surroundings, chatting away with Hazel. They had been wonderful, traveling up from Passaic, though Aunt Em's phlebitis had taken a turn for the worse. And Bradford, sharing her dismay over the funeral, the viewing of the body, Toby's shattered skull patched up beneath a wig that didn't quite match his hair, the rouged, dead cheeks. "He wanted to be cremated," Bradford told her sadly. "Not that the Hansfords ever gave a damn about what Toby wanted."

Throughout the wake Marianne sat on the same chair, wanting desperately to be with Karen, to deal with her sorrow in private. But people spoke to Marianne offering condolences, people she could not remember ever having met, people she did not know, did not care about, and would never see again. Even as she spoke—"Thank you," "You're so kind," "Yes, do call"—her numb

mind wandered, hearing bits of conversation from those
who sat briefly on the sofa next to her chair.

"Yes, I think Nixon can do it." The statement was
made by a bald man in standard funeral dress—black
worsted suit, long black tie, white shirt front—to his
similarly attired companion. "He's the only one who
can open China up."

"Talk about a can of worms. Do we *really* want China
opened?"

"Sure. With close to a billion prospective Coca-Cola
guzzlers, why not? It's a big market, Bud. Big. This
Canadian friend of mine—he's president of Armature
Sewing Machines—was in Canton last year . . ."

Canton. China. Marianne thought of her father and
mother. Were they dead, too? Had they perished years
ago without her knowledge, without her having the opportunity to properly mourn them?

". . . they say there are Americans still there. Missionaries and business people who got trapped . . ."

Her parents hadn't been trapped, they had chosen to
stay. And they had sent her away. Did they ever think
of her? Did Sarah and William wonder what had become
of their daughter? If they were here now, in this cold
room, would they be a comfort? It was hard to say. So
few could really comfort her now. Only the thought of
Karen, so tiny and defenseless, made it bearable.

"Toby had such great promise . . ." Two women had
replaced the men on the sofa, the amber-haired one
sipping a Manhattan. "So young, what a pity. I was
telling Oscar at the funeral that Toby . . ."

Toby. Her heart ached with a frightening, hollow pain,
pumping gray bleakness through her veins. She could
put the Olivers out of mind, tuck them back into their
corner, but how could she manage without Toby? She
didn't want a fond and loving memory. She wanted *him*.

Guests were beginning to leave. In a few minutes she
could do the same. The wake had lasted two and a half
hours, an eternity. Of the Hansfords only Hazel had
been solicitous, urging Marianne to eat, bringing relatives over to offer condolences. Neither Dorothy nor Ed

Hansford had approached her once. Not one word of commiseration, not one sign that she, their son's widow, was present. It seemed that as far as they were concerned she did not exist. Their avoidance was a snub to which Marianne now, at the end of this terrible day, felt indifferent. With Toby gone, she told herself, they are out of my life forever.

But the Hansfords were not that easily dismissed.

CHAPTER V

FOUR DAYS AFTER THE FUNERAL ED HANSFORD'S LAW-
yer, Tom Barstow, came to Marianne's small Ithaca
apartment and offered her fifty thousand dollars for her
daughter.

"Karen will have the world with a ribbon tied around
it," was the way he put it. A tall man with stylishly
groomed salt-and-pepper gray hair that suggested a hair-
piece, he had established himself on a chair without
being asked. "She'll have all the advantages a kid could
possibly have, a beautiful home, education, trips abroad,
you name it. They'll treat her like a princess. Mrs.
Randover, the housekeeper who raised Toby and Hazel,
has offered to come back. You know what a good—"

"Of all the—!" Marianne shot up from the green sofa
where she had just seated herself, her face flaming with
anger. "You can tell the Hansfords to go to hell! Now
get out!"

"A moment—if I can finish," he continued pleasantly, ignoring her outburst. "You'll have visitation rights,

44

of course. They want full custody, naturally, but once a month—''

''Out!'' Marianne strode to the door, holding it open. ''Come on, on your feet! Out! And don't come back!'' she warned, slamming it behind him.

Two days later the Hansfords announced their intention of taking the matter to court, claiming that Marianne was an unfit mother. The internationally known law firm of Barstow, Barstow and Smith would represent them.

To fight the Hansfords, a near penniless Marianne had to beg, borrow, and scrounge for money. Uncle Bob, solidly behind her but in modest circumstances, gave what he could. Bradford sold his car, his share in a small business venture, and enlisted a friend, George Gold, a junior partner in a fairly respectable law firm, to take the case at a reduced fee.

For Marianne the hearing was sheer torture. Still grieving over Toby, she had to sit day after day in an overheated, claustrophobic courtroom listening to lies and twisted half-truths while Mrs. Hansford, dressed in elegant black, put on a show of poignant sorrow.

The judge, the Honorable Titus B. Bell, upon whom so much depended, was a stocky, broad-shouldered man with heavy features, the sort of character who would appear more at home in football gear than in judges' robes. He had a reputation for conservativism. A churchgoer, a firm believer in family, flag, and Mom's apple pie, he was not a judge Marianne's lawyer would have elected to appear before had he been given the choice.

''Bell's a stickler for rules,'' Gold informed Marianne. ''He believes very strongly in upholding the good old red, white, and blue moral code. If he sniffs anything offbeat in your lifestyle, widow or not, we're in trouble.''

''Can't we get someone else?'' Brad suggested.

''We could try. But with court calendars so crowded it would make the whole procedure a long-drawn-out one, and even then you'd be taking a chance. There's worse than Bell. No matter who says what, judges are not impartial arbitrators. They all have their prejudices.''

The Hansfords could not only procure the best legal advice, they could also afford to hire Dr. Phillip Zarden, a $150-an-hour psychiatrist experienced in child custody cases. Marianne had to make do with a court-appointed shrink. Each psychiatrist was to examine both his client as well as his client's adversary.

To say that Marianne did not take too kindly to Dr. Zarden when he came to Ithaca to interview her would be a gross misstatement. He angered her. A thick-lipped, cigar-smoking man, he looked more like a cartoon politician than a behavioral scientist. He had probed into her past with an emphasis on sex that seemed unnecessary, if not prurient. Or maybe he was simply trying to earn his fat fee.

Her own psychiatrist, Dr. John Hansen, though better-looking and more pleasant, seemed inept, if not disinterested. But, of course, this case wasn't going to make him rich.

The hearing dragged on and on. Marianne had known the charges against her and realized the Hansfords would try everything in the book to discredit her. She had expected a rough time.

But nothing like this.

Dr. Zarden was on the stand. He was being questioned by the Hansfords' attorney, Tom Barstow, who conducted himself with an assertive suaveness Marianne had previously found irritating but now found frightening.

"You say you gave Marianne Hansford a mental status examination. Would you please explain, Doctor?"

"Certainly. I observed her, her behavior, her gait, her manner of approach with me, her dress, her affective or emotional tone as we discussed her marriage, her relationship with her husband and his parents."

"And what is your conclusion?"

"Her dress was rather sloppy, but appropriate, I suppose, for a young college student: scuffed shoes, faded jeans, oversized man's shirt. She greeted me with a fairly courteous manner, but after that her attitude steadily deteriorated. She was not very cooperative, at times overtly hostile. I would say this young woman harbors a great deal of irrational anger."

Irrational? Marianne thought. God Almighty! Two heartless people, her putative in-laws, who had treated her like dirt underfoot, were suing to take her child from her and she was supposed to be placating and friendly? Yet there was a lesson to be learned here, one that she was slowly mastering. Never show your enemies how mad you can get. She shouldn't have lost her temper and ordered Barstow from her apartment or told Zarden that his questions smacked of Peeping Tomism.

Tom Barstow adjusted his tie. "Dr. Zarden, I also understand you interviewed the police who broke the news of her husband's death to Mrs. Hansford."

"That's correct. They reported that Mrs. Hansford seemed to be in some sort of trance. They observed a packet of marijuana on the floor under the coffee table, but could not be sure if Mrs. Hansford was under the influence of drugs. At the time she was holding the child in her arms. The baby, obviously in need of a diaper change, was screaming, but the mother paid no attention to it."

People see what they want to see, Marianne thought angrily. A presumption had been made that was totally false. It sickened her. Marianne tried to screen the voices out. She concentrated on the water pitcher on the table in front of her, then on the judge. His eyes were closed. Concentrating? Bored? Or was he dozing?

"Dr. Zarden, you describe Marianne Hansford as hostile, angry, and resentful. What effect, if any, would that kind of behavior have on her relationship with her daughter?"

"In my opinion I believe it would have a harmful and negative effect on Karen."

Brad leaned over and whispered, "What an ass!"

When George Gold got up to cross-examine Dr. Zarden Marianne wondered how he was going to handle this pretentious phony. George, admittedly, had no experience in family law. This trial would be a new undertak-

ing for him. "He's bright," Brad had assured Marianne.
She hoped that was enough.

"Dr. Zarden"—George gave him a big smile—"you
say that Mrs. Hansford appeared hostile?"

"Indeed."

"Don't you think she had a right to be when, instead
of being interviewed, as she had expected, she found
herself in analysis, with you asking questions about her
sex life that were not pertinent to the matter before the
court?"

"Not at all. I think her sexual attitudes as well as her
general behavior are important. . . ."

"Even the question about her possible indulgence in
oral sex?"

The judge's eyes popped open.

"Certainly. You see—"

"Never mind. Let's go on to the next question. You
mentioned the police report of Marianne Hansford's reaction to news of her husband's death. Isn't it true that
at moments of shock some people will go numb, freeze?"

"That may be true. But in my observations I have
found the contrary is more normal. Great emotional
upset, weeping, often hysteria."

"I see. And you also took it as a sign of neglect that
the baby's diaper was wet."

"Sopping," Dr. Zarden smugly corrected.

"Do you think that perhaps Mrs. Hansford was too
stunned to be aware of the baby's diaper at that moment?"

They were splitting hairs. Marianne felt tired, too
tired to listen. Her bones hurt. She felt as though she had
aged a century since the two policemen had knocked on
her door. She needed Toby.

"Furthermore," Dr. Zarden was saying, "I find that
Marianne Hansford has a reputation for promiscuity."

Marianne, shocked out of her lethargy, angrily rose
from her seat but was immediately pulled down by
Bradford.

Dr. Zarden went on. "We know for a fact that she
cohabited with her late husband for a year before they

were married." The doctor's face glowed with dark self-righteousness. The judge's ears seemed to lift.

"And prior to that had several affairs. . . ."

"It's a lie," Marianne muttered between gritted teeth. "A damned lie!"

"In fact, I have a witness who will testify that he and Marianne Hansford were intimate several times a week up until the very moment she became engaged to her future husband."

"Bailiff," the judge instructed, "will you call the witness?"

When Sam walked through the swinging doors Marianne felt like shrinking into the floor beneath her feet. She thanked God that Uncle Bob was not there. Or Aunt Em. Especially Aunt Em.

"Do you swear to tell the whole truth . . . ?"

He looked the same. Blond good looks, tennis tan, that little smile on his lips that she used to think charming. Why were the Hansfords doing this to her, dredging up an old love affair? And why had this bastard agreed to testify? Money? Maybe Ed Hansford's business connections would help Sam finance his Senate Campaign.

". . . and you say you would *sneak* her into your fraternity house. Wasn't that against the rules?"

The truth, she supposed, was damning enough. All over the country girls were sleeping with boys, having sex without benefit of clergy. People were accepting the sexual revolution as a fact of life. Would the Honorable Titus B. Bell?

It was the sixth day.

Barstow had Marianne's psychiatrist on the stand. "Dr. Hansen, you say you interviewed Mr. and Mrs. Edward Hansford in their home?"

"Yes. I found them cold, composed, condescending, at times patronizing."

"To you," Tom Barstow said with a small smile. "But in your studied opinion, that wouldn't affect their ability to parent, would it?"

George Gold was on his feet. "Objection! Leading question."

Tom Barstow continued. "Now, Doctor, would you consider Mr. and Mrs. Hansford emotionally able to take on the role of loving mother and father for this child?"

"I was given to understand that Karen would actually be put under the care of a Mrs. Randover."

"A mature woman who has raised their own two children."

"Yes, but—"

"And isn't it true that the Hansfords are in a financial position to give Karen a secure home? She won't want for the basics, in fact she will have many advantages denied the average child."

"Yes, but—"

"And the younger Mrs. Hansford. What visible means of support does she have? How will she be able to provide for the child?"

"An uncle has offered to assist her." Dr. Hansen looked put upon. Support was not his department.

"Am I given to understand that this uncle . . ." Barstow consulted his notes. "A Mr. Robert Parker, is well off, that his financial status is on a par with Mr. Hansford's?"

"No, but—"

"I take it, then, that Marianne Hansford will have to go out to work. That means she will have to find a sitter, one that probably does not have Mrs. Randover's qualifications—"

"Objection!" George bounced up on his toes. "The statement presupposes a fact." George was a short young man, energetic, like an impatient schoolboy always in motion even when seated. Unfortunately, he had none of Tom Barstow's cool command.

The Hansfords' testimony was brief and, Marianne feared, compelling. Their concern, each of them testified, was solely for Karen's welfare. In their opinion, for Karen to remain with Marianne would be detrimental to the child's healthy growth. The mother's background was dubious. Born in China of parents who chose to stay on after the Communist takeover. They wondered (over George's objection) if Karen would not be exposed to un-American ideas.

Marianne felt that the only two things going for her in that entire hearing were Brad's testimony as a character witness and her own. Brad stoutly denied that his friendship with Marianne was other than platonic.

"You expect the court to believe," Tom Barstow asked with a knowing smile, "that your association with such an attractive young woman had no sexual involvement?"

"Believe according to your own biases, Mr. Barstow. There *are* friendships between men and women, whether you think so or not."

Led by George, Marianne told the court of the Hansfords' disapproval of her marriage, of how they had not been interested enough to attend their son's graduation and had only made overtures when the baby was born. George tried to leave the judge with the impression that the Hansfords were attempting to get custody of Karen simply as an act of revenge against Marianne, who had "appropriated" their son.

But again the Hansford attorney managed to punch holes in her testimony, saying that Marianne was only reading her own hostility into the Hansfords' attitude.

"When a concerned father and mother see their only son marrying a girl beneath him socially, a girl who is also a person of loose morals—"

"Objection!"

By the final day, Marianne could not bear to look at the Hansfords. But she felt their presence, their palpable animosity, saw them without turning her head: Ed, who sat upright, expressionless, only a blink of an eye now and then to indicate he was alive and breathing; and Dorothy, who came every day wearing a different black outfit, trimmed in mink at the collar and cuffs or roped with pearls or collared with a discreet bit of white lace. Subtly but expensively chic, every hair in place, Dorothy nevertheless managed to portray a distraught woman whose only concern in life was the welfare of her granddaughter.

Marianne knew that she should think realistically, prepare herself for the possibility . . . No! she vowed to herself, shaking her head violently. I'm not going to let these loathsome people beat me! I'm going to win! And after this is all over I am never, *never* going to be put in such a humiliating and helpless position again.

She turned slowly to face the Hansfords. They're so damned sure of themselves, she thought bitterly. Of course, they can afford to be.

The Hansfords were trying to concentrate on what Judge Bell was saying, but Marianne's penetrating gaze was too powerful to ignore. They both turned toward Marianne, the smug expressions in their eyes quickly fading when they saw the pure hatred in hers.

The judge apparently had been fitted with bifocals since his last appearance. He fussed with them now, removing them, polishing them with a white handkerchief, replacing them on his nose. The court sat and waited while he shuffled papers, made several notations, conferred with the court reporter, then with both psychiatrists.

They went on waiting. Dorothy on the other side of the room was calm, a small smile teasing her raspberry lips. She whispered something to Ed, who stopped tapping his fingers on the table. Marianne sat frozen, her hand like ice in Brad's.

The judge cleared his throat and looked up, his eyes magnified by the thick lenses.

"I have listened attentively to both sides of this case. Custody battles are always difficult to decide. Fortunately, the child in question is still an infant, and so the litigation on her behalf will, I hope, have no harmful effects." He drank from a glass at his elbow. "I find this case has important, if not fundamental, ramifications. . . ."

Oh, God, Marianne groaned inwardly, why doesn't he get on with it?

"Now we have here grandparents who . . ."

He was reviewing the entire case, going over it point by

point. At that rate they might be there for two days. Marianne, who had eaten no breakfast and no dinner the night before, felt faint.

"I myself find that psychiatric opinions are often misleading. We have here a good example. Two doctors interviewing the same persons with widely differing views. The question of the young woman's morals . . ."

The heat in the room had been turned up. It must be at least eighty degrees, Marianne thought. There were no windows, only the garish fluorescence of perpetual day.

". . . considering that some cases are settled out of court. However, in this instance . . ."

Brad whispered, "Are you all right?"

Why did people keep asking her if she was all right? Of course she wasn't. How could she be, sitting day after day through anxiety that was sheer torture? Yesterday she had said she would win. Today she didn't see how it was possible.

". . . in the last analysis a mother-child relationship, unless the environment is totally inappropriate—which may be debatable here—is one that this court finds it cannot sever. Karen Hansford belongs with her mother, though we believe that some sort of supervision . . ."

Had she heard right? Was it true?

"Therefore, the court awards custody of Karen Hansford to her mother, Marianne."

Yes! Yes! It was true! Brad squeezed her hand and grinned. A sob caught in her throat, her eyes filled with tears. She had won! Karen was hers! Oh, God, it was true. True! Her baby was hers. The little five-fingered hand, the tiny, tiny nails, the squashed-in nose, the crimped ears, the sweet breath, the daughter Toby had given her. Hers.

"I didn't think old Bell would come through, but," Brad said as he slapped the steering wheel emphatically, "as George says, you never know. I guess Bell figured motherhood—come what may—was too sacred to be tampered with."

"Thank God!" Marianne was ecstatic. It was over

and she had won. "God, it's so wonderful!" She turned to Brad. "Is it true what George says about the Hansfords appealing?"

"I don't think they're serious. They'd just like to wear you down. Ignore them."

"I wouldn't put it past them. I wouldn't put *anything* past them. But I'm not going to worry about it now. I'm starved. Can we stop somewhere to eat?"

They found a roadside diner. Marianne ordered steak, french fries, corn on the cob, cole slaw. She ate everything that was set before her, including a basket of rolls and apple pie à la mode.

"It's great to see you dig in," Brad said, watching her eat.

"I'd almost forgotten how good food can taste. Even this. Now all I have to do is get my life in order. I'm not going to let anyone trash me again," she said vehemently. "I'm going to be a somebody. Does that sound juvenile?"

"It depends what you mean by a somebody."

"Someone who has money, recognition, power. Let's face it, we live in a world that respects winners. If you're rich and important, people look up to you, envy you. I'm going to be important, Brad—not *as* big as the Hansfords but *bigger*. Wasn't it a Kennedy who once said that living well is the best revenge? Watch me, Brad. This isn't after-trial euphoria. I'm going back to finish my degree. Then I'm going to find a job with a future. It can be done, I know."

"If you're serious, what about the economics of all this? Let me help."

"No, Brad. You've already done enough. I refuse to take another penny from you. I'll get a part-time job, apply for a loan. We had a little in the bank, and there's the income from Toby's trust. It should go to Karen, if not me. Don't worry, I'll manage."

It was night when they left the cafe, cold and frosty. Brad turned the heater on as they drove.

"If there's a heaven—and, like Uncle Bob, I sometimes

have my doubts," Marianne said, "I can see Toby looking down at me and smiling. Funny, it's still hard for me to believe he's dead."

"It's too soon," Brad said. When would it not be too soon? he wondered. When can I tell her it's time to consider another man in her life? Like me. He kept his eyes on the road, thinking that "soon" was relative.

"Marianne," he said almost grimly, peering at the dark road ahead of him, "there's something I've got to say." He turned to her. Her head was thrown back on the seat, and her eyes were closed.

"Marianne?" She was sound asleep.

CHAPTER VI

WHEN MARIANNE GOT BACK TO ITHACA SHE GAVE UP her apartment and moved into a two-bedroom house, sharing it with a grad student, Hazel Dalton. There were two reasons for her move. Paying a split rent was cheaper, and Hazel, like Marianne, was a single mother with a young child trying to make it alone. Together they could adjust their classes and work schedules so that one of them would always be at home with the children.

It seemed like an ideal arrangement, but in reality it was less than perfect. Hazel, a robust girl three years older than Marianne, with a cap of sandy hair that frizzed into tight curls in wet weather, was an indifferent housekeeper. Actually, as Marianne soon realized, "indifferent" was a generous way to describe Hazel's complete lack of interest in maintaining even the minimum standards of health and safety.

The girls had agreed at the outset that they would take turns with household chores, Marianne one week, Hazel the next. But Hazel seemed to be operating on another track. No matter how Marianne coaxed and lectured,

Hazel always "forgot," allowing the dirty dishes to stack up in the sink, the beds to remain unchanged, the trash to overflow. Marianne, raised in Aunt Em's compulsively tidy house, where everything had its place, finally decided it was less of a problem to clean the mess up herself.

Hazel, except for the housekeeping, was easy to get along with. More importantly, she was good with the children, bestowing a bubbling affection impartially on both. The fact that she never spoke of her husband, from whom she was supposed to be divorced, or mentioned the circumstances of their separation, led Marianne to suspect that Hazel's husband was probably fictional and that little Jimmy was illegitimate. Not that it mattered. Least of all to Jimmy. He was a placid two-year-old, happy with his bottle and a beloved rag doll that he sucked on when not using his thumb. To Marianne he seemed a mite slow, behind Karen, who was already trying to stand, though Hazel maintained Jimmy was simply a late bloomer.

Marianne found two part-time jobs, one in Uris Library and another in a local dentist's office, where she came in on Saturday afternoons to do the books.

She was carrying a full load now. It was seven days a week of work and classes and long hours of study at night—a punishing routine. But she had Karen. Karen was her fun, her relaxation, her inspiration. A laid-back Hazel wanted to know what Marianne was trying to prove.

"You're a real grind if I ever saw one," she accused. "Don't you ever relax? It isn't healthy to let work and the kid make up your whole life. How's about me getting you a date? I know this English instructor, good-looking, smart. You'll like him. Come on, Marianne. We can ask the gal next door to sit with the kids. It'll only be for a few hours."

"Thanks Hazel, but I'd rather not."

"Marianne, for Pete's sake, you're still young. . . ."

"I know, Hazel. But I'm not interested."

She missed Toby, especially when she couldn't sleep.

She would lie there in the darkness, listening to Hazel snore from the next room, watching the luminous clock on the bureau, staring at its hands slowly making their rounds, and think of Toby. She would review their life together, going over that first moonlit walk on the beach, remembering their wedding, how he had kissed her fingers one by one after he had put the wedding ring on; Toby in the kitchen, tucking the flour sack around his waistband; Toby holding Karen. Toby smiling . . .

"Time will heal," Uncle Bob told her. His letters came frequently now, once, sometimes twice a week, and always there were words of encouragement, of affection. Even Aunt Em, who rarely wrote, sent her a postcard: "Saw your stuck-up in-laws' picture in the paper. That Dorothy looks like the cat that swallowed the canary."

Marianne tried not to think of the Hansfords, but it was impossible not to. She had gone through the simple legal process of reassuming her maiden name and was inclined to believe this would serve to irritate them even more. She didn't trust them. Brad had told her not to worry about an appeal on the custody decision. But she did worry. She had no money and no way to raise it if they took her into court again. She couldn't—wouldn't—go to Uncle Bob a second time. She knew he'd insist on helping her if the Hansfords reopened the case.

There were times when she had the urge to take Karen and flee, to get on a Greyhound and put as much distance between her and the Hansfords as she could. But she knew that by doing so she would only defeat herself, her plans for her future and Karen's. She did not want to live hand-to-mouth, hiding in some hole-in-the-wall town like an illegal alien. She wanted Karen to have everything the Hansfords could give her—and more.

One afternoon she received a letter from Barstow, Barstow and Smith, the Hansfords' legal representatives. The sight of those three names on the envelope set her heart pounding. This is it, Marianne, she told herself. Here's that summons that Brad told me not to worry about. For a moment she was tempted to tear it up, pretend she had never seen it. But finally she opened it and read:

Re: Tobias B. Hansford.

Dear Mrs. Hansford:

This is to inform you that according to the
provisions of your late husband's trust,
the monies therein are reverting to his father,
Edward W. Hansford. The income of said trust
will be terminated as of the first of April,
1972.

If there are any questions . . .

It could be worse, Marianne told herself, standing in
the darkening living room, her face strangely elongated
and pale in the flawed mirror that hung above the green
brocade sofa. It could have been the Hansfords trying
for custody again.

It could have been worse, but it was bad enough.
Marianne needed that income. It was a struggle each
month to come up with her half of the rent, to pay her
share of the utilities, to buy groceries. It didn't seem
possible that just a couple of jars of baby food and a
case of formula could cost so much.

Well, all right, she told herself, tearing the letter again
and again. Was she going to let the Hansfords watch
while she went under? No way. Things were not all that
bad. She had reapplied for a scholarship and another
loan and, if approved, the money should be coming to
her at the start of the next semester. In the meantime
she'd get another bookkeeping job. She'd fit it somehow, somewhere, into her schedule. If she had to, she'd
draw time out of her sleep. Who needed more than five
hours, anyway?

Now she knew what people meant when they talked
about surviving. It was slogging through day after day,
counting pennies, buying second-hand books and second-
hand clothes, cheap soap powder, the inexpensive hamburger that shrank to a dime in the pan, bruised apples
in the "reduced" bin, and day-old bread. Every extra
little item was haggled over in self-debate: Can I afford

it? It was trying to wind your tired mind up once more to go over that tricky chapter on Business Law so you could get a good grade on your midterm, because good grades were now imperative. It was fearing even the slightest cold; a day off was money lost.

It was hard.

Sometimes at night, too tired to go on, she'd take a sleeping Karen from her crib, wrap her in her blanket, and sit holding her, rocking on Hazel's rickety, squeaky chair, singing the only lullaby she knew.

> Sleep, baby, sleep.
> Thy father watches the sheep.
> Thy mother is shaking the dreamland tree
> And down falls a little dream on thee.

One Sunday morning Marianne got a call from Ginny, Brad's sister, who had baby-sat Karen during the trial. Marianne had met all four of Brad's sisters. The three who were older than Ginny were married to husbands who seemed cast from the same mold: golf, football, and beer addicts. Nice guys but, like their wives, uninteresting. Ginny, on the other hand, did marvelous oil portraits of children, was an opera buff, loved a wide assortment of "characters," and wouldn't live anywhere else but Manhattan. She was married to a doctor, Leo, a liver specialist, who was homely in a rather distinguished way and who shared many of Ginny's enthusiasms. Marianne liked them both.

"How nice to hear from you!" Marianne exclaimed.

"Yes . . ." Ginny hesitated. "Marianne . . ." Her voice sounded far away, tinny. "Marianne—I'm at Laura's—something's happened."

Laura was another of Brad's sisters. Eighteen months older than Ginny, she lived in Syracuse with her husband and three children.

Marianne's throat constricted. "Brad? Oh, God! Something's happened to Brad."

"Well—yes. There's been an accident."

The word "accident" drove terror through Marianne's heart.

"What?" She took a deep breath, trying to steady her voice. "Was it a bad one? Is he hurt?"

"No . . . oh, I don't know how to tell it. . . . Marianne . . ."

Marianne had never heard Ginny so distraught. It made her own fright worse. "Please, Ginny!"

"It happened yesterday. . . . Brad was visiting and he—he was backing his car out of the garage when he . . . oh, God!"

Marianne's hand on the phone had turned damp.

"He . . . Brad ran over Carlie." Carlie was Laura's four-year-old daughter.

"Was he . . . is he . . ."

"Carlie was killed instantly."

"Oh, my God!"

"It wasn't Brad fault. . . ." Ginny's voice broke. Marianne felt sick, shock and dread washing over her in a wave of nausea. How could a mother endure such a loss? If anything like that ever happened to Karen . . .

"It was one of those terrible things that doesn't seem possible," Ginny went on. "Brad didn't see Carlie. You know how kids are. She just darted across the drive under Brad's wheels. He couldn't have stopped in time even if he had seen her."

"Oh, Ginny, I'm so sorry, so sorry. Laura?"

"She's under sedation."

"And Brad?"

"That's what I called about. Everyone in the family is irrational. Until they gave Laura that shot—she was screaming 'murderer! murderer!' It's been awful. Brad just sits in that spare room with the shades drawn. He won't go to the funeral. He says it would be an insult for a murderer to go to the last rites of his victim. He says he might as well be dead, too. Talk like that. I can't reason with him. He won't talk to any of us. I thought maybe if you . . ."

"I'll be there as soon as I can," she said quickly. "I'll leave Karen with Hazel and catch the next bus out. And

Ginny . . . thank you for calling and telling me this. You know how much I care for Brad."

Marianne found Brad sitting on the edge of the bed, his head in his hands.

"Brad?"

He lifted his face, white and drawn with pain. "What the hell are you doing here?" he asked in a harsh voice. "I told Ginny not to call you. You shouldn't have come. Please, Marianne, I don't want to see anyone."

"Brad." She went in and knelt at his knees.

"Go away," he said, not looking at her. "I told you. . . ."

She took his hands. He tried to pull them away, but she held on. "Brad, it wasn't your fault. I want you to know that. *You're not to blame.*"

"But *I* did it. No one else."

"No. You were no more to blame than Toby making a left turn and running into a truck he didn't see."

"It isn't the same thing. How can you compare the two?"

"It's a happening over which you had no control."

"But I did."

"You *didn't*. Can't you get that through your head?" He looked at her, his eyes clouded with misery.

"Oh, Brad . . . don't do this to yourself," she protested, her throat tight with pity.

"Why did you come? Why?"

"Because you're my friend."

"Fine friend. I could have made sure that kid was in sight. I should never have started that car. . . ." He turned his head away. "You should have stayed in Ithaca."

"Brad, you *are* my friend. The minute you heard about Toby you rushed over. You comforted me. Let me do the same for you." Marianne sat down beside him and put an arm around his shoulders. "Please, Brad . . ."

He turned to her, tears brimming in his eyes. Suddenly, pressing his face into the hollow of her neck, he began to cry, great heaving, wracking sobs that shook his body.

Marianne had never seen a man cry. Uncle Bob had not even wept when the mother he loved had died. And now Brad—who had always appeared the tower of impenetrable masculine strength—sensible, sane Brad was sobbing like a baby. She held him just as she held Karen, stroking his back and soothing him, saying over and over, "It's all right, all right, I'm here."

After a long while Brad's sobs subsided. His head lay still against her breasts. She eased one arm over his shoulder and was trying to reach the box of Kleenex on the side table when his arms suddenly went around her.

He lifted his tearstained face. "Marianne—I love you."

His voice and eyes held an intensity she found as disturbing as his tears. "I know you do, Brad."

"You don't understand."

Ginny appeared in the doorway. "Can I help? I thought I heard someone crying."

"It's okay," Brad said, releasing himself from Marianne, plucking a Kleenex, blowing his nose. "Okay. I just had myself a good bawl on Marianne's shoulder, that's all. I'm better, Ginny, really."

In July Marianne took and passed her CPA exam. She was a full-fledged accountant now and could have found a job at a good salary in a firm that wasn't averse to hiring women accountants. But she wanted more than that. She wanted to be associated with a prestigious multinational company where she would have a chance to rise above profit and loss ledgers. She was determined to erect an impregnable fortress for herself and her child. She wanted to build a career that would give her the money and power to be free of worry about the Hansfords forever. That thought alone was what kept her going through those dark months, through the days of illness, through anxiety and exhaustion. When I'm through with this, she kept telling herself, everything else will be a piece of cake. I'm going to make it. I know I am.

Marianne was six months away from her degree when,

like so many MBAs, she was interviewed by representatives from large corporations who came to campus each year to cull the best and the brightest. She thought she did well, thought she had a good chance. Employers under pressure from recent passage of the Equal Opportunity Act were now hiring women. "Give us a call when you get to New York," she was told. She did.

Either it was naiveté or blind optimism—Marianne never could figure which—but the reality was far different from what she had imagined. No one was sitting in the towered kingdom of High Finance watching and waiting for Marianne Oliver.

There were jobs. And when Marianne followed up on the promising interviews she had had at Cornell she was full of hope. But the job descriptions—assistant manager, executive aide—were merely euphemisms for glorified secretaries and file clerks. These companies wanted "tokens," women who would sit at desks with fancy nameplates but who would execute menial clerical tasks, employment that would make her long, hard fight to earn a respectable degree a mockery.

Exxon, RCA, Seagrams.

"Do you have to start from the top?" Hazel asked one afternoon. Hazel had preceded Marianne to New York and they lived in a fifth-floor walk-up in the unfashionable section of Greenwich Village. The two young women had finally been forced to hire a babysitter, the landlady's daughter, a lame, unmarried girl who had a passion for eating other people's food and who left their refrigerator and cupboards bare when she came to sit for Jimmy and Karen. But she was good to the children; they liked her, and she was on call.

"I'm not starting from the top," Marianne said. "Those companies happen to offer the best opportunity for someone looking for a career with a future."

But not *her* future, it seemed. The "quotas" for women in middle management were already filled. Sorry. But would she consider their secretarial pool? Lots of women advanced from IBMs and steno pads. Marianne, if she had learned anything, knew they didn't. Most, if not all, qualified women who joined the clerical staff usually got stuck there.

Hanover Trust, IBM, Billings, Bendix.

All the same. She began to wonder if the Hansfords had any connection with her being turned down so consistently. Ed had friends in high places in the business world, but who they were and where they were placed she didn't know.

Brad thought it highly unlikely. He couldn't see stone-faced Ed Hansford asking people not to hire Marianne Oliver. "Someone would be sure to place you as the mother of his grandchild. Word would get around," he wrote. "People would say, 'That custody battle, remember? What a mean bastard.' No. Ed won't take the chance of appearing petty and vengeful. Ed, being Ed, will want to maintain the impression of a good loser, dignified and aloof."

"Ed may not want to 'appear' petty and vengeful, but I know better. I wouldn't put anything past Dorothy Hansford. Ed would just be carrying out 'Mother's orders,' " Marianne replied bitterly.

In early November Brad came into New York for an interview for a teaching position at New York University. He still had another year before he completed his doctorate but it gave him a perfect excuse to check up on Marianne.

Marianne, Brad had concluded early on in their friendship, had a surprising capacity for love and hate—surprising because to the casual acquaintance she seemed so well integrated, so much on an even keel. She was fiercely loyal, but once a person had betrayed her—like Sam—or had declared themselves her enemy—like the Hansfords—she turned against them with a quiet but determined vehemence. She might deny that the Hansfords had soured her, but ever since the custody hearing a subtle change, an almost imperceptible hardening, had occurred in Marianne.

Only toward Aunt Em and her real parents did Marianne seem ambivalent. Aunt Em herself, from what Brad could gather, had wavered between fondness and resentment during Marianne's growing-up years. But maybe that was true of many parents who loved their children one moment and could happily exile them to

Zagorsk the next. As for the Olivers, Marianne did not seem to believe them dead, as he and Uncle Bob had sometimes argued. Was it because she still hoped to hear from them, hoped to find in them the blood kinship she thought she had been denied? Or was it simply a hidden anger against them for their long silence, an anger she hoped to confront them with one day?

He loved Marianne but had given up, at least temporarily, on trying to make her see that his love was more than a friend's or a big brother's. He wasn't going to push her. He knew she'd only say "I don't love you like that, Brad. Maybe we ought not see each other so often. Maybe we ought to cool it." He didn't want that, he didn't want to give up having her arm tucked in his, her face turned to him with that wonderful warm smile. Someday, if he was patient, the chemistry would change. Someday. He hoped.

Marianne was running so low on money that soon she would have to take any job she could get just to keep herself in subway fare and stockings. Karen was talking now, toddling around the apartment, getting into the cupboards and drawers she could reach. Marianne wanted to move; the neighborhood was not safe, not a place to bring up a child even for a short time. People were being mugged in broad daylight. She never went out at night.

Then Hazel, who had filled out tons of applications, was interviewed for a position in the Department of Education in D.C. and got the job. She would be moving in two weeks.

Marianne could no longer afford to wait for her big career opportunity. She had to take what she could find. The morning after Hazel had given notice, Marianne went down to Lambert, Kramer, and Nichols, an accounting firm, and applied for a position. Their personnel manager, a young man with brown curly hair and a PR personality, was impressed by her qualifications.

"Yes," he said, "we do have a position opening up in our tax department, dealing with the less complicated returns. I'm sure you could handle those without trouble."

Patronizing bastard. But she kept on smiling, her lips growing stiff as he went on.

"We've never hired a woman accountant, but Mr. Lambert is up with the times. Women's lib and all that." He winked. "He'll have to give the final okay, of course. But with my recommendation and this"—he tapped the application—"I think it's safe to say you're in. Mr. Lambert isn't here right now, but why don't I set up an appointment for three o'clock on Wednesday?"

Marianne went back to the apartment, telling herself she'd only be there temporarily, just long enough to find something else. She was *not* going to be discouraged. But, damn it all, if she had been a man she would have been snapped up before she had even finished her MBA. She told herself she wasn't bitter, but she was.

As soon as she got in the door that evening Hazel told her she had received a phone call. "Didn't catch the name, but here's the number."

Marianne poured herself a cup of coffee before she went down the hall to the phone. When the voice at the other end said "Billings Corporation," Marianne's heart did a double flip-flop. She gave her name and after a long, agonizing minute was referred to a Mr. Cartwright. They had a place for her in their accounting department, he said. Among other things, she'd have the responsibility of checking progress reports from subsidiary companies. Was she interested?

Marianne did not hesitate. "Yes. Very much."

She knew she was overqualified for the job, that it was one that any well-trained bookkeeper could handle. But Billings offered potential that a small-potatoes firm like Lambert, Kramer, and Nichols couldn't match. And she'd have her foot in the door. Once inside, it would be up to her to make herself visible.

After she hung up she stood for a few moments, oblivious to her drab surroundings, as confidence surged through her veins, flushing her cheeks. She'd prove herself at Billings. She knew she had the brains and the will to be more than a flunky in accounting. They were going to notice her. And soon.

CHAPTER VII

THE BILLINGS CORPORATION HAD STARTED OUT AT THE turn of the century as a small midwestern factory making farm implements. As it grew it expanded from hoes, tillers, spades, and post drillers to tractors, harvesters, and army tanks. In the fifties it began to acquire subsidiaries—feed and seed outlets, a chain of hardware stores, a tire company, a coast-to-coast string of nurseries, Amalgamated Transport's fleet of long-distance trucks, and GUMCO Oil. By the time Marianne arrived at its headquarters in New York City, Billings was a large corporation with branches throughout the country.

Though Billings was not one of the giants, it was large enough to appear formidable to a young girl just out of college. But Marianne would not allow herself to think of Billings as formidable. Challenging, yes, but not formidable.

The controlling bloc of stock was still held by the Billings family. Jim Olmstead, Jr., the present chairman of the board, had come into a large chunk of it from his father-in-law when he married Carol Billings. His decisions, however, were never made alone but were arrived at by a consensus of the top brass. Frequently guarded from the public as well as from Billings's own employees, these official points of policy nevertheless reached the lower strata in the form of rumors. Directives came down the line as cryptic memos.

She'd been there eight months when she worked out a way to simplify the system of collecting the information that was sent quarterly to stockholders. Her method eliminated duplication and, in a small but important way, decreased the seemingly endless flow of paper—and earned her a promotion to a supervisory position.

Though her salary did not equal the salaries of her male counterparts, she welcomed the money. Still faced with a mountain of debt incurred during her custody battle, she also had her daily expenses to contend with. New York, even in 1972, didn't come cheap.

She had moved out of the East Village soon after she had started at Billings. Her new apartment on West 20th Street in Chelsea was an improvement over the old. But not much. It was larger, true; the plumbing worked, there were no scampering sounds at night, and she could actually see a tree if she stuck her head out the window and craned her neck. Then, too, the district, aside from being within easy commuting distance to her job, had its charm. Once the habitat of famous writers like Brendan Behan, Dylan Thomas and Thomas Wolfe, it retained remnants of its old gentility with its brownstone houses and the Victorian Gothic Chelsea Hotel, sprouting turrets and chimneys. But her building was old, and the rooms had a musty smell that no amount of air freshener could disguise. Marianne looked forward to the time when she had paid off her debts and could afford something better—an apartment where the paint wasn't flaking from the woodwork and the kitchen was larger than a broom closet.

Her promotion in so short a time had boosted her morale. The longer she worked at Billings the more she realized how lucky she had been. Billings was the right place for her. She wasn't kidding herself about what lay

ahead. She knew that except for a dogged few and a
token female here and there, women had a hard time
breaching the barrier that held them back from managerial and executive posts. But she had studied the success
stories of those who had made it, noting their emphasis
on the psychological differences between competition
and teamwork, both important in the corporate structure. And she was also prepared to find the field booby-
trapped by men who resented female trespassers. Her
one big asset was self-confidence, reinforced by her
victory over the Hansfords and her survival at Cornell.
If she could win those battles and carry away her MBA
as a trophy, then she could win the war here.

The system wasn't going to beat her, she told Brad;
she was going to beat *it*.

She had no desire to be "one of the boys," but neither did she want to be whistled at, patted on the behind, or propositioned. Her boss, chief accountant Horace
Blake, posed no problem. He was a sober, gray person,
polite but distant. Even his praise for her streamlining
program had been dryly impersonal.

Actually, there were only two men who gave her a
hard time. Some nerd in Systems and Harold Bundt in
the Tax Department. Their suggestive remarks she ignored, the invitations for lunch or an after-work cocktail
she firmly but politely refused. But when Harold Bundt
stopped at her desk one afternoon and put his arm
around her, his hand cupping her breast, she gave him a
resounding smack that could be heard clear up to the
president's penthouse, where Jim Olmstead, Jr., a friend
of Bundt's father, sat on the not-too-frequent occasions
when he was in town.

Marianne was called into Horace Blake's office the
next day and was prepared to discuss the incident. To
her surprise, Blake said nothing about Bundt or the slap.
Instead, in a flat voice he launched into a little speech
that Marianne guessed was a stock preamble to dismissal. She was told what a good job she had done at
Billings and how much she was appreciated. But profits
were down and expenses running high. The corporation

was cutting back, winnowing staff, and since Marianne had very little seniority they would have to let her go. With a recommendation, of course.

Marianne did not believe a word of it. Bundt, his male ego bruised, had pulled strings. Horace Blake was only following orders from above. However, she realized it would be foolhardy to antagonize Blake by going over his head. She would jeopardize their relationship, on which she must for the time depend. Tactfully, she requested permission to discuss her situation with Jim Olmstead.

"If that's what you'd like to do, of course," Blake said. "But you'll find him—ah—rather inaccessible."

Not in the least discouraged by Blake's negative prediction and ignoring a coworker's comment about having more sass than brains, Marianne called Olmstead's office. A thin voice told her that Mr. Olmstead was in conference. Moreover, his calendar was filled for the next three weeks. "Why don't I get back to you when he has free time, Miss Oliver?"

But Marianne was too angry now to let the matter drop. Replacing the phone, she reached down to the bottom desk drawer and retrieved her purse. Flipping it open to the inside mirror she carefully applied her lipstick. She tucked a stray strand of hair into the French twist at the nape of her neck and fluffed out the side curls. Lowering the mirror, she adjusted the wide collar of her Giorgio blouse (picked up at Loehmann's, bless Loehmann's), a rich blue and ivory striped silk that enhanced her creamy complexion and brought out the blue in her eyes. Feminine, she told herself but nicely understated.

Then she went out in the corridor, where she caught an up elevator. She'd be frank, businesslike, state her case concisely. She would also point out that Billings was too modern an operation to tolerate sexual harassment. Was sexual harassment a phrase that might unsettle Mr. Olmstead? She had never met him, and the reports received about him conflicted. Some said he was hard-nosed, others that he was an affable man. A good many in the accounting department agreed that the real brains behind the chairman was his wife, Carol Billings, daughter of the company's founder.

Confronted by the receptionist, Marianne introduced herself and said she had spoken to Olmstead's secretary and had been promised an appointment. Never mind that the promise had been for some indeterminate future date.

She was waved through a pair of glass doors into a lounge carpeted in plum wool that sank under her heels. On one wall hung a large Mondrian that Marianne assumed was an original. A hatchet-faced woman came out from an inner sanctum.

"Miss Oliver, I'm Mr. Olmstead's assistant and I believe I've already explained that Mr. Olmstead can't see you," she said firmly.

"Yes, I'm aware of that. I'm hoping I might catch him between appointments. I've a matter of importance to discuss and it won't take more than a few minutes. I'll wait."

"It won't do you any good to . . ."

But Marianne had already seated herself on the mauve sofa. Taking a notebook and pen from her purse, she began to scribble, the image of a busy junior executive who couldn't waste a moment. With a sigh, and not wanting to make a scene, Miss Hatchet Face sat down at her desk and began tapping at the keys of an IBM with fastidious delicacy.

A half hour later the glass doors opened and a small, birdlike woman dressed exquisitely in a black sable coat and a tiny sable-trimmed hat entered.

The secretary rose, her sharp-featured face creased in a smile. "Mrs. Olmstead, how nice to see you!"

Marianne stole a glance at the chairman's wife. She had seen her picture once in the *Times*, a blurred, inky image that showed a woman with her mouth open and her eyes closed, caught by the camera flash in surprise.

Now, even in her sable coat and that darling little hat, she was not what Marianne would call attractive. She was too short— five feet, five-foot-one at the most. She had a large nose. Seen in profile, it resembled one of those long false noses stuck on in comic fun, perching above her mouth and little round chin. Marianne was wondering why Carol Olmstead, with all her money, hadn't had a nose job when she turned suddenly, meeting Marianne's eyes, her own keen and lively.

"How do you do, Mrs. Olmstead," Marianne said, getting to her feet. "I'm Marianne Oliver. Accounting."

Mrs. Olmstead's smile transformed her face. It was the kind that negated the nose, that twinkled her bright eyes and radiated warmth and charm. Marianne liked her at once.

"Waiting for Jim?" she asked.

"Yes."

Miss Hatchet Face growled something in Carol Olmstead's ear.

She nodded and turned back to Marianne. "Why don't you come inside and we can both wait together?"

Marianne didn't need a second invitation.

Olmstead's office had bronze-tinted windows running from floor to ceiling across two sides. The windows looked out on a vista of Manhattan's skyscrapers poking their serrated heads through a yellow mist. Signs like beacons lit up the gloom. REVLON, CALVERT, TOSHIBA. A plane, its landing lights on, crawled like a bug across the murky sky. Carol pulled the drapes, shutting out the view.

"New York under smog makes me think of poison gas," she said. Turning to the desk, she pushed a button and lamps sprang to life. The desk, of ponderous polished wood, held an intercom, a glass globe, and a caddy of sharpened yellow pencils. Mrs. Olmstead motioned to a leather couch flanked by two goosenecked brass lamps.

"So you're in accounting," Mrs. Olmstead said, seating herself beside Marianne, drawing off her gloves.

"Since last July."

"I was interested in accounting when I went to school. But Daddy said it wasn't a ladylike subject. You can tell how far back I went."

Marianne laughed. "I'm afraid that attitude hasn't changed very much."

"Well, I suppose not. Speaking of change, what do you think of the new GTE retrieval?"

"Great. It works like a dream."

Carol went on to discuss it in a knowledgeable manner, surprising Marianne, who thought a chairman's wife would take little interest in such mundane things as office equipment. One word led to another, and soon Marianne was telling Mrs. Olmstead why she wanted to see her husband.

"I'm sorry to say I'm not too surprised," Mrs. Olmstead said after Marianne had finished. She was thoughtful for a moment. "You've got to remember that men founded and developed corporations and institutions like Billings. My grandfather and his father before him made the company a place where men could work and feel secure. Then suddenly women come along wanting in. The men feel threatened. But they're going to have to accept us. Whether they like it or not. They'll just have to realize that we women have a lot to give. Because we aren't steeped in hoary tradition, we can bring a fresh perspective, a new way of solving problems, to corporate policy. And that's all to the good."

They went on chatting until Jim Olmstead arrived. Tall, large-boned, with white hair receding at the forehead, washed-out blue eyes, and a white, bristly moustache, he had the appearance of a man who had once been athletic and handsome. His wife introduced Marianne and explained that Horace Blake was letting Ms. Oliver go.

"Who?"

"Horace Blake, he's our head of Accounting. I'm sure you've met him. Thin hair, bifocals, red nose. Blake is trying to trim staff. And, of course, Miss Oliver has no seniority to speak of. But Jim, I have it on good authority, she's one of our best."

Marianne had to admire the clever way Carol was handling the situation. No mention of Bundt. No hint that Blake was only following orders percolating down from Jim Olmstead himself. Only that Blake had acted in what seemed a logical, cost-effective manner.

"Well, now." Jim cleared his throat. "There must be some mistake. Of course we can't let Miss—ah—Miss Oliver go."

To Marianne's relief, the whole episode was glossed over. Apparently Blake felt that since Marianne's dismissal hadn't been his decision in the first place, there was no point in making an issue of it. The few jokes and snide remarks that lingered for a week or two were soon dropped for other, more interesting items of office gossip.

One of the pleasant aftermaths of Marianne's encounter with the top brass was the friendship that sprang up between her and Carol Olmstead.

Marianne liked Carol and she knew Carol liked her. Still, Marianne was hard put to understand why the older woman—who must have had many intimate friends as well as scores of acquaintances of her own age and social status—should seek her out. At least once a month she telephoned Marianne and asked her to have lunch with her. "I'm in town for a little shopping." Or, "I'm upstairs, dropped in to see Jim. How's about a bite at the Four Seasons? My treat."

The third time they met Marianne discovered part of the answer.

"Frankly, Marianne," Carol said over poached sea bass at Le Madrigal, "I envy you. Not so much your looks—although God knows I wouldn't mind having that face—but for being born thirty years after me. Women today can get ahead. It's still not easy, I realize, but doors are opening. In my day they were shut, and you had to be a real bruiser to jimmy them open. I wasn't even allowed to try. Daddy, for your information, was an A-one bastard. He never forgave Mom for giving him three daughters instead of sons. Women, to him, were basically useless. There was nothing any of us could do to please him. The only good thing I ever did, according to Daddy, was to marry Jim. For some crazy reason, which I'm sure he never tried to fathom himself, he took a liking to Jim. I like him myself. He's a sweet guy, a little laid back, intelligent—not brilliant, you understand, but intelligent—and reasonably faithful.''

Marianne got the picture: a nice guy, but nothing to match the sharp-witted, clear-thinking Carol. It substantiated the rumor that she was the brains behind Jim Olmstead. She wondered if Jim Olmstead brought the corporation's problems home to her or if she actually sat on the board. Carol, without being asked, explained.

"Daddy was a son of a bitch. A mean, grasping, narrow-minded son of a bitch. When I married, he said— and it was just like the old jackass to put it in writing— that when he retired, his Billings shares were to go directly to Jim. If that wasn't enough—cutting me out like that—he specified that under no circumstances would a female member of the family be allowed to participate in the running of the company. Fortunately, he didn't make a blanket no-woman ban. That was probably because Daddy never imagined that a woman could invade his tidy, masculine boardroom. A daughter might get there by reason of inheritance, but for some little typist or steno or sales manager to work her way up? No way.'' She paused to take a sip of water.

"Did it make me bitter? You bet. It didn't matter to my two sisters, but it did to me. I can see him now, dark hair, the gray touched up by his barber to make him look younger, trim—no paunch, thank you—and the brown eyes like gimlets. Except for the nose, I'm his female counterpart. I didn't want to resemble him, to be *anything* like the old tyrant.''

She was silent while a busboy removed their plates and a waiter refilled their coffee cups. "I don't have any daughters of my own; two boys, neither of whom shows the least inclination toward Billings. One is a musician— violinist—in the National Symphony. The other is a journalist and lives in Paris. If I had a daughter I would try to break Daddy's will. But I don't.''

"Isn't there some way you can still do it? For yourself, I mean.''

"Not for myself. It isn't worth it. A lawsuit might cause a panic among the stockholders, get the board all

stirred up. The next best thing"—she gave Marianne
one of her scintiltating smiles—"is a proxy daughter.
You."

Marianne felt a sudden tightness in her throat. She
wanted to hug Carol, that funny little woman with the
big nose and carefully arranged dark hair, so fine you
could almost see the skull shining through. "I—I'm flattered. I don't know what to say."

"You don't have to say anything, my dear. I've been
watching you. To say you're smart would be an understatement. You've got great potential. You're not afraid
to take risks, you're goal-oriented, you have a knack
with people. . . . Oh, I could name a half dozen things.
In my opinion you'd make a fine executive. Not tomorrow, but someday. And it goes without saying you've
got to work hard for it. I think you will. It's about time
women broke up that exclusive all-male club."

Marianne reached across the table and pressed Carol's hand. "You could have been that fine executive."

"I know."

Marianne considered herself lucky to have found such
a mentor, one whom she admired and who was so strongly
behind her. In the back of her mind she suspected that
Carol might be using her as an instrument of revenge
against her dictatorial father, that in some way she was
paying him back for his low opinion of her and of women
in general. But even so—and who could blame her for
wanting revenge?—she felt that Carol's admiration and
affection were genuine.

"Now," Carol said, "tell me a little more about yourself. I know you're widowed and have a little girl, Karen.
What's she like?"

Marianne leaned back in her chair, her face softening.
"Karen? How can I describe her? Beautiful, intelligent,
even-tempered . . ." She laughed, amending, "Well, most
of the time. She's three now. I'm thinking of preschool,
a place where she can play with other children. I don't
want her growing up feeling deprived because she's an
only child."

"Were you one?"

"Well—yes. As far as I know. I—well, it's a complicated story."

"Tell me."

"It might bore you."

"Marianne, if I find it boring, I'll let you know."

Marianne had been working a year and a half at Billings when she was offered another promotion. She would
be an assistant to Mr. Gunther, visiting the various
Billings subsidiaries, troubleshooting, and reorganizing
accounting systems so that they were in line with the
parent company's. It was an important advancement in
her career. She called Brad to arrange a celebration
dinner for the following night and then rushed home to
tell Karen.

When Marianne got home she noticed a car parked
across the street in a red zone. It was an Alfa Romeo
Spider Veloce, similar to the one Toby's mother had
owned. A woman was at the wheel. The evening light
was too uncertain for Marianne to make out the face,
but she could have sworn it was Dorothy. Marianne was
debating whether to cross the street to have a closer
look when the car suddenly started up and, nearly
colliding with a truck, whipped out into traffic and
drove off.

Marianne stood there watching the car, its red taillights winking at the end of the street as it turned the
corner. Was Dorothy Hansford watching her apartment?
Two weeks earlier Marianne had received a letter from
Dorothy asking if she might see Karen. "A meeting can
be arranged anywhere you like," she had written. Marianne had torn the letter up and tossed it in the trash.
And just the day before yesterday another letter: "How
can you be so heartless? I think you are . . ." Marianne
hadn't finished reading it.

Was a frustrated Dorothy still trying to gather incriminating evidence to prove her an unfit mother—a live-in
lover, a garbage bin full of empty vodka bottles, a parade
of seedy-looking characters coming and going? Or maybe
Dorothy and Ed would attempt something more drastic.

Like kidnapping. They could hire someone to snatch Karen. Just yesterday she had read that a divorced father had kidnapped his small son. She wouldn't put kidnapping past the Hansfords. Once they got their hands on Karen, they'd take off for Europe, South America, Florida. They could afford to go anywhere. By the time Marianne had climbed the stairs to her apartment she had convinced herself that the Hansfords were planning to steal Karen.

She cancelled her celebration dinner with Brad and instead spent the next two evenings searching for another apartment. By the weekend she and Karen had moved to the Upper West Side.

"It's about time I moved up anyway," she told Brad, who had come over earlier to help.

They were sitting on the green brocade sofa, empty cartons of deli takeouts on the coffee table before them. Karen was asleep in Uncle Brad's lap, her thumb stuck comfortably in her small mouth.

"You call Amsterdam Avenue up?" Brad asked.

"Nearly up." Marianne removed Karen's thumb from her mouth. Karen stirred, settled more cozily under Brad's chin, and replaced the thumb. "It was all I could find on short notice." Marianne again tugged the offending thumb from her daughter's mouth.

"You'll wake her," Brad said. "Let her be."

"And risk her having buck teeth?"

"That's an old wives' tale."

"Like hell."

"You know," he said, his voice edged with exasperation, "sometimes you get a wrong notion and nothing can shake you."

"Thumbsucking's not a notion, that's . . ."

"I don't mean just thumbsucking. Take this idea of the Hansfords trying to kidnap Karen. Of all the crazy—"

"It's not crazy. Nothing connected with the Hansfords is crazy."

"They wouldn't."

"They would."

"Marianne, you're becoming irrational. You—"

"*Shhh*. I'd rather not talk about it. Okay?" she said, and after a small silence she added, "You're not mad?"

"No, why should I be? It's your obsession, not mine. And speaking of obsessions, your career means a lot to you, doesn't it? I know you've worked hard for your success. But maybe there are some limits . . ."

"I love working at Billings, Brad. It's a growing organization with a promising future for somebody like me. And don't tell me it's either my career or Karen. Karen will always come first. I've fought too damn hard to keep her. When I think . . . But you know all that."

"Yes." He gave her a warm smile. "I was there, remember?"

Brad's hair had darkened since college days and he had lost his freckles. Marianne, who had never paid much attention to Brad's looks, decided he had become a very attractive man. And as a bachelor, he was highly eligible. Now teaching at NYU, it was no wonder that, as Brad had once quipped, lady colleagues and female students often waylaid him in NYU's hallowed halls with all kinds of propositions.

Why, she thought, half amused, as they chatted on, he's such a nice guy I could almost proposition him myself.

In June of 1977 Marianne was invited to a Cornell reunion in Ithaca. Until then she had avoided alumni bashes. She had mixed feelings about Cornell. There were the good ones, when she thought about the happy but short time she had spent there with Toby, and sad ones, when she remembered his sudden death. Her subsequent struggle to keep going, to finish her education, she did not care to think of at all. But Brad was going, and several classmates she hadn't seen in a long time would be there, too.

"You need a weekend, for God's sake!" Brad said. "You haven't had one day to yourself for years. If you can't get a sitter, Ginny will be glad to look after Karen.

How are you going to keep in touch with old friends and meet new ones if you don't get out and circulate?''

"I meet lots of people. And if you're talking about a man in my life, I've already got one. You." She laughed. "Why, I do believe you're blushing. Are you? You nut! Okay, okay, I'll go!"

In preparation she did some serious shopping, a luxury she hadn't given herself time to enjoy before. Since working at Billings she had bought her clothes in a hurry, during a lunch break or while making a quick foray to Macy's or Gimbels on a Saturday afternoon with Karen in tow. Her purchases had been mainly outfits she could wear on the job, mannish suits and no-frill blouses, the standard uniform of career women of the seventies. But now she took a half day off, browsing through Bendel's and Bergdorf Goodman. Shocked by the outrageous price tags, she had to keep telling herself she could afford it now. All her debts were paid off, and she owed no one except herself. She could finally afford to splurge.

She bought two daytime dresses, one a light wool, shading from melon to peach, the other a pale gray linen. Because evening dresses were too costly at these stores, even for a splurge, she got one at Altman's, a turquoise sheath that floated two chiffon streamers from the scooped-out back.

At the last minute Brad was unable to make it. An English physicist with whom he had scheduled a meeting later in the month had moved his visit forward, and Brad did not want to miss him. Hearing this, Marianne began to have second thoughts herself.

"So you're going to stay at home because I'm not there to hold your hand?" Brad needled.

"Okay! Okay! I'm going!"

She went, and after she got to Ithaca she was glad she did. There had been a transition, new buildings, new shops, a mall that hadn't been there before. It was fun to see the changes in her classmates. John, who had had an aversion to shoes, haircuts, and clean jeans, in a custom-tailored three-piecer, making it big at IBM. Jackie done up like a Las Vegas showgirl, false eyelashes, married and divorced twice. And Hazel, slimmed down, her frizzy hair straightened, a good-looking husband on her arm.

It was on the last night at the dinner-dance that she met Gregory Windham. He was introduced as a hotshot mover and shaker, owner of Windham Mills and assorted subsidiaries, class of '61. A dark-haired, classic executive type, he had what Aunt Em would call "wicked eyes." Their chemistry was instantaneous. A mutual attraction so overwhelming it took Marianne completely by surprise. He was not exactly her type—worldly, authoritative, a bit macho, she suspected—yet he had a certain audacious charm she found hard to resist.

They drank champagne and danced all night, and Marianne willingly accompanied Gregory back to his hotel suite. Verbal preliminaries were unnecessary. They had known from the first that making love was not only desirable but inevitable.

When Gregory closed the door behind them and she went into his arms, his chest hard against her breasts, his hungry mouth claiming hers, she wondered how she could have gone so long without this feeling of exhilaration. Sex she had had, yes. One or two times with a man she'd met at a dinner party—couldn't even remember his name—and the car dealer from whom she had bought her Mazda. Sex without passion. But this was different, this was fire, molten flame burning her flesh, her breasts, a furnace in her loins.

Marianne held him tightly, savoring his strong mouth, running her hands up the bunched musles of his back.

"*Mmm*," he growled, coming up for air, resting his mouth in the little hollow of her throat, nuzzling the side of her neck. "To think I almost missed that reunion, almost missed meeting you."

"Me, too."

"Marianne . . ." He lifted his face and looked down at her for a long moment. Then swiftly, with an impetuosity that took her breath away, he rained kisses on her face, her cheeks, her chin, her nose, her eyelids, his searing, insistent mouth bruising her own. Gripping the skirt of her gown with one hand, he shimmied it up over her thighs, and with the other he yanked at his zipper.

"Wait," she whispered, slipping out of his arms. Her wrists quivered and electricity crackled as she pulled the turquoise crepe de chine over her head, revealing a wispy bra of coral lace. She dropped her dress, and before she could get to the bra, Gregory bent his dark head and through the filmy cloth took a nipple in his mouth, teasing it with his teeth.

She reached back and unsnapped the bra and he peeled it free with his teeth, letting it fall to the floor to join the heap of green silk. Going back to the nipple, now taut, smooth, round, and darkly pink, he took it between his lips, sucking, worrying it with his tongue, sucking again in deep indrawn gasps.

Marianne felt as though ice was running down her spine, and she shivered. She tried to help him undress, but in their frenzied haste arms, legs, and clothes got tangled and they tripped, falling to the carpet, rolling over and over, consumed with laughter. When Marianne tried to get up he caught her around the waist, forcing her down, pinning her shoulders to the floor, covering her body with his.

"I can't wait," he murmured hoarsely.

Her legs, as if they had a will of their own, spread to receive him, and he entered her with a jolt that tore a small cry from her lips. He filled the aching void between her legs with a pleasurable, enormous hardness, moving back and forth in quickening glides.

"Don't come," she whispered.

But he didn't hear her, his plunges grew deeper, more rapid, until he stiffened with a low groan, bursting inside her.

"Sorry," he apologized in a mumble, kissing her forehead. "But that's what you've done to me. I'll make it up to you."

And he did. It was a night of pure sensual pleasure. Gregory, magnificent naked, with black curly hair furring his broad chest, took her to bed, and in a slow, leisurely fashion that increased in tempo and heat he made love to her. With his hands, mouth, and tongue he kissed, licked, and sucked every crevice of her quivering body, the crook of her elbow, the cleavage between white breasts, her belly, the inside of her thighs, her clitoris, swelling under his tongue until in an agony of suspended anticipation she seemed to explode, ripples of ecstasy coursing through her body.

Later, under the shower, she shed tears, thinking of Toby. She remembered that first night they had made love at the Sea Shell Inn, the white moonlight pouring in through the lace-curtained windows onto their naked bodies. "Was I all right?" she had asked afterward. "Super," he had said, kissing her tenderly. Now she knew the truth. Toby, even in his relative inexperience, had been aware of her awkwardness. He had praised her ineptness because he had loved her. She hadn't had an orgasm. She hadn't even known what one was. If he had lived, would they have grown and matured together, experimenting with their lovemaking? Could he have made her as happy as Gregory had tonight? But she ought not to compare the two. Toby had been hardly more than a boy, the first real love of her young life.

Gregory Windham liked to think of himself as a self-made man cast in the same mold as his grandfather, who went to work in the mills at twelve prior to the passage of child labor laws and rose to be the owner of Windham before he died. But Gregory was third-generation Windham, and while his early years at the plant had been anything but easy or pleasant, he had started his career with advantages his grandfather never had.

Gregory admired self-made men. He felt that those who started at zero and with bare hands fought their way up to success were the real heroes of the world. Hard-working and self-disciplined himself, he had little use for idlers, whiners, or losers. He sought the company of people in business and the arts who had made it the hard way to wealth and power.

He also had a discerning eye for potential. He was

good at picking employees who were quick to learn, who in a short while could take over important positions, places of trust and authority, thus freeing him for overall management. But as for placing women in high executive slots, he couldn't see it. They didn't have the training or the stamina. Not that he didn't applaud or wasn't fond of intelligent women—Marianne was a case in point—but on a corporate board? No way.

Marianne's ambition to get there—she had mentioned it only in passing during their brief, passionate, and, to Gregory, unforgettable encounter—didn't make her any less attractive to him. He relished her spirit as much as he did her lovely face and beautifully responsive body. Marianne. Now *there* was a woman.

Marianne returned to her apartment late in the afternoon on Sunday. Still full of Gregory and the wonderfully wild night they had spent together, she absentmindedly went through the small pile of mail that had accumulated in her absence. A phone bill, three organizations asking for money, an appliance store throwaway, and a *Ms.* magazine. Under it was a letter with a foreign stamp. She picked it up slowly, her hand trembling as she stared at it, a thin, bluish envelope with black, slanted script.

It didn't seem possible, but here it was, like a ghost taking on flesh, the letter she had never really given up waiting for these past twenty-nine years. *Mrs. Sarah Oliver,* the return address read. *Sixty Donfeng Road, Canton. PRC.* The People's Republic of China.

Her mother had written at last.

CHAPTER VIII

"**M**Y DEAR DAUGHTER . . ."

Marianne paused. Torn by a sudden burst of anger, she wavered on the edge of destroying the letter, tearing the opaque rice paper page into a dozen strips. She drew breath to calm herself down, then began to read again. The writing was steady, clean-stroked, with only a slight embellishment to the capitals.

My dear daughter:

The years have gone by, I know not where,
but you have never been far from my thoughts.
Circumstances have made it impossible for me
to communicate with you. But now that China
and the United States have established relations
it is my fondest hope that we can get
together. My one regret is that your
father won't be here. He died in September
of 1967. His death still seems unreal to me.
But I will not dwell on that. Is there some

way you can come to Canton? I would travel
to Passaic but am presently unable to. I
do want to see you, Marianne. You are my
only child. Please write and let me know.

Fondly,
Sarah

It's not the sort of message *I* would have sent to a
daughter I hadn't seen since infancy, Marianne thought
as tears came to her eyes. She doesn't say anything
about being sorry for not having written sooner. "Fondly,"
no reference to love. Short, succinct; there isn't one
personal question in it. Have you married, any children,
what are you doing, do you remember me?

Marianne tried to tell herself her disappointment, colored by the memory of childhood rejection, was irrational. She ought to give Sarah Oliver the benefit of the
doubt. Maybe, as Uncle Bob had once pointed out, her
mother had been too ill to write. "I would travel . . . but
am . . . unable to." Maybe she was still in poor health.
Or maybe her mother had felt that the Parkers had
assumed the role of parents and that it was best not to
intrude. There could be a dozen rational excuses for her
mother's silence. She mustn't condemn her out of hand.

Marianne tried to see the situation objectively. But she
couldn't. The gnawing sense of injustice remained. *Three
decades* had gone by since she had left China. And
finally her mother had decided to write. Too late. What
did it matter now? Why didn't she tear the letter up, toss
it away with the rest of the junk mail? Sarah Oliver had
no rightful claim on her. Sarah Oliver doesn't exist, she
thought. I won't go, of course. I might answer the
letter—it would be petty not to—but to travel the thousands of miles to Canton? Out of the question.

As she dropped the letter in the "To Be Answered"
file the front door slammed open.

"Moms?"

She turned to meet the running figure in jeans and
candy-striped T-shirt, her arms wide, lifting her seven-

year-old jewel, twirling her around, covering her face with kisses.

"Oh, Moms! Moms! Stop! I can't breathe!"

"Miss me?" Marianne asked, giving the child an extra squeeze before she put her down.

"Oh, yes! Mrs. Hobbs and I had such fun today. We went to the zoo and there was this funny man who fell down. Mrs. Hobbs said he was drunk, didn't you, Mrs. Hobbs?"

"Yes. So he was. She was a good girl, Mrs. Oliver. Minded real fine." Mrs. Hobbs's eyes under a scruffy black felt hat reflected unspoken criticism. While Marianne's housekeeper reluctantly accepted the necessity of a widowed mother working to support her child, she did not approve of weekends away from home, no matter what the reason.

Mrs. Hobbs stooped, gathering Karen in one arm to kiss her. "I have to be going now, honeybunch."

"Let me pay you," Marianne said.

Later, while Marianne hastily assembled supper for Karen and herself, the doorman announced that a messenger was coming up with some packages.

There were three of them, each with two dozen long-stemmed roses nestled in green tissue, each with a card that said, "I love you. Gregory."

He called as she was putting Karen to bed. "I've been trying to remember the color of your eyes. Brown? Blue? Green? No, no, *gray*! Gray, and fantastic like the rest of you."

She laughed. "You're sentimental, Gregory. And not very original. Thanks for the roses."

"Not very original either. I hope you like them."

"Actually, I'm allergic to roses."

"Oh?"

"I'm kidding. They're lovely."

"I meant what I said on the card. Could I come over and give you a free demonstration? You'd be under no obligation to buy."

"Not tonight, Gregory. I'll call you later."

Karen, her jaw moving rhythmically, asked, "Who's that?"

"A man I met at Cornell. What's in your mouth, young lady?"

The jaw stopped.

"Okay. Give it to me."

A wad of bubble gum was sheepishly deposited in Marianne's palm.

"What's his name?" Karen asked curiously. "The man on the phone."

"Gregory Windham. He went to Cornell, too, but before I was there."

"Is he nice?" Earnest dark brown eyes questioned.

"Very." A sudden picture of their lovemaking, naked limbs entwined and heaving, flashed through her mind, and she found herself blushing. "He lives in New York, too. You'll meet him."

"Is he as nice as Uncle Brad?"

Nice was not a word Marianne would use in connection with Gregory. Volatile, dynamic, and tender at the right moments, yes. But nice was too bland.

"You'll like him," Marianne said.

"Does he have any kids?"

"Two boys. Charlie and Paul." Gregory had been married for ten years, divorced for three. Unlike the few divorced men she had known who had complained sourly about their ex-wives, Gregory spoke of his former spouse with respect, if not regret. Marianne liked that.

"Are they my age?"

"No. They're older than you. Both are away at school. And speaking of school, young lady, did you get your homework done while I was away?"

"Yes, Moms. We had to do a project about a foreign country. I wrote it about China. I told the teacher I had a granny there."

"That's true."

Two years earlier Karen had befriended a little girl her own age who had come to stay briefly with her grandmother and grandfather in the apartment next door. Karen had wanted to know why *she* didn't have a granny, too.

For Marianne, the Hansfords were difficult to talk about. The details of her struggle for Karen's custody was something Marianne thought the child was too young to understand. Instead she had answered Karen as honestly as she could. She explained that her dead father's parents lived in another city, that they and she had quarreled and were not on friendly terms. This seemed to satisfy Karen. As for the Olivers, Marianne pointed out that the distance between Canton and New Jersey made visiting impractical. And again Karen accepted Marianne's word without question.

But now Karen delved. "Why don't Granny and Grandpa Oliver ever write, Moms?"

"As a matter of fact, I heard from Granny today." The hard place in Marianne's heart that had been scarred over for so many years considered the letter. How much simpler, she thought, it would have been if I had lied to Karen and told her the Olivers had died, just as Emma had once advised Uncle Bob to do with me. Simpler. Nothing is simple. The questions would have been asked in any case. We all want to know where we come from. The daughter or son who has been adopted, lavished with love, still asks questions. What was my real mother like? Who was my father? Granny? Grandpa? The desire to know, to have roots is strong.

Once again Marianne had to fight back tears. "She wrote that Grandfather died," Marianne said.

"Oh! How sad!" A cloud crossed the upturned face.

"Before you were born, darling."

"Are we ever going to get to see Granny?"

"I'm thinking of it."

But, of course, she wasn't. She had already decided against Canton.

"Can I go, too?"

"You have summer camp," she reminded. Should I go? she asked herself. Just out of curiosity, if nothing else? It would be interesting to see what her mother was really like.

"I wouldn't mind missing camp," Karen said hopefully.

"And there's the camp play," Marianne pointed out. "They count on you to take a leading role."

"Oh, Moms, that isn't true." Karen's finger probed for a bit of left over bubble gum on a back tooth. "They always pick me for the bad fairy or the witch."

"Some witch. Take your finger out of your mouth."

"Oh, Moms." She giggled, throwing her small arms around Marianne's neck. "I love you."

For a few moments Marianne rested her face against her daughter's warm cheek, closing her eyes, letting a happy tide wash over her. This is what Sarah had missed, she thought, all this love; love that seeps through the skin and runs in the blood. One's own, one's kin.

She would go to China, she decided suddenly. But she'd go alone. Maybe her mother did love her, and always had. She would never know unless she went and saw for herself.

Marianne had no difficulty in getting leave from her job. She booked a flight and made reservations at a hotel through the China International Travel Service. Marianne's cable to her mother was answered within a few days: "Will meet you at airport."

Bradford, glad Marianne had made the decision, promised to look in on Karen while she was gone. He envied Marianne her trip. His interest in China had spurred him to continue his language lessons with Jimmy Wu, a Chinese colleague at M.I.T.

"Sorry I can't go with you and practice my Chinese on the natives, though I'm learning Mandarin, not Cantonese. Wu tells me there's a big difference. Next time, maybe."

Gregory Windham surprised her by saying he had business in Hong Kong and would meet her there for a few days after her visit with her mother.

"It's like being given a candy apple for having gone to the dentist," she told Gregory. In two weeks their relationship had quickly developed into the shared intimacy of a long-time affair.

"That bad?"

"Yes—and no."

She had been ambivalent from the start, and her feelings swung from regret to anticipation and back to regret again. Yet she now felt she had to make the trip. It had become a challenge. She had prepared herself for several contingencies, sure that she could handle them all: disappointment, a perfunctory welcome, a tearful one. By and large, she told herself, it won't make that much difference. I have Karen, Uncle Bob, Brad, and now Gregory, people who love me. My mother has always been on the far edge of my life. And whatever happens won't really matter.

But it did matter.

Coming into the noisy, crowded airport waiting room after passing through customs, Marianne looked around for her mother. Sarah had written that she would be wearing a dark blue cotton jacket and trousers with a bright red scarf around her neck. Most of those in the milling beehive were either army personnel or travelers in Western dress, tourists, businessmen, and Overseas Chinese (those Chinese who lived in and were citizens of other countries), Nikons and Yashicas slung from arms and necks. The average Chinese of the People's Republic, Marianne had been told, did not travel by air. Nor were they permitted in the airport unless they had official authorization.

Marianne, though tired, felt calm. She had had a tedious flight: New York City to Seattle to Tokyo, where the aircraft had sat on the ground for three hours because of some minor engine malfunction. Her neck felt stiff, the result of napping in her seat at an awkward angle. And she needed a shower.

"Marianne?"

The voice was low, and when she turned to confront the smiling speaker she had a moment of shock.

Based on Emma Parker's long-ago, fuzzy description she had expected a fairly tall woman with brown hair and a dimple at each corner of her smiling mouth. The dimples were there, but hard to find in a face that seemed prematurely webbed and furrowed. She might have been tall once, but now she was slightly stooped and thin, very thin, almost skeletal.

"Sarah." Marianne could not bring herself to say "*Mother*."

"Marianne." No embrace, but a handshake. "It's good to see you. Is this your luggage? I have a friend waiting outside in the taxi."

The friend was standing at the bottom of a flight of shallow stone steps, dark, pouched Oriental eyes glimmering behind black-framed glasses.

"This is Dr. Chen," Sarah said.

Taller than her mother, he wore the same blue uniform as Sarah and the people in the small crowd of Chinese who peered curiously at them from behind a wire-fenced barrier.

"How do you do, Miss Oliver?" His English was faultless, his handshake energetic. "Welcome to Canton."

The taxi was a ramshackle Russian-made sedan of the fifties, maroon in color, dented in the front left fender and with a smashed, lopsided headlight. The young driver pinched out a cigarette before he started the car, maneuvering it out onto a tree-lined street. It was late July, hot, muggy, and overcast with an oppressive pall. People thronged the gray sidewalks and bicycled on the roadway in ranked files like schools of fish, each clad in the same blue cotton. They all seemed to have identical haircuts, short with just the tips of the ears showing. Occasionally a woman wore her hair in tightly braided pigtails. Otherwise it was difficult to distinguish between male and female.

"Is today a holiday?" Marianne asked, observing the tide of humanity.

"No holiday," Dr. Chen explained. "We have very few. New Year's, Liberation Day, the Spring Festival. But people go to factory and office at staggered hours. We have many workers in Canton. It's a busy city."

They turned a corner where a crowd was gathered around a tall, wide bulletin board.

"They are reading the daily newspaper," Dr. Chen said. "There is much interest in what is happening in Beijing now. Probably you have heard in the States: Mao Zedong died last September, and his widow, Jiang

Qing, along with three others, has been arrested for
trying to control the government. They are known as the
Gang of Four."

"Yes. I've read about the trial."

Dr. Chen left Marianne and Sarah off at the Dong
Fang, where Marianne had reservations. It was a large,
rambling hotel built around a courtyard with greenery,
graveled walks, and clipped bushes. Marianne's room,
in the older section, was austere, the faded, cranberry-
colored carpet worn, peeling up from the floor in the
corners and along the base of the lime-green walls. Thermos jugs of water, one hot, one cold (the water was
undrinkable for Westerners, her mother explained), stood
on a scarred bureau along with two cups turned downward on saucers and a china bowl which held several
packets of tea. Marianne, glancing in the bathroom, saw
the broken tiling on the floor and faucets that leaked a
steady drip-drip into a cracked porcelain sink. There
was no air conditioning, and the single electric fan,
positioned on the windowsill and whining from side to
side, gave no relief.

"You must be tired," Sarah said. She was sitting on a
cane-bottomed chair, her spine straight, her ringless hands
folded in her lap.

"Yes, I am," Marianne said flatly, suddenly uncommunicative.

Sarah had said very little on their ride from the airport.
Dr. Chen had done much of the talking, while Sarah, in
composed silence, had listened attentively to Dr. Chen's
minitravelogue. She did not seem ill at ease now, but
Marianne felt a strain. Usually adept in social situations,
Marianne was uncomfortable. This stranger, her mother,
was a closed book, and it did not appear as though she
was ready to open it. Bradford had warned her about
that. "Your mother is not Chinese, but she's always
lived in that culture," he had said. "It might have effectively colored her attitudes. Remember, they show warmth
only to family and kin."

"But I *am* family."

"Then you must remind her," he had said.

Now Marianne, not knowing where to begin, asked, "Would you like a cup of tea?"

"That would be nice."

Marianne fixed two cups, pouring the steaming water from the Thermos jug. The tea was strong and scalding hot. Beads of sweat formed along Marianne's hairline.

"Are you still teaching?" Marianne asked politely.

"Yes. I could retire—we can do that at fifty-five—but I want to go on while I'm still useful."

"What do you teach?"

"Literature." She did not elaborate but smiled again at her daughter. The smiled annoyed Marianne. It seemed fixed, without purpose.

"Where are you living now?" Marianne felt she was pulling every bit of information from her mother with tongs.

"With Dr. Chen and his family. His sons have adopted me. To the Chinese it is unfortunate if you do not have children to support you in your old age."

The statement somehow put Marianne on the defensive. Nice people adopting an old lady because she had no one to care for her.

"But the Chen boys must have known you had a daughter," she said. "And surely when you retire you'll get a pension."

"Daughters always belong to their husband's family. But I see"—she glanced at Marianne's ring finger—"that you did not marry."

"I did marry. I'm widowed."

"Oh—I'm so sorry."

A prickly silence fell between them. As the moments ticked away Marianne fought a rising anger. The fan droned back and forth, back and forth, lifting a corner of the thin scarf on the bureau every time it passed. Outside in the corridor a mysterious thumping, as if someone was dragging heavy luggage, passed the door. Sarah cleared her throat but did not speak. Marianne, unable to control her irritation any longer, said, "Aren't you going to ask me anything about my marriage, my hus-

band? Aren't you interested enough to wonder if I have
children?''

"I was waiting for you to tell me," Sarah said calmly.
"I don't like to pry.''

Pry! Marianne tried hard to keep her voice at a reasonable level, but it simmered with anger. "What was
the purpose of my coming to Canton if we're going to sit
in a hot room just looking at one another?''

"I don't want you to tell me anything unless you feel
you want to.''

It was like shadowboxing with a fall of feathers. "Aren't
you curious, concerned, interested?" she demanded.

"Because I don't ask doesn't mean I'm not concerned.''

It wasn't reserve, as Brad had said. It was an icy wall,
one that Marianne suddenly wanted to batter down with
her fists. "I don't believe that," she snapped, not both-
ering to hide her bitterness. "If you had cared you
would have written to me, you would have tried to
contact me. Twenty-eight years! Twenty-eight! And nothing but silence." Marianne paused, her heart racing, her
cheeks hot. She had warned herself not to bring up the
past, but she couldn't help it. It was here now, all the
disappointments coming back to claim her.

Sarah only sighed resignedly. "I know, I know.''

Suddenly Marianne felt defeated and ashamed. She
looks so frail and defenseless, Marianne thought. Yet
her shame did nothing to lessen her anger. She had the
terrible urge to weep. But over what? She couldn't give
herself a logical answer. That was the distressing thing.
If she, Marianne, had spent a bleak, cruel, deprived
childhood, then her anger would be justified. But her
early years, thanks to Uncle Bob, who had never stinted
on love, had been good ones. He had given her kindness, understanding, a secure home. Why then bear
animosity toward this poor creature, Sarah Oliver, whose
colorless face turned to her now in mild surprise?

Lost dreams, Marianne thought, answering her own
query. The child who had hoped and waited was still
there. Behind the sophisticated facade, the burnished hair
swept into a neat butterfly bun, the Soprani linen sheath,

the Estée Lauder blusher, the little girl still knelt at the window watching for the postman to bring a letter that never came.

"Sometimes," her mother said sadly, "things happen we cannot predict."

What things? Marianne wanted to shout.

Instead she got up and went to the window on legs that were damp and sticky in their nylons. Standing there looking over the courtyard and the small pond, its green surface flecked with diffused sunlight, she fought for self-control. She had known the meeting with her mother would be difficult, awkward, perhaps even painful. What she had not anticipated was her own intense reaction, the ferment that must have been building for years suddenly spewing out. It disturbed her. She did not like to think that Marianne Oliver, the careerist, the level-headed professional who had been able to meet potentially explosive situations at Billings with a cool dispassion, could come apart so easily.

Behind her, Sarah murmured, "I'm sorry."

Marianne turned to face her mother. Suddenly her anger had dissipated. She felt tired and weary. "I am, too. But . . ." She shrugged. "It doesn't help to dwell on what should or shouldn't have been done. Tell me." She took another deep breath. "Tell me about my father. When did he die?"

Sarah wet her lips, her eyes filming over.

"If you'd rather not talk about it . . ." Marianne offered.

"No. It's only right for you to know. He—he was killed in the summer of '67—ten years ago. During the Cultural Revolution, by a band of Red Guards."

"How awful."

"Yes," her mother said. "It was a—a misfortune."

"I would think that such a murder would have made you want to come back home. Didn't you want to leave then?"

"This is my home," she said quietly, with an obdurate turn of her mouth. "Mao Zedong made many mistakes, not the least of which was the unleashing of the

Red Guards, but the basic tenets of the revolution are still sound. Whether the western world liked Mao or not, we have to remember that he brought a bankrupt, famine-stricken nation together and put it on its feet. He found a way to feed the hungry, tend the sick, free the coolie and peasant. He gave the Chinese their rightful dignity.''

"You really believe in Red China," Marianne said.

"The People's Republic of China," she corrected. "Yes, I do."

Marianne said nothing, not wishing to pursue a political argument. She wasn't equipped for it. What's more, she didn't care. She had come to Canton to see a mother who had suddenly reappeared in her life, not for a lecture on revolution.

The next day Marianne went to visit her mother at the Chens'. They lived on Donfeng Road, not far from the memorial to Dr. Sun Yat-sen, in a house situated behind a wall that ran the length of a city block. Dr. Chen greeted her at the double gate. One gate to screen the compound from the street, he explained, the other to keep out evil spirits. According to him, the Chen compound, consisting of a half dozen buildings, had been in the family since the Ming Dynasty. After Liberation the buildings as well as the main house had been divided up into living quarters for a dozen families.

The House of Chen now reflected little of its past grandeur. Tiles were missing from the roofs, which must have been magnificent with their curved eaves and *kui longzi*—glazed figurines of mythical dragonlike creatures. Paint was peeling, lattices broken, shutters missing. Former gardens were now narrow, dusty lanes littered with refuse and strung with dingy drying laundry.

The Chen quarters, far more ample than those of many Cantonese, the doctor pointed out, consisted of three bedrooms, one each for his married sons, their wives, and their children, and one for himself and his wife and an unmarried daughter. Sarah had been given a small partitioned room just off the kitchen that was reached by crossing a tiny courtyard overgrown with creepers and a few dispirited stalks of bok choy.

Sarah, showing Marianne her room, with the iron cot, the one chair, the rickety small table she used for a desk, saw the dismay in her daughter's eyes. She thinks I'm poor. She feels sorry for me, Sarah thought. I *am* poor by her standards, but I've reached that stage of life where it takes so little to make me content. I was never one for possessions, and they mean less to me now than ever. The Chens are my family; I belong. I have a place in their household. I am respected at the University. I have my memories, some unpleasant, but there are good ones, too.

"This is your father," she said, pointing to a photograph high on the wall. Beneath it on a small shelf was a vase that held his ashes.

"Do I look like him?" Marianne asked.

"The hair and the eyes—a little." Sarah suddenly felt the familiar ache in her throat. Ten years and she couldn't get over his death. It had been cruel, wanton. Not so much the way he had died—that was bad enough—but to be taken from her in the prime of their lives was the real tragedy.

"It's a shrine, isn't it?" Marianne said, motioning to the urn.

"I suppose you could say that." How could she ever explain to Marianne that the ashes and the photograph kept William alive for her? That she had never accepted his death, never would. Had it been wise to write to Marianne? Perhaps she should have left well enough alone. But the child had been in her thoughts ever since the day she had kissed her goodbye and sent her off. How could she make her understand? How could she give the reasons behind her long silence without betraying the ideals which had guided both William and herself? She sensed that Marianne thought her hard, uncaring. But it wasn't true. It was just that through the years she had lost the knack of intimate conversation. And this grown person was a stranger, not the baby she had held in her arms. How could she break the barrier, reach this angry woman? She didn't know.

"Tell me," she said timidly, "a little about your life. You must forgive me for not asking sooner."

Marianne gave her a brief history, the sort of résumé one might exchange with a seat partner on a long flight. She said nothing of the Hansfords or her struggle to keep Karen. "Do you have a picture of Karen?" Sarah asked when she had finished.

Marianne produced the picture from her pigskin wallet.

"Ah," Sarah sighed. "How pretty she is. And she looks so intelligent."

"She is," Marianne agreed, softening.

"I wish that I could see her."

"We might arrange it," Marianne said slowly.

Mother and daughter gazed at the photograph: Karen grinning impishly into the camera, her eyes dancing under a dark fringe of curling hair. Side by side they stared, a quiet string of moments drawing them together, the first thin thread of a possible tie. But it was suddenly broken by Dr. Chen's voice from the courtyard.

"Sarah!" he called loudly, "bring your guest into our parlor for a cup of tea."

The "parlor" consisted of frayed wicker chairs, a long, ornately carved teakwood table (a Chen heirloom, saved miraculously through years of turmoil and revolution), and a potted ginger plant. It was as Spartan as Sarah's alcove. The scrubbed tile floor was without a carpet. A wall hanging—a paper scroll depicting a fog-shrouded mountain—tried but failed to hide the dangling electric wiring that powered a single feeble light bulb. There were no windows in this room, only the front door, which led to the compound lane, and the one at the rear, giving entrance to the courtyard. A son, two sisters-in-law, Dr. Chen's wife, who was a large-boned woman with graying hair, and a grandson were waiting for them. The child, shy in the presence of this foreigner, was eight or nine, Marianne judged, his bowl haircut growing out in pointed thatches at the nape and over the ears. He stood between his father's knees, gazing at Marianne with a mixture of awe and curiosity.

Dragon Well tea was served, along with bean curd pastries. Everyone spoke English, if only a few polite words. Dr. Chen, aside from practicing medicine at the local clinic, taught a language class at the University. "Whatever is in vogue at the moment," he said. "It used to be Russian. Now it is English."

The conversation touched on superficialities: the humid summer weather in Canton, the best places to eat, the most interesting sights to see. Sarah contributed little. She sat, her face blank, as if she were gazing inward. Teacups were refilled. Dr. Chen made some remark about President Carter's gesture of friendship toward the People's Republic, continuing in Ford's and Nixon's footsteps. The child, feeling a little more secure now and somewhat restless, left his father's knees. He touched his aunt briefly on the arm and traced his finger lingeringly along the flowered carving of the table, pausing at Sarah's chair. Coming out of her trance, she drew him onto her lap, her arms going around him, her chin lifting to kiss the crown of his head, her cheek bending to rest affectionately against his.

Watching them, Marianne felt as though a knife had run through her heart. It hurt. She could accept that her mother could only give her a handshake if she thought that Sarah wasn't capable of giving more. But it wasn't true. She could be as loving, as maternal, as any woman. But not to her. Never to her. The feeling of rejection and anger returned, a sour ball in Marianne's stomach. She regretted coming to Canton. I'll stay out the planned five days, she thought bitterly, and put as good a face on things as I can. I'm not ready to admit to myself, or to those at home, that my visit has been a failure.

When she said goodbye to her mother on Saturday, Sarah suddenly bent forward and gave Marianne a cool, dry kiss on the cheek.

"I'll write," she said. "And you must answer."

"I will," Marianne said, not sure that she would.

CHAPTER IX

Rather than fly to Hong Kong, where she was supposed to meet Gregory, Marianne took the through train. She wanted to see a little of the countryside, which Dr. Chen had assured her was picturesque. The car in which she rode was air-conditioned, filled with Japanese and Americans on package tours. Each double seat, backed with lace doilies and comfortably upholstered, was provided with jugs of hot water, tea, and cups, which stood on shelves jutting out from the curtained windows. By contrast, passengers in other cars, the ordinary Chinese, traveled in humid heat on hard benches, men, women, and children packed together with their baskets, their bedrolls, and their tin buckets of rice and tea.

What most those poor people think of us, Marianne wondered, riding in such grand style? It was a question she had asked herself more than once when she had purchased a pearl bauble or cloisonné vase to take back to the States as souvenirs. The prices of these items were often more than the Chinese salesgirl made in a month. Perhaps this contrast between the haves and have-nots gave Sarah, who still believed strongly in the Chinese revolution, pain. Perhaps she resented the rich foreign tourists like Marianne who hunted for bargains the Chinese could never afford. If so, she kept her displeasure, like her other feelings, to herself. Who could guess what Sarah thought?

With a heavy sigh, Marianne turned to the window as the train picked up speed and the engine, hauling its long, swaying tail behind, rumbled across a high embankment. Below them the still waters of flooded rice paddies reflected rows of green shoots and a blue sky speckled with drifting white clouds. Marianne, chin on hand, gazed at the fleeting hamlets, mud-walled, thatch-roofed huts clustered along puddled lanes where ducks and spindly chickens and a random pig or two rooted in the clay earth. Neatly ordered gardens of cabbage, celery, and melons gave way to fields tilled by lumbering bullocks or sinewy, barefooted peasants who, too poor or unlucky to possess a draft animal, trudged behind plows. Black-pajama-clad Hakka women wearing fringed straw hats bent to their tasks, ignoring the train, a familiar sight in its twice-daily passage. Now a narrow road paralleled the train, crossing a short, high-arched bridge. Over it a man, bent double, was hauling a cart loaded with bricks and lumber, his back, arms, and muscle-bound legs straining as he moved forward at a slow, bobbing pace.

As Marianne watched she thought of her mother again. Sarah's face seemed to haunt her. Marianne would have preferred to put the previous five days behind her, but the bent peasant pulling his cart recalled Sarah's frail, round-shouldered figure. The patient acceptance of a harsh life. Why had her mother remained all these years in China? Duty, she claimed. But to Marianne this was an unsatisfactory explanation. The more Marianne pondered the riddle of Sarah, the more elusive the answers remained. As a child, Marianne had invented a picture of Sarah, had even, in fantasy, imbued her with speech. The reality had been very different. There was so much she didn't understand, might never understand. Perhaps she shouldn't have come to Canton.

At Shenzhen, the border town, English-speaking officials came through to examine passports, visas, and declarations. On the Colony side, beyond the infamous barbed-wire fence put up by the Chinese and reinforced by the British, who felt that Hong Kong could not take any more refugees, the procedure was repeated.

An hour later, after traversing the New Territories and their rows of concrete tenements, Marianne arrived at Kowloon's Hung Hom station. There she took a cab through the tunnel to Hong Kong Island and the Mandarin Hotel, its scrawled M rising above the noisy traffic on the street below. Gregory had reserved a room for her on the third floor, filling it with red roses and sprays of white orchids. A note expressed his regret at not being able to meet her, but he would be held up at an important conference until two o'clock. "I love you. Can't wait."

The Mandarin, though an old hotel, kept up with modern times, offering all the amenities of air conditioning, push-button draperies, TV,, and a bathroom that gleamed with silver faucets and polished tile.

Marianne stood under the shower for a long time, scrubbing her torso, shampooing her hair, closing her eyes, letting the water pour over her. Her long hair was a nuisance. She would have it cut when she got home. Home. She missed it. She missed Karen terribly. She missed her laughter, the snapping, ballooning bubble gum she tried to hide from her mother, the white, tender nape of her neck as she bent to read. Marianne wondered what Karen was doing now. The time difference was so confusing. Was it afternoon at Camp Mennehauouk or evening? Was Karen swimming in the little lake bordered by pines or sitting in the mess hall, eating supper, a scum of milk on her upper lip as she chattered with a friend?

If it weren't for my promise to meet Gregory, she thought, I'd fly back to New York tomorrow.

Gregory. Her mood lifted as she thought of him. He

was more complex than his hearty, outgoing manner would lead one to believe. Only last week she had learned from the mutual acquaintances who had introduced them at Cornell that Gregory was a generous, though anonymous, contributor to several philanthropic organizations. He had also endowed a scholarship at Cornell using not his own name, but that of a favorite professor now deceased. This anonymity was so uncharacteristic of Gregory, who was not at all shy when it came to claiming recognition for his business exploits, and it only proved what Marianne already knew. Beneath the tough, aggressive exterior, Gregory possessed a streak of altruism that he preferred to hide.

Aside from this admirable trait, Gregory was fun, a marvelously wonderful companion. Dining sumptuously with him at prestigious restaurants, attending cocktail parties of the rich and sometimes of the famous, sitting center aisle at opening nights had been new and exciting experiences. It had been so long since Marianne had enjoyed herself, years since she had had a really good time, laughed so heartily, and been so easily amused.

Gregory owned an elegant townhouse on Riverside Drive where he gave wonderful parties. There, surrounded by Jay Spectre decor, Edo panels, and contemporary furniture upholstered in Clarence House leather, Marianne had met a variety of people from both business and the arts—bankers, musicians, actors, corporate lawyers, artists. But no matter how illustrious or interesting the guests might be, Gregory's presence seemed to charge the atmosphere with a special kind of electricity. He radiated vitality. He was the spark that got things going, that moved others to be at their best, their sharpest, their wittiest.

But there was more. He had wanted Marianne to meet his boys and had arranged that they have lunch together at Astor's in the St. Regis. Marianne had been a little late, coming in breathless, and had seen Gregory before he saw her. He had been standing on the other side of the lobby. Only one of the boys had been there (Charlie, she later learned), dark-haired like his father, a tall, gangly teenager. The boy had said something and Gregory had put his hand on his shoulder, smiling at his son, a look of such tenderness in his eyes that it had melted Marianne.

It was these little things, gestures, moments of tenderness, that endeared Gregory to Marianne as much as the admiration—and passion—he aroused in her.

Dressed in a cool, light robe, her still-damp hair tied back with a scarf, she sat reading the *South China News* when a knock on the door and Gregory's peremptory "Marianne!" brought her to her feet.

"I didn't expect you for another hour—" Marianne began.

"I cut the damned conference short."

He came into the room, a package tucked under each arm, bringing with him, as always, a dynamic air of *joie de vivre*. Dropping the packages on the floor, he pulled Marianne into his embrace, a man taking possession, his mouth claiming hers, demanding a response. And she gave, gladly, willingly, crushing her hungry mouth to his, dissolving at the feel of his hands on her body. Oh, it was good to be held, to be kissed, to be *wanted*.

"How'd the visit go?" he asked, looking into her eyes, his own soft with understanding.

"Not too well," she answered ruefully. "I—I can't talk about it now."

"Sweetheart, I'm so sorry." He held her close, caressing her hair. "Don't think about it. I'll make it up to you. I'm going to see that you have one hell of a good time here in Hong Kong. You've earned it." He kissed the side of her neck. "I want you to be happy. I love you, remember?"

Her robe had fallen open, and his hand slid inside under her arms, stroking her back, sliding erotically over her buttocks, pushing his erection into her groin.

"You know now why I cut out of that meeting, don't you?" He leaned his mouth against her forehead.

"Yes . . . Gregory—I . . ." Her voice became still as his hands moved, finding her breasts, cupping them, stroking the nipples with his thumbs. Then, bending his head, he took one of the rosy buds in his mouth. Marianne's breath quickened with pain and pleasure. She pressed Gregory's dark head to her breast.

"You—you're in a terrible hurry," she managed.

"Aren't you?" he asked, lifting his head.

He began to undress swiftly, divesting himself of coat, shirt, tie, trousers, shoes. He grabbed her arms, drawing her into his embrace again, his naked hairy chest scratching her tender skin, his mouth drifting over her face, planting kisses on her temples, her cheeks, her lips. Reaching behind, he jerked the blue scarf from her hair, releasing a silky cascade over her shoulders.

"Don't think about anything but me," he ordered softly.

"I'm not. I won't."

Naked on the bed, they gave themselves up to each other, a mutual passionate assault that roused Marianne to new heights of awareness of pure sensual pleasure. She loved his dark, strong hands, hands that stroked or could touch with feather lightness the curve of her hip, the hollow of her pelvis.

She cried out when he entered her, gripping his shoulders as spasm after spasm shook her body.

Afterward, with ice clinking in glasses of gin-and-tonic in their hands, they sat up in bed while Marianne opened Gregory's gifts.

"It's like Christmas when I was a kid," Marianne said, her face flushed with excitement. "But I have nothing for you, Greg."

"That's an understatement if I've ever heard one."

She laughed, undoing the silver ribbon of a long box. From a nest of tissue paper Marianne withdrew a cream-colored silk kimono embroidered front and back with white, blue, and gold chrysanthemums, the green, velvety leaves so real they seemed ready to be plucked.

Another box held three cashmere sweaters and a tweed skirt of purest wool. She hesitated before she opened the jeweler's box, then drew in her breath. Nested on ruby velvet were a pair of diamond earrings and a chain of alternating gold beads and small sparkling diamonds.

"Oh—it's beautiful, beautiful! This must have cost you a small fortune." Marianne lifted the necklace from the box. "But I can't."

"You can't what?" He took the diamond and gold chain from her and hooked it around her neck. "That's what I like about you. You're a holdover from another century. 'I can't,' " he mimicked. "Of course you can, you're my love and deserve nothing but the best."

She had learned by now that Gregory was given to platitudes, but they were delivered with a kind of candor, an almost boyish sincerity that charmed her. She loved the way he infused time-worn phrases with new meaning. His delivery, his voice, whatever he said expressed exuberance, a volatile message that said he was glad to be alive. She liked that. It made *her* glad, too.

The gold beads and diamonds nestling between white breasts were cool and heavy. And wickedly expensive. A gift for a mistress or a favorite concubine. They made her feel terrifically seductive and alluring.

"I'm starved, darling. Shall we go out for lunch?" Taking her hands, Gregory lifted her to her feet, kissing the tip of her nose, his eyes suddenly misting over. Her heart flew out to him, her lover, the giver of joy.

After a delectable lunch at Henri's, Gregory took her on what he termed "the Cook's tour." With a patience that surprised them both, he drove the rented Mercedes in stop-and-go traffic, crawling inch by inch through the central district at a pace that was notorious for reducing drivers to sweating fury.

"No hurry," he said, touching her hand, leaning over to plant a kiss on her cheek. "You'll get a good chance to see the city this way."

"What a contrast to Canton."

Canton had been thronged with bicycles but very few cars (and those either taxis or Red Flag official limousines). Except for the horns of the buses and the tinkling bells of the cycles, there had been little noise. But Hong

Kong's jam-packed streets rocked with a cacophony of sound. Horns blared, drivers swore, tires screeched in a crush of trucks, vans, buses, and taxis.

"Things are still booming, I see," Gregory commented.

Everywhere it seemed buildings were going up to the jarring, tooth-rattling notes of pneumatic drills; high rises, their steel girders like ribbed cages, soared above the clamorous bustle below. And the signs! The bold calligraphy of Chinese in neon and cherry-red paint vied with English placards strung across storefronts, swinging above the sidewalks and streets, announcing restaurants, tailor shops, money exchanges, jewelry and department stores. A pressure of human bodies, mostly Chinese, moved along the pavements, girls tripping by in jeans or tight skirts, men in business suits and ties, in dungarees and shirtsleeves, in shorts and T-shirts.

Gregory parked the car in a public garage. "I want you to see Ladder Street. It's unique to Hong Kong."

Ladder Street proved to be a series of shallow steps that climbed a steep, narrow alleyway. Here, on either side, Chinese merchants had set up shop cheek by jowl, their wares spilling over from interiors festooned with merchandise to outdoor baskets and stalls, flowers, vegetables, desiccated shrimp, dried mushrooms, octopuses, spices, tea, plastic shoes, and parasols. The jabber of many voices in a foreign tongue, the cries of the haggling customers and vendors, shouting children, the pop of a firecracker, the hiss of outdoor grills, the steady clop-clop of feet funneled down and around Marianne and Gregory like a roiling river. Gregory, pointing out objects of interest, had to shout in Marianne's ear to be heard over the din.

"I love Hong Kong," he said, pausing at a fruit stand where piles of tangerines and stalks of green bananas were displayed in reed baskets. "It's a city on the go. Frankly commercial. No apologies. People are not only here to make a buck, but to double, triple, quadruple that buck. Men have come here with only a few coins in their pockets and built empires. Tough, smart, adventurous, willing to take chances."

"You like that," she observed.

"Yes, I do. I like challenge. I like competition. I like matching wits with men who are geared up to do me in. I like winning. And I don't mind hard work. I thrive on it."

Marianne smiled. "Them's my sentiments, too."

"You." He gave her an affectionate, fatherly smile. "You're too ambitious for a lovely lady."

"Gregory." She took his arm suddenly, turning him around so she could look up into his eyes. "You're patronizing me," she said flatly. "And I'm not the least flattered."

"I didn't mean to patronize you, sweetheart."

"Not intentionally. But tell me honestly, if I were a man and said I wanted to play for high stakes, try my luck in the big game, would you have said I was too ambitious?"

"No, but . . . ."

"No buts. You've got to get over the notion that women can't compete with men in the business world."

"Oh, Christ, Marianne, I'm not that backward. I've got women working for me, smart as whips. I admire women—and men—anybody with brains."

"Just as long as you don't forget," she said, kissing his cheek.

He put his arm around her shoulders, holding her tightly for a long moment. *Marianne,* he thought. She was special. Not like any woman he had ever known. Sophisticated, beautiful, wonderful in bed, not jaded like most of the women he knew, but unique, as if she was just discovering passion. He admired her cool poise, loved that wonderful smile that lit up her face. He liked the quick way she zeroed in on him in an argument. Intelligent. A woman you could have a decent conversation with. Yet feminine. A womanly woman. He was falling in love with her.

"Let's get the car," he said, resisting the urge to hustle her back to the Mandarin and to that wide, wide king-sized bed. "I want to show you the Tiger Balm

Gardens, a crazy place built by a Chinese patent medicine king. And Aberdeen.''

"Is Aberdeen that Chinese fishing village?''

"Right. The people live on the water in sampans and
junks. Many of them used to boast that they never set
foot on dry land. I don't know whether that's true anymore, but they're still there, anchored in that cove, the
way they've been for nearly a century.''

Hours later, returning to their hotel, Gregory took a
wrong turn and found himself driving through the outer
fringes of a slum section, a part of the city he would
have preferred to miss.

"This wasn't on the tour,'' he said apologetically.

"No, I wouldn't think so.''

Hovels scabbed the hillsides, shelters erected from
packing cases, discarded, rotting, sea-soaked lumber and
rusting metal. Tar paper shacks with sagging walls and
gaping doors leaned tipsily against one another. The
stench of mold, of unwashed bodies, of running sewers
and human feces penetrated the air-conditioned Mercedes.

"Mostly refugees from the Mainland,'' Gregory explained.

"It seems they haven't bettered themselves,'' Marianne said, appalled and saddened by the squalor that
was before her. "Canton and the countryside around it
might be poor, but it's a park compared to this.''

"No rice paddies, for sure. But most of these people
are probably earning more than they could ever earn in
the People's Republic.''

"Maybe. But it's still low wages, cheap labor to those
who employ them, isn't it? I suppose that's what gave
Hong Kong its impetus during the sixties. Without these
refugees the companies here couldn't undersell in the
markets of the world.''

"It's no secret, Marianne, that labor costs are the
biggest factor in production.''

"Right, but . . .''

"But what? You mustn't think that the poor aren't
benefiting from Hong Kong's wealth. Many of these
people would starve without the thousands of jobs that

have opened up in the last few years. Take my word for it, sweetheart, they're still better off here than under a regimented society."

"It wouldn't seem so," Marianne said doubtfully.

"Of course they are. As soon as government gets a handle on housing, the slums will disappear. Furthermore, the unions are beginning to make headway here, and labor is demanding higher wages."

"Which means the big money will pull out."

"Possibly. There's another factor to consider. The Colony's lease runs out in 1998. Maybe the whole area, Hong Kong, Kowloon, the New Territories, will revert to China."

"So that means a communist Hong Kong."

"Not necessarily. The betting is that the People's Republic will leave the island the way it is, highly capitalistic. As it goes now, trade with the Colony generates needed hard cash for the Mainland."

"I just wish all of this wasn't done on the backs of the poor."

"Listen, sweetheart, let me give you a tip. If you're going to get anywhere at Billings, or wherever, you can't be sentimental. You'll get yourself run over by the stampeding mob, pushed out of the race to sit on the sidelines with your principles and your sentiments."

"You're not going to tell me that the corporate elite are all monsters without humanity."

"You missed my point. I'm as human as the next guy. You know that. But I keep my public or business life separate from my private life. You have to in this cockamammy world."

"You're probably right. But frankly, this squalor"— she waved toward the dismal scene, the smoking outdoor cooking fires, the ragged children picking among the heaps of rubbish—"gets to me."

"Foolish, lovable, tenderhearted girl. You ought to be in the movies, or sculpting, or writing novels—"

"Gregory!"

"Okay. Okay. I can't change the world, Marianne. I don't want to. I do what I can to help, but that's the

private side of me." He gave her earlobe a playful
tweak. "C'mon sweet, don't look so down. We're out to
have a good time, remember?"

They had been invited by Albert Sung, a Hong Kong
multi-millionaire who often did business with Gregory,
for dinner the next evening. Sung had built himself a
mansion on the Peak, high above the swarming crowds
and tumultuous roar of central Hong Kong. It was an
interestingly designed residence combining East and West.
It had a Chinese tiled roof, curved at the eaves and
ornamented with *kui longzi* that shone gold-red in the
last rays of the setting sun. Contemporary sliding glass
walls gave a panoramic view of the harbor.

The interior was what Marianne secretly labeled "sub-
dued opulent." In the spacious entryway a huge gilded
figure of the Chinese imperial lion stood on hind legs,
glowering fiercely. The only other furnishing here was a
small lacquered table over which hung a scroll with
Chinese calligraphy. The light fixtures were of Swedish
cut glass.

Mr. Sung greeted them warmly.

"My wife will join us shortly," he told Marianne and
Gregory, guiding them into a vast room where Chinese
brocades and hand-rubbed teak blended with Widdicomb
and Heritage chairs and tables.

"This is your first visit to Hong Kong, Miss Oliver?"
Albert Sung asked after they had given their cocktail
orders to a white-coated manservant.

Sung was a stocky man of medium height with a
fleshy face. His jet-black hair, receding from a round,
high forehead, was streaked with gray.

"I trust Gregory has been showing you around?"

"Yes. Fascinating city."

"I'm glad you find it so."

He spoke with an accent that held a slight Oxford
cadence.

They were on their second martini, discussing Aberdeen, when Mrs. Sung—Lily—appeared.

She was in formal dress, a shimmering Paris creation,

the neckline slashed to the navel, the skirt molding a
superlatively proportioned figure. Lily was not beautiful—
the mouth was too full, the nose too flat—but her smoldering eyes under black pageboy bangs exuded the kind
of feline sexuality that would bring any man to attention.

Her smile as she shook Gregory's hand and then Marianne's was polite, hostessy.

"Long time no see, Gregory," she said.

At dinner, however, which was served on gold-
rimmed Sèvres and handwoven linen, Marianne sensed
displeasure, if not anger, simmering beneath Lily's social smile. Though her manner as a courteous hostess
remained, a sudden sharp look, a shrug, a fleeting pout
directed sometimes at Gregory, sometimes at her husband, piqued Marianne's curiosity. Had Mrs. Sung
planned something else for this evening, something more
interesting than entertaining her husband's business associate and his girlfriend, Marianne wondered. Or did
she resent the relationship between Gregory and Albert?
The two had been friends long before Lily's arrival as
Mrs. Sung on the Peak (she was his fourth wife), and
their conversation was sprinkled with reminiscences that
effectively cut both she and Lily out.

Marianne did not mind. She found the early days of
Windham and Sung interesting. She enjoyed hearing about
the frantic, sweaty push to get quick orders of fifteen
hundred pairs of jeans or a thousand polyester blouses
out to wholesalers in New York ahead of the competition. The innovative sales pitches to prospective buyers,
the clever tactics to acquire smaller yet stubbornly resis-
tant companies, the power plays among the high and
mighty intrigued her.

After dinner they adjourned to what Sung called the
"cozier" study, a fairly good-sized room, the floor strewn
with Tianjin carpets and furnished with Chinese antiques.
They were being served cognac and coffee when a manservant entered to inform Albert that he had an urgent
call from London.

Some minutes later Marianne excused herself and found
her way to the powder room. She had drunk a little too

much wine and the air conditioning, turned abnormally low and blowing coldly on the back of her neck, had given her a headache.

The marble bathroom, glitteringly plumbed in gold, had mirrored walls that reflected a half dozen Mariannes. She studied these images, smoothing out a small frown with her fingertips, telling herself she really must get more sleep or she would develop bags under her eyes. Oh, but Gregory was worth it, she thought, smiling at herself. To be so loved.

She hugged herself, her eyes shining, her mind already picturing the night to come, the feel of Gregory's taut, naked body pressed to hers, the electricity running through her blood, charging her senses.

She caught herself going pink and turned away, a small, embarrassed smile still curling her lips. Really!

Somehow she missed her way in the plush-carpeted corridor, and it took her a few minutes before she got her bearings and retraced her steps. The door to the study was slightly ajar. Marianne had her hand on the knob when she heard her name spoken by Gregory.

"Marianne. I told you the other night—"

"She's a whore!" Lily hissed in a low, tense voice. "Your whore. And you had the rotten brass to bring her here. You bastard! I told you, Gregory, when this started that I didn't give a damn what you did in London, New York, Zurich, who you married, who you screwed. But here in Hong Kong you belong to me."

"Now, wait—hold on a minute, will you? Damn it! You and I had an understanding—"

"No! Send her home! If you don't, I'll tell Albert everything. I'll give him an earful. . . ."

Marianne stood for a moment in stunned disbelief.

"I'll let him know all about us, the times you and I . . ."

Marianne did not wait to hear more. Turning, she hurried blindly down the corridor to the powder room. Locking the door behind her, she sat down on the little ice cream parlor chair in front of the wide mirror. Angry, hurt, she stared at her reflection, the diamonds at her ears and throat glittering in the fluorescent light. *In Hong Kong you belong to me.* Why had Gregory brought her to this place? Why? *You and I have an understanding.* Gregory and Lily had an understanding. Albert knew nothing about it. He would be given an earful unless Gregory sent Marianne home. *Your whore,* Lily had called her. Damn Lily! Damn Gregory!

She could accept his past affairs, the women he had slept with before he met her, shadowy figures at a safe remove. They were not part of her life. She didn't want to know about them. She didn't want to see or meet them. Couldn't he understand how humiliating it was to be taken to the home of a former mistress, to sit there all through dinner while Lily sized her up, secretly sneered at her? Maybe Lily wasn't a *former* mistress. Maybe he had been sleeping with her while Marianne was in Canton. Maybe it inflated his male ego to have two of his women together in the same room. She didn't know. She wished she didn't care.

Somehow Marianne managed to get through the rest of the evening wearing a neutral smile on her face, putting in a few words at the right moments, and finally thanking her host and hostess as she and Gregory went out the door.

As they drove back to the hotel Gregory asked, "What did you think of Sung?"

"Interesting."

"Interesting is an adjective that covers a wide range from 'he's a bastard' to 'at least he wasn't boring.' "

"He wasn't boring."

They wound their way down from the Peak, the lights of the city below glimmering through a luminescent haze.

"Do you have to sit over there?" Gregory asked. "Come closer."

She didn't move but stared straight ahead, her face expressionless.

"What's the matter?"

"I'm glad you asked that question," she said icily, turning to face him. "Very glad. Lily Sung is the matter. I'm not an eavesdropper—it wasn't intentional—but I overheard her little speech."

"So that's it."

"Hell, is that all you've got to say?" She stripped the earrings from her ears, then tried to undo the clasp of the necklace. But her hands were shaking too much. "Why did you take me there?" she demanded.

"Marianne, listen—"

"I don't want to listen. Just take me back to the hotel."

Gregory suddenly pulled off the road and stopped the car.

He turned to her angrily. "You're going to listen whether you want to or not. Lily means nothing to me. Absolutely *nothing*."

"*She* thinks she does," Marianne hissed.

"Hear me out, will you? I had an affair with her— ongoing, I'll be honest—for a number of years. I'm not proud of it. It was a dirty thing to do to Sung. Circumstances—I won't go into that now. But it was over even before I met you. The day after I got back from Cornell I wrote to Lily telling her it was finished. I had been meaning to tell her that for some time. Knowing you— well, it just gave me the push I needed. She said she understood, but couldn't we be friends? When I came to Hong Kong she called me at the Mandarin. She said she knew we were through as lovers but that didn't mean we couldn't speak to one another. Later Sung invited me to dinner. I told him I was entertaining a special someone from New York. 'Bring her along!' he said. He insisted we come. I thought Lily knew about it, I thought she had meant what she said. She didn't."

Marianne sat, hands clasping the earrings in her lap, staring ahead at the streetlight flickering through the trees.

"You don't believe me."

"Gregory—"

"No, don't say anything. I understand how you feel. I should never have taken you to Sung's. I wouldn't want to hurt you for the world." He touched her cheek and she turned her head. "I love you, Marianne. I'm not placating you." He traced her mouth with a finger, then leaned over to kiss her softly. "It's God's truth."

"Gregory . . . I . . ."

"Will you forgive me? Please?" His eyes pleaded.

Had she blown the whole episode out of proportion? Gregory's relationship with her had never been anything but open and loving. Would he lie to her now? She didn't think so. Was it fair to condemn him because he had made an error in judgment? And really, that's all it boiled down to.

"Marianne?"

She turned to him and smiled, then she impulsively linked her arms about his neck. "Why not?"

Later, lying in Greg's arms, Marianne forgot about Lily. The postcoital euphoria sent her mind floating, thinking dreamlike thoughts, her fingers idly tracing the hairs along Gregory's wrist. That this man could bring her to such total ecstasy still amazed her.

"Marianne?"

"*Mmmm?*"

"You've never said you loved me."

"Don't you know?"

"I want to hear you say it, darling."

"Oh, Gregory, of course I love you. I love you very much."

She was packing. Her large suitcase, open on the bed, was nearly full, the small carry-on beside it waiting for the overflow.

"Do you have to leave now?" Gregory asked. "Can't you stay over for another day or two?"

"There's nothing I'd like better, but I promised Gunther. And work is piling up. It's okay, we'll see each other again."

"We'd better. I wish I could go with you. But there's that damned meeting with Taijo Limited. In fact"—he looked at his watch—"I'm late for it now. Sorry I can't take you to the airport."

"No problem, darling. I'll catch a cab."

At the airport she got through customs only to find there had been some mixup. The hotel had made reservations for Wednesday instead of Tuesday. The plane she was supposed to be leaving on in an hour was full. She couldn't get a confirmed reservation until the next day. Frustrated, Marianne had little choice but to return to the Mandarin.

When she finally got back to the hotel and was given another room, she put in a call to Billings and left a message for Gunther explaining that she'd be a day late. Looking at her watch, she saw it was four o'clock. Gregory's meeting was probably over by now. She started to dial his room number when she thought, no, I'll surprise him. In a way she was glad of the delay. On the way to the airport she had already begun to miss Gregory. Funny, she had thought, how quickly a man can become such a big part of your life.

Locking her door, she went down the carpeted hallway to the elevator. It seemed to take forever to get to the floor below. At room 512 she paused before she lifted her fist and gave a decisive knock.

"Who is it?" Greg called.

Marianne, disguising her voice, put on the lilting accent she had heard so often these past few days and called, "Room service!"

Gregory opened the door. He was in his undershorts. The look of astonished dismay on his face was quickly followed by an obvious attempt to block her view. But it was too late. Marianne had already seen her. Lily. Lily without a stitch of clothing standing in the doorway of the bedroom.

Marianne turned away and ran back down the corridor, dimly aware of Gregory calling after her. She couldn't think. Tears blurred her eyes. She kept seeing Lily, the smug smile, the way one arm leaned casually against the doorjamb. *It's over. She means nothing to me.* She couldn't wait for the elevator. Where were the stairs? There must be stairs. Every hotel had stairs. She hurried down another corridor. "Exit" in red above a door. She climbed quickly, her breath coming in short gasps, her heart pounding. *Fool! Fool! Oh, God, what a gullible fool.*

Once in her room, where she thought she could let it all out, she found she couldn't shed a single tear. She felt frozen, a block of sharp-edged ice congealing her heart.

The telephone rang. She stared at it, not wanting to answer, sure it was Gregory. But the phone's strident piping persisted and she finally picked it up. It was the switchboard. Would she call the long-distance operator? A Mr. Bradford Young from New York had been trying to reach her.

She waited mechanically, dull-headed, waited with unshed tears burning her eyes for the call to come through. Why should Brad be telephoning? She didn't want to talk to him, she didn't want to talk to anyone. Not now. If Brad only knew . . .

Suddenly the thought struck her that Brad wouldn't be calling long distance unless there was some kind of emergency. A life-and-death matter. An illness, a death. Who? Karen? It had to be Karen. Karen at camp. Marianne's ear, pressed to the phone and echoing with crackles and splutters and the sound of distant, piping voices, strained to hear. Something had happened, something terrible. She was sure it was Karen. Nothing else would make Brad put in an "urgent" call. Karen had had an accident. She had fallen and had hit her head on a rock. She was unconscious with a fractured skull. Or had she swum out too far in the lake and drowned before anyone could reach her? Oh, God! Why had she ever left New York?

Terror and guilt tightened her throat so that when Brad's voice came over the static-fractured distance she couldn't speak.

"Marianne? Marianne, are you there?"

"Yes." She cleared her throat, trying to free her trapped tongue. "What—what is it? Not—not Karen." Please God, not Karen."

"No. It's Uncle Bob. He's had a stroke."

She was ashamed of the relief that washed over her, a shame quickly replaced by incredulity.

"Uncle Bob? A stroke? But he's always been so healthy. A little high blood pressure—"

"He's in the hospital. Marianne, I'll be straight with you. It doesn't look good. His chances are slim."

"But how? Only two weeks ago we talked, he was playing golf, enjoying himself." She swallowed and tried to pull herself together. "I'm leaving as soon as I can get a plane out." She'd go to the airport and wait. Maybe she could get on that seven-fifteen. "I'll fly directly to Sarasota."

"Let me know your schedule and I'll meet you. Do you want me to bring Karen?"

"No. I don't think it's a good idea. She's too young."

"I'll call your Aunt Em and tell her . . ."

But she wasn't listening. A stroke. His chances were slim. She didn't want Uncle Bob to die. He wasn't going to, he mustn't. He couldn't. He was father, uncle, grandpa, friend. Dead was forever. Dead was Toby being buried again, going down into the deep earth in a casket. When she hung up the tears she could not shed earlier coursed down her cheeks.

She was throwing things into her suitcase when Gregory pounded on the door.

"Why the hell did you run off so fast?" he demanded when she opened it, leaving the chain on.

"Go away, Greg! I don't want to speak to you! I don't *ever* want to see you again."

"Marianne—"

"Go back to Lily," she screamed. "Leave me alone!"

She slammed the door shut in his face and bolted it. Then she locked herself in the bathroom so she could not hear his pounding or the sound of his voice. She sat on the side of the tub weeping. To have come to this.

Allowing herself to be taken in by a man who had fed her the big lie. "I love you." "You're great! Fantastic!" A charming, handsome bastard. And now Uncle Bob was lying in a hospital bed, fighting for his life.

All the way back to the States and across the country to Sarasota she wore sunglasses to hide the puffy, red-rimmed eyes that had so recently been aglow with happiness and love.

CHAPTER X

HE DIED AN HOUR BEFORE HER PLANE TOUCHED DOWN. Her reaction when Brad told her—his comforting arm around her shoulders, his voice gentle—was one of angry disappointment. No tears, no grief, only this crazy resentment. Uncle Bob had let her down.

Though her logical mind had examined the possibility of his death, she wasn't emotionally prepared for it. Over the plains of Texas, the breadth of Louisiana and Alabama, she had composed little conversations with Uncle Bob, snatches of memories she would share along with her insistence that he must get well. He would recuperate, she had told herself. He would get better, go into physical therapy, learn how to restore speech, limbs, whatever part of his body might have been effected by his stroke. He would be good as new. Uncle Bob loved life; he was *not* going to die.

She recalled an incident of her childhood—she must have been ten—when she and Uncle Bob had gone bird-watching at the Great Swamp sanctuary. It had been a cold, icy December morning, and patches of swamp had frozen over. Bob, spotting a redtail with a broken wing in a clump of withered grass, had gone out to rescue it when the ice suddenly cracked under him. Marianne watched in shock as he went down thigh-deep in frigid water.

"Don't come!" he warned her as she started out to help. He tried to wriggle free, but his feet seemed to be wedged under some object and he couldn't move them. Marianne, certain he had sunk into a bog, began to cry.

"Hey, Sis, this isn't time for tears!" he called. "Go over to the road and wave your arms at the first car that comes along. Mind—don't stand in the middle, but to the side."

It was a lonely byway with little traffic—none, it seemed, on this day. The cold, still air nipped at her nose and the tips of her mittened fingers. She shoved her hands in her jacket pockets and stamped her feet, then ventured out on the potholed macadam to peer down through the arch of naked-limbed trees. It took a half hour before a truck came into view. The driver, a farmer, stopped and, hearing Marianne's story, quickly followed to where she had left Uncle Bob.

"Hope he hasn't froze to death," the farmer muttered.

Marianne remembered how the farmer's remark had congealed her heart with fear. As they walked back through the woods Marianne's mind had already pictured the scene they would find: Uncle Bob gone, swallowed up by the swamp with only a lone hawk wheeling in the winter sky to mark the spot where he had gone down. And, she recalled with a vividness that flooded her with a sudden unbearable nostalgia how, as they approached, Uncle Bob, still mired in mud, had waved at them, calling out cheerfully.

Marianne had wept as they drove home. "Now, now, Sis. Did you think a little accident like that could finish your old Uncle Bob? I'm too tough to die."

But not tough enough.

An anguished, miserable Marianne did not like to ac-knowledge that her irrational response to Uncle Bob's death arose from her unhappy encounter with her mother and her disastrous experience with Gregory. Why, she asked herself, had Uncle Bob had to die at a time when she was at such a low ebb? She realized her anger—at herself, at a fate that had taken one of the dearest people from her—was selfish, and she was ashamed of it, so ashamed she could not confess her feelings to Brad.

"I know you said not to bring Karen down." Brad spoke as they drove out on the palm-lined highway leading to the outskirts of Sarasota, where the Parkers had bought their retirement home. "But I did."

"You *what*?" she demanded, relieved to switch her painful thoughts to something she could honestly get mad about. "That's taking one hell of a lot on yourself. I told you I didn't *want* Karen here—especially at a funeral. It's no place for a child. And then you have the gall to bring her anyway. How could you?"

"Now wait a second. Listen, will you? That kid is growing up without a sense of family. She doesn't have brothers or sisters, cousins, aunts or uncles, just the Parkers and me, Uncle Brad, and a mother who isn't home much of the time."

"Well! That ties it!" She knew she ought to stop, calm down, that Brad was acting in her interest, no matter how misguided. But she couldn't. "I went to see my mother and took a few days off in Hong Kong. Was that so terrible?"

"You know that's not what I'm talking about. I mean a job that has you working fifty hours a week plus most weekends—"

"Don't! Don't give me that sexist crap, especially now. If I were a man raising a child alone, you wouldn't throw working overtime up to me. It so happens I have to earn a living. I hold a job, a good one, that happens to include some out-of-town trips. Jesus! And as for sisters and brothers, that sentimental trash is for the birds. How often do you see your family? When's the last time you visited Ginny? Or your mother? And they only live in Rochester."

"I talk to Mom every Sunday morning. And whether

I visit Ginny once a week or once a month doesn't really matter. I grew up with them, I have memories of belonging."

"Oh, shit! And what's this got to do with a funeral?"

"A funeral is a time when a family gets together. Not as happy an occasion as a wedding, but it does bring people closer."

"I can't say that the last funeral you attended brought you any closer to your relatives."

His ears turned a fiery red. "That's damned unfair! Christ! You would bring that up."

It *was* unfair—cruel, really—but she had so much anger and grief boiling inside she couldn't keep from lashing out. She hated herself for it, yet, consumed with emotion, was unable to take the words back.

"You know damn well they all finally came around. Even Laura."

"I just wanted to point out—"

"It doesn't have anything to do with Karen, does it? We're talking about now. Right? Uncle Bob, who means something to Karen even though she hasn't seen him all that much. There'll be Bob's brothers and sisters, maybe a few kids. Let Karen have the pleasure of knowing she's included in a clan."

"Some pleasure. People crying, Uncle Bob all gussied up in a satin-lined coffin. It might give her nightmares."

"Maybe. But she'll also know that she has cousins—a couple of times removed, maybe, but family."

"There you go again. Family. Just what the hell am I supposed to do about it?"

Suddenly she began to cry. Great wracking sobs shook her body, tearing her apart. Brad pulled over to the shoulder of the road and took her in his arms, where she continued to weep against his chest, blindly accepting the tissue he pulled out of the glove compartment. She didn't seem able to stop. Clutching the tissue, she went on crying, her breath coming in gasps between the shattering sobs.

"Jesus, I'm sorry, Marianne. Please don't cry. It's going to be all right."

She shook her head. "It—it doesn't seem as though *anything* is going to be all right."

"Yes. You'll see. Things go bad in Canton?"

Again she shook her head, this time in the affirmative.

"Well, it was sort of expected, wasn't it?"

"Yes." She sniffed, blowing her nose loudly, looking up at him briefly through tear-blurred eyes.

He didn't ask her about Hong Kong. He knew she was meeting Gregory Windham there. She had told him. Although he had said nothing, she had sensed his disapproval. He had met Gregory and hadn't liked him. Marianne, not wanting to make a point of it, had not asked him why.

"I'll be all right." She blew her nose again. "Let's not fight. You're too dear a friend for that."

"I should hope so."

"I want you to come live with us in New York, Aunt Em. If it's your phlebitis you're worried about, you could spend the winter months in Florida and the rest of the time with us."

They were sitting on what Aunt Emma referred to as the "veranda," a tiny wooden porch with a worn plank floor that had been tacked on to the front of the stucco house as an afterthought by a former occupant. The house faced west, supposedly to catch the distant bay breezes, but today not a leaf or a blade of grass stirred in the limp heat. A languid stillness hung over the cottonwoods. The birds, hidden in their green-shadowed depths, had ceased their rustlings and had become silent. Somewhere up the street a lawnmower droned. Aunt Em's rocker squeaked. The torpid air reminded Marianne of Canton and Hong Kong. Depressingly so. She should never have gone. Canton, maybe, because if she hadn't made the trip she would always wonder about her mother. But Hong Kong she could have done without.

She couldn't understand how the woman she had become—sophisticated, knowledgeable, mature—could have reverted to the same vulnerable girl that had fallen in love with Sam. Granted, Gregory wasn't Sam. He had

the sort of charm and vibrancy—and gentle tenderness—
Sam lacked. But it was just these qualities that drew other
women to Gregory. And he to them. Gossips had told her
that in the past Gregory had found many women attractive.
But at the time it hadn't mattered. She was meeting him
in Hong Kong to have a good time, not to fall in love.

In love, my God!

Was faithfulness outmoded? Was it "in" to be promiscuous, or was she being judgmental, a moral Aunt
Em in disguise? Perhaps it was no big thing to sleep
around, to change bed partners. Though she didn't go
in for the sport herself, she didn't condemn it in others.
But when a person was in love, or *said* he was in love,
you'd think he'd wait—at least a couple of hours—
before he slipped between the sheets with someone else.

It wasn't funny. It hurt. A pain under her ribs that
wouldn't go away. Yet hurting, hating Gregory, she
found herself wondering how it would be in the days and
weeks ahead. She would miss him. She would miss his
air of confidence and authority that somehow made her
feel strong, too. She would miss the murmured conversations they had as she lay in his arms after lovemaking,
the sound of his deep, vibrant voice, the feel of his lips
in her hair.

"Marianne," Aunt Em said, bringing Marianne back to
the present. "It's dear of you to ask me."

"Nothing dear about it, Aunt Em. And the invitation,
I might add, is not made because I need a babysitter for
Karen. I just don't like to think of you having to go it
alone down here. You need someone in case of illness,
an accident, whatever. We ought to be close by."

Emma rocked, fanning herself with a palm leaf fan,
the tiny swirl of air lifting a gray tendril of hair from her
shiny forehead. She had become even stouter through
the years, her chins increasing. Her sausage arms, bare
in sleeveless poplin, had grown large and ropy.

"Marianne, would it hurt your feelings if I refused?"
she asked gently, turning to her, resting the fan on her
ample lap. "I—had other plans. Now that Bob's gone—
God rest his soul—I have to make a life of my own."

"Why, yes, of course." Marianne looked at Emma in mild surprise. She had never thought of her as having a life of her own. Emma Parker had always been Bob's wife, his right hand, Marianne's substitute (if irascible) mother, a housekeeper, fixer-upper, waitress, and all-around handy companion. Marianne had thought that Emma Parker had been perfectly happy in these roles and would be miserable without them. Now she was talking about plans, a life of her own.

"You mustn't think I was unhappy," Emma said perceptively. "I wasn't. I loved Bob, I loved my house. It was home to me, the only real one I ever had. But every once in a while I had this urge to take off and see the country," she said dreamily. "But Robert hated to travel," she sighed. "It didn't make me love him any less. No woman could have asked for a better husband. But he was a homebody. Now that he's gone, I think I'd like to travel a bit."

"What about me?" Marianne couldn't help asking. "I must have made you feel tied down, too."

"You did come as a little surprise."

"Oh, really, Aunt Em," Marianne cajoled, "it wasn't a little surprise, it was a big surprise, and—my guess—not a very welcome one."

"Now why'd you say that? Don't tell me." She gave Marianne a broad smile. "Funny how things and feelings change over the years. I never thought I could talk to you this way. Maybe it has something to do with Bob going and you and me having both been so close to him. But the truth is, in those early days there were times when I could have wrung your neck, I was that jealous. Well, wouldn't you be if you were in my place? You two jaunting around on Sundays, working together in the woodshop, talking a blue streak as if I wasn't there. Nobody likes to be shut out."

"Of course not. Oh, Aunt Em—"

" 'Twasn't your fault entirely. You were just a child. Now and then I'd tell myself that and feel guilty. I was brought up by relatives, too, so I knew how it felt to have no father or mother and a pair of cranky adults laying down the law. Anyway . . ." She gave a heavy sigh. "I did the best I could by my own lights, I suppose. You turned out pretty good, even if I did a lot of hollering about wiping your feet at the door."

"It was more than muddy shoes, Aunt Em."

"More? As I recall, you weren't always sweet and obliging, either. I didn't keep a list, but I can remember a few things, like running to Uncle Bob every time I looked cross-eyed at you, and getting mad at me, calling me an old-fashioned worrywart because I brought your overshoes to school when you forgot them on purpose. I had the notion maybe you were a little ashamed of me."

Marianne felt her cheeks grow warm. "Aunt Em, I didn't mean—"

"It's all right. We all do things we ain't proud of. But if you want to sit here and dig into the past and do a tit for tat, I'll go along."

"Of course not. Tell you what." She leaned over the arm of her chair and kissed Aunt Em on the cheek. "If you forgive me, I'll forgive you."

Emma smiled and, reaching across, patted Marianne's knee. "It's a deal, Sis."

When Marianne returned to work she was confronted with a crisis.

Several months earlier she had taken over the supervisory position vacated by her immediate boss, who had quit Billings for a job in another company. She was put in charge of her circuit, gathering information for stockholders from the Chicago, Cleveland, and Atlanta holdings with emergency trips to other companies when she was needed. She had a staff—two aides and two secretaries.

During her absence Harold Bundt, transferred from Tax and now working directly under Blake, filled in for her. She wasn't especially thrilled at having Bundt sit in her office even for a short while, but she reasoned that she'd be back at Billings before he could do much damage.

In the pile of unfinished business waiting for Marianne when she returned was a report she had been working on, a study of the building and leasing policies of Billings's various offshoots. In the course of her duties she had noticed that there was no coherent industry-wide plan for warehousing inventory; that Crescent Manufacturing, makers of industrial carpeting, for instance, stored their product in scattered depositories that they leased at high rates. Figures showed that if Crescent built their own warehouse they could save money over the long haul. Others would do better by leasing. But until now there had been no guidelines, no dollar-and-cents percentages by which managerial people could make comparative judgments.

She had not yet composed the final draft of the report she planned to present at the next meeting of the Finance Committee, an adjunct of the Board of Directors headed by Felton Knox, an older man who many years earlier had married into the Billings family.

Much to Marianne's surprise, the Finance Committee had called a special meeting in her absence at which Harold Bundt had presented the same idea.

Coincidence?

She doubted it. From her observation, Harold Bundt was a methodical plodder with little creative imagination. Moreover, he couldn't possibly have learned that much about Cresent or the other companies in the short time she was away. He didn't like her. Though he made a pretense of cordiality, she sensed he was still smoldering because she had not only had the temerity to slap him, but had also successfully avoided being fired because of it. His contempt was expressed in odd and unnerving ways: a sneer as he held a door open for her, forgetting her name, or referring to her as "that little lady."

Marianne was convinced that Harold Bundt had stolen her brainchild. She had placed the draft of her report in a locked drawer, but prying it open would have been easy. How to prove it? The papers were there as she left them. He must have Xeroxed and then replaced them. She had spoken to no one about her proposal, and if she accused Bundt of filching the report, he could easily refute it.

There was more. In addition to appropriating her plan, he had discovered a minor error in her figures in the Consolidated Statements of Capitalization. Marianne rarely made errors, but she was fallible, and this had slipped through. From what Marianne was able to learn through a friendly secretary who had taken minutes at the Finance Committee meeting, Bundt had blown up this error to outrageous proportions. He had also exaggerated the times that Marianne was absent because of family matters, implying that domestic concerns interfered with her performance at Billings. Plainly, Bundt was playing up to the Finance Chairman. It was well known that Knox looked with less than relish at the notion of women assuming executive roles. The married ones, especially, he felt, ought not to take on responsibilities that needed their undivided attention.

Though Marianne knew she wouldn't lose her job over this episode, her prospects for promotion at Billings would be seriously damaged. She had to do something quickly.

She managed to obtain a copy of Bundt's presentation to the Committee. He had cleverly altered her report, changing some of the language, rearranging tables, and inventing a few charts of his own. Bundt's revisions would make it more difficult to accuse him of theft. She wondered, then, if he had kept the copies (assuming he had made them) of her notes or if he had destroyed the lot.

Taking a leaf from Bundt's book she stayed late one night and, using a master key, went through his files, then his desk. Luck was with her. There, under a stack of legal pads, she found what she was looking for. But now that she had the incriminating copies, how could she prove Bundt had made them? Again it was her word against his, and Felton Knox would naturally lean toward Bundt.

Through the years Marianne had never presumed on her friendship with Carol Olmstead by asking her to intervene on her behalf. Advice was sometimes solicited and given, but Marianne knew that her mentor preferred her to make her own way. Except in an emergency, Carol had once said.

This was an emergency.

Fortunately, Carol was not off on one of her Parisian jaunts but at the Olmstead townhouse in New York. Marianne arranged a lunch date at Lello's and brought the copies and her own typed draft.

Carol wore a brimmed hat of Italian straw that made her face look smaller and her nose sharper, but her dazzling smile was there, and the warm hug. "I've been dying to hear about your trip to China. How was it?"

"So-so. But I'll tell you all about it later. There's something that's come up at the office."

Marianne explained as briefly as possible. Carol did not waste time with such mundane queries as "Are you sure?" Instead she heard Marianne out and when she was finished said, "I could speak to Felton—he listens to me—but I think it would be much more effective if it appeared that you were handling this matter on your own. Arrange an appointment with Felton. When you see him, come flat out with your accusation against Bundt. Ask for a three-way session in which you can confront the bastard, then put Bundt through a grilling. Try to get a fourth party. Maybe Horace Blake. He has a reputation for being equitable."

The meeting was held in Felton Knox's office, furnished to his taste with deep chairs of worn leather, the floor scattered with bear and deer rugs. The walls bristled with hunting trophies, a brace of antique dueling pistols, and ancient musketry. Felton was a tall, thin man with wiry white hair cut close to a pinkish skull and a jaw like an Army sergeant which, in fact, he had once been.

He may not have liked women who aspired to rise above the rank of secretary, but he was a gentleman. On his feet at Marianne's entrance, he gave her a friendly smile as he motioned her to a chair.

Harold Bundt, already present when Marianne came

in, was turned out in conservative charcoal gray even to
his socks. He greeted Marianne politely without a sign
of nervousness and with none of the condescension he
had shown toward her before.

He's playing it cool, Marianne thought. A man in
command who sees no reason to defend an accusation
that is patently false.

Horace Blake joined them. To Marianne his nonde-
script appearance—the blue eyes behind glasses, interested but nonjudgmental—had a calming effect.

Knox tersely summed up Marianne's assertion, which
Bundt denied in a level voice.

"You could have copied your own scribbling," Bundt
stated, allowing himself a hint of a smug smile. "After I
might add, you read *my* report."

Marianne, prepared for this sort of statement, ignored
it. She asked Bundt detailed questions about warehousing
policy at Crescent that had not appeared in her notes,
the answers to which only someone who had worked
closely with the project would know.

It wasn't long before Bundt got tangled in a web
of inconsistencies. Cornered, his imperturbable facade
dropped like the mask of a poker player who's been
caught pulling an ace from his sleeve.

"Listen you—you bitch!" he lashed out. "Ever since
you've been here you've been brown-nosing your way
from one promotion to another. Not to speak of what
you've probably been laying out. Everybody knows how
you suck up to the chief, pretending to be his wife's
friend. And the mistakes you make—my God! The—"

Blake interrupted Bundt's tirade. "Did you steal Ms.
Oliver's proposal?" he demanded.

"Hell no!"

Felton Knox, his clean-shaven jaw set at a pugnacious
angle, tapped two fingers on the report before him,
touched an onyx inkstand, straightened a pencil. Obviously Bundt's outburst did not sit well with him. Whatever his faults, Marianne knew he was of the old school.
He might harbor his own private thoughts about female

employees, but he would never voice them—or permit others to voice them—in a lady's presence. Especially in the sanctity of his office.

Blake, doggedly on track, remarked, "Mr. Bundt, the evidence points to some kind of chicanery."

"Bullshit! Fel," Bundt appealed, "are you going to believe this babe or me?"

Obviously the "Fel" was too much for Knox. Bundt should have been aware that the head of the Finance Committee didn't care to be addressed as "Fel" by middle-management nonentities, even if their fathers did go deer hunting with Jim Olmstead.

"I think," he said evenly, "you and I'd better have a talk."

The meeting was over.

Bundt resigned the following day.

A few weeks later Marianne was offered the position as assistant to the head of Crescent Manufacturing in Cicero, a suburb of Chicago. It was a line rather than a staff position. She would be dealing directly with the lifeblood of Billings, working for a productive money-making unit rather than shuffling papers at corporation headquarters. Furthermore, she would be in a position to have a say about policy. It was no secret that in order to advance at Billings line experience was essential.

Marianne was congratulated all around and Accounting gave her a send-off, a catered buffet supper. Blake made a brief speech and said the expected things: a job well done, excellent record, intelligent, innovative employee. They would miss her in Accounting.

Three years later she would be reminded of that complimentary farewell speech. But by then her relationship with Blake would have changed radically.

CHAPTER XI

"I THINK THE CRESCENT JOB IS A WISE MOVE," BRADFORD said.

"You do?"

Having packed Karen off to bed, Marianne was sitting with Brad on the sofa in the living room. Feet propped on a glass coffee table, they sipped on balloon glasses of Napoleon brandy Brad had brought in to celebrate.

"Why so surprised? I was never against your career. I just felt that pouring heart and soul into it at the exclusion of everything else was—is—a crazy way to live."

"You're wrong. It's the only way to go, Brad, the only way to get ahead. A woman has to work twice as hard to prove herself."

"Twice as hard is not eighteen hours a day, counting Saturdays. Since you came back from Hong Kong you've set yourself a killing pace, as if someone were riding herd on you with a bullwhip."

"I'm tying up loose ends before I leave," she protested.

"I can't believe there's that much winding up to do.

You have a competent staff—shift some of the load onto them."

"Okay. So I'm a workaholic, always was." She didn't tell him that one of the reasons she had thrown herself into her last days on the job at Billings with an almost frantic zeal was to erase Gregory Windham from her mind. Charts, graphs, figures, balance sheets served to blot out his face and dull the remembered sound of his voice, his laughter. The more hectic her daylight hours, the more midnight oil she burned, the more exhausted she felt, the better she slept at night. She sought deep sleep without dreams that would haunt her. She wanted to forget Gregory, Gregory's hand in hers as they climbed the stone steps of Ladder Street, Gregory leaning across a candlelit table, Gregory teasing, Gregory holding her tightly in strong arms.

That first week when he had called she had cut him short, yanking the telephone cord from the wall plug. At work she had left instructions that she was out to Gregory Windham. The boxes of roses he had sent she tossed into the garbage. She had returned the diamond necklace and earrings by insured mail. The cashmeres, the wool skirts, assorted scents, purses, and bracelets he had given her she had donated to the Friends of the Poor rummage sale. She didn't want to think of him, to be reminded. He was something that had never happened. Screw Gregory.

"I'll miss you," Brad was saying.

"Me too." Marianne smiled ruefully, then impulsively planted a kiss on his cheek. When he winced, she teasingly gave him another. "But there's always AT&T. Or Sprint. We can fight long-distance."

"It isn't the same thing."

They were down to the last of the Napoleon when their talk turned to gossip about Cornell, friends, husbands, wives, and who was living with whom.

"Incidentally, I hear you've got a new love interest," Marianne said. "Sabrina what's-her-name."

"Sabrina née Donaldson."

"Wasn't that the gal the Hansfords were trying to push on Toby? With a lot of help from herself."

"Same one. She's been married and divorced since Toby's time."

And her lovers, Brad supposed silently, have been legion. Sabrina's claim that she had gone into therapy to cure her "hangups" and was now ready for a commitment Brad took with a grain of salt. Meeting her at a cocktail party, Brad had taken her home. Her sensuality, the way she moved under and over him, served as an excellent antidote for the blues. Marianne had been in Hong Kong with Gregory at the time, and the thought of those two together—arms linked, roaming an exotic city by day, making love by night—depressed him.

Sabrina was forgetfulness. Her velvety body, the full, firm breasts with their puckered pink tips, the bushy triangle at her loins, her long-fingered, deft hands, the caressing, mobile mouth, the wet, papery tongue that licked and tantalized, all of it in motion, acted like a pain-killing drug. She took him out of the snake pit, and he needed that. She swore that she was crazy about him, had been since they had made it at the Hansfords.

Though Brad believed only half of what Sabrina said, her flattery bolstered his ego. Her intuitive awareness touched him. He could never love Sabrina. Marianne would always stand in the way of any woman he might love, but Sabrina eased the harshness of his monkish existence the way other girls had failed to do.

"We're not living together," Brad said, almost defensivley, wondering why he should feel that way. Did Marianne expect him to remain the virginal big brother while she played around with men like Gregory?

"You mean not yet."

The asperity in Marianne's voice surprised Brad. Could she be jealous? Fat chance.

"You're far too good for that alley cat," Marianne went on. "A one-night stand now and then, maybe. But not a live-in arrangement. She'll drive you nuts."

"She has her good points."

"I bet." She laughed. "Well, more power to you, Brad. Have fun."

Did she mean that? Sure she did. Sure.

If Brad approved of Marianne's new job, Karen did not. She didn't want to move, didn't want to change schools, didn't want to be separated from Frankie, her very best girlfriend. Upset, tearful, the child put Marianne's heart in a vise. She had expected some opposition, but not this storm of protest.

"Darling, don't cry." She took Karen in her arms, kissing her wet face, settling her on her lap. "They have schools just like Broadmoor, and you'll find wonderful friends there, too."

"Not like Frankie." Karen and Ginny's daughter had become inseparable companions since they had started school in Manhattan.

"I bet you there's a little girl out there right now who wears glasses, has a fat blond braid down her back just like Frankie, and who needs a friend. She's probably waiting for someone like you."

The dark brown eyes, moist and questioning, looked up at Marianne. "Are you making that up?"

"Let's call it an educated guess. She might not be blond or wear glasses like Frankie, but she'll be about the same age and just as much fun. And"—she brushed a lock of hair from Karen's forehead—"I know someone else who's waiting. Want to guess?"

The dark, curly head shook.

"A little puppy. Sparky, the poodle you've always wanted."

"Oh, Moms! Really, really?"

"Really." It was a bribe, but one that Marianne convinced herself she had to offer. The job in Cicero was important not only for her future but for Karen's as well. Karen was never going to experience the hardship she herself had gone through at Cornell or face the same demeaning treatment she had received from the Hansfords. Wealth and power, Marianne had once vowed. That was still her goal. And though getting there involved grueling and sometimes less-than-inspiring work, she was slowly making it. Crescent was one more step up the ladder.

But there were moments, rare and disturbingly honest, when she asked herself if it was really Karen's welfare that drove her to succeed. Was it pride in her professionalism, the consuming desire to prove she was "good enough," that goaded her on in hot pursuit of success? Or was she propelled by an overriding desire for revenge?

Marianne didn't probe these possibilities often. The day-to-day problems at home and at work gave her little time for introspection. It was only on those occasions in the dead of the night when, tired and unable to sleep, forcing her mind from memories of Gregory as she tossed and kicked at the tangled sheets, her thoughts moved from one into another and the uncomfortable questions arose. Inevitably she would answer them by telling herself it didn't matter what her motives were. It didn't change a thing. She had set herself on a course she could no more reverse than she could alter the flow of her blood or the beat of her heart.

Marianne found a small clapboard house in Oak Park, a once-affluent suburb of Chicago within easy commuting distance of industrial Cicero. What intrigued Marianne was its resemblance to the home in Passaic where she had grown up. It had similar low ceilings and doorways, a small parlor, a tiny bay-windowed dining room, a large, old-fashioned kitchen, and steep stairs ascending to the upper story.

It was furnished—or, rather, overfurnished—in 1920 Sears catalog style: ponderous sofas and dusty velour armchairs decorated with embroidered linen runners. The back yard ran narrow and deep under two spreading oaks, their leaves beginning to bud in the sharp March air. Lilac bushes draped the weathered wooden fence on one side, and on the other withered morning glory waited for their spring resurgence.

What was most important to Marianne was the way

Karen took to the house. Mourning over the apartment on Amsterdam Avenue ceased once Karen saw the back yard and assessed its possibilities for Sparky.

"We can build him a doghouse right—right"—her arms flailed— "right over there by that tree. And he can have all that space to run in."

The stairs fascinated Karen. She must have clattered up and down the staircase that first day a dozen times, telling Marianne that Frankie would *love* it and couldn't they have her come to visit soon?

Marianne congratulated herself on her decision to rent the house. Though the street was seedy and rundown, it was homey. Aunt Em and Brad would approve.

Marianne lost no time in acquiring a housekeeper. She interviewed half a dozen prospects before she employed Mrs. Beebe, a stout woman in her forties, widowed with grown children. She was a cheerful, maternal woman, and from their conversation Marianne guessed she was permissive rather than strict.

With Karen happily under the care of Mrs. Beebe and enrolled in a good school all in the two weeks she'd allotted to the tasks, Marianne reported to Crescent. She knew the manager, Si Ludlum, from previous visits, since Crescent had been on her circuit. They got along fairly well. It had not been that way in the beginning. Because she had traveled as Jay Gunther's assistant in the old days, Ludlum had assumed they were sleeping together. He had persisted in making snide remarks about Gunther's good luck, the perks in having a foxy chick he could tuck in with after a day's hard work. Since Jay hadn't bothered to set Si Ludlum straight, Marianne had taken it upon herself to do it. She told Ludlum his insinuations were unfounded, if not insulting. They were beneath him, her, Gunther and Billings. Simply because a man and a woman were doing a job together didn't make them bedmates. Later, when Ludlum learned that Gunther was gay, he had apologized to Marianne. Ludlum's basic attitude hadn't changed, but she had accepted the apology with good grace. From then on their relationship had improved. But now that

she was coming to work at his right elbow she didn't
know what to expect.

Ludlum wasn't happy about it and said so.

"Look, Marianne . . ." He had never called her by
her last name. "I know you're a bright lady with figures
and balance sheets. But how are you with a wrench? It's
not that you'll be asked to crawl around in dirty pants
tightening loose nuts, but you've got to understand a
little about stamping machines, creels, conveyor belts
and such. The mechanics and machinists on our repair
crews are all men. Same with the assembly line. The
guys like to know there's someone in the front office
who knows his left hand from his right and isn't too
proud to come out on the floor when they're in a tight
spot. You can see the problem, can't you?"

"I'm afraid not, Si," she said calmly. "It happens I
can tell a wrench from a drill. I also know what a skew
chisel is, as well as a quick-release ratchet and a Phillips
screwdriver." Thanks to Uncle Bob, she might have
added. Uncle Bob had allowed Marianne to tinker along
with him in his workshop, since Em nearly forbade her
in the kitchen.

"That's home workshop stuff," Si said gruffly, nevertheless eyeing her with a little less condescension. He
was heavyset, with a paunch that hung over his belt, not
exactly the picture of a man who could scoot under
sliding valves or climb over gear wheels himself.

"I learn fast," Marianne assured him, making a mental note to bone up on company machinery.

She hadn't been at Crescent a month when a me-
chanic came by to tell her that a tufting machine had
broken down. Ludlum was out of the office and the shop
foreman was home sick. It was a new piece of machinery,
one the men were still unfamiliar with, and they were
stymied.

She went out to have a look. Recalling the blueprint
she had studied religiously, she thought she saw the
problem. Getting down on all fours, she asked for a
Stillson. With the men hanging over her shoulder, murmuring advice and unintelligible asides, she worked the

oily bolt behind the needle bar, shifting her knees, trying
for better leverage. When her wrench slipped off for the
third time, she inadvertently muttered, "Oh, shit!"

Behind her there was a sudden silence. Still on her
knees, Marianne turned. The men looked at her, then at
each other. Finally, like a cloud passing from the face of
the sun, grins broke out. Nothing was said. But Marianne knew she had been accepted.

She brought out the blueprint and the crew gathered
around it, studying the diagram, discussing pros and
cons. There was no hesitancy, no hanging back, no
skepticism. Her input was received with the same con-
sideration as that of any of the mechanics. Together
they worked out the problem, and fifteen minutes later
the needle bar was moving again.

The experience exhilarated Marianne, giving her as
much satisfaction as balancing a difficult worksheet. She
may have ruined a pair of pantyhose, a good skirt, and
several fingernails, but she had made an impression as a
person rather than a woman, and it broke the ice at
Crescent.

"You're a trier, I give you credit for that," Ludlum
told her later when heard about the incident. "A trier."

From him it was an accolade.

The following Christmas Marianne and Karen flew to
Sarasota. Emma had not sold the house as originally
planned but kept it as a base where she could return
between trips and for the holidays. They were joined
there by Brad and his sister Ginny and her family, who
were vacationing in St. Petersburg. The reunion between Frankie and Karen was accompanied by squeals
of delight, a joy later tempered by a spat over who had
grown the most. Both girls were beginning to shoot up,
and according to Uncle Brad, the mediator, Frankie had
the edge. "Sorry about that, Karen," he commiserated.
"Maybe next year."

Emma had decorated the house festively with silver
tinsel that shivered each time the door crashed open to
admit one of Frankie's younger brothers. Looped under

the ceiling across the dining and living rooms, the tinsel
dangled with paper figures of Kris Kringle, gilded choir-
boys, and moon-faced angels. The tree, a seven-footer
sprayed with artificial snow and twinkling with tiny lights,
dominated the cramped living room. The heap of gaily
wrapped gifts under its boughs acted as a magnet for
small detectives that rattled boxes, trying to guess their
contents.

"What's your Aunt Em so uptight about?"
"She gets nervous around kids."
Karen and Frankie, best friends again, were reclining
on striped cushioned lounge chairs in the backyard. Both
were slurping on dripping Popsicles, Karen's grape,
Frankie's orange. An exasperated, almost beside herself
Emma, feeling beseiged by so many youngsters, had
banished them all from the house until suppertime.
"Then why'd she invite us?" Frankie tossed a braid
over her shoulder.
"She doesn't know herself. That's what she told Moms.
She says she'll never be able to clean up the mess."
"What mess?"
"I guess your brothers aren't too good about picking
up after themselves."
"They're on vacation. When we're at home Mother's
very strict. She really cracks the whip."
"My mom does too."
"But yours isn't around all the time like mine."
"No. She works." Karen ran her tongue over the now
bare Popsicle stick.
"Well, mine doesn't. Sometimes I wish she did. But
then we'd miss doing a lot of neat things—like going to
the Brooklyn Zoo or to lunch or ice-skating at Rocke-
feller Center—or playing tennis. She's teaching me how
to play tennis."
"Moms said if I wanted to learn she'd hire a pro to
teach me."
"Oh, wow! That's great!"
"Yes," Karen agreed without enthusiasm. "She doesn't
know much about tennis, but she knows a lot about

birds. And she says when she has the time we can go out to the Forest Preserves to bird-watch.''

"Neat."

"Maybe in the spring, she says, if she isn't too busy."

"She sounds like she's busy a lot."

"I guess so." Karen tucked her Popsicle stick under the lounge cushion. "She's got an important job."

"When I grow up I'm going to have an important job, too."

"Not me," Karen said. "I'd rather play tennis with my kids."

On Christmas afternoon Marianne and Brad, escaping from the hubbub of overexcited children, took a stroll down the road past an orange grove awash with the perfume of blooming trees.

Catching up on news since their last letters, Marianne said, "So you and Sabrina broke up?"

Brad tweaked a tiny bloom from an overhanging limb, crushing it in his fingers. "There wasn't much to break up. Seems she was seeing someone else in between the times she was telling me what a great guy I was."

"Par for the course, isn't it?"

"Yup. She ran off and married the other great guy last week. I think you know him. Gregory Windham."

Marianne's step did not falter, although her feet suddenly felt like lead. The smell of orange blossoms seemed to suddenly overpower her with their heavy scent. This is crazy, she thought, grinding her teeth. I'm over Gregory, have been for a long time. He means nothing to me. Nothing. Let Sabrina have him.

"I must say they deserve each other," she said evenly. Why did Brad have to tell her? There was no reason to mention his name. It spoiled the day.

Marianne didn't want to hear about Gregory Windham, didn't want to remember. Yet his face was as clear in her mind now as it had been in Hong Kong. Standing in front of the mirror at the Mandarin, heads together, smiling at their images, Gregory's look had wrapped her in warmth and love. False love, false warmth. While the other woman had been patiently waiting on the Peak, saying, *"In Hong Kong you belong to me."*

Brad stole a glance at Marianne. She was taking it pretty well. Better than he had expected.

"Seems a weird stroke of fate," Marianne said, "those two getting together."

"You could say that." Brad felt a twinge in his gut. Fate had had nothing to do with it.

It was he who had brought Sabrina and Gregory together. Bumping into Gregory one evening at the bar in the Algonquin, they had spoken a few words. From the gist of this brief conversation, Bradford had gathered that the Algonquin was a favorite watering hole of Gregory's when he was in town. The next evening Brad had returned, bringing Sabrina with him. Recalling it now, he had to smile. He had never thought of himself as a matchmaker. But Sabrina's enticements were beginning to pall, and she zeroed in on Gregory like a rifle sight on a target. Bold and sassy in silver lamé, with silver earrings jingling from rouged earlobes, she seemed to have captivated Gregory. Brad feared that he was too savvy to swallow Sabrina's bait, but apparently he had. Either that or he and Sabrina were both tired of sleeping around and had decided to try a new arrangement— commitment. When Brad read of their elopement in the paper he poured himself a drink, lifted it to the unseen couple, and cried, "Hallelujah!"

He had hoped that Gregory's marriage would take him out of Marianne's life forever. Maybe it would end that faraway look she sometimes got in her eyes. She still thought of Gregory. Just now, at the mention of his name, he had seen the fleeting frown of regret. He didn't want Gregory to have her, even in her thoughts. He didn't want any man to have her. He had once stepped aside for Toby, his best friend. Never again. Someday soon the right moment would come and he could tell her how he felt. That he loved her. He hoped she would be ready then, able to look at him as much more than a friend.

CHAPTER XII

DESPITE HER DEMONSTRATED ABILITY WITH BLUEPRINTS and wrenches, Marianne's relationship with Ludlum remained on a less than congenial level. Si's criticisms—and there were many the first six months—were couched in terms that made it clear he hadn't changed his opinion of women as company executives. Marianne, keeping a rein on her tongue and careful not to overstep her authority, ignored the sniping and went on with her job. As time wore on Ludlum occasionally mellowed enough to halfheartedly commend her. But his grudging compliments were few and far between.

When she suggested innovations, he groused. He didn't like her proposal to delegate some of the decision making to floor managers, rather than having every problem dumped on the front desk. He also put thumbs down on Marianne's plan to conduct employee performance reviews.

"Christ, Marianne, the men will scream bloody murder and have the union on my back."

She tried to explain a review's advantages, but he

wasn't buying it. "Why don't you let *me* handle the guys in the shop? Okay? The floor out there's my beat. I understand those bastards better than you. Hell, I've been working with some of them for twenty years. They'd never stand still for a machine clocking them every time they go out for a leak. Forget employee performance. It's a lot of baloney anyway."

Sometimes Marianne felt as though she were walking a tightrope with Ludlum watching to see if she'd lose her balance and fall. Yet Ludlum was no fool. He did a good job of running Crescent. Under his jurisdiction the plant had doubled in size, and its profits had increased accordingly. But Marianne felt progress could move at a faster rate. She saw places that cried out for improvement, costs cut and waste reduced. She itched to get in there and show Ludlum how. But there wasn't a chance. Not yet. Patience. Wait and work hard, she told herself. When Ludlum sees that I'm an asset, not an inept female or a competitor out to get his job, maybe he'll finally give me the responsibility I deserve.

While Marianne was contending with Ludlum she received three letters in rapid succession from her mother. These were lengthy missives which Marianne, rushed for time and at a loss as to what to say, answered in short notes. Her mother scolded her for her brevity. It galled Marianne. She remembered all the years she had waited for a letter, would have gone down on her knees and thanked God for a postcard, and received nothing. Now her mother dared to criticize her brief letters. Sarah's correspondence was long, detailed, and beautifully written, but oddly without warmth. She told about her pupils at the University, the courses in English literature she was teaching, the weather, botanical flowerings, and new hotels that were going up. But there was little that was personal. Nothing that conveyed her thoughts, her wishes, her inner feelings. Nor did she ask about her daughter's well-being. There was no "Are you happy? In love? Do you think of me? Please write and tell me about yourself."

And what could Marianne have said? Her routine at Crescent was beyond Sarah's experience or comprehension. The language of operating revenues, net income, and machine loading forecasts would be as unintelligible to Sarah as Chinese was to Marianne. She did include truncated reports of Karen's progress in school, her dancing lessons, her taking up and discarding of the flute. But how could Marianne explain the obscene graffiti chalked one night on the house wall, or their dog, Sparky, who received a police summons for having bitten the postman on the leg? Graffiti was unknown in Canton and dogs, once forbidden as pets because they consumed precious food, were still rare. Nor could she see how the small catered dinner parties she gave for business associates would interest Sarah. Reports of *bifteck Bercy au Père* served on Limoges porcelain and eaten with baroque, gold-plated knives and forks, Château Margaux drunk from Steuben crystal, and laps draped in Irish linen would only serve to reaffirm Sarah's belief in the imminent downfall of the decadent West. The cultural gap between Marianne and her mother was as wide as the personal one.

In speaking of Sarah to Karen, Marianne would gloss over these differences. She would describe the house in which Grandmother Sarah lived, the Chins, the food they ate, the kitchen woks in which it was cooked. Karen's question—why doesn't Grandma come to visit? —Marianne parried by saying that Sarah was too frail for such a long trip.

"We'll go see her one of these days," Marianne promised.

Karen's recent questions concerning her grandmother Oliver and the ones she was beginning to ask about the Hansford grandparents unsettled Marianne. Her daughter was searching for family ties, just as Brad had intimated. When Karen saw her friends with fathers, brothers, and sisters, Marianne guessed her daughter felt her own lack keenly. What Karen was too young to know was that the facade "nice" families put up to the world often hid situations that did not bear close scrutiny. Dissension, rivalry, threats, and curses went on in nearly every kind of household.

Though she couldn't give her daughter a traditional family, she did shower her with an abundance of affection and love. But there were only so many hours in her day; that was the rub. There was too much Marianne was missing—school gatherings, prize days, teacher conferences, recitals. There was no time for walks through the zoo, picnics in the park, the little outings she herself had enjoyed as a child. I'll make it up to her, she would think. She didn't ask when. Karen was growing so quickly, a preteen now, an adolescent tomorrow. Time was passing.

One night after Karen had given her mother a detailed account of a schoolmate's neat father, Marianne wondered again if she should remarry.

Who? Whom could she have as a husband? Brad, maybe? He said he loved her. But she wasn't sure how he meant it. She didn't love him the way she had loved Toby or even Gregory. Marrying Brad would be like marrying a brother.

She thought of other possible candidates, who were few indeed. Her doctor? She had dated him a half dozen times. Twice divorced, two years younger than herself, attractive, intelligent, but he lacked sparkle. But Karen liked him. To bind herself in marriage to a man she did not love for Karen's sake would eventually prove punishment for both of them.

Nor would such an alliance solve all her domestic problems. She would still need a reliable housekeeper, something she hadn't had since Mrs. Hobbs. References, Marianne discovered, meant little or nothing. Mrs. Beebe had lasted two months. Coming home early from the plant one afternoon, Marianne had found her sprawled on the big chair in the living room in front of the TV, glassy-eyed, reeking of pot.

The current housekeeper was a black woman. Mrs. Eddlestone was loud and aggressive in public but a sweetheart at home, strict with Karen, fighting any show of sentimentality that would reveal a vulnerable heart. Marianne could only hope that Mrs. Eddlestone would have more staying power than the others.

Then there was Forest Avenue itself. Already shabby when Marianne moved in, it was steadily sliding toward urban blight. A robbery had been reported several doors away the first week Marianne had been in residence. A month later two women had been accosted and mugged while walking their dog in the alley behind their home. It would be a few years before the community of Oak Park would pull itself up and become a fairly safe suburb as well as a model of civic integration; meanwhile, the push of a poorer black population had alarmed the middle class, who had decamped in great numbers. They had left behind their tree-shaded streets and their most famous native son's legacy. Frank Lloyd Wright's home and the twenty-five other Prairie School structures he had designed, with their low, ground-hugging lines, still attracted tourists, giving Oak Park a modicum of fame. But Frank Lloyd Wright, long dead, and the Studio Foundation carrying on in his name were less than reassuring when Marianne had to park her Volvo on dark nights and climb the porch-shaded steps to her front door.

It was on one of those nights that she asked herself if she should relocate. She could move to Fox River Valley or Oak Brook or north to a lakefront condo. But it would mean uprooting Karen again. The child had established her territory on Forest Avenue and had made many friends there. And what of Mrs. Eddlestone and Sparky?

No, they would stay. After all, she reassured herself, it couldn't be worse than Manhattan.

In May Marianne had a visitor. Jim Olmstead came to Chicago to attend a seminar on corporate management and Carol traveled with him.

"Jim doesn't give a hoot or holler about corporate management," Carol told Marianne over lunch at the Lodge. "If he doesn't know about it now, he never will. It's just a good chance to get together with old college buddies."

The Lodge seating was arranged in banked tables rising in tiers around a dance floor, now vacant. Dimly lit and full of fake rusticity, it served expensive and, to Marianne's taste, undistinguished food.

"Horace Blake's in Chicago, too," Carol added. "He's looking over a possible acquisition. Tobins Plastics, I think he said."

Horace Blake, since Marianne's departure from New York, had been elevated to the board as assistant to the finance chairman, Felton Knox. He was now in charge of new acquisitions, inspecting and approving companies Billings might be interested in buying.

"Blake's a good judge," Marianne said.

"I agree." She looked older; the skin under her makeup had grown crepey. But the spirit and warmth were still there.

"What's with you?" Carol asked, giving Marianne her sudden, dazzling smile.

"Oh, I'm doing fine."

Carol lifted the brim of her hat to observe Marianne. "What exactly does 'fine' mean? Having trouble with Ludlum?"

"I wouldn't say trouble." Marianne was reluctant to complain.

"But he's a bastard, blocks you at every turn, right?"

Marianne, buttering a roll, shrugged.

"I wish you'd quit that 'loyal to the boss' crap with me. Me. Carol, your old friend. What's he, one of those macho leftovers, afraid of a woman?"

Marianne frowned at the roll. "Partly. And partly afraid of trying something new. 'Rocking the boat,' he calls it. When I try to initiate something different he says, 'We're running a business here, not an experimental lab.' "

"He's got a good rep back at headquarters. Not spectacular, but solid. Crescent shows a comfortable profit each year."

"I'm aware of that. But I feel the plant could do better. He takes everything I suggest as criticism. Change, according to him, no matter how small, costs money, and in times of high interest rates it's stupid to take chances. Well, he's got a point. For the short term. But it's poor strategy not to make a few sacrifices now that will pay off in the long run.''

Carol's small, blue-veined hand covered Marianne's. ''You're right, of course. And I can appreciate how frustrated you must feel. Do what you can. Tough it out. And learn. That's one of the big reasons you're there—to learn.''

Carol's words gave Marianne the boost she badly needed. Her mentor was still watching, as she had promised. There had been long stretches when Marianne, losing touch with Carol, had felt she had been forgotten. Her move to the Cicero plant, made in high expectations, had become a dead end, it seemed, a place where she would be stuck for the rest of her career. But Carol had given her renewed purpose, a sense that she was still working toward a goal. If in the recent past Marianne had sometimes asked herself why she was knocking herself out, why the long, tiresome hours, the attaché case stuffed with papers going home on weekends, she now had the answer. To learn. To go on to something bigger and better. Her future still depended on her, what she did, how she handled herself.

''I'm in there trying,'' Marianne assured.

''That's my girl.''

One afternoon in early June a tapping on Marianne's office window brought her head up. A man was standing on the other side, his face pressed against the glass, his nose flattened, his grinning mouth grotesquely widened. She did not recognize him until he laughingly withdrew his face. Gregory Windham!

Her heart turned over with a disturbing thump as he came through the door. Dressed in a light three-piece blue suit, his white shirt contrasting with his suntanned skin, his dark eyes glowing with health, he looked vitally handsome. She had forgotten how handsome.

''Long time no see,'' Gregory said. ''Had business in Chicago and thought I'd look you up.''

''I can't imagine why,'' she said starchily.

"Because I wanted to see you, Ms. Oliver. I've missed you. Aren't you going to ask me to sit down?" He pulled a chair out from the wall and drew it close to Marianne's desk. "You look fantastic!" He smiled, studying her for a moment. "Great! Cut your hair, didn't you?"

"Yes."

The phone rang. Marianne spoke into it, avoiding Gregory's amused, admiring eyes. The call was from the printer, who was in the process of putting out a brochure on Crescent products. Something about a delay. His voice babbled meaninglessly in her ear. She couldn't concentrate on what the man was saying. She had to ask him to repeat it. But again the voice went through her without registering. Damn Gregory, why was he here? She didn't want to see him. He belonged to the past. It irked the hell out of her to see him sitting there as if he had only to present himself and she would fall into his arms.

"Can't we get together?" he asked when she got off the phone.

"What would be the purpose?"

"You never really let me explain about Lily."

"Explaining about Lily seems to be a minor vocation with you."

"There was a reason . . ."

"How many reasons can there be for a naked lady in a man's bedroom, and the man not exactly overdressed himself?"

"If you had answered my calls or letters you'd know the real story. You treated me as if I'd become a leper."

"You did."

The telephone rang again. Marianne picked it up and said, "Call me back in five minutes."

"Is that all you're giving me, five minutes?" He laughed, undeterred. "Can't we go out to dinner tonight and talk about it?"

"There's nothing to talk about." The old pull, the old charm. The vitality that seemed to brighten the dingy sameness of Crescent's workplace. Sitting at ease in his

handsomely tailored Huntsman blazer and navy trousers, his handmade pale blue Sea Island shirt and silk
Sulka tie, his crossed legs showing feet shod in Lobb
shoes, he looked every inch the successful corporate
nabob who had just Concorded over from Bond Street
to pick up a subsidiary or two. Attractive, self-assured,
he still diminished all the men she had ever known.

"I understand you're married now," Marianne said.

"The marriage is in a state of what is known as falling
apart," he said lightly. "Sabrina and I, according to all
indicators, will soon be going our separate ways. It was
a mistake in the first place, Marianne," he noted soberly.

"Sorry about that," she said with a show of indifference. Why should she care about Sabrina and Gregory's
marriage? What did it have to do with her life?

"Are you?" His look was quizzical, yet probing, a
look that unlocked emotions she had thought long tamed.
They came rushing out, freed from their barred cage.
She'd missed him. She missed their shared laughter,
their good times. She missed the verve he had given to
her life, the excitement. She missed his lovemaking. She
had a sudden fierce longing to be crushed in his arms
again, a desire to feel his nakedness against hers, to
have the darkly furred chest bruising her white breasts,
the mouth ravaging her own. There was also a nostalgic
wish to be cradled tenderly, seeking sleep nestled close
to his beating heart.

"I still love you," he said.

With a will that had been forged during nights of tears
and despair, Marianne curbed her desire. Coolly rational
now, she quoted with feeling another disappointed lover:
"Frankly, my dear, I don't give a damn."

His thin, sensuous mouth twisted in a wry smile. "I
find that hard to believe." He rose and looked down at
her. "Don't you?"

"No."

She watched as he left, threading his way through the
outer office, the secretaries following him with their
eyes, a handsome man with dark curling hair, broad

shoulders, and purposeful stride. Gregory Windham. She wondered if Lily was still waiting for him in Hong Kong.

One morning in late June Marianne, after having paid a visit to one of Crescent's faltering wholesalers in Batavia, decided to swing down Route 31 and have a look at Tobins Plastics in Aurora. Carol had written her that Billings had acquired the company on Blake's advice. Blake felt that a little updating of machinery and staff would turn it into a good investment. Meanwhile, they could use it as a tax write-off. Marianne was curious to see how Tobins had applied their infusion of new capital.

Finding the listing in the phone directory was easier than finding Tobins itself. After many wrong turns and backtracking she finally located it off Prairie Avenue on a side street near the railroad. A half-block-long, one-story brick building, it stood behind an overgrown hedge of forsythia and mock orange. The sign "TOBINS PLASTICS" had lost the P and one S.

Marianne had some trouble with the front door, which seemed to be stuck. Going in, guided by a sign, she made a right turn and found the offices. They were eerily silent, the desks empty, chairs drawn in, the typewriters and computers cloaked under transparent hoods. There was no one in sight. It was the noon hour, but even in the worst-run establishment a few employees remained on duty.

"Hey!"

The voice startled her. It came from a door leading into an office at the far corner of the room behind a bank of files.

"What do you want?" A man in shirtsleeves appeared. He carried a holstered gun on his hip.

"I'm looking for the plant manager."

"He ain't here. What can I do for you, miss?" He moved closer, passing through a dust-moted ray of sunshine.

Marianne was on the point of identifying herself when some instinct held her back.

"I wanted to see about an order for . . . ." She hesitated. Plastics. That covered a multitude of products. Take a stab at it, she told herself. ". . . containers. Who are you?"

"Caretaker."

"I don't understand. Are you people going out of business?"

"Don't know. I'm just hired to keep an eye on the place."

"How can I reach the manager?"

"Mr. Brewer's out on the West Coast. Took a job with Teledyne."

"And his replacement?"

"I think it's some fella by the name of Art Corey."

Art Corey. The name rang no bell. There was something very weird about all this, very weird.

"Did Mr. Corey say when the new machinery would arrive?"

"Nope."

"Mind if I have a look at the plant?"

He eyed her suspiciously. "What for?"

"Just curious."

"Yeah. How do I know you're not counting the typewriters, looking for an easy way to get in? A good market for hot computers these days, ain't there?"

"Now, listen—"

"I think you'd better amscray, sweetheart." He moved closer, his hand on the holster. "Go on, beat it!"

Outside, Marianne told herself there had to be a logical explanation for the vacant desks, the silent phones. Maybe the entire work force had been given a leave until the new equipment was installed. Maybe the offices themselves were to be renovated—new desks, a new carpet, paint on the walls and the latest in computer technology moved in.

Should she call Mr. Brewer at Teledyne? Who was Art Corey? Should she try to find out from Horace Blake? Art Corey. He was probably some young, dynamic assistant manager in Atlanta or Dallas being brought up to reorganize Tobins. So why worry? God knew she had enough to occupy her mind at Crescent. She couldn't be responsible for Billings acquisitions. Tobins was not her concern.

And yet it nagged at her. The unlit, dust-moted room, the rows of hooded typewriters, the vacant chairs. What did it mean?

A month later Marianne went back to Tobins, feeling, irrationally, like a criminal returning to the scene of a crime. The forsythia and mock orange were ranker, the patch of lawn sere and overgrown with crabgrass. The legend on the brick wall still read TOBIN LASTICS. The double glass doors at the entrance were locked. Pressing her nose to the glass, Marianne saw a strip of carpet and, above it, the glinting reflection of herself.

She went around to the side door. Locked. At the back in the alley the shipping dock stood empty, swept clean, the roller doors fastened.

Had Billings made a turnaround concerning Tobins? Maybe after reevaluating the financial forecast of the company they had decided it would be too unprofitable a venture, and they were putting it up for sale. Or were they simply phasing it out?

She did not discuss her little adventure with Ludlum. But that night she called Carol Olmstead.

"Would you know if Billings is selling, or has sold, Tobins Plastics in Aurora?"

"Tobins? No. But I could find out. Why do you ask?"

"I smell a rotten fish there, Carol. I could be wrong. I'll tell you more when I hear from you."

The next day Carol returned Marianne's call.

"Tobins is still on our books. Loans totaling $350,000 for the months of May, June, and July. One for $50,000 pending for August."

"I see," Marianne said slowly. The plant had not been in operation in June or July. There had been no sign of machinery having arrived, no sign of life. The situation was what she had suspected and dismissed, only to have her suspicions rise to the surface again. Someone had received $350,000 and simply walked away with it. Tobins was a dummy company, a fake set up to milk Billings. Were there others like it that Billings was carrying, small acquisitions that required loans and showed a loss on the balance sheet?

She told Carol about her visits to Tobins. "There might be a perfectly logical explanation. But I feel something's wrong. I'd like to come up to New York and have a look at the books."

Marianne flew to New York on a Wednesday, using the excuse of family business to explain her trip. She took Karen with her.

Mother and daughter were drifting apart. Marianne, trying to juggle her job at Crescent—and now this business with Tobins—saw herself losing touch with the dearest person in her life. Of course, Karen, now twelve, was at an age when she preferred the company of her friends, when extracurricular activities absorbed a great deal of her time. But she was less inclined to share her thoughts with Marianne than she had been when she was younger. Not secretive, yet Karen was growing out of the habit of "saving up" things to talk over with her mother.

In many ways Mrs. Eddlestone had become a stand-in for Marianne. She had been taking Karen to her church, an evangelistic denomination, The Reformed People of God. It appealed not only to the black population of Oak Park but also to white blue-collar workers and to those who seemed to be on the fringe of society. Marianne saw no harm in Karen's interest. With Uncle Bob an agnostic and Emma a now-and-then Methodist, she herself had somehow skipped religion.

The trip to New York, Marianne hoped, would give her time with Karen. Lunches and museum tours and shopping. Karen herself was eager and happy to be going. She would be seeing her old friend Frankie, with whom she was still carrying on a passionate correspondence. They had already spoken to each other on the phone about Karen's coming visit and had arranged a full, complicated itinerary.

As it turned out, Marianne was grateful to Frankie and Ginny for taking Karen under their wing. Combing Billings's books and microfilms took longer than she had expected. It also had to be done without arousing suspicion, which meant she was at the office in the very late afternoon, sometimes staying on through half the night. Mornings found her too exhausted to whip up enthusiasm for a long day's outing. She tried, but Ginny, seeing the white, strained face, persuaded her to rest. "You're asleep on your feet, Marianne. I'll take over. I don't mind. I'm enjoying it."

By three A.M. on Saturday she thought she had found what she was looking for. Farrow Cannery at Heron Bay on the Gulf Coast of Alabama had been acquired by Billings two years earlier. The corporation had loaned it over $200,000 at low interest for the purpose of buying new fishing boats and renovating the plant. Farrow had paid the interest on the loan but nothing on the principal. It was still operating at a loss.

Further delving into microtaped files revealed that Blake had also personally investigated Farrow, recommending its purchase and the subsequent loan.

The next day, with Carol's blessing, Marianne booked a flight to Mobile. At the airport she rented a car and drove out to Heron Bay. She could not find Farrow. Inquiries at the post office revealed that ten years earlier a good-sized shrimping concern named Farrow had operated out of Heron. But after a hurricane had destroyed its fleet and demolished the cannery, Farrow went bankrupt and never reopened.

There was no doubt now. Someone had set up dummy companies and simply pocketed the money. It may have been more than one man. He certainly needed accomplices. But from all indications, the main culprit emerged as Horace Blake.

CHAPTER XIII

"**I** F YOU'D ASKED ME A YEAR AGO ABOUT THE POSSIBILITY of Horace Blake being involved in something like this, I would have said, 'Him? No way!' " Marianne shook her head. "He's the last person I'd suspect. He simply doesn't fit."

Marianne and Carol were sitting in the Billings boardroom at one end of the long, mirrorlike table set with emptied ashtrays, silver pitchers, and glass tumblers. The aroma of fresh lemon polish stirred in the draft of the air conditioning ducts. It was late Monday night; the cleaning crew had come and gone.

"No," Carol agreed. "He doesn't look the criminal type. But neither did the Boston Strangler."

Marianne had gathered facts and figures in a report, making two dozen copies for the Board. In addition, she had obtained two separate tapes on which was recorded the voice of Horace Blake speaking to the directors. On replay he came through clearly, his clipped monotone recommending the purchase of Farrow, then Tobins.

"I still don't understand how he got away with it," Marianne said.

"He banked on trust. Blake's been with Billings for over twenty years. He built a reputation for scrupulous honesty. Of course, we'll do a thorough check of those early years, but I'm willing to bet that the facts will show a clean record. He *was* honest."

"Something or someone must have turned him around," Marianne said.

"I can't imagine who or what. He leads a very prosaic life. We didn't know him too well—he's always been a private person—but from what I've been able to gather, his wife is a bit of a social climber. She spends money, but not extravagantly. Certainly not beyond Blake's salary. They have a girl and a boy in college, also well within Blake's means."

Carol brought a gold case out of her purse and extracted a cigarette.

"A new habit?" Marianne asked, surprised.

"No. I only smoke when I'm upset. Like now." She struck a match and lit up, drawing deeply, exhaling, watching the smoke drift across the table. "I've always maintained that too much financial authority in one man's hands is asking for trouble. On the other hand, I can't blame the Board for not becoming suspicious. Horace has always had a spotless record—conscientious, savvy. We bought Coleman Metal Works, I remember, on his recommendation, and it's been a honey. Who would guess that he'd slip in a few dummy companies?" She took another drag, letting out twin streams of smoke from pinched nostrils. "There might be others besides Farrow and Tobins. We'll have our auditors go over the books."

"Was he bonded?" Marianne asked.

"As a member of the Board, probably not. Daddy made it a rule. He used to say, 'If you can't trust a director, you can't trust anyone.' That's one of Billings's problems. It still has a foot in the last century."

Marianne pushed her hair back from her heated face, tucking it behind her ears. The fraud she had uncovered in the last few weeks—the extent of which was still unknown—would reflect negatively on the corporation. Blake's capacity to cheat by using his position as financial officer was not a plus for Billings. But it wasn't Blake himself she thought about. It was the challenge of solving an intricate, high-stakes puzzle.

Marianne said, "What astounds me is the chances he took. Any one of us might have paid a visit to Tobins or Farrow. When you were in Chicago you knew about Tobins and could easily have gone by."

"What? Jim waste his time inspecting a plastics plant? Blake knew that the chairman—and his wife—had more interesting, if not better, things to do. And as for Felton Knox, why should he check on a member of his own team?"

Carol tapped ash from her cigarette. "He just might have gotten away with his little game if it hadn't been for you, Marianne."

"It was just a lucky break."

"Don't be so modest." She stubbed out her cigarette, grinding it into the ashtray. "Then, to sum up, Blake acquired deadbeat companies, or nonexistent ones like Farrow, through Billings and gave them low-interest loans. To avoid embarrassing questions he paid back a small interest but kept the loans and, of course, the acquisition money."

Marianne nodded. "Then he must have laundered those checks. To do that he'd have to have at least one accomplice. Or it could very well be an innocent party, one that had no idea of what Blake was up to."

"Right. We have to find out what route those checks took before we can collar Blake."

"What do you suggest?" Marianne asked. "The FBI? The FTC?"

"Not yet. If we blow the whistle on Blake now he may be able to cover his tracks. He's clever, I'll give him that. I've got a better idea. I know a good man, a lawyer who has dealt with fraud cases. I'll get him on it and see if he can trace the money."

"Do you think there might be other fake companies?" Marianne asked.

"Maybe. But we'll let that possibility ride for now. It would take too long to have auditors come in and make a thorough search. Meanwhile, Blake would guess that his little scam was in the process of being discovered. Let's keep this under wraps until we get more information. My suggestion is that you go back to Crescent and wait until we're ready."

Returning with Karen to Oak Park the next day, an exhausted Marianne slept through the flight, coming awake only as the plane began its descent into O'Hare. Looking at a silent Karen as they rode home in a taxi, Marianne felt a familiar surge of guilt. She had meant to have a long, chatty conversation with Karen on the plane, catching up, as it were. Instead, she had dozed off. Somehow she had lost sight of her pledge to reforge mother–daughter ties on this trip. She and Karen had done nothing together except share a hurried lunch at the Tavern on the Green. Yet it had been impossible to squeeze more than that from her overcrowded schedule. Even her late evening dinner date with Brad—whom she hadn't seen in months—had to be canceled. I'll see if I can get a month off at the end of the summer, Marianne thought, planning ahead. Karen and I will go camping. Maybe Yellowstone Park. It isn't as if the future is suddenly closing down on us with no chance to do things together. Once this mess is out of the way, I'll have more time for Karen. I'll *make* more time, she vowed.

Three and a half weeks later Carol called to tell Marianne the money had been traced.

"Don't ask me how it was done. I can guess there was some arm-twisting and a few dirty tricks. But apparently money from Tobins was routed to Joe Brewer in California. It was a sum considerably more than Brewer, the legitimate owner, had been willing to take for his run-down plant, the difference going to Blake through a third party named Art Corey. How much was involved we still aren't sure."

"And Farrow?"

"Done the same way, using a go-between called Dowell."

"So we've got Horace Blake."

"I think so. Brewer has already flown the coop. But we have a deposition from Dowell. I've informed the directors about our findings and the consensus is to confront Blake and give him a chance for restitution. There might be two million, more or less, he has bilked from the corporation. Not a staggering amount, when you consider our assets, but we don't like the scandal going public."

"I understand."

"I want you to come up for a meeting this Wednesday. Tell Ludlum you have family business, anything. He doesn't have to know."

Marianne checked into the Manhattan Regency early Wednesday morning with the usual nervous and depressing feeling of being pulled in opposite directions. Karen had asked her mother not to go. After months of rehearsing her drama class was putting on *Madama Butterfly*. The premiere performance would be that night.

"Sweetie, I *hate* missing it," she had said. "I've looked forward to seeing you as Cio-Cio-San. I'd give my right arm to be here, honestly. But this meeting is very important. I can't skip or postpone it. You do understand?"

If Karen had pleaded, wept, shouted, thrown a tantrum, Marianne would have felt better. But the pale, "Yes, Moms," the crestfallen face, the sad acceptance had torn at her heart. What could she do? It was so hard to explain to a child how even a run-of-the-mill job precluded a mother's availability for school functions. That kind of mother belonged to a vanishing breed. She loved Karen; she wanted to be with her. But she also knew she couldn't quit Billings. It was her security and Karen's.

On impulse, she went to the phone and dialed her home number. Mrs. Eddlestone answered.

"Miz Oliver? Sorry, but Karen't ain't here. She's gone over to the school. They'se dress rehearsin' before the big do tonight. I plan to be sittin' in the front row."

"I wish I could be there, too."

"Yeah. Ain't it a shame?"

"Tell her I called, will you, Mrs. Eddlestone? Oh, and please say that I love her and will be thinking of her tonight."

"It'll help some. She cried a little 'cause yo' ain't here."

Marianne hung up feeling the pit closing in on her again. Damn! she swore under her breath, clenching her fists, damn! Why am I so upset? Kids are resilient. Karen's probably at the school now, joshing with her friends, trying on her costume, fixing pompons in her hair, with no thought of me.

She was unpacking her suitcase when the phone rang.

"Blake here."

The familiar, colorless voice startled her. It was as if a ghost had suddenly materialized. How did he know she was in New York, at the Regency?

"Yes, Mr. Blake." Had he been told about the meeting? He must know. It was called for three that afternoon.

"I wonder if we can have lunch," Blake said.

"I'm sorry, but I'm already booked." She wasn't, but the last thing she wanted to do was to have lunch with Blake.

"Perhaps I can meet you afterwards in the hotel lobby," he said, refusing to be put off. "It will only take a few minutes. Say two o'clock?"

Marianne found it difficult to refuse. What did he want? Ought she to tell Carol? She decided against it, feeling well able to handle Blake herself. A few minutes of conversation was little to ask and could alter nothing.

"I'll be there."

He was on time.

"They're putting me on the carpet this afternoon," he

said, getting right to the point. "I'm sure you're well aware of it."

She nodded but said nothing. They seated themselves in the corner of the lobby, facing each other from the depths of deeply upholstered chairs. If she had thought Blake would look ill, crestfallen, or worried, she was wrong. He presented the same neat appearance: polished shoes, conservative suit, and plain tie. His pale face was cleanly shaven, looking not much older than when Marianne had first come to work for him.

"I understand you were the person initially responsible for this inquiry," Blake said.

"How did you—"

"Does it matter?" he interrupted. "You know as well as I that what goes on upstairs at Billings is not a well-kept secret."

Leaks, rumors, slips of the tongue, Marianne thought. But it must have been recent. Both she and Carol had been very tight-lipped about the matter in the early stages.

"I need a favor," Blake said.

Marianne braced herself. Was he going to bribe her? Have her go back on her report about Tobins and Farrow? He knew she couldn't. Impossible. Even if she had wanted to, it was too late.

"I was wondering," he went on, "if you might put in a good word for me."

Marianne met his eyes questioningly. "I know you to be a fair man," Marianne replied carefully. "But I don't know how much of an impression a character reference would make in view of recent . . ." She paused, thinking of a polite way to describe the filching of two million dollars. ". . . ah, events."

"You might say you knew I was desperate for money."

Desperate. A word so packed with emotion seemed odd on Blake's lips. Was there actually some passion boiling behind those bland features?

"*Were* you desperate for money?" she asked coolly. "Two million dollars' worth?"

"I want you to soften them up. Ask them to give me an unbiased hearing. Just as I did for you."

She knew he was referring to the Bundt incident. He had been on her side then, backed her. But this was different. *She* hadn't been caught with her hand in the till.

"I'm sure if you offer restitution they will go easy on you," Marianne said.

"It would take me years. Some of the money is gone. Some—well, I can't put my hands on it right away."

Marianne asked, "Investments?"

"You might say," he replied stiffly, as if her question was out of order.

"I'm afraid you will have to be more specific than that, Mr. Blake."

"I'll sign a note promising to pay back a certain amount each month."

"Without revealing where the money went?"

"I don't see why that's relevant." His thin mouth closed with a downward turn.

His attitude is hardly repentant, Marianne thought. Blake's cool self-possession would not sit well with the Board. Its conservative members would expect a hand-wringing, broken culprit, not a man who acted as if he had been accused of pilfering a few postage stamps.

"You could speak to Mrs. Olmstead," he said suddenly. "Point out the excellent service I've given Billings for over twenty years."

"My opinion won't mean much," Marianne said finally.

"It will count. You're very close to Mrs. Olmstead. And we all know how much influence she exerts on the chairman."

"You overestimate the importance of my friendship with Mrs. Olmstead," Marianne said defensively.

"I don't believe I do. You've moved up the ladder faster than anyone I can recall. I've known men who were stuck in accounting for ten years before they got a promotion."

"You think my progress was due to Mrs. Olmstead?" Marianne asked, getting angry. "And not my own ability?"

"Oh, you're quite able. I don't question that. You forget *I* promoted you myself. But you also have pull. It helps."

"Mrs. Olmstead is my mentor. It's an accepted fact that young people, especially women, coming into an organization need the support of someone who knows the terrain."

"*I* had no mentor," he said arrogantly. "I made it on my own. My job performance speaks for itself."

Marianne, who had always thought of Blake with sober objectivity, suddenly came close to hating him. His superior air, the self-made man looking down on the spoon-fed Johnny-come-lately infuriated her. What right had he to challenge her? Or was she angry because she had expected him—as the Board would expect him—to plead?

Marianne looked at her watch and rose to her feet. "I'm sorry, Mr. Blake, but there's nothing I can do."

The board meeting that afternoon was anticlimactic. The atmosphere was as solemn as that of a meeting of funeral directors deciding what to do with a questionable corpse. Since Blake had been on the Finance Committee, Felton Knox, its head, conducted the hearing. Most of the board was present, but, aside from Knox and Jim Olmstead, she had never met any of them face-to-face before.

Marianne gave her testimony, honing it down to a concise report. The investigator Carol's lawyer had hired explained how he had traced the money from Billings to Brewer and Dowell back to Blake.

Next one of the firm's independent auditors issued a cut-and-dried summary. He concluded with a statement that amounted to a lecture on the role of auditors. He pointed out how it was almost impossible for them to uncover the existence of small dummy companies that came and went if the figures balanced. It was up to *somebody*, he claimed—the treasurer, an executive vice-president, the controller—to spot a suspicious pattern.

"Two companies don't make a pattern," defended Felton Knox.

When Horace Blake spoke he emphasized his long tenure with Billings and how he had given the corporation the best years of his life.

"This lapse is regrettable," he said almost impassively. But Marianne noticed as he talked that a convulsive twitch appeared in one eye, indicating a less-than-tranquil state behind the composed facade.

Blake continued to be vague about what he had done with the money. Nor was his case helped by the way he characterized his theft.

"My actions were wrong, I'll admit, but the amount is far, far less than what a large corporation like Billings has made over the years by undercutting small competitors, putting them out of business, and then buying them up cheaply."

"That's a despicable accusation!" Felton cried.

"But true. You gentlemen might recall Metzner's, to cite a recent case. They manufactured garden tools. We went after them, running big sales in our own chain in the towns where they were located. Rakes and hoes and mowers at half price. When Metzner's filed for bankruptcy we snapped them up."

Marianne had to admire Blake's guts. At the same time she realized his attempt to brush off his crime with the implication that "everybody steals" was inadequate. According to Blake, his theft was only a matter of degree.

Blake went on to suggest they settle the matter amicably. "To go public would affect the value of Billings stock. It might cause a substantial drop. I know you gentlemen would not want that."

Felton Knox, who had been getting redder and redder in the face, sprang to his feet. "That does it! Are you blackmailing us, Mr. Blake? Well, answer, damn it! Are you?"

"No, sir, I was merely—"

"You defraud Billings of two million dollars—and God knows how much more we haven't been able to trace—and you're talking about settling!"

Restitution, Marianne knew, would not be enough. The Board was out for blood.

Horace Blake was arrested and booked an hour after the meeting adjourned. He was freed on $200,000 bail into the custody of his wife. Two days later on a chill autumn morning Nancy Blake found her husband slumped over his desk in the study of their Westchester home. He had shot himself. There was no note.

CHAPTER XIV

"**I** NEVER DREAMED HE'D KILL HIMSELF," MARIANNE said to Brad. "I'm still in shock."

He had stopped off in Chicago for a few days while en route to the West Coast, and Marianne told him the whole sordid tale over dinner at Hugo's.

Seated in a wickerwork booth, they had an angled view of the splashing fountain in the center. An expensive restaurant, Hugo's provided an imposing if not scenic ambience where customers dined among live trees potted in Italian marble tubs. Waiters busied themselves at tablesides tossing salads or torching beef.

He watched as she toyed with her spinach salad. "What has it been? A week?"

"Yes. His wife called me, Brad. It was awful. She said if it hadn't been for me, Blake would still be alive. I can't blame her. She made me feel as though I had put that gun to his head."

"That's a lot of crap. Why should *you* feel guilty?"

"But—I do. Do you remember when I first arrived at Billings how I promised myself I'd become highly visible? I've succeeded. The Board certainly knows who Marianne Oliver is now. Blake asked me to put in a good word for him. And I didn't.''

''I can't understand why you should feel so responsible for Blake. You acted the way anyone with integrity would have done.''

''I'm not too sure about the integrity. I exposed a man who once defended me when I needed him.''

''You mean the time Bundt *stole* your report? But Marianne, *you* hadn't done anything wrong. The fact remains that Blake ripped off his employer to the tune of several million and didn't want to take the rap for it. *It's not your fault.*''

Brad passed the basket of rolls to Marianne. ''Are they hounding Mrs. Blake to give the money back?''

''Yes and no.'' She selected a roll. ''It seems that Nancy Blake received none of the benefit from the more than two million her husband stole. She knew nothing about it until the news appeared in the papers.''

''What do you think he did with that money?''

''No one really knows.'' She folded her hands around her wineglass. ''That's what puzzles me. Why did he do it? Why did he embezzle nearly three million dollars? For a fat bank account in Switzerland? He hinted that he had invested at least some of the money, but no one has a clue where.''

''Well, he's dead now. His secret went with him to his grave.''

Marianne sipped absently at her wine. ''Brad, there are so many whys connected with Blake. He could have retained a good lawyer, promised to give back the money, maybe gotten off with a short prison term. Sixteen months, something like that.''

''Sixteen months in jail might seem like a lifetime to someone like Blake. *I* don't know.''

They ate for a few minutes in silence.

''Did I tell you my good news?'' Brad finally ventured. ''The Chinese have invited me to lecture at the South China University in Canton in the fall.''

''You can give regards to my mother,'' Marianne said.

"I'll do more than that. I plan to get to know her."

"That won't be easy." She sighed. "Not a nice thing to say, is it? Maybe *I* make it hard. I really don't mean to, Brad, but somehow I can't seem to put aside my childhood resentments. I can cope with my feelings toward Aunt Em. We even had a heart-to-heart talk when I was in Sarasota, and though there was a lot that wasn't said, I think we came to a kind of understanding we've never had before. Why can't I do that with my mother?"

"She's still a stranger, Marianne, and you've known Aunt Em all your life."

"No. It's more than that. When I saw my mother or when I read her letters now I'm reduced to the same abandoned child. It's ridiculous. I've been a big girl for a long time. Sometimes I wonder if we're all still children dressed up like adults."

They were on their dessert—an apricot torte—and coffee when Brad said carefully, "By the by, I bumped into the Hansfords the other day."

"Great. I hope you didn't bother with hello."

"As a matter of fact, I said more than hello. Dorothy and I had a little chat."

Marianne pushed her plate aside irritably. "I can't imagine about what."

"She'd like to see Karen."

"That case is closed, Brad."

"Marianne," he said impatiently, "it's been almost twelve years."

"I don't give a damn if it's been a hundred."

He watched the color flush her cheeks, her hand trembling as she reached for her wineglass. "Weren't we just talking about adults? I thought you prided yourself on your ability to judge without becoming emotional."

"How else can I judge two people who tried to take my child from me? Spying on me, sending me hate mail."

"You can't be sure. You never opened those letters."

"Dorothy wasn't writing me love notes, I'm sure. And

don't give me that bullshit about depriving Karen of grandparents.''

"They've changed," Brad persisted. "They're sorry for the custody brawl, stopping Toby's trust fund. They want to make amends. They'd like a reconciliation.''

"Now that I've made something of myself? When I needed their support they couldn't have cared less.''

Brad agreed. "People change. They're getting on, looking into their sixties and having second thoughts. Dorothy seemed sincere.''

"I'm glad you said 'seemed.' They never liked me, Brad, and never tried to hide it. Because they've suddenly decided they want a granddaughter why should I come running all eager and forgiving? I don't trust them. And neither should you. Dorothy can put on a great act.'' She set her jaw. "Meeting again with the Hansfords is out of the question.''

In late November Karen caught a bad cold that left her with a hacking cough. Marianne suggested she stay home from school for a couple of days, but Karen begged to go. Her drama club was rehearsing *A Christmas Carol* and she had the role of Mrs. Cratchit.

On Tuesday at noon Marianne got a call at the plant from Mrs. Eddlestone. Karen had been sent home by the school nurse with a fever of one hundred and two. She had pneumonia and the doctor had put her in the hospital.

It was as though Marianne herself was stricken. She felt ill; she would never forgive herself. Instead of going to work she should have taken the day off. She should have nursed her, watched over her, taken her temperature every hour. She should have had a doctor look at Karen. She should have . . .

Should, should, should, the word pounded into her skull as she paced the green waxy floor of the hospital corridor. The doctor had come and gone. Karen had responded well to medication, he had told Marianne. Bed rest and she'd be fine. "There's no point in your staying, Mrs. Oliver. She'll probably sleep through the night.''

Marianne couldn't bring herself to leave, to go back to a house that would seem empty without Karen. She didn't trust the doctor. He was too young, too casual. Should she call in another?

She consulted a Dr. Timmons—a chest specialist. His diagnosis was the same. She's okay. Could be worse. Responding well. Not to worry.

Karen, weak, pale and thin, was released after two days. Marianne remained home from work for another five days. She knew Karen was in capable hands with Mrs. Eddlestone, but Marianne wanted to mother Karen herself, to hover over her, see she took her medicine, ate nourishing food, wasn't tired by too many visitors or too many phone calls. She only wished they were spending this much time together under better circumstances.

When Marianne returned to her desk the following Monday she noticed the pink memo before she got out of her coat. It was from Ludlum. She didn't have to read it; she knew what it said. She herself had okayed more than one pink slip for employees in the past. "Your services are no longer required." Ludlum was giving her two weeks notice.

No explanation. Just a quick chop of the ax.

With the memo in her hand, Marianne went into Ludlum's office. He was on the phone. "Be with you," he mumbled. Marianne stood and waited, feeling angrier and angrier as Ludlum obviously made no attempt to cut his call short.

She stared at him deliberately, long and hard. He gave her a weak smile and hung up.

"What's this all about?" She waved the memo at him.

"Sorry, but we have to let you go. You're not here half the time when we need you. We had this big rush order come in and I had to handle everything myself. You're just absent too damned much."

"Now, look, Mr. Ludlum, you know that's not true. I've put in more time—"

"Wait!" He held up a hamlike hand. "I know you have

problems at home. We all do. Sorry about the kid. But we can't run a business on sentiment.''

"Sentiment, my eye. You know damn well I've done a good job here. It's just an excuse. You've been trying to find one ever since I came. It galls you to have a woman in the front office, especially when you want your buddy, McClosky, to have my job.''

"I told you the real reason. There's no point in discussing it. *I'm* boss here. And when I say you go, you go.''

Marianne swallowed her fury. She wouldn't give this bastard the satisfaction of making a scene.

"Very well,'' she said in a controlled voice, "I'll see what I can do.'' She turned to leave.

"Don't go crying to Billings!'' he shouted after her. "They already know. Won't do you any good.''

Marianne didn't believe him. She knew Ludlum did not have the final word. When her anger cooled, she considered possible plans of action. Carol would be the logical person to get in touch with. But she and her husband had left two weeks earlier on a trip.

Who could she call? It had to be someone at Billings. Gunther? But he wasn't important enough to do her any good. Tustin? Jerry Spake, vice-president and treasurer? Loaden, planning? Felton Knox?

She made a list of all the members of the board and called each of them in turn.

No luck. Tustin thought Ludlum was the best person to decide such matters. Spake said it was bad policy for the Board to intervene in personnel problems. Loaden shared his view. Cramer, who'd been absent at the last board meeting, wanted to know who she was and why she was calling. Felton Knox, along with the remaining Board members, couldn't be reached.

She had accomplished nothing. No one at Billings was available or willing to help her. Apparently her uncovering of Blake's fraud had left no lasting impression. For the first time since she had read the pink memo she realized she was facing the loss of her job. She had complained about Crescent, been bored and frustrated there, but it was a status position she had earned.

When she thought of starting over again, anonymously doing work for which she was overqualified, waiting for promotion, trying to make herself noticed, going through the same motions she had been through at Billings, she felt sick. Si couldn't be counted on to give her a decent recommendation. The long hours, the weekends lugging her attaché case home stuffed with papers, the talks she had given the sales force—all nullified by Ludlum, who had fired her because she "had taken too much time off for personal reasons."

She spent a dismal week working up a résumé, still unable to believe she had been sacked. In all her working life she had *never* been fired. It was humiliating. She thought of consulting a lawyer. Didn't NOW have some kind of legal arm whereby employers could be sued for sex discrimination? It probably took years for such a lawsuit to get to court.

On Monday, out of desperation, she phoned Felton Knox again. This time he was in. She explained her situation in brief without giving any hint of anger or self-pity.

He said, "Is that Si Ludlum you're talking about?"

"Yes."

There was a short mumble she didn't catch. "What?"

"Thought he retired. Should have if he hasn't." Another mumble. "Miss Oliver, let me get back to you tomorrow."

Felton Knox was not exactly a supporter of Marianne's and she expected little if anything from him. His "tomorrow" might mean next week, next month, or never.

After she hung up she put in a call to Brad. She hadn't wanted him to know Ludlum had given her her walking papers—what could *he* do about it?—but she needed to talk to a friend.

Brad was sympathetic and practical, too, reviewing a variety of options. Marianne could wait until Carol returned from her trip, she could sue, hunt for another job, ask for a board hearing—alternatives Marianne herself had considered.

"You know," Marianne said, "I can't help wondering if the Hansfords might not be behind this. No—wait, Brad. It's not all that illogical. Ludlum's had plenty of time to fire me. Why suddenly now? The last time you and I spoke, you said the Hansfords wanted a reconciliation, and I refused. Could be they're retaliating."

"Marianne." His voice held the kind of strained patience she found irritating. "Be reasonable, if—"

"Do me a favor, okay?" she interrupted. "Try to find out if those two know each other. Ed Hansford and Si Ludlum."

"You're jumping to conclusions, aren't you?"

"It's possible, Brad."

"After all these years?"

"Why not? Can't you see it? They *hate* me. They'd do anything to—"

"You have absolutely no proof. What you do have is a wild imagination."

Marianne felt the heat of an angry flush rise from her neck. "Did I imagine the way they treated me at Toby's funeral? Dorothy blamed his death on me. *Me*. You were there at the wake, at the hearing, you know what adders they are."

"Granted. But if the Hansfords wanted you fired, why wait until now?"

"Opportunity. A friend in high places. A combination of circumstances."

"It isn't logical. . . ."

"The Hansfords aren't logical," she practically screamed. "The trouble with you, Brad, is you see everything through the eyes of a physics professor, trying to figure people out like a mathematical equation."

"The hell I do!" he shouted. She had touched a nerve. He resisted being labeled a bloodless academic. "It doesn't take much to figure that you've got this paranoid complex—listen to yourself!"

"Forget it!" She slammed the phone down, feeling more miserable than ever. She hated to fight with Brad, but why was he suddenly taking up for the Hansfords?

Marianne's troubles that winter of cold and ice seemed to follow one upon the other. Karen had been seriously ill, she'd lost her job, had tried unsuccessfully to get Billings to support her, and she was on the outs with Brad. She was beginning to wonder what was next when what next happened.

Two days after she had spoken to Brad her car's brakes went out. She took it into the local garage. A week, they told her. From experience she knew it would be closer to two, very possibly three. She was given a loaner, an Audi that stopped dead in the middle of Michigan Avenue traffic the first afternoon she used it. She had gone to pick up some books for Karen at the Art Institute for a class project on impressionist art. After calling the garage, she left the car and took the train home.

It was dusk when she got off at her stop. Coming through the revolving spiked iron gate she was suddenly conscious of someone close behind her. People, she told herself irritably, were always crowding your heels. In a hurry. But the two passengers who had left the train when she did had gone on ahead, and there had been no one on the platform. Where had this person come from?

She felt uneasy. It wasn't quite dark, the streetlights were on, but there were no pedestrians and few cars. She hurried, the hairs on the back of her neck prickling. If she could just get to the corner and turn it she'd be on Olive Street, where there'd be a Kroger's and some late shoppers. The footsteps behind her kept pace. She didn't dare turn around. The trees grew tall here, their spreading branches making a dim cave underneath.

She was crossing the alley when the heavy breathing behind her got louder. Terror gripped her, and before she could break into a run an arm shot out, a hand muffling her scream. The ironlike claw dragged her into the alley. Marianne, her heart lurching in black panic, arched her back, struggling to get free, her fear-crazed mind refusing to believe that it was her legs that were frantically kicking, her throat and tongue that were silently shrieking for help. This was something that happened to other women, in the newspapers, on television, in the movies. And yet here she was, caught, desperate, terrified, her heart crashing against her ribs.

What magnified the horror was her attacker's muteness. No words, no voice, only animal grunts, a jungle beast with its prey firmly hooked in its talons. Terror pulsed against her eardrums. The hand was smothering her, she couldn't breathe. She would be raped, murdered. To die like this in an alley. God, no! She managed to work her lips free and bit down on sour flesh with all her strength. There was a yelp. The hold slackened. Marianne broke loose and whirled. But her back was to a brick wall and she couldn't get past the large, menacing hulk wearing a ski mask. The hulk knocked her into the wall so hard that her head rang with the impact of skull on stone. She saw the flash of a knife. This was it, this was . . .

Her assailant gripped her shoulder to steady her. She brought her knee up and—more by chance than aim— got him right in the testicles. He yelled, doubling up.

Marianne plunged past and ran, her ankle twisting as she dashed out of the alley.

When she arrived home, shaken and terrified, she was surprised to find her bag was still dangling from her left shoulder. If the motive had been robbery, why hadn't her attacker slashed the strap of her bag, grabbed it, and run? What had he wanted? Rape? Or just plain murder? Later, with knees that couldn't stop trembling, she took the police to the scene. There she found the books she had dropped.

"Any idea who it might have been?" she was asked.

"It was a man. Except for his height, which seemed about eight feet at the time, I can't give you any kind of description. I have no idea who it was."

*   *   *

"Miss Oliver?" It was Felton Knox returning her call a week late. "How are you? Good. I've spoken to Ludlum and the problem we discussed has been resolved. You're to report for work in the morning, and if you have difficulties, let me know."

"Thank you, Mr. Knox." Marianne struggled to keep her voice even. She was so relieved she wanted to cry. "I appreciate—"

"Quite all right, quite all right. Anything to oblige a loyal Billings employee."

Marianne, putting the phone back in its cradle, let out an astonished, "Well, I'll be damned!" Felton Knox had come to her rescue. Would wonders never cease? Had someone along the way converted the old die-hard, made him see that women had their own worth in management?

Hardly.

Several weeks later Carol, passing through Chicago, explained it to Marianne at lunch at the Drake.

"I got the whole story from Jim, who got it straight from the horse's mouth. Felton hates Si Ludlum's guts. They were in the Army together in Korea, both with desk jobs in the same outfit. Seems Felton applied for compassionate leave because his young wife was critically ill. The clerical staff was shorthanded at the time; if Felton left, it meant that Ludlum would have to work his time off until Felton came back or was replaced. Ludlum conveniently *lost* Felton Knox's request for leave. Fortunately, Mrs. Knox recovered, but when Felton found out what Si had done he lit into him and the two had to be separated before they killed each other."

"I don't understand. If Knox bears such a grudge against Ludlum, why hasn't he had him removed from Crescent?"

"He'd like to, but he can't. When Billings took over Crescent it was with the agreement that managerial employees who had seniority could remain until retirement, if they so chose. Si Ludlum chose, and Felton couldn't do a thing about it. So I imagine he was more than pleased to go over Si's head and reinstate you. Just a small way of getting his own back."

"And all the time I thought Felton Knox had joined my fan club."

Carol laughed. "Don't give up. He might yet. How's it been going?"

Marianne made a wry face as she pushed a slice of orange over the remains of her fruit salad. "Strained. Large, explosive silences when Si and I have to be within three feet of each other. He talks to me through an interpreter."

Carol reached across the table and pressed Marianne's hand. "Just hang in there, it can't be for too long. I'm glad you're still with us."

Two months passed. Marianne again felt dead-ended, as if she had reached the last stop on a trunk line to nowhere. What she had once thought of as high visibility had long since sunk into anonymity. She heard little from Carol and nothing from the Board. No hint of promotion, no call to lofty places. She wondered if her differences with Si Ludlum had hurt her chances. The year 1982 had passed. Suddenly it was 1983. Karen started high school, enlarging her circle of friends, girls who were talking about boys now, about who was going steady, who was dating whom. They played Van Halen and The Police. They whispered secrets, closing the door of Karen's room when Marianne walked past.

Karen was a pretty girl. Black curly hair, dark eyes, and a smile that dimpled. Marianne would look at her and feel her heart contracting with love. Considering that the teen years were supposed to be rebellious ones, a period in life when mother and daughter suddenly began quarreling, she and Karen had few differences. Karen observed Marianne's curfews and rules without fuss. Though she protested her mother's ban on eye makeup and skin-tight jeans, she gave her mother little trouble.

Yet they weren't friends. The closeness Marianne promised herself she would cultivate and achieve never came to pass. It bothered Marianne. She hadn't given up. There was still time, she told herself. When Karen got past early adolescence she'd turn to her mother for advice, for confidences. They would talk, laugh, and share; they'd be like sisters. But there were moments when Marianne had the uneasy feeling that this possibility might elude her. Something valuable was slipping through her fingers, something she was unable to grasp or hold on to.

For a few months that spring she became involved with a man, Roger Vance. She had met him at a party given by the parents of one of Karen's school friends. Forty-eight, an airline pilot, he had traveled the world, mostly in the Orient, where he had been an interested observer. She liked him. He was good company and helped her feel that she was still an attractive, desirable woman. He was competent in bed, but he set off no fireworks. There were times when Marianne, lying beneath him as he panted over her, wondered if she was being unrealistic to expect a replay of Gregory. Or even of Toby, whom she had loved so much.

Yet Roger filled a need. Marianne was still young, full of vital juices, and not ready to commit herself to celibacy.

"He's a nice guy," was the only way she could describe him to Brad when she wrote.

"Which covers a multitude of omissions," Brad countered in his next letter.

But when Roger Vance asked Marianne to marry him, she knew she couldn't. Tactfully, as gently as she could, she broke their relationship off.

In the spring of '83 Carol wrote Marianne and told her that Billings was in the throes of acquiring Ashland Corporation and several of its subsidiaries under favorable terms.

The only drawback is that they want us
to take Casey Textiles along with the
package. And you know—except for several
big concerns—how textiles have been phased
out, done in by foreign imports. Casey's
been in the red for two years. We might

sell it. But I was thinking that if it had *any*
possibility, I might suggest to Jim that
we put some bright young go-getter in
charge and see what *she* can do. How's
about it, Marianne? What do you think?

An elated Marianne answered immediately:

　　. . . all false modesty aside, you couldn't
have considered a better candidate. I'm
ready, have been for a year. I'm more
than prepared to take on a job bigger than
the vice-presidency (assistant manager) at
Crescent. I've got ideas, the drive,
experience. Changing from wools to polyesters (I've already boned up on Casey's
product) won't be a problem. When I came
to Crescent I knew zilch about carpets,
but now I could give you chapter and verse
on cut or loop pile, tufting, dyeing, or
finishing. I don't think the switch would
be dramatic. I guarantee that in a month
I'll know more about false twists, winding,
texturing, air jet bulking—you name it—than
the man who's running the plant now. But,
of course, what you'll be looking for at
Casey is someone who can gear up production,
someone who has an eye on the market and can
go after new outlets. . . .

While Marianne waited for Carol's reply she immersed
herself in study of the textile industry, trying to analyze
why some companies had succeeded while others had
failed—an elusive quest, since no two firms seemed to
agree on a formula for running a profitable textile
enterprise.
　　However, by the time Jim Olmstead called and asked
her to meet with the Board, her mind was so crammed

with tables, figures, and technical and scientific terms she felt like a walking how-to and what's what of the fabric trade. She had waited a long time for this opportunity, and she knew she was ready.

CHAPTER XV

THE BOARDROOM HADN'T CHANGED. THE LONG TABLE, with its mirrorlike shine, set with squat, utilitarian drinking glasses placed one inch from the top of the yellow legal-sized pads, the black onyx ashtrays two inches to the left, and the lineup of sharpened pencils to the right, was just as Marianne remembered it. On the far wall the life-sized portrait of Grandfather Billings still presided benignly over the pulled-up leather swivel chairs, his thin, pinched nose sniffing the lingering aroma of lemon wax not yet polluted by tobacco smoke.

With the exception of Cramer and Tod Moss, they were all there. Jim Olmstead, Richard Tustin, Jerry Spake, Henry Loaden, Felton Knox and William Gaines—a tough battery of interrogators. Marianne, dressed in checkered Scottish tweed and a gentian-blue silk shirt sat to the right of the chairman.

She was nervous. But in control. This would be a first for Billings, a woman to be considered as president of a subsidiary. In addition, they might think her too young.

But she wasn't going to let gender or age throw her. Somebody had to be first.

The meeting was called to order, minutes read, a few items of preliminary business mumbled and shuffled through before Jim Olmstead got to the main item on the agenda.

"Ms. Oliver, glad to have you with us this morning." There was a general murmur, with twitchy smiles all around. "You have been highly recommended for the presidency of Casey Corporation, and we have met here today to determine whether you are the best candidate for the position. As you are probably aware, Casey has been operating at a loss, so our new president will be coming in at a disadvantage. It will take a great deal of know-how to make this a going concern again. We need someone with a clear understanding of the obstacles, someone able to devise a workable plan. Quite frankly, hoisting Casey out of the red ink will be an unenviable job."

He isn't going to make this too easy, Marianne thought. Starting out on a negative note. The palms of her hands felt damp. She resisted the urge to wipe them on the sides of her skirt.

"Let's get to the specifics," Joe Spake said when Olmstead had finished. A lean, gray man with a receding hairline, he had the sharpest, coldest blue eyes Marianne had ever seen. "Miss Oliver, you've been in carpeting and are probably familiar with wools and felt synthetics. But you will be dealing with clothing fabrics at Casey: Dacron, nylon, polyesters, and so on. Can you tell us something about Dacron, for instance?"

It was as though he had asked her to give the history of the written word. Where to start?

"Dacron—as you probably all know—is a DuPont trade name for a substance made from ethylene glycole and dimethylterphthalate, amorphous in its original form. Like most man-made fibers, the filaments are formed by melt extrusion through spinnerets. These are machines that resemble showerheads, and the fibers come through looking like spaghetti. They are then stretched to about four times their original length. However, Dacron is more complicated than that. It is available in various forms: filaments, staple, tow, and fiberfall, to name a few. You are probably acquainted with some of its—"

Henry Loaden stared at her as if she had lost her mind and she abruptly switched gears.

Marianne knew this was her one and only opportunity to prove herself. The Board wanted solid information and realistic profit goals. She provided them. She embarked on the presentation she had worked up and honed to perfection, explaining the properties of the fibers that made up the different fabrics and the complicated machinery utilized in spinning the fibers, recommending the most cost-efficient type of equipment, pointing out the need for new, computerized weavers that were expensive but would pay off handsomely in the long run.

"Ms. Oliver," Henry Loaden interrupted, "I'm sure we've all been impressed with your knowledge of the technical side of textile manufacturing, which is important, I grant, but you will have people directly under you who have years of experience in the how-to. What is critical is your ability to run a company successfully, to see that Casey stockholders earn a respectable dividend. How are you at handling labor–management problems, forming policies of production, and so on? In short, tell us why you think you are capable of heading Casey."

The technical quiz was over.

"I think I'm well able to perform as president of Casey." Did she sound boastful? Overconfident? This was no time for shy modesty. She had to sell herself. "At Crescent I worked out a cost-effective program that would have saved the company a considerable sum."

"Was it put into operation?"

"Unfortunately not." She resisted the impulse to tell them that Ludlum was stubbornly set against new ideas, especially those coming from a woman. No sour grapes here. "However," she continued, "I have my plan with me and can outline it for you." She opened a manila folder.

"Just leave it with the secretary," Loaden said. "She'll have copies made and we can study it later."

"Miss Oliver." Joe Spake, taking his turn, addressed her. "You've had a chance to study Casey's figures, I presume. What do you think?"

Dismal. The plant seemed headed for the chute. "They don't paint a rosy picture, do they?" She flashed him a smile before she lowered her eyes to the sheet of figures she had extracted from her folder as if to peruse the tables of bad news she knew by heart. "But I think we can change that." Was she right to use the royal "we"? "High interest rates are not to our advantage, nor is the current rate of inflation. But I think if we reorganize along the lines I've outlined in the proposal I'd like to distribute—cut waste and increase efficiency—we can become more competitive. There are many areas yet to be explored—possibly the manufacture of luxury fabrics—like silk—where we could have a corner on the market. I think putting out a quality product is of prime importance—Crescent's success in the past was largely due to this factor—and then we must institute a sales campaign with strong incentives for clothing manufacturers to buy our products. These two goals are basic for Casey, and they are attainable, even though the outlook now may seem dim."

Tustin, a bony man with a head and face like a cadaver's, frowning and silent until now, spoke up. "Miss Oliver, we have to make sure you're going to be able to delegate authority as well as interface with top management. I understand that Si Ludlum let you go last year."

Marianne felt as though the room's temperature had suddenly dropped to five degrees above freezing. She had been afraid of this, had prepared herself for it, yet it unnerved her. Her contretemps with Ludlum might be the sticking point. The Board knew about it because she had called each of them and asked for their help.

"Yes. That's true. It was a misunderstanding over time taken away from the job."

"Time for domestic problems?"

"Five days," Marianne said. Did her voice hold a

tremor, her face show edginess? "My daughter was seriously ill."

"I see. You have a child."

It was a statement so close to an accusation Marianne was tempted to retaliate by shouting, "Damn it, so do you!"

Instead, she replied evenly, "Karen has responsible care. I've not neglected her, nor have I neglected my work."

Jim Olmstead broke in unexpectedly. "Tustin, we're getting into matters here which have no bearing on this review. We are questioning Miss Oliver on her ability to perform, not on her personal life. She has an excellent record with Billings. And I think you all remember the affair with Blake."

The muscles in Marianne's midriff relaxed. Saved. After Jim's less-than-enthusiastic introduction, she hadn't expected him to come forward with such strong support. Bless Carol. She had primed him. Bless her a thousand times.

The balance of the meeting was taken up with mundane points—inventories, plant equipment, depreciation information—with which Marianne had no problem.

When it was over they said they'd let her know their decision in three or four days.

When Jim Olmstead's secretary finally called, saying he would like to speak to her, Marianne felt like the defendant in a long, arduous trial who was about to hear the jury give its verdict.

"Miss Oliver? Jim Olmstead here. How are you this afternoon?"

"Fine. And you?"

"As well as can be expected."

Was that good or bad?

"Well, Miss Oliver, it has fallen upon me to give you the news." There was a pause. "Will you hold for a moment? I have another call."

What news? Good or bad? Why was he prolonging the

torture? What call could be more important than this one?

"Miss Oliver? Sorry. First let me repeat that Casey is no prize. . . ."

He was softening the blow. Telling her she wouldn't want that falling-down plant if it was handed to her on a platter, that she was lucky not to be stuck with it.

"However, if anything is to be done with this particular concern, I think you are the person who can do it. Let me be the first to congratulate . . ."

They had given her Casey.

Before she went back to Oak Park to wind up her affairs, the Olmsteads gave a black-tie celebration dinner party in her honor. Marianne asked Brad to be her escort.

"You look very distinguished," she said when she opened the door to him at Ginny's apartment where she was staying.

"It's rented," he said, smoothing down the lapels of his tux. "The sleeves are a little short."

"No. You've just got very long arms. But if you don't put your elbows on the table no one will notice. Turn around. Nice." She had never realized how broad his shoulders were, although God knew she had leaned on them often enough.

"Speaking of nice fits," he said, "you look *très élégante*."

"Think so?" She was wearing a navy matte jersey sheath with a plunging neckline, a gown that outlined and flattered her figure. Her jewelry was understated: an antique gold brooch pinned below the right shoulder and antique gold earrings. "I'm glad you could make it on such short notice."

"I'll have you know I had to break a date for this gala event. Is it going to be fun?"

"Probably not. I would guess the entire Billings Board and their wives have been invited. The conversation most likely will consist of long-term debts, joint ventures, the International Monetary Fund, and guano."

"What?"

"Fertilizer. Billings has just taken over Santa Cruz Fertilizer, a Peruvian company."

"Should be fascinating."

The Olmsteads lived on Riverside Drive in one of the elegant old limestone mansions that had a view of the Hudson. Grandfather Billings had bought the place from a down-and-out Tammany politician. The Olmsteads had furnished their home with items gathered on their world travels: Louis Quatorze benches and chairs, carpets from Turkestan and Morocco, Greek amphoras, Italian Renaissance panels, and Japanese screens, to name but a few. The effect just escaped cluttered.

Tonight the Lalique chandeliers and Tiffany lamps were ablaze, casting bright illumination on the formally attired men and expensively gowned women clustered in the drawing room for predinner drinks.

To Marianne's surprise, there was only one other board member present among the invited—Felton Knox.

"I knew you'd seen enough of that gang for a while," Carol told Marianne.

They were a mixed group. Some of the men were golf cronies of Jim's, tanned, leather-faced, hearty outdoor types; some were professionals, a lawyer and his wife, an orthodontist and his live-in girlfriend who owned a string of boutiques, and an English publisher who did "naughty books." The talk was pleasant, light, sometimes interesting, occasionally witty.

Dinner, served at eight on antique Wedgwood china, was accompanied by three different wines in Steuben glasses: white for the shrimp, a Rothschild Beaujolais with the beef, and a port with the charlotte russe. It was a hearty but simple meal, deliciously prepared and unobtrusively served. And none of the women—or men—mentioned calories or diet.

As they were returning to the drawing room Carol took Marianne aside. "Come into the library," she whispered in a conspiratorial tone. "Our guests will excuse us for a few minutes. I want to talk to you in private."

After the doors were shut, Carol turned to Marianne

and said knowingly, "Brad is such a fine young man. Any chance of a romance blossoming there?"

Marianne laughed. "Carol, you know there's not. It's too good a friendship to spoil with romance."

"What a thing to say! At your age, you shouldn't be down on romance. I realize your relationship with Gregory Windham went bad—I won't ask why—but that shouldn't put you off."

"I'm not against romance," Marianne said uncomfortably. "It just isn't the number-one priority in my life right now. As for Brad, he's my best friend—what more can I ask?"

Carol sighed disappointedly. "I suppose romantic attraction can't be turned on at will."

"No. And I hope I haven't sounded short. I don't mean to. I do appreciate your interest. I can't begin to thank you—"

"For Casey? No thanks are necessary. You did it all yourself. No favors asked or given. Okay?" She smiled at Marianne, one of her warm, lively, huggable smiles. "There is a business matter I wanted to ask you about. Billings is interested in a chunk of real estate on Long Island—they want to expand Green Thumb. The land happens to belong to your erstwhile father-in-law, Hansford."

At the name Marianne's lips tightened in a grim line.

"It would be a complicated deal—I can't go into it now. I know you have no love for the man, but—to your way of thinking—can he be trusted to be fair and not pull anything shady? We have our lawyers looking into it, but I still believe a personal opinion is important."

Marianne said, "I see," as if a cold lump had settled in her throat.

"Oddly enough, we've never had dealings with Hansford before. He seems to have an okay reputation—at least we haven't heard anything to the contrary—but I thought it wouldn't hurt to get your input. Do you feel you can give me an unbiased assessment?"

"I'm not sure." Could she? Her advice was being asked. It was important. Suddenly, for the first time, the full impact of her promotion hit her. She was president of a company now, and what she said would have importance in the decision making of Billings's top brass. It was a heady feeling, a feeling of power, the power she had worked toward for so many years. What made it doubly sweet was that her initial use of that power would be in connection with Ed Hansford. Another spurt of adrenaline shot through her veins. What she said next probably wouldn't ruin Hansford, but it would start a rumor—"I heard he's not very reliable"—and rumors once circulated could cripple a business deal.

"We think he's anxious to sell," Carol explained. "Maybe too anxious. I never met the man myself, but I'm told he's a real poker player."

"It's true. Ed Hansford is hard to read."

Here was her opportunity for reprisal even in a small way. She could tell Carol that Hansford was not a man of his word, that in fact he was no better than a thief.

She'd be guessing, of course. Outright lying. As far as she knew, which was little, Ed Hansford had a pretty clean record. Still, the temptation was strong. When she thought of the wrongs the Hansfords had perpetrated against her, she found reprisal hard to resist. Even if she had no proof, as Brad maintained, of the Hansfords' attempt to kidnap Karen or of Ed's hand in her trouble with Ludlum, she would never forget their cold hostility after Toby died, their fight to wrest Karen from her.

But did she really want that kind of retribution? Inventing gross falsehoods smacked of spite, not revenge. The string of lies she could inflict as vindication seemed terribly mean and petty. Wasn't *living well the best revenge*, as she had once promised herself?

And she would be living well. She had moved up in the world to a place where she could afford comfortable quarters, a limo to take her to and from work, beautiful designer clothes, a good school for Karen, travel, all the rewards that accompanied a top executive's position.

"You seem to hesitate," Carol said.

"I'm trying to sort out my feelings." She drew a deep

breath and finally answered. "I have nothing but contempt for Ed Hansford. But to be perfectly truthful, I'm ignorant about his business practices. I'm afraid I can't be of much help."

A compassionate look had come into Carol's eyes, and Marianne realized that some of her inner struggle must have shown. Her forehead felt clammy, her cheeks hot. When she remembered how many times she had sworn to get even with the Hansfords, remembered how their evil shadow had hung over her life for so long, she wondered again how she could pass up this opportunity. Was she a typical soft-hearted female, as Gregory had once claimed? No, she decided, that isn't it. Stooping to slander is just not my way.

"I know you hate discussing the Hansfords," Carol said gently. "I thank you for your honesty. That's a quality I've always admired in you, Marianne. I'm sure now, more than ever, that Billings made a good choice."

"Why, thank you, Carol. But without you—"

"None of that, now. Incidentally, have you decided where you're going to live? You ought to buy yourself one of those renovated brownstone duplexes."

"Don't they cost the world?"

"You can afford it now. You're going to be making good money, Marianne. Besides, it will be a tax write-off."

"I hadn't thought of it that way."

"You have to get used to thinking big, Madam President."

"Somehow, I don't think that's going to be an insurmountable problem," Marianne said, breaking into a broad smile.

CHAPTER XVI

Cutting her ties in Oak Park and Cicero would have caused little emotional trauma if it hadn't been for Karen. Marianne said goodbye to her neighbors, a few friends, and Ludlum without too much regret. But Karen's parting with her schoolmates was wrenchingly tearful. And there was Mrs. Eddlestone. Marianne urged her housekeeper to come with them to the East Coast, but Mrs. Eddlestone refused.

"Don't know nobody in New York," she said. "Not a soul. I got family here."

Searching her mind for a way to ease Karen's unhappiness, Marianne hit upon the idea of sending her to the private girls' school Frankie was currently attending in upstate New York. She called Ginny, asking for her opinion about Rexford Academy for Girls, and received an enthusiastic response. Karen's sniffles tapered off on overhearing the conversation. She hadn't thought about Rexford. Naturally, it couldn't replace Oak Park High, but . . .

By the time the enrollment papers were filled out and

sent off, Karen had sold herself on Rexford. Speaking long distance to Frankie, Karen's voice had the old joyful lilt to it.

Settled, Marianne thought, the biggest load lifting. Everything is clicking into place.

Marianne put up at the Harley while she went house hunting. A real estate broker, an effusive young man who had asked her to call him George, had done the preliminary footwork. When he came to pick her up at the hotel he was optimistic.

"So—it's a brownstone you want. I think we can find one to suit you. I've got several fantastic buys on my list."

"They're popular, aren't they?"

"With space at a premium and rents out of sight? You bet. People don't want to live in the sticks the way they used to. Commuting is a hassle. And you gotta admit, Manhattan is fun city with dozens of restaurants to choose from, nightclubs, theaters, museums, shops, you name it. Something going on all the time. A brownstone gives you a shot at home ownership in a crowded city where condos and apartments are the norm."

The brownstones were built before 1910 as one-family row houses. Designed for the large upper-middle-class Victorian household, they had comfortably accommodated numerous offspring, dependent relatives, and a retinue of servants. But as the city grew these affluent Victorians fled to greener pastures, and their homes were converted into hotels, cheap rooming houses, or apartments, many of them falling into neglect and ruin. The reverse movement of people back to the city had started in the late fifties, and as the years advanced the brownstones became more and more appealing.

The first three houses Marianne was shown required extensive restoration, and Marianne didn't feel she wanted to go into prolonged contention with carpenters, painters, and plumbers.

"If you want a perfect 'as is,' " George said, "plus a good neighborhood, there's not much choice. I do have one in the Museum District. Expensive. The owner is asking three-five-0."

"Three hundred and fifty thousand. That's a little more than I care to pay." On the far chance that Casey wouldn't make it—though she was determined it would—she didn't want to be stuck with a big mortgage. "But let's look at it anyway."

It was love at first sight. Banked in oriel windows, rising five stories above the pavement, it seemed to have come straight out of the TV series *Upstairs, Downstairs*. The spiked iron fence that marked its perimeters and the fretted gate that led to the cellar set it off from its cheek-by-jowl neighbors. The arched doorway had above it a carved cornucopia of fruit and a stone bust of what must have been the original owner.

Inside, partitions and walls had been removed to form spacious, high-ceilinged rooms. The original wainscoting had been preserved, as well as the "wedding cake" moldings and the green mosaic glass on doors that led from the living to the dining room.

"A good buy, one of my best, even with the asking price." George, sensing a sale, waxed enthusiastic. "There aren't many like this left. Dandy renovation job. First class. If you like it, we might even get the owner to knock off a thousand." He followed Marianne up the stairs. "The first two stories are one unit, the upper three are rentals, four apartments. This place would pay for itself."

She'd have to get a bank loan for most of the down payment. Could she allow herself to go into debt? Big debt?

"This is the master bedroom and bath."

There was a tree outside the window, its leaves turning yellow, a tree she could watch from her bed as the seasons moved through it, bare in winter, budding in spring, full-leafed in summer, throwing sunlit shadows on the floor.

"There are two other bedrooms, two baths," George said.

The room she would choose as Karen's overlooked a small, enclosed garden. Neatly hedged, it had a bed of yellow mums, a little flagged path, and a stone bench. She could almost hear Karen exclaiming, "Hey, Moms, that's neat. Maybe we could get Sparky back." Karen would love the garden.

"I'll take it," she said.

To hell with money, she thought. Casey isn't going to fail.

The Board hadn't set any time limit, but Marianne knew she had to get the company out of the red while the accountants could still use it as a tax write-off. In the meantime, it was hers. Billings would advance a modest loan to modernize within limits. They were not about to sink large sums into an operation with an uncertain future.

When Marianne inspected the plant she was relieved to note that it was not nearly as out-of-date as she had been led to believe. Improvements in machinery and floor plan had been made only five years earlier. Two of the latest multiphase looms had been on order when the plant was sold and only needed payment to get prompt delivery. The chief difficulties, as Marianne saw them, were low productivity and poor sales, problems that know-how, hard work, and determination could solve.

The second week after she had installed herself as head of operations, manager, president (she hadn't decided on a title yet), she called a meeting of Casey's employees: managerial, clerical, and the mill workers.

"I'll put it to you bluntly," she said, standing before them, looking into a sea of faces, some blank, some wary, some fearful. She knew what they were thinking: new management means changes, new people brought in, old hands let go. It was true. On that point she could give them no reassurance. But her message was not entirely pessimistic.

"The future of Casey depends on you—on all of us. It's no secret the factory's running at a loss. Either we get back on the credit side as soon as possible or we face a shutdown. I'm instituting a system that's been tried successfully elsewhere. You'll be able to buy into the company, have a voice and share in its running, a share in its profits. A good quarter, everybody gets a bonus, money plus stock, according to input. If things get rough, you—and management as well—will have to take a cut."

She reorganized the sales force, weeded out middle management, hired experts in the fields of advanced technology, chemistry and marketing. When Brad came down, at her invitation, for the grand tour, he was visibly impressed.

"You have a going concern here," Brad shouted above the whine, stamp, and clap of mechanized looms tended by women who wore ear protectors.

"Not going enough," Marianne hollered. "Let's get back to my office."

"We're operating, but just," Marianne said, closing the door on the distant clanging. "Sit down, Brad. Excuse the art deco furniture, but now isn't the time to replace it, especially when I've turned down a request to refurbish the women's lounge. I'll get to both in time."

She sat behind her desk, a varnished block of plastic wood. "Brad, this company has the potential, but right now it's in heavy competition with at least a dozen others in the polyester field. When I spoke to the board I mentioned novelty fabrics. But I've been thinking more and more about silk."

"Silk?"

"Casey has done some silk. They supplied fabric for ties, scarves, umbrellas. We have a good setup here. One plus is that silk, like man-made fibers, doesn't require spinning, so our equipment might not take that much converting. What got me thinking was the way silk is coming back into the marketplace. It faded from fashion when polyester came on the market and stayed that way for a long time. But now the latest designer shows from Paris and Italy feature silk as they never have

before. And in this country there are already manufacturers who are turning out silk apparel. Royal Silk and
Imperial have been conducting ad campaigns for a year
and a half now. I'll have to check them out, see if I can
get figures on their sales. It seems to me the field is
promising. If I can locate a cheap source of raw silk—''

"Why look further than China?" Brad interposed.
"Now that China has opened its doors to trade you'll be
able to buy what you need there. How cheap I can't say,
but certainly more reasonably than silk from Japan or
Brazil. Japan's into autos and high tech these days,
leaving China as the number one silk producer."

"China?" She pushed her hair back and tucked a lock
behind her ear. "There's a tariff on textile imports, but I
don't know how it applies to silk, since we don't raise
silkworms commercially in this country. But a phone
call can check that out. So . . ." She gave him a quick,
bright smile. "What do you think?"

"I think it's a fine idea."

"*Mmmm.* It has possibilities. No, better than that,
probabilities." Silk. Polyester would still be the mainstay of Casey, but she could use a profitable sideline.
She would start off on a modest scale, and if that proved
successful, expand.

"What do you know about the silk making process,
Brad?"

"Not a hell of a lot. First there's the silkworm, who is
fed mulberry leaves, then spins a cocoon. . . ."

"Oh, Brad. Every school kid knows that."

"That's my limit." He grinned.

"It doesn't matter. I can get all that information from
one of my experts." She leaned forward, spreading her
hands on the desk, her eyes shining the way they did
when she was on to something new and exciting. "What
I want to know is how I go about contacting the right
people in China to arrange a meeting."

"You might try the Federal Trade Commission for
starters. Incidentally, remember my telling you I'd been
invited to lecture at the South China University in Can-

ton? Well, NYU has just confirmed my leave of absence. It would be terrific if we could be there at the same time.''

Marianne consulted with Carol, who thought her idea had merits, and then started putting the project in motion. Directed to CHINATEX as the proper agency, she wrote to them, indicating Casey's interest in buying raw silk, describing Casey's operation, and stating that she, as president, would represent her own company.

Marianne had decided to deal directly with the Chinese rather than sending the plant manager or someone else in her place. She didn't want to negotiate via telex or uncertain telephone connections, giving instructions long distance. She wanted to be there to make a change in plan, if necessary. For instance, she wasn't quite sure whether importing silk in the reeled or raw stage would be more cost-efficient because of lower tariffs than silk yarn already "thrown," or perhaps dyed silk. That decision couldn't be made until she had seen the product, tying it to a price range within which she could bargain.

Though she had been given full responsibility at Casey, Marianne thought it politic to present a review of her proposed venture to the Board. There were a few mumblings and a pointed question or two, but the general feeling was one of indifference. Marianne had the feeling that most of them—including Felton Knox—had already written Casey off. This negative attitude, instead of discouraging her, stimulated her all the more. She'd show them. She would make Casey work. When the profits started rolling in, they'd sit up and take notice.

She got her team together. Her new secretary was an indispensable member. Hollis Albek, a tall, raw-boned woman, had been sent over by the head of office personnel at Billings when Marianne first came to Casey. She proved to be as excellent as her credentials indicated. Efficient, quick to learn, able to make decisions on her own, she was far superior to any secretary Marianne had had in the past. And far more reserved. But Mari-

anne was not complaining. It was more important that
she have a competent secretary, however chilly, than a
bungler who oozed good fellowship.

In addition to Hollis, Marianne would be taking a
contract lawyer versed in international transactions, a
textile expert who could judge the various grades of silk
with competence, and an American-born interpreter of
Chinese descent, Jimmy Kwong.

Passports and visas were readied. Affairs at Casey
were arranged so that the plant manager could take
over, freeing Marianne to leave at a moment's notice.
But weeks melted into months with no word from China.
Her application had been received and was being considered, she was told in answer to her numerous inquiries. Brad, already in Canton, tried to find out if Marianne's
petition had fallen into some bureaucratic crack or gotten lost in a maze of official correspondence.

"Sorry," he wrote, "there doesn't seem to be anything I can do. I've learned that patience is the key word
in dealing with the Chinese. I'd advise you to resign
yourself to it."

In late March Marianne attended a textile industry
conclave in Atlantic City. When she went over the official program and read that Gregory Windham was listed
as one of the speakers on a symposium titled "New
Trends," her first instinct was to forget the convention
and return to Manhattan. She had no desire to be anywhere near Gregory. But then she thought, why should I
leave? She had come to the convention to pick up a few
pointers from her competitors, to see the latest inven-
tions in robotic machinery and dyeing techniques, and
she'd be damned if she was going to turn tail and run
because Gregory was among the hundreds present. With
luck, she wouldn't meet up with him at all.

She thought she saw him the following day. A man
resembling him was sitting at the bar of the cocktail
lounge in her hotel. She had gone there to meet a whole-
saler with whom Casey had been doing business. The

man at the bar did not see her enter, and when she sat down she took care to do so with her back to him. Just in case. However, curiosity got the better of her, and a few moments later she turned her head, only to find him staring at her. It *was* Gregory, but a Gregory she hardly recognized. He looked thin, haggard, with dark bruises underscoring his eyes. He lifted one finger in recognition, gave her a bleak smile, then turned back to the bar.

He doesn't want to talk to me, she thought with surprise. He looks terrible, she noted. Probably burning the candle at both ends. Booze and women will do that. Partying, no sleep, and he wasn't a kid anymore.

Was she disappointed? Had she wanted him to come to the table, ask if he could buy her a drink, sit down, have a conversation, plead with her to go out to dinner? Not really. Not more than any woman who found it ego-serving to be pursued by an attractive man she could turn down. Only he wasn't allowing himself to be turned down. It was just as well. She had put Gregory out of her life. He was nothing to her except someone she once, unfortunately, had loved.

In the bar mirror Gregory studied the back of Marianne's head. He could almost guess what she was thinking about him. Hung over, guzzling hair of the dog, on the way to getting drunk again. He wished he was drunk, wished he could drown himself in booze so he wouldn't have to think, to remember. He couldn't face Marianne, he couldn't face anyone. He was afraid he'd start to bawl again. How long had it been since they put Charlie underground? Tomorrow it would be a month to the day. He thought he was doing fine until he saw that kid. Seventeen, eighteen, he had the same dark brown cowlick and dark eyes with lashes that girls always envied. He was at the booth helping his dad push subscriptions to a new textile publication.

"It's a great little magazine," he had told Gregory. "It's really hot!"

That was one of Charlie's assorted quips. "It's really

hot!'' Hearing that cracked voice say it put a knife
through his gut. Never mind about parents not having
favorites; Charlie had been his. He should have tried to
work it out with Ruth, not said okay when she wanted a
divorce. She had let herself go, gotten fat, sloppy. Said
he was unfaithful, so why should she care about making
herself attractive? Well, maybe it was his fault. Maybe
he could have been a better husband. Oh, Christ. He
didn't know. Charlie was gone. Charlie . . .

He looked up at the mirror and saw that Marianne
was talking to a fat little man with a pipe. Seemed
familiar. A jobber, he thought. Marianne looking smart
and beautiful in blue wool, a froth of white lace at her
throat. If he could only have married her instead of
eloping with the oversexed lightweight like Sabrina. It
had been an impulsive, stupid thing to do. Sabrina was
ninety nine percent glitz and little else. But Marianne—
Marianne *was* real. Smart, gorgeous, and loving. Proud
as hell. She had dumped him because of Lily. Couldn't
blame her. It was such a crazy set of circumstances,
Marianne probably would never believe the truth, how
Lily had contrived that situation at the Mandarin. Damn
Lily.

He watched as the jobber got up and left. Marianne
was gathering papers, her purse. On impulse he rose and
went over to her table.

"Hello, Marianne. May I sit down?" He saw the
doubt on her face. "I'm sober—no kidding."

She studied him for another long moment, her gray-
blue eyes still wary, though the edges of her mouth had
relaxed.

"Be my guest."

He sank down, twisting his lips in a grimace. "You're
looking great—as usual. I saw in the papers where you'd
been made president of Casey Textiles. Congratulations."

"Thank you."

He lapsed into silence, staring at his drink. He should
have stayed put, not barged in on her. He felt awkward,
didn't know what to say, which was a laugh. Gregory
Windham always knew what to say.

"Something troubling you?" she asked, breaking the silence.

He looked up and saw the question in her eyes. "No." He wasn't going to beg for sympathy. Hell, he hadn't sunk that low.

"You've lost weight," she said.

"Well, yes, I've been on a crash diet. Battle of the bulge. I guess I overdid it a little." Another twisted smile. "How's tricks?"

"Fine."

"Could I buy you another drink?" Without waiting for her answer he turned to signal the cocktail waitress and in doing so caught the eyes of a man who had just walked through the door. Ken Parrot, an old buddy from the early Windham days. Ken made a beeline for his table.

Gregory introduced Marianne, hoping Ken wouldn't ask to join them.

"Hey!" Ken said, easing himself uninvited into a seat. "I've been wanting to get together with you, old guy. I'm so sorry about Charlie. I didn't get a chance to talk to you at the funeral, but me and the wife were there. It's a shame—such a nice kid."

Gregory looked down at his drink and said nothing. Marianne remained silent.

Ken cleared his throat. "Well, I see where three's company." He gave Marianne a quick once-over as he got to his feet. "So long. See you around."

Again alone with Gregory, Marianne's voice registered shock when she spoke. "I didn't know about Charlie. . . ."

Gregory took a firmer grip on his glass. He didn't trust himself to speak.

"I'm so sorry," she said softly. "I'm so sorry. If you don't want to talk about it . . ."

"No. I'm okay." He gulped the last of his drink and again beckoned a waitress. After he had given his order, he said, "I just have a few bad moments now and then. Charlie came down with leukemia a year ago. We thought we had it licked, but last month . . . He didn't make it."

"Your ex-wife, how . . ."

"Ruth is quietly—or not so quietly—having a breakdown. I wish I could."

"I can't think of anything worse than losing a child," Marianne said, her voice folding around him, reaching out to his pain. "I don't know what I'd do if . . ." She touched Gregory's hand. He grasped hers, holding on, suddenly flooded with a wave of black grief. It scared him.

His voice, on the edge of breaking, said, "I'm not going to make an ass of myself. Maybe I'd better go."

"Don't go," Marianne pleaded. She didn't think Gregory should be alone. "Have you eaten today?"

"I don't remember—a hamburger at breakfast, maybe."

"I'm taking you out to dinner."

"Now, look, Marianne, I can't stand people's pity." His tone echoed the old assertiveness.

"As a matter of fact, I'd like some dinner, too. I haven't had mine yet. And I'd like you to come with me. Okay?"

Over dinner they talked about the import tariffs the textile industry was proposing to Congress. Marianne kept the conversation going whenever it seemed to lag by discussing Casey, what she was doing there, that she was planning to go to China. Gregory mentioned that he, too, would soon be traveling to China on business. Midway through a sentence she realized he wasn't listening. His shadowed eyes seemed to be gazing through her.

He was thinking of Charlie. He hadn't heard a word about tariffs, Casey, China. His thoughts were on his son, a young man who had just begun to live, his future cut off, the lonely look of his grave. Why Charlie?

"I'm sorry," Marianne's voice broke in. "I should have realized that I'm doing to you exactly what people did to me when Toby died. Talk about everything but what was really on my mind. I only met Charlie once. Tell me about him."

She had leaned forward, and he knew the interest he saw on her face was sincere. "You would have liked him, Marianne. Charlie was a likable kid. Twenty when he died. Twenty. Likable and smart. Started to read when he was two. Crazy about flying kites. In fact, he designed a few. There was one of Charlie Chaplin. He did it from old photographs, got the face and that little black mustache just right."

He talked on. It was as though a floodgate had suddenly been opened. He couldn't seem to stop himself. He told her all about Charlie's childhood, his penchant for taking his toys apart and attempting to put them back together, how he wished now that he and Ruth had tried harder to make a go of their marriage.

"Charlie was very close to his mother. We both loved him. That should have held us together. But it didn't. You see . . ." He paused suddenly, shook his head, then gave her a wry smile. "Jesus, I didn't mean to make this a therapy session. Probably bores the hell out of you."

"No, I like listening. I'm finding out things about you I never knew before."

"Is that good or bad?"

"Good."

"Does that mean you've forgiven me?"

"For Hong Kong? No."

He wasn't sure whether she was kidding or serious. "I know it looked bad—incriminating—and I don't blame you for walking away. But sometimes, Marianne, things aren't the way they seem. If I could explain . . ."

"You don't have to, Gregory."

"But I want to. Please. Just listen."

"Do I have a choice?" There was the ghost of a smile in her eyes.

He took her hand and held it for a long moment. "You don't know how many times I've gone over this in my mind. Trying to tell you what really happened. I guess the best way to begin is to say something about Lily. I don't mean to give you her life history, because she's never talked much about her past. When Sung married her, he didn't pick her out of the gutter—though she'd once been there. By the time Sung met her she was a high-class call girl with an apartment of her own, a car, a few pieces of good jewelry, and a strong ambition to marry well. She did. As Mrs. Sung she became a lady, a polished hostess—you saw her in action—a good conversationalist, someone her husband was proud to bring his business associates home to. But Lily never lost her aggressive, guttersnipe instincts or her insatiable appetite for men." He paused for a moment. "The biggest mistake I made in my life—and God knows, I've made plenty—was starting an affair with her. She's the type who, once she's got her hooks in, won't let go. I'm telling you this so you'll understand what happened.

"When you left for the airport that day I went to my meeting. I got back to the hotel around three-thirty and the room seemed empty, dead. I missed you. I'm not much good at being alone anyway, but this was really bad. I decided to shower, change, and go down to the bar, where I could at least hear live people talking around me.

"I was through with my shower and was getting into my shorts when I heard a sound behind me. It was Lily. Lily wearing nothing but a little gold locket around her neck. Somehow she'd sneaked into my hotel room—she'd done that before—and had hidden.

"She said, 'Hi, Greg.' Just like that. I've never hit a woman, but I came as close to it then as I ever hope to be.

" 'You've run out of whiskey,' she said. 'I'm having room service bring up another bottle. Jack Daniels, is it?'

" 'Listen . . .' I was ready to give her the word when there was a knock on the door and a voice saying, 'Room service'—and you know the rest. That's it. I can't blame you for thinking the worst. I still love you, Marianne."

She looked at him out of wide eyes, their blue-gray

depths liquid with compassion. She wasn't thinking about
Lily or Hong Kong. He had the feeling that she had only
half heard his explanation and apology. That look was
for Charlie. It got to him. His eyelids burned, his throat
suddenly felt raw. If he stayed a minute longer he'd cry
for sure.

"Listen, thanks for the dinner, the talk," he said
hurriedly. "I have to run now . . ." He picked up the
check and rose. "Will you be around for a few days?"
He could feel the tears pressing. He was supposed to be
a man, damn it. "I'll call. Okay?"

He needed a drink badly. What had gotten into him?
Talking with Marianne and the way she had looked at
him made him suddenly remember how he, Marianne,
and Charlie had had lunch at the St. Regis and how they
had laughed at some silly joke Charlie had told. Memories like that tore him apart. A whiskey neat burning his
insides would help.

Once Greg reached his room and poured himself a
drink, however, he found he didn't want it. The stuff
would only make him feel worse. He sat on the edge of
the sofa with his face in his hands. He'd been working
too hard, fighting a takeover of Windham by Stevens,
that strike in Georgia, the first vice-president going over
to GMC, sales hitting a plateau. And Charlie. Everything at once.

Marianne sat in the coffee shop gazing pensively into
space. What a strange turn of events. She had never
imagined speaking with any degree of civility to Gregory
again, never dreamed she would feel anything but hostility toward him. Charlie's death had shaken him profoundly.

She had told Gregory that she was finding out things
about him she hadn't known before. And it was true. In
the past she had been aware of his love for Charlie but
never of how deeply that love had been felt. Gregory's
charm, his vibrant personality had hidden a man more
tender than she realized. It was this man she could
forgive.

*   *   *

He was still sitting on the sofa when he heard a knock, followed by Marianne's soft voice.

"Gregory? Gregory, it's Marianne."

He opened the door. "Greg, I want to help if I can." She held out her arms.

He went into her embrace and let her hold him, the first time in his adult life he had been held by a woman other than his mother.

They sat together for a long time on the sofa, Gregory nestling against Marianne's shoulder. They talked. They didn't speak of Charlie again, but reminisced about happier times, parties they had been to, people they had met.

It was inevitable, Gregory later thought, that he should make love to Marianne that night. There was something strangely virginal about her, as if the grief she had shared with him had made her shy. He had to coax her with words and kisses before she'd let him undress her. But he forced himself to take his time.

Slowly, his hands moving over her satin-smooth skin, he caressed and stroked until he felt her relax under him. He bent and kissed her lightly on each breast, then rested his mouth a few moments between them, the firm white globes pillowing his face. She had the most beautiful breasts of any woman he'd ever known. Just holding and touching them excited him.

Taking one flushed nipple in his mouth, he sucked and nipped and sipped until it hardened in his mouth. Her moan of pleasure put a wild edge to his desire. He brought his head up and kissed her hard and hungrily, fanning kisses over her face, blazing a trail to her throat and back to her mouth again. Soon she was matching him in frenzy, her hands clutching his shoulders, sliding smoothly down his back. When he lowered himself to find the honey sweetness between her legs she began to spasm at once. Excited beyond endurance himself, he flung himself over her, raising her quivering buttocks with his hands and plunging deeply inside, the velvety suction receiving him with a responsive upward movement. Oh, he loved her, he loved the feel of her, the moist feminine heat, the final explosive burst that jolted his spine.

"I'm never going to let you get away from me again," he murmured, holding her tightly in his arms.

CHAPTER XVII

On April first Marianne finally received the go-ahead from CHINATEX. A committee would be attending the Canton Trade Fair on the fifteenth, and they would like to do business there.

She immediately cabled Brad and had him make hotel reservations for the "Casey Five," as she called them. "A good hotel, please," she urged, remembering the drab, humid room in the old wing of the Dong Fang and its ineffective revolving fan.

"I'll do my best," Brad wrote back. "Your mother and I have become great friends. I find her amazingly up on contemporary literature, considering the years our books have been banned in China. Modern fiction by American authors is in short supply. You might bring a bagful of paperbacks when you come. Nothing overtly political or pornographic. Alice Walker, maybe, or Eudora Welty. Your mother's looking forward to seeing you and so am I! I'll make the hotel reservations open-ended, since you didn't give me a departure date."

Marianne couldn't guess how long she'd be gone, but

she had been told to prepare for at least three weeks. It seemed an excessive amount of time for a transaction that in the West—given thorough preparation—might take three or four days at the outside. Gregory was going to China, also to Canton. He would be negotiating not only for silk but for cotton as well. At first Marianne thought the coincidence too pat. Had he hurriedly made arrangements just because she would be there?

"Hurried? Hardly. I've had this in the works for fourteen months. Finally got Sung to goose them into action. But I'm not complaining." He smiled, taking her in his arms. "If I'd known you'd be in Canton at the same time I wouldn't have cared how long it took."

They had resumed their relationship as lovers, spending weekends together when Marianne wasn't visiting Karen at Rexford. Sometimes he went with her. He was very charming to Karen, interested in what she had to say, exchanging anecdotes of his own boarding school days.

Karen thought he was cute; he made her laugh. Was Marianne going to marry him?

"Of course not," she told her daughter. "He's just a friend."

It wasn't for want of being asked.

"I'll put it simply and clearly—for the third time, I might add—notice I'm keeping count?—will you marry me?"

"Gregory, I think we ought to wait."

"For what?"

They had just seen Paul Newman in *The Verdict* and were in Gregory's white Maserati on their way to the Hors d'Oeuvrie atop the World Trade Center for a midnight snack.

"You're putting me off, Marianne, a delaying tactic. And for a reason. You still hold Hong Kong against me."

"No. Really. I've forgotten about it."

"What then? I've got it. You think I have some pretty young thing stashed away in the Village."

She laughed. "I trust you, Gregory."

"You're not saying that as if you really mean it."

"But I do. You're my one-at-a-time lover."

"That sounds like a half-assed recommendation. I'm a marrying man, sweetheart. I haven't even suggested we live together. I want you to be my wife."

"I know. And I love you for it."

"But not enough to marry me."

She was silent for a few moments, trying to think how she could explain, without hurting him, that she *was* unsure of herself, still watching over her emotions, jealously guarding herself against hidden disappointment.

"Greg—why don't we let it ride a while? We enjoy each other's company. I love being with you. We never seem to run out of things to talk or argue about, whether it's corporate takeovers, white knights, the Saudi lobby, or just plain gossip. We both like Woody Allen, the old Raymond Chandler mysteries, strawberry shortcake, oysters on the half shell, seltzer. I love going to bed with you. You're a wonderful lover, passionate and tender . . ."

"Marianne," he interrupted, "you're beginning to sound like a commercial, trying to sell yourself on Gregory Windham. I want you to be in love with me the way I'm in love with you. I want you to be my wife. I want to be the father of your children. Is that so hard to understand?"

"No." And that was one of the problems. She did understand. Gregory, she felt, wanted the kind of woman who would give herself over completely to him. That was one of the reasons he wanted to marry her—aside from love—because she was organized, practical, and competent. She sensed he wanted a first-rate *hausfrau*, just as he insisted on first-rate executives on the Windham board. A capable wife who could manage the maid, the cook, the gardener, and, in a pinch, if things went awry, step in and fix a leaky faucet or whip up a beef Stroganoff for thirty guests.

"Why do you want to wait?" Gregory asked.

"What's the hurry, darling? Right now I'd rather not have any commitments until I get Casey in the black."

"I wouldn't object to you going down to the office every morning."

"Object?" She gave him a sharp look.

"Just kidding." He leaned over and kissed her. "But, Marianne, I'd hate to see you making Casey the exclusive focus of your life."

"Isn't that what you did with Windham Mills?"

He laughed. "Okay. You win this round. But I'm warning you, I don't give up easily."

Before Marianne left on her trip she went up to see Karen again. To Marianne's dismay, she found her daughter glum and uncommunicative.

"What's the matter, hon?" Karen had been so ecstatically happy at the beginning of the semester and on Marianne's last visit with Gregory had laughed at his jokes, telling a few of her own. She had spoken of the tennis club she had just joined and her English lit teacher who, she was sure, was going to give her an A. Something had gone wrong.

"Nothing." A dispirited "nothing" that was loaded with meaning.

"Bad grades?"

"Nope. They're okay."

They were sitting on one of the twin beds in the room Karen shared with Frankie. Karen's half was characteristically neat while Frankie's looked as if a high wind had whipped through, scattering books, papers, candy wrappers, and dirty socks over chairs, the glass-topped desk, and the floor.

"Did you and Frankie have a fight?"

Her head lowered, Karen nodded. Then, looking up at her mother, a tear clinging to one of her lashes, she said, "She's changed." Her throat worked. "Moms, she's like somebody I don't know anymore."

"Why is that?"

"Well, she's got this dumb boyfriend. He's a nerd, a total nerd. She spends all her time with him. He works in a bicycle shop over in Williamstown. She can't even go to a movie with me like we used to on Sunday afternoons." The pain of rejection was written into the little worry wrinkles across her forehead.

"Maybe it's just a temporary crush." Marianne put her arm around her daughter, holding her, feeling her softness, the fragile, childlike bones. How pathetically vulnerable they are, she thought. "Frankie will get tired of him. He's something new in her life. When the novelty wears off, you and she will get back on your old footing."

"No, Moms, I don't think so. She's bonkers about him."

Bonkers, the desperate terminology of young love.

Marianne squashed the urge to shake her daughter. "What do you do for socializing? Getting to meet people that aren't at the school?"

"Oh, I've gone with Tilly—she's in my art class—to the Church of the Blessed Angels. It's like the one Mrs. Eddlestone belongs to in Oak Park. The choir is great. Really super. Nice people. They're all very friendly, lots of kissing and hugging, like one big happy family. I've thought of joining."

"I can't see any harm in it. But don't go whole hog. Those people can sometimes be fanatics."

"No, Moms, they aren't. They're ordinary people, only they *believe* in something."

To Marianne the earnestness on Karen's face was like an accusation. *They* believe, the message read, what about you? Missed out again, Marianne thought. Should I have sent her to Sunday school, gone to church? How was I to know my daughter would resent my lack of involvement in some kind of institutional religion? And how, where, would I have fitted it into my schedule?

"Honey, if you aren't happy here . . ." Marianne began.

"Except for Frankie it isn't too bad." She plucked at the bedspread, loosening a thread, twisting it between her fingers. "I'll be okay." She gave her mother a bleak smile. "I'm just not going to room with Frankie anymore."

Marianne stroked Karen's hair, black curls like her

father's, cut close to her head. "I love you, darling. Whatever happens, I love you." She gave the young shoulders another hug. "I want you to join me in Canton on your spring break. There's so much to see in China. We could take a cruise on the Yangtze, see the Great Wall. And you'll have a chance to meet Grandmother Oliver."

"Sounds neat," she said without enthusiasm.

Two representatives from CHINATEX and Brad were waiting to meet Marianne when her plane touched down at Baiyun airport. Before she debarked she saw that the red lettering across the upper face of the terminal had been changed from Canton to Guangzhou. Pinyin spelling had been adopted in 1979 to simplify or "romanize" the Chinese language, her mother had written. And though most foreigners, including Marianne, went on calling it Canton, Marianne now made a mental note to remember the altered name. Peking was Beijing, Mao Tse-tung was Mao Zedong, Tibet Xizang, and so on. She didn't want to appear touristy or like the cartoon American traveler who did not feel it important to learn a few minor facts about his host country. She had come to China on business and she wanted to be taken seriously.

Introductions were made by Jimmy Kwong, Marianne's interpreter. A young man with a round face and black, lively eyes behind glasses, he spoke Mandarin as well as Cantonese.

"Mr. Lu, Mr. Wei, this is Miss Oliver."

They shook hands. Marianne would meet the other members of the Chinese team later.

Brad hovered behind and over the others, grinning at Marianne in delight.

The remaining Americans were named, hands shaken. Hollis Albeck, then Art Schultz, their lawyer, and lastly Jerry Cooper, the textile maven, a man somewhere in his sixties who had been in Canton twice since "it went Red."

Two black Mercedes limousines, polished to a mirrored gloss, awaited them. Brad managed to slip into the one that would carry Marianne, settling himself in the back seat with her and Mr. Lu. Mr. Wei had gone in the second car.

"Sorry I couldn't do better with hotel reservations," he told Marianne. He had managed to book Marianne and Hollis into the White Swan, a world-class hotel built as a joint venture of the Chinese and a Hong Kong consortium. But the men in the party would have to stay at Renmin Mansion, a hotel which catered to overseas Chinese visitors and the overflow of Westerners during the fair. "Getting a room in this town at this time of year is next to impossible."

"Don't apologize," Marianne said. "I didn't give you much notice."

Mr. Lu, turning to Marianne, said in English, "Dr. Young speaks the truth. We have many more guests this spring than we planned. However, I shall do my best to see your people moved to the White Swan as soon as quarters become available."

"Thank you, Mr. Lu. You speak very good English."

"Not so good. My accent needs improvement, but I thank you."

As they drove down Jeifun Road through the heart of Canton Marianne was struck by the changes that had taken place since her last visit. Whole blocks of apartments, tall buildings housing new hotels and commercial offices, had gone up in the intervening years, giving the city a more urbanized, Western look. Traffic had increased. Bicycles still moved in wheeled phalanxes, but the buses overflowing with passengers had multiplied. In addition, she saw a greater number of automobiles—official cars, taxis, and quite a few Japanese Toyotas and Datsuns that looked suspiciously like private conveyances, unheard of in 1977.

But the biggest change was on the sidewalks, where a whole new life had sprung up. Booths and open-front stores sold sweets, spices, housewares, tea, baskets, white funeral wreaths, lamps, and musical instruments. Hung from tree to tree along the outer edges of the pavement, clotheslines displayed T-shirts, sweaters, blouses, dresses, and jackets in bright, fluorescent colors. People paused to finger, try on, and barter, jostled by those who were inspecting wares set out on canvas ground covers. These were heaped with bananas, pineapples, oranges, bok choy, and bunches of celery, the farmers with their hand scales measuring out, weighing, calculating. Crates of chickens and geese squawked and honked, scrawny necks and yellow bills poking through slats. A dentist with a foot-pedal drill attended a customer, mouth opened wide, a barber trimmed hair, a shoemaker hammered.

"It's so different," Marianne observed. "I knew there had been changes, but I didn't expect this."

"Since it's my first visit," Brad told her, "I can't say. But what you see is the free market. It's been permissible for a couple of years now for the peasant to sell his surplus after he's met his state quota. As for the shops—small enterprises, they're called—they help solve the unemployment problem. People 'waiting to be assigned' —that is, without a job—may set themselves up as private entrepreneurs if they can beg or borrow the necessary capital."

"And their clothes!" Marianne went on in a tone of surprise. "Nothing like the Mao uniforms, men and women alike in blue cotton, that I saw when I was last here. I wouldn't say they're New York chic, but the colors—and they have a little style. Not bad, not bad."

Mr. Lu smiled. "Guangzhou is a port city, Miss Oliver. It has always been a little more Western than, say, Wuhan, where I come from."

They crossed the bridge to Sha Mian Island and pulled up at the roofed entrance of the White Swan. The limousine that had deposited the men at the Renmin stopped behind them. Hollis got out.

"Take a nap," Mr. Lu advised Marianne. "Have a rest. This afternoon we take you and your party on a tour of the city. Tonight a banquet at the Datong restaurant. Six o'clock. Is this all right?"

"Yes, thank you."

Brad got out and escorted the two women into the hotel, where they registered.

"Brad, would you like to come up?" Marianne asked.

"For a few minutes. I know you'll want to relax for this afternoon's schedule. The Chinese can set a mean pace."

"I wish I could skip the sightseeing," Marianne said as they rode up in the elevator. "I've already seen the Sun Yat-sen University, the Peasant Movement Museum, and the Exhibition Hall of the Revolution."

"Better not. They take a good deal of pride in their historical institutions."

"I know. Good relations. Solid personal rapport, Jimmy Kwong keeps telling me. He clued me in as to what to expect all the way over."

Once they reached the suite, Marianne immediately sank down on the sofa, kicking off her pumps, which had become two sizes too small since their stopover in the Philippines.

"You look exhausted," Brad said, fixing himself a drink and sitting down beside her. "I'll leave if you want."

"No, stay. At least until you finish your drink." She was glad Brad was there. He gave her a sense of the familiar, as if she were still anchored safely in Manhattan. Despite her sophisticated executive status, she hadn't traveled much. Her previous visit to China had been her first trip to a foreign country. China, then as now, seemed overwhelming in size as well as in population. And the Chinese businessmen she had to deal with—were they as enigmatic as her business colleagues had indicated? Or were they like every trader, like every good poker player—inscrutable.

"How's Karen?" Brad asked.

"So-so. She and Frankie aren't getting along. She's jealous because Frankie has cut her off in favor of a boyfriend. She'll get over it when she meets her own heartthrob." She turned to him. "Tell me what you've been up to. How's school?"

"Fine. I'm enjoying it. I have a group of dedicated, bright students. We manage amazingly well with my broken Chinese and their fractured English. The only complaint I have is their damned refusal to challenge me. They won't ask questions the way they do at home. 'Why do you say that, Dr. Young?' or 'What do you mean?' 'Isn't it possible to do it this way?' "

"You're an authority figure to them, Brad. By the way, have you seen my mother?"

"Several times. She doesn't look very well. Bad color, shortness of breath. I asked her if she was thinking of retiring and she said no, there was too much to do."

"She said the same things to me in 1977."

"They've had to reorganize the school because it had been closed down during the Cultural Revolution, and they're still working at it. She's looking forward to seeing you."

"Yes, I know. She wrote as much." Marianne shook the ice cubes in her glass. "I'm going to make an effort this time. But I can't do it all."

"No. But halfway sometimes isn't enough."

"Meaning it's up to me to go the extra mile?"

"Wouldn't hurt that badly, would it?"

The banquet that night at the Datong was held in a room off an open terrace that looked down over the Pearl River, where fishing boats were returning from a day at sea. The water had a brown, muddy look. Little choppy wavelets crested with foam broke in the wake of a motorized string of barges. A breeze fanned the diners. The entire Chinese team was present: Mr. Lu, Mr. Wei, Mr. Hsu, Mr. Chang and Mr. Boa. When Marianne had asked for a list of the team's full names, she got it but was told by Jimmy that "Mr." was a form of address adhered to by all except family.

They did not, as some Westerners would have it, all look alike. Nevertheless, Marianne thought it a good idea to associate a physical characteristic with each of their names, at least until she got to know them better. Mr. Lu, in his mid-thirties, had clearly defined, handsome, lean features. Mr. Hsu was a tiny man, large-eared, solemn-eyed. Mr. Wei, plump-cheeked, owlish behind dark-rimmed glasses, an older version of Jimmy Kwong, smiled at every remark whether he understood it or not. Mr. Chang, she learned, was their interpreter, a young man in his twenties with a longish face and slightly protruding teeth, while Mr. Boa, an older man, had a narrow, furrowed brow and a high-bridged nose.

Preliminary toasts of *mao tai* were offered. Marianne tempered her consumption of the 180-proof liquor by sipping small amounts. She wasn't about to risk getting high and making what might be a fatal slip at the beginning. So much depended on first impressions. When the host, again according to custom, placed a small amount of food from the serving platter—a sauced slice of fish filet—on her dish, she accepted graciously, commenting that it was delicious. She had learned to use chopsticks on her first trip to China and through practice before her current visit had become adept. The height of the table, several inches above the norm at home, helped. There was less distance to go, less chance of a morsel slipping ignominiously into her lap.

Talk at the table was of the Canton Opera Troupe they would see the next night. "You must not judge it by comparing it to your own opera," Mr. Lu said. "If you listen closely and watch the actors you'll understand and enjoy."

The silk expert, Jerry Cooper, sitting next to Marianne, leaned over and, shielding his mouth, said, "Enjoy! Ha! Noise you wouldn't believe. Banging and crashing and screaming, enough to drive you up the wall. And this guy says enjoy!"

A short, heavyset man with a wheeze, Jerry had beetling gray brows that moved expressively, twisting, rising, or coming together in a frown when he talked. And he talked a lot. Marianne knew he had no great love for the Chinese (can't trust them, he had told her at least a dozen times), but she had brought him along because he had been recommended as the best silk specialist in the

States. She had been informed that he could tell the quality of reeled or thrown silk by a cursory examination. He knew the difference between voile and georgette, pure dye and spun silk, while Marianne, like any lay person, could only hazard a guess by the feel of it. His advice would be invaluable. She had hoped that his public comments would be confined to fibers and fabrics. But now as the liquor flowed she found herself anxious about what Jerry might say next. Fortunately, he got into a conversation with Art Schultz about his former employer, ITT, and its troubles with Congress.

Nothing that had to do with business was mentioned during the meal. It was purely social, a get-acquainted affair, but Marianne knew the Chinese were astutely sizing her up, as she was them. The host, in the person of Mr. Lu, sat opposite the entrance door, as was customary. Marianne, as the honored guest, sat to his right. Mr. Lu answered questions about the modernization of China in a polite but ambiguous way. Marianne identified him as a charming but intellectually agile diplomat. She filed this information away for future reference. The other Chinese remained mostly silent, murmuring now and then in their own language or listening closely to their interpreter's translation. Later Marianne would discover that all but Mr. Boa understood and spoke English.

Course followed course, Shao Xing chicken, crab with scallions, straw mushrooms with shrimp, and fresh papaya for dessert. Ten minutes after hot, wet towels had been served and used for freshening, the host rose, signaling that the banquet was over. Kwong lingered behind in conversation with the headwaiter. His purpose, as he had informed Marianne beforehand, was to find out the "grade" (A, B, or C) of the banquet they had been given. It would be Marianne's obligation to reciprocate at a similar level.

On the sidewalk outside Art Schultz took Marianne aside. "Any chance of us getting rooms at the White

Swan or the Garden?" A man in his late forties, he was tall and thin, with earnest eyes sunk in deep sockets. "Anything that's an improvement over the Renmin. They have all three of us jammed into one room, no room service, no air conditioning, the water can't be used to brush your teeth, and the restaurant wouldn't qualify as a two-star greasy spoon. My ulcer's been acting up again."

This was the first she had heard of Art Schultz's ulcer. Schultz had been to China before. He ought to have anticipated a few inconveniences, and if he had an ulcer he thought might flare up he should have told her when the venture was still in the planning stage. While she might sympathize with Art's sick stomach, there would be problems enough without having a disgruntled and complaining participant on her team.

It was nine o'clock in the evening when she and Hollis were dropped off at the White Swan. As they entered the lower lobby Gregory and Brad, who had been sitting side by side on overstuffed maroon chairs, rose as one.

"Marianne!" Gregory covered the distance between them in two strides. Folding her tightly in strong arms, he kissed her with a thoroughness that took her breath away. She struggled free with a forced laugh.

"Greg! Please!" Embarrassed, conscious of Brad's masklike countenance in the background, she tugged her jacket back into line. "Let's not make this a production."

"Why not?" Greg asked, reaching for her. "I'm happy to see you."

Marianne sidestepped him. "Hello, Brad. You two have met?" Of course they had. But she felt awkward and couldn't think of anything to say.

"More than once," Brad said. "Didn't know Greg was going to be in Canton."

"I thought I mentioned it." She hadn't. But, damn it, why should she feel apologetic? So she hadn't told Brad she and Gregory were back together. So what?

"Couldn't wait," Greg said, his eyes fastened on Marianne. He did not seem at all affected by Brad's displeasure. "So I pushed my schedule ahead."

Gregory linked his arm with Marianne's, drawing her closer. Marianne did not resist. Why did he have to be so demonstrative in front of Brad?

"Shall we try the bar upstairs?" Marianne suggested in a bright, artificial voice. "See what they can do in the way of a drink?"

Hollis had already disappeared toward the bank of elevators.

"I think not," Brad said tersely. "I'll be on my way. I'll call you later, Marianne."

Gregory, watching him leave, said, "What's he ticked off about?"

"He's not ticked off."

"The hell you say. Doesn't like me, does he?"

"He's not wild about you."

"You're telling me. He's the one who introduced me to that lollipop Sabrina. I think he did it on purpose." He brought her close and kissed her again. "Let's have that drink at my place. I'm staying at the Garden."

"Gregory . . ."

"I want to make love to you, woman. How's that for being up front. Of course, I could say I want to f—"

"Don't," Marianne interrupted, putting her fingers to his lips. "I hate that expression. I'll come. But I have to be back here at a decent hour."

"What's decent? Ten o'clock in the morning?"

"No! Midnight, you idiot, one or two at the latest."

"You're joking."

"I'm not. I know the Chinese aren't going to keep track of my hours, but I'm a woman doing business in a foreign country. . . ."

"Really?"

". . . and I have to watch myself. The Chinese have a strict moral sensibility and I don't want them to get the impression that they're dealing with a loose woman."

"Too late. They've seen right through you from the start. Marianne Oliver, hotter than a firecracker, a centerfold who'll bed anything in pants . . ."

"And I thought it was a secret. Anyway, there's Hollis."

"Hollis, my God! You can't mean you have to act like Ms. Celibacy for *Hollis*?"

She grinned. "Why not?" His look of mock dismay made her laugh. Standing on tiptoe, she kissed his forehead. "Okay, you talked me into it."

Alone with Gregory holding her tightly, Marianne felt laughter rising in her closed throat, joy that the day, thank God, was behind her. Gregory's mouth and hands were the magic, blotting out the little unpleasantnesses, the bumpy flight, the split hotel reservations, Art Schultz's ulcer, Jerry's snideness, Brad's disapproval, Hollis's stony silence. Here, high above the soft, twinkling darkness of the Cantonese streets, the door had closed on worry. Though she hadn't had more than snatches of sleep in the last twenty-four hours, she felt awake now, alert, her nerve ends tingling.

"Aren't you going to undress me?" she asked against Gregory's shoulder.

"*Mmm*," he growled, grinding his swollen crotch into her loins.

Marianne giggled at Gregory's rumbling. "What will Hollis think?"

Finally naked, he held her again. "I love you, Marianne." And she clung to him, her cheek pressed to his, a sudden moistness blurring her eyes.

Propped on an elbow, Gregory gazed at her for a long while before he bent to kiss her. She drew him down to her bare breasts, desire and tenderness coursing through her veins like golden honey. A few moments later he began to make love to her, her aroused senses rushing to meet, to reciprocate. Why couldn't this feeling last—the feather-light kisses that tickled along her belly and between her thighs, the coarse, curly hair running through her fingers, the sure, strong hands that caressed, the mouth that made her tremble? He was such a marvelous lover. Every touch was orchestrated to give pleasure, to

fire her hunger for more until she was beside herself
with sweet agony and he entered her, pinning her to the
bed with masterful strokes, bringing her to a shuddering
climax.

The afterglow of their lovemaking satisfied Marianne
almost as much as the sex: lying there, cheek to chin
in the circle of Gregory's arms, the tension flowing
out of her, relaxed, drowsy, content, speaking in low
intimate tones.

"Marianne." Gregory turned his face, kissing the side
of her head. "You *are* incredible, you know."

He had said it many times before. But now, delivered
in a deep baritone voice that seemed to come from the
bottom of his soul, with the wonder of his love force
still strong within her, that simple, mundane declaration
touched her deeply.

"I thought I was in love with Ruth." He pushed
himself up on an elbow, his darkened face barely visible
in the thin shaft of light coming through the bathroom
door. "We were both young, and she seemed to be
everything I wanted in a woman. Seemed. It didn't take
long before I discovered she was frigid—maybe it was
my fault, but I don't think she really *liked* sex. And she
had a caustic tongue. She got her kicks out of putting me
down. No man can take that for long." He traced her
lips with his finger. "But you, Marianne . . ." He bent
and kissed her on the mouth. "Beneath that prim talk
about loose morals, you're an extraordinarily passionate
woman. What's more, even when you're angry—and
you get that way when I forget myself and go a little
macho—you don't come at me with bare fangs."

"Don't fool yourself," she chided. "I'm pretty capable of gnawing big chunks out of you."

"Maybe. But I have this fond—and, I hope, not
mistaken—belief that you love me."

Did she? *Could* she? Gregory had the sort of solid
strength she admired. He's a mature man and I'm a
woman, she thought, not the young, wide-eyed girl who
married Toby—poor, darling Toby, who never had a

chance to be more than a boy. Gregory loves me. And when I'm with him I feel stimulated, alive. He can be gentle and tender and dominant, but loving. He's intelligent, enterprising, successful. Then why don't I set a date for the wedding? It's nice lying in bed with Gregory, warm body to warm body, talking cozily. What would it be like to have Gregory at home, my husband, a man who shares my interests, a man who will listen to my problems and support me, a man who loves me?

"Marry me?"

"Well—I'm thinking about it."

"I'd be good to you, a model husband. You wouldn't have to give up Casey, if that's what you want. Or you could come work for me."

"Offering me a job, too. My, my, aren't you generous?" she mocked.

"I wouldn't mind having you on my team. And it would be a good thing for you, too."

"In what way?"

"Corporate infighting can get very rough. I'd see you weren't caught in the crossfire. I'd protect you."

She pushed herself up on the pillows, feeling as though she had been dashed with a bucket of cold water.

"You're going to *protect* me? Gregory, I'm *not* Little Red Riding Hood."

He laughed. "Sweetheart, it's only natural for a man to want to protect the woman he loves. I know that sounds like a throwback to sidewhiskers and high-button shoes, but I don't mean to be literal. At least, I hope not. I respect you for wanting to be independent." He took her in his arms. "Just give me the time to get used to it."

Cradled next to his heart, she relaxed. What if he wasn't exactly the man she would like him to be? Maybe she expected too much. Gregory had his faults; he admitted them. Wasn't that the first step toward change? She wasn't naive enough to expect miracles, but he could learn to love her as she was, not as a beautiful woman whose career was one step above a hobby, but as on equal.

The last thought drew a heavy sigh.

"What's the matter, hon?" he murmured, his lips in her hair.

"You," she said, turning, and lifting a smiling mouth to be kissed.

CHAPTER XVIII

IF MARIANNE HAD THOUGHT SHE WAS FINISHED WITH SIGHT-seeing that first afternoon in Canton, she was wrong. The Chinese seemed to feel that foreigners abhorred a time vacuum, a free hour in which to be on their own. There was so much to see and the visitors must see it all. It didn't matter whether they had come on tour, on a diplomatic mission, or to trade; the established rounds must be made. The Casey Five were trooped through the Temple of Six Banyan Trees, dutifully following their guide up the nine flights to the top, a puffing Jerry and muttering Art bringing up the rear. They called at the Huaisheng Mosque and the Catholic Cathedral, where Chinese adherents in this year of religious tolerance came to pray. They endured a three-hour opera, applauded gymnasts and folk dancers, and sat through a theater performance without understanding a word. They oohed and aahed at the pandas and golden monkeys at the zoo, fed carp in the pond at the Orchid Gardens, and watched young people roller skate at the Cultural Park.

"I don't think I want to see another panda or hear another screeching falsetto," Art complained.

"Grin and bear it," Marianne told him, wondering again if she had picked the wrong man for the job.

On one of their morning tours they had stopped at the Zhong Shan University, where Marianne's mother taught, but Sarah had already gone for the day. Marianne hadn't seen her mother since her arrival, though they had spoken over the school phone. They had arranged a meeting that subsequently had to be canceled because at the last moment Mr. Lu had announced an excursion to White Cloud Mountain.

"When are we going to get down to business?" Art wanted to know as they examined glazed Sung pottery at the Guangzhou Museum.

"Soon, I hope," Marianne said. "But, Art, this isn't your first visit. Certainly you knew it would take time."

"Time, sure, but working out contracts, not fooling around with this stuff."

"We're in China," she said shortly.

Jerry, who also had been the route before, didn't complain so much as make wisecracks that were sometimes amusing but more often embarrassing. He didn't seem to see the necessity of watching his language or keeping his voice down. Marianne could only hope the Chinese delegation wouldn't be offended.

Hollis was the most adaptable and conscientious of the group. She took copious notes, typing them up in the evening, wrote letters, and sent and received messages from Casey through the telex. She made no demands, quietly trailing along through the sweating humidity in her long-sleeved shirtwaists and sensible low-heeled shoes. If she was bored, tired, glad, or sad her imperturbable manner gave no sign.

By contrast, Jimmy Kwong enjoyed every minute of this Canton venture, expressing his emotions openly. He had been to Canton many times and loved the city. The scenery, the food, the sidewalk barter, the tea shops, even the jingle of bicycle bells delighted him. He laughed easily and joked with his counterpart, Mr. Chang. He

shopped in the native stalls for paper cutouts, raincoats,
dolls, masks, coral figurines, Chinese fiddles, and bottles of *mao tai* to bring to his relatives in New York.
Marianne liked him. She liked the way he kept the
team's lagging spirits up, the way he could josh Art out
of his sour mood and exchange salty banter with Jerry.
Kwong claimed to be in love with the pretty desk clerk
at the hotel. "A real China doll," he said. And though
the girl was abashed at his forward American style, he
felt she liked him. He swore he was going to take her
home.

It wasn't until the fourth day that Marianne felt the
Chinese were getting closer to the main purpose of her
visit. Marianne and her party were taken to Foshan, an
old city that had once been the capital of the province,
some ten miles south of Canton. Noted for its Shi Wan
pottery works, it also had a silk factory. Here Jerry put
aside his caustic manner and became soberly professional.
   Marianne, having read everything she could lay hands
on about silk, knew, at least academically, how the
process went from worm-moth to fiber. Still, she found
the reality fascinating. The white cocoons bobbing in hot
water immersions beneath the hum of intricate machinery
seemed a far-fetched, if not impossible, beginning for
the end product, bolts of smooth, lustrous silk. The
factory girls, wearing white caps, a cross between surgi-
cal and shower caps, worked with dextrous fingers, de-
taching and feeding filaments from the cocoons into
porcelain eyelets where it was rapidly wound on reels.
The Casey people were told by the guide that these
women had been carefully trained to blend several filaments into a single thread of uniform diameter, an operation that required a quick, practiced, and skillful eye.
This reeled or raw silk was what Marianne was interested in.
   However, Jerry had suggested she might want to consider the silk after it had been thrown—that is, converted to yarn. Installing machinery for the necessary
degumming (removing the sticky sericin left over from

the cocoon) had to be balanced against higher prices and increased tariffs.

As they passed the clacking, humming reels Jerry advised, "I wouldn't bother with Canton silk. Too hairy. Your best bet is silk from Suzhou, Shanghai or Hangzhou."

They moved on to the throwster room, where the silk threads were being twisted into strands strong enough for weaving, their own entrance coinciding with that of a group of some thirty-five tourists. The noise from the machinery was deafening, and they stood herded together, trying to hear the guide above the roaring, clanking din. The lecture went on and on, a meaningless murmur. It was hot under the glaring fluorescent lighting. The smell of shaving lotions, colognes, stale tobacco, and human bodies, deodorized though they were, was stupefying. People got restless, shifting from foot to foot, jostling one another. One woman with fat arms kept taking pictures, raising her camera above the crowd, urging, "Please move your head, *please*." Marianne, who was standing on the edge of the group, suddenly felt a fist punch the small of her back. She lost her balance. For a sickening moment she tottered and would have fallen into a large, rotating wheel if Kwong hadn't caught her. She clung to his shirtsleeve, a clammy sweat breaking out on her forehead as she stared at the huge, relentless wheel whirring at a dizzy speed.

"What happened?" Kwong's face under the strong light had a dusty pallor.

"Somebody pushed me." She looked over at the crowd, now moving on with the rest of her party, who had been unaware of her near miss.

"On purpose?"

"If it wasn't on purpose it was pretty damn close to it."

"But who? Who'd want to do something like that?"

"Beats me. I can't even tell you who was standing behind or next to me. I was trying to hear the guide and not paying attention."

"I'm certain it was an accident. Or perhaps someone

too absorbed to notice you, like the lady who was taking pictures."

"That's one hell of a way to get a good shot. I could easily have been sucked into the whole works, reeled, twisted, and thrown into someone's silk pajamas by now." She gave Kwong a shaky smile, though the picture of herself broken and bleeding, limbs severed, head crushed, sent a chill wave of nausea through her.

"I'd like to leave," Marianne added, her kneecaps still trembling. "Would you tell Mr. Lu? I think I've seen enough."

The next afternoon they were taken for the second time to the Canton Trade Fair. Unlike the first visit, which was a hurried trek through all the exhibits, they went directly through Gate Four to the Hall of Textiles. Here they were given time to inspect a rich display of silks China was currently producing.

"Beautiful," said Marianne, running her hand over a flowered brocade with a peony-pink and apple-green design.

"You are interested in our raw silk?" Mr. Lu asked.

"Yes. The thrown silk, too."

"Ah, thrown. More expensive."

The ice was breaking; they were on the verge of talking price. And Marianne was eager to go on, even if it meant holding a meeting in the hall with people name-tagged in plastic milling about bolts of pongee, lamé, and tussah. She waited while Mr. Lu spoke to his delegation. There was chatter back and forth.

"What are they saying?" Marianne asked Kwong in a low voice.

"They are discussing the availability of thrown silk. I think they'd prefer you buying the raw."

"If they make the price of thrown too high, I'll have to."

Mr. Lu turned to Marianne. "We hope you've had an enjoyable day. Now we take you back to your hotel." There was no indication that their tentative attempt at finding a price of some kind, any kind, would escalate into a little hard bargaining on the short ride to the White Swan. Marianne gazed out of the limousine window, swallowing her frustration as Kwong and Lu rattled away in Chinese. She had managed to feign far more patience than she had felt these past few days as the Casey group had inched through crowded, dust-moted museums and tramped over graveled park paths, the milky heat like a damp sponge melting her makeup, leaving streaks of sticky sweat down the back of her dress. It was during such moments that she empathized with Art, who knew he had work piling up at home while he stood restive in front of a gilded, pot-bellied Buddha, burping bird's nest soup behind a shielding hand.

When the car stopped for a light, Marianne noticed a department store mannequin done up in a powder-blue pantsuit that had been fashionable at home two years earlier. The Chinese were catching up, Brad had told her. Yet a few minutes later she saw a man bent double, harnessed to the shafts of a cart, a human beast of burden hauling a heavy pile of bricks. Like the peasant she had seen years earlier on the bridge, he was not an uncommon sight. Two thousand years of catching up. How patiently these people dragged their loads, plodding along, eyes fixed on the pavement, one foot set before the other, sinewy leg muscles straining. They were working toward the new life, a promised future that might or might not come. Patience was the key word. And here she was grousing about a few days.

She couldn't blame Lu for this lengthy prologue to the main event. It was the Chinese way. This was how Lu had been trained to do business. What seemed to her like an annoying delay was probably routine for him. Certainly he was more communicative than she had expected a Chinese to be. She had learned more about him in four days than she had about Hollis in several months. Lu had gone to school in Shanghai. He was married and had one child—all that was allowed due to the country's overpopulation. His wife worked as a statistician in a Shanghai steel mill. Marianne's first impression of him had been correct: a charming man, courteous and smoothly wary, fielding Marianne's more probing personal questions with good-humored tact.

Brad had told Marianne that once trust and friendship were established with the Chinese the rest was easy. With Mr. Lu she had no problem. She wasn't too sure of Chang. Though he was ostensibly the interpreter, he rarely spoke directly to her. Did he disapprove of her, find that dealing with a woman on an equal basis was disconcerting? Wei, Hsu, Boa were friendly enigmas. They shook hands, nodded, smiled, watched. Were they giving her good grades? Maybe they wanted a couple of days to assess and debate. Or were they taking another prospective customer on tour, giving him or her the A banquet in the interim? She knew that Gregory was scheduled for the "Chinese treatment," as he called it, but whether it was with the same team she did not know. Of course, Mr. Lu would never tell her. And, for that matter, Gregory probably wouldn't, either.

Maybe she ought to be grateful for some free time, Marianne reflected later in her suite. It would enable her to catch up on news of Casey via long distance, if she was lucky enough to get a decent connection. The day before she had tried to reach Karen and, after a five-hour delay, had finally spoken to her, a disjointed, unsatisfactory conversation.

"Yeah, yeah, I'm okay, Moms. What? I can't hear you, you've got to talk louder."

"Did you get the airline tickets?"

"Tickets? Yeah. I got them. What? I can't *hear* you."

With extra time at her disposal, Marianne could make another stab at talking to Karen. She could also arrange a meeting with her mother.

Sarah Oliver refused to come to the hotel even when Marianne offered to send a car for her. She said places like that—meaning palaces of Western decadence, Marianne supposed—made her uncomfortable. There was no privacy in the Chen home, so Marianne suggested they have lunch in a restaurant of Sarah's choosing.

She picked the Dong He, a lunchtime cafe located in East Mountain River Park where the Cantonese ate, not because the food was particularly good but because it was cheap.

As Marianne taxied to the restaurant, she marveled at all the people and activity. The streets were as alive with bike riders at eleven in the forenoon as they had been at seven in the morning and would be at six in the evening. Over a million and a half people in the city alone, not to speak of the five or so million in the surrounding countryside. Whenever Marianne thought of the vastness of China, with its teeming millions, and how by the year 2000 it was estimated that the population would reach 1.2 billion, it boggled her mind. She wondered how any government, regardless of its political persuasiveness, could cope. Maybe that was why her mother was such a staunch believer in Mao. Whatever else could be said about him, her mother claimed, he had unified China, bringing a war-torn country out of chaos, setting up the structure to deal with famine and disease. He had given the Chinese the dignity of national pride by pinning the People's Republic to the map of the world.

Marianne was thinking of this when she drew up to the park's entrance. Sarah was waiting for her, standing beside the moongate set in a white wall.

"Hello, Mother." Not waiting for the embrace she sensed wouldn't come, Marianne kissed the sallow cheek. "It's good to see you."

Thin, her brow more deeply lined than when Marianne had last seen her, she pressed Marianne's hand with her own damp one. The sun, high in a blazing blue sky, beat down like a punishment, glancing off the white wall in pulsing waves of heat.

"You look lovely, Marianne." Her mother's eyes lit up for a moment.

A compliment. Surely that was a good beginning. Marianne followed her mother through the gate.

The restaurant, built on the edge of a lake and surrounded by gardens and shade trees, looked cool and inviting. The interior, however, was a disappointment. Despite the stand of tall bamboo growing up through the roof, it had a fast-food-chain decor. Chrome chairs upholstered with cracked peach vinyl were pulled up to shaky, chrome-legged tables spread with stained plastic tablecloths. There were no menus.

"You must order for me, Mother."

Sarah conferred with the waiter, an acne-skinned young man in a soiled white jacket.

"Would you prefer perch or chicken?" she asked Marianne.

"Either will do."

While they waited for their meal, Marianne spoke. "I'm sorry I wasn't able to get away sooner. But Mr. Lu, who seems to be head man of the CHINATEX team, has us on a tight schedule."

"They like to show foreigners notable points of interest."

"I've already seen most of the 'notable' places, if you remember. But I suppose it's one way to get to know the men I'm dealing with. Incidentally, I understand a member of the team was a student of yours. Mr. Wei."

"Wei Ma—a big man, round face?"

"Yes, that sounds like him. He plans to call on you."

"He was an excellent student. One of my best."

When their food came, Sarah handled her chopsticks with dainty precision, giving attention to her food. The chicken, cut into strips and mostly bone, brought to mind the scrawny fowl Marianne had seen strutting about in courtyard doorways.

"How have you been feeling?" Marianne asked, breaking the silence. She wondered why her mother, who could write such long, descriptive letters, had so little to say face to face.

"All right. And you?"

"Fine." Marianne waited for her mother to pick up the conversational ball but she didn't, so she went on, "Does it get much hotter than this in the summer?"

"Oh, yes. The temperature often stays in the nineties

in July. We have lots of rain, too, so you can imagine how humid it is."

"And no air conditioning."

Her mother gave her a blank look and went back to eating, holding her rice bowl in one hand and chopsticks in the other. Like the natives of her adopted country, she was serious about the business of dining.

Four Chinese men came in wearing greasy peaked caps and sat down at the table next to theirs. They stared at Marianne and Sarah as the Chinese will do to Westerners who have strayed off the tourists' beaten path.

"Aren't you going to eat your lunch?" her mother asked.

"I'm not very hungry." The chicken was undercooked and greasy. But the rice was edible and Marianne picked at it.

"What are you teaching now?" Marianne asked, trying again to initiate a discussion.

"The same. American literature."

Another silence. The heat, odorous with steamy cooking smells, seemed unbearable. Perspiration had gathered at the back of Marianne's neck, under her arms, behind her knees. Her discomfort added to a growing feeling of resentment. Though she fought it, her rancor increased, sprouting, branching out like an insidious, noxious weed. She knew she ought to stop herself but couldn't. I might as well not be here, she told herself. What the hell am I doing here? Sarah is simply going through the motions of being a mother. It's the same farce, the same hypocrisy. Nothing has changed since the last time. Nothing. No warmth, no interest, not even curiosity.

"Would you like some tea?" Sarah offered politely.

"Yes, I think so."

She would forgive her everything if only Sarah would show some semblance of love. Even Aunt Em—querulous, unpredictable, sometimes unkind—had shown more affection.

"Perhaps you'd like sugar?"

"No, thanks, Mother."

Maybe I'm not making enough effort, Marianne reflected. I'm letting her set the mood and tone of this meeting, accepting the chill politeness without attempting to break through it. I can't give up.

"Mother?"

"Yes?"

"Karen is coming over next week."

"Here, to Canton? Oh, my!"

She smiled, the tired face lighting up like the sudden flare of a match. In that smile Marianne suddenly had a glimpse of the younger woman, the hair brown then and drawn up in a neat bun, the cheeks fuller, the eyes shining. Marianne had been cheated of that woman, the years of her mother's youth. The thought made Marianne sad and bitter.

"Karen will have what we call spring vacation, a week off in April that usually coincides with Easter."

Her mother wiped her mouth with a scrap of cotton handkerchief. "Do they still make schoolchildren celebrate religious holidays?"

"They don't celebrate. Those holidays have more or less become secular." She didn't want to get into a church–state argument. She changed the subject.

"If I can get the time I thought the three of us might spend a day or two in Hong Kong. Would you like that?"

"No. I wouldn't," Sarah said.

The look in her washed-out gray eyes was close to fear. Is she afraid, even now, to leave the country, Marianne wondered, afraid the authorities won't let her back in?

"It would do you good to get away." Marianne pressed the point.

"I don't feel the need."

"Don't you have any curiosity as to what's going on in the world out there?"

"You mean Hong Kong? Dog eats dog in Hong Kong. The peasants who thought they would find paradise there are coming back. Your newspapers don't print stories about those people, the disillusioned and the starving and the sick whom nobody wants in Hong Kong.''

But why do so many remain, why do so many like it, she wanted to ask but didn't. Another touchy subject. She was beginning to think that getting through this lunch on polite terms with her mother was all she could bargain for. Why had she deceived herself that there would be more? Brad was always pushing her about her family, about grandparents, as if she was at fault because she hadn't provided them for Karen. It wasn't like giving your child a new bicycle for Christmas or a dog for a pet. Was she to blame because her mother and father had abandoned her, because the Hansfords had proven grasping and cruel?

"Brad tells me," Marianne began, trying again to steer clear of controversy, "that you and he have become friends."

"I like Bradford. A nice young man. But then, I'm partial to college professors. I should be, I married one." A smile twitched the corners of her mouth. "Your father and I both came from academic families, you know."

"There isn't too much I *do* know about you and Father."

"Oh? I'm sorry. I thought maybe Emma might have discussed this with you."

"Emma didn't seem to have much information. Not even a photograph." Marianne hesitated before she slid the phrase in, smoothly, deftly, like a knife. "And you never wrote."

Her mother's face took color. She looked down at the table. Her fingers, finding a few crumbs of rice, trembled as she swept them up and deposited them in the bowl.

"Yes—yes—it's true."

Now why did I have to bring that up? Marianne thought, castigating herself. It was uncalled for. Childish and mean. Her mother could no more recall those lost years and relive them than could Marianne.

"I'm sorry," Marianne murmured. "I shouldn't have . . ."

"No, no. I can't blame you for . . ." Sarah picked at another grain of rice. "You see . . ."

"Mother . . ." The sallow, flushed cheeks, the trembling hands stabbed at Marianne's conscience. Suddenly she wanted to embrace, to hug the small, shrunken figure, to say "Mother, I'm sorry. I want to love you. I really do."

"Mother . . ."

"Yes?"

Why couldn't she say it? She tried, but the words did not come out as she intended. "Mother—tell me about your—our family, my grandparents on your side and Father's."

Sarah, fiddling with her teacup, seemed to be collecting her thoughts. "You are interested?"

"Certainly."

"Well—your father's father tutored private pupils. His main interest was Chinese literature. Originally he was from Oakland, California, but when he received a small inheritance he came to China with his wife to continue his studies. That was in the twenties. Your father was born in Shanghai. *My* parents were teaching at the American School in Shanghai, and their people before them were missionary teachers in Africa. So you see, it was only natural for William, your father, and I to continue on with a scholastic career. I . . ." She lifted her eyes to Marianne. "I was hoping you would do the same."

"Teaching never appealed to me. I was drawn to numbers and math in school, so I went into business."

"You enjoy—business?" The word was dropped like a faintly repellent stone.

"Very much."

A silence. Their teacups were refilled. The quartet of Chinese, quaffing beer along with their food at the adjoining table, had become boisterous, laughing and talking loudly.

"I know you won't agree with me," Sarah said slowly, picking her words with care, "but it's not what I'd call a commendable profession."

Marianne stared at her.

"Private enterprise has only one objective—profit, which *I* equate with greed."

Marianne, hot in the face, exclaimed, "That's a distorted, utterly false view!" The little food she had eaten churned sourly in her stomach. "It's that so-called 'greed' that makes the wheels turn, gives jobs to people—and well-paid jobs, not forty *yuan* a month!" Her voice was rising. She knew it, but it didn't seem as if she could control the volume of her anger.

"Then why have your companies looked to the Third World for cheap labor, China included?" her mother wanted to know. "I suppose your company is thinking of employing Asian workers, too."

"If I have, I don't apologize. Our competitive system has made us the greatest country on earth. And China? Still dragging its feet in the Middle Ages. Just look—the Chinese are still beasts of burden, while our people, even the poor, are riding around on wheels. I say hurray for the USA and its capitalists. Three cheers for the best system in the world."

Marianne, hearing herself, could hardly believe her ears, the smug jingoism coming from her own lips. It was the kind of dumb flag-waving that gross-mannered Jerry Cooper would indulge in, not sophisticated Marianne Oliver. She was allowing herself to be goaded into a heated debate that was fast degenerating into a mindless squabble. How had it happened? How had she gone so quickly from compassion to anger?

"I suggest you read your history," her mother continued calmly. "Find out how China was kept from entering the twentieth century by the British, French, Germans, and, yes, the Americans, too. Surely you've heard of the Opium Wars, when the Chinese government was forced to accept the importation of opium?"

Marianne nodded but did not answer. There was no sense in going on. In a sudden flash of insight she saw that her own anger had been provoked not so much over ideological differences as by the knowledge that her mother had made Marxism the number one priority in her life. Everything else, even her daughter, was secondary. It hurt.

"Look, Mother," Marianne said in a conciliatory tone, "let's not fight over politics. You have your views, I have mine. Can't we find a mutually agreeable topic?"

Sarah's chin quivered. "You're right. It's thoughtless of me. I apologize."

"I'm just as much at fault."

"No. I'm older—and, in a sense, your hostess." She paused, lifting the cup in an unsteady hand, then putting it abruptly down.

"Is something wrong?" Marianne asked. Sarah's face had gone ashen.

"No. I'm all right."

Marianne again felt remorse and pity. Her mother seemed so frail. An untidy strand of gray hair had come loose over one ear, giving her an oddly vulnerable look. Marianne wondered once more about her past. In their correspondence she had asked Sarah about her life during the decades following the revolution. But Sarah had either ignored her questions or answered evasively. It was obvious she did not want to write or talk about those years. It was as if they had not existed. Maybe her mother felt that Marianne wouldn't understand her involvement with the Chinese Liberation. Maybe there were things she had done in Mao Zedong's name that didn't bear repeating.

"Are you through eating, Mother? Suppose we sit out of doors. It's so hot in here. There must be a bench or two under a tree near the lake."

"I'd love to, but I've an appointment with a student at half past two at the house and will barely make it."

"Let me drop you off." She had asked her taxi to wait.

"If it's no trouble."

Afterward, in the taxi on the way to Dr. Chen's, Sarah sat, spine straight, almost rigidly, hands folded in her lap, her eyes focused on the back of the driver's head. Marianne's attempts at conversation were answered in monosyllables, as if she had been dismissed back at the Dong He. It irked Marianne. Had her earlier compassion been a waste? Why had she thought Sarah vulnerable? This woman was built of iron. Sarah could make appropriate small talk, come to the defense of her beloved China, even sound human at times, but on the inside she was hard core. Ideologists were like that—people who held tenaciously to their narrow doctrines, willing to be burned at the stake rather than budge an inch from their beliefs. Sarah Oliver was a revolutionary first, a teacher second, and maybe somewhere down the line a mother, a simple biological accident.

At Dr. Chen's outer gate Marianne said goodbye. "I'll let you know when Karen arrives." She planted a kiss on Sarah's unyielding cheek.

"Yes, do that."

She certainly seems in a hurry to be rid of me, Marianne thought. We've had our little get-together and now she's glad to be home. She will slip back into her comfortable routine and quickly forget that she and I have disagreed on almost everything. Perhaps she'll even succeed in putting me out of her mind.

To Marianne, however, the afternoon left a haunting, tormentingly bitter aftertaste.

Sarah stepped carefully over the high sill of the moongate, watching her feet as she started across the broken flags of the courtyard. Weeds trampled into dust, a basin left out by Mrs. Kang, a plastic bottle, a pile of cement rubble, all had to be carefully negotiated from the gate to Chen's door, which today seemed miles away.

"Ni Haoi." The greeting startled her. Old Wang with his granddaughter.

"Ni Haoi." She knew he wanted to stop and chat, but she couldn't. Not now. She was dizzy, so disoriented she was afraid she'd fall.

Once inside the house she clung to the back of a wicker chair, her breath coming in short gasps, the knifelike pain in her chest nearly strangling her. Then she slowly made her way across the small inner courtyard to her alcove. The Chens were not at home, not even Grandma or the boy. She was grateful for that. She didn't want sympathy or concern. It would be a trial to speak to anyone with a hammer pounding against her ribs.

She found the pills and, placing one under her tongue, sank down on the bed, her head in her hands, listening to the heavy pump of blood while the pellet dissolved. She ought to carry those pills in her handbag, have them wherever she went. One of these days she wasn't going to make it. But she wouldn't think of that.

Ahhh! The pain. Gingerly she stretched out on the cot, cupping her hand over her erratic heart as if to protect it.

She stared at the white plaster wall where a picture of Mao Zedong hung. It was no longer considered correct to display his picture in public. The large portrait of him in Tian An Men Square had been removed several years earlier, and people now spoke of him only as the father of Liberation, wanting to forget the decades afterward and how he had grappled to bring China out of its poverty.

She hadn't forgotten. She never would. In 1982 she had made the long and difficult trip to Beijing, sitting up for two nights in a "hard seat" from Canton. She had stood in line for hours in the square together with thousands of others in a biting wind, tasting the yellow dust sweeping down from the northern plateau, waiting to get into the Memorial Hall for a view of the Chairman's body.

It had been worth it. The sight of Mao lying under the red hammer and sickle flag in his crystal coffin had moved her. It had been an experience she would never forget: the shuffling feet padding slowly, solemnly past the bier, the awe on the faces, young and old. Mao had been and still was a symbol of hope.

How could she make Marianne understand? Ah, Marianne. Worlds divided them, lifetimes. Marianne was lost to her. The baby she had held, the miracle of life, had disappeared into a void. She could cry when she thought of it. But she had long since ceased to weep. Too many tears had been shed. Now there was only an ache in her throat, a rawness when she thought of the baby that once had been hers. And now this woman, this pretty, strong-willed girl who was a stranger had come back.

She had hoped that Marianne would bear more than a physical resemblance to William, perhaps have the same smile, the same gentleness. But there was nothing of Marianne's personality that she could see as William's. She reminds me of my own mother, Sarah thought, the stubborn line to her jaw, the gray-blue eyes that blaze when she's angry.

Why was she so harsh with Marianne? She didn't want to be. Was it because she wanted the child back, all those years to live over again?

She shifted her head on the hard pillow, the pain in her chest ebbing. No one but Dr. Chen knew about her heart. She had sworn him to secrecy. She hated to have people coddle her. If the University found out, she'd have to retire, and she wasn't ready. Too much to do. Dr. Chen had accused her of being single-minded. She couldn't deny it. Perhaps that's what she and Marianne had in common, their obsessive drive. The same genes, the same blood.

Pleasantly tired now, she closed her eyes, her hands falling to her sides. Marianne's infant face appeared on her closed lids, the whorl of blondish hair, the foreshortened nose and little pink cheeks.

"Sleep, baby, sleep"—the old lullaby she once sang came back to her—"Thy father watches the sheep. . . ."

CHAPTER XIX

ART SCHULTZ WAS FLYING BACK TO THE STATES. THE ulcer gnawing at his vitals had failed to respond to Maalox or to the bluish substance a Chinese doctor had prescribed. The pain, he assured Marianne, was killing him. Jerry Cooper, who had sent for his wife and was at the airport to meet her, agreed that Art looked terrible.

"It's those snakemeat balls they've been feeding us at the hotel," Jerry said to Marianne while a green-faced Art waited impatiently for his flight to be called. "He's got weak intestines, poor guy."

"Better than a weak head," Art said sourly.

"Speak for yourself, shyster."

Marianne finally saw what she should have seen earlier: the two men did not get along. It was just as well one of them was leaving and that the one was Art. She could always get a good lawyer, but a silk expert would be hard to replace.

Art said, "Sorry to do this to you, Marianne. I'd recommend Harry Bancroft as an alternative. Harry was in that Cyber Systems deal here in China, so he has experience. I'll give him a jingle when I get back to New York."

"Thanks, Art, but things will move faster if I have Carol Olmstead send someone. It isn't that I don't trust your judgment, but Bancroft might be busy or hard to reach or too expensive for Casey's budget."

After Art had departed through the monitored gate, Jerry said, "I don't know why you're in such a hurry to get counsel. The Chinks—"

"Chinese," Marianne corrected sweetly.

"Okay. Chinese. They've only met with us once in the last three days. And then in the hotel lobby, for Christ's sake. And they're changing the team. Putting in guys we've never seen before. An old trick, trying to confuse us, soften us up so we'll give them whatever price they ask."

"You ought to know better than that, Jerry. Their working methods are different than ours."

"They don't trust each other, that's the problem."

"Of course they do. They're all employed by the same board of directors, aren't they?"

"Yeah, Mao, the Great Chairman in the Sky."

Jerry had his own problems. His wife, Candy, flying in from Hoboken, had been—was (and would prove to be) the principal one.

"I'm her third husband," Jerry had confided in Marianne. "She had rotten luck with the first two. One was a drunk and the other was a miser and beat her. Poor kid. And she's such a wonderful little girl, never had much, but I'm gonna bust my ass to see she gets a break, some of the goodies in life she's missed."

"How long have you been married?"

"Six months. And still on our honeymoon. I hated to leave her. Men are attracted to Candy, she can't help it. Not that she goes in for any funny stuff, but she's young—only twenty-two—and kinda gullible, trusting, thinks everyone is on the up-and-up. A girl like that's an easy mark for guys on the prowl."

"If you're worried," Marianne had suggested, wondering how someone who had made two marriages could still remain gullible, "why don't you ask her to join you?"

"Money. I'm short."

"No problem. I'll advance you some of your salary."

"Hey! You mean it? That's great!"

So they were here now at the Guangzhou airport waiting for Candance Cooper, the virginal femme fatale. And when she finally came through customs to Jerry's expansive embrace, Marianne did a double take. She had expected a gorgeous blonde, taller than Jerry, young, with a sweet yet come-hither look. Candy was young, but not twenty-two; in fact, it would be stretching it to say she would see thirty-two again. Short, with a big, swollen bottom outlined by tight pants and large breasts straining at a bright sweater, Candy was not exactly what Marianne would describe as a head turner. She wore oversized gold hoops in her pierced ears, several gold chains around a truncated neck, and—except for heavy eyeshadow and a screen of unbelievably long false eyelashes—no makeup.

"Pleased to meet you, Miss Oliver." She gave Marianne a limp handshake. Every finger on both hands sported rings, one ostensibly a diamond engagement ring with a stone so big that if real must have put Jerry in hock for the rest of his life.

"Please call me Marianne. We're so glad you could come. And I hope you forgive Jerry for not being able to get better accommodations. Canton is very crowded this time of the year."

"That's all right, Marianne." She took her husband's arm, smiling, blinking her brushworks up at him. "I don't mind. I think it's going to be fun. Jerry says the shopping here is wonderful. He says they have fabulous pearls. The girls at home will just turn green when I come back with real pearls from China."

"Well, sweetheart, they cost a little more—" Jerry began.

"Now, you know you promised your Candy." She leaned up and kissed him.

He smiled and squeezed her shoulders. "In that case, you know what they say, sugar—a promise is a promise."

The next morning after breakfast Marianne became ill; the classic stomach upset, vomiting, and diarrhea. Only very soon it became apparent that this was not just an ordinary case of the queasies. It was the kind of sick nausea that went beyond discomfort: a wracking, gripping distress that had her moaning in misery. She was alone. Hollis had gone out in search of a carton of Winstons. To Marianne the suite seemed like a deserted ship, tossing and rocking and heaving with its single helpless passenger stretched out on the tilting deck in a half-comatose state. Her roiling stomach had lodged a sour ball in her throat and thickened her tongue. Her head ached. She felt so wretched she did not wonder that people in similar circumstances wished for a quick death.

The phone rang. Ought she to answer it? Or was it ringing in her head? It went on ringing and ringing, then suddenly ceased. Silence now. Blessed silence. The room took a few turns and she hugged the pillow under her cheek to steady herself. She was drifting down into an uneasy torpor when the shrill, persistent sound of the phone brought her drugged eyes open again. She reached out, missed, reached again.

"Hello. What d'you want?"

"Marianne?" It was Brad.

"I—can't—talk. I'm—oh, God!" She moaned, dropping the phone, heaving herself off the bed, and stumbling into the bathroom.

When she got back, sweating and shivering, the phone was dead.

Ten minutes later Brad knocked at the door. Marianne managed to crawl out of bed to let him in.

"What is it? You look awful!"

"Thanks—thanks very much." A vise twisted her stomach, squeezing the air from her lungs. "Something—I ate. Uh-oh! Excuse!" Again she staggered to the bathroom.

A few moments later Brad appeared in the doorway.

"Go 'way, Brad." She leaned against the sink, her head drooping.

Brad found a washcloth, wrung it out in cold water, and dabbed at her mouth, wiped her forehead and cheeks. The refreshing coolness sponging away salt tears and sweat brought a small whimper of relief.

"How long has this been going on?" Brad asked.

"Don't know. Feels—like forever."

"Something you ate at breakfast?"

"Maybe. Oh, God, I feel so weak. I never, *never* get sick." Her knees buckled and she clung to his shirt front.

"You're going to the clinic," he decided. "We'll have to wait too long for a doctor to get here."

"I don't need . . ." Her thick tongue, like wet toweling, groped for the word "doctor."

"You haven't got an ordinary gastric complaint, Marianne. You're going to the clinic!"

He bundled her into a cab and held her close as they drove to the Foreigners' Outpatient Clinic at the First Hospital.

Brad's inexpert Chinese explained the problem. Marianne, dimly aware of her surroundings, gagged at the smell of ether, alcohol, and some pungent, sweet odor she could not define.

"I was right." Brad's voice came to her from a long distance through a dark fog. "He's going to pump your stomach. Nothing to be afraid of—just some mild poisoning."

There were frightening sounds and the sensation of her stomach being turned inside out. She felt a pounding in her head as she slid into blackness.

Later, in the taxi, she emerged from the nightmare holding tightly to Brad's hand. His arm was around her shoulders, her head nestled against his chest. Sunlight and shadows flashed in streaks across his knees.

"You okay?" Brad asked, looking down at her.

"Yes." She lifted her chin. "I think so."

But so weak, exhausted, as if the blood had been drained from her body leaving a thin, watery residue of fear. Fear of what? She shifted her head and Brad's arms adjusted to her move. How solid he was, how comforting. What was there to be afraid of?

"The worst is over," he said. "All you need is a little rest."

Her eyelids drooped, and when she opened them again she was in her suite. How did she get there? Did he carry her through the lobby? Up the elevator?

She sat slumped in a chair, watching as he turned down the bed.

"Shall I help you undress?"

Her head still hurt. How had she managed to get sick when she had so much to do? Send instructions to Casey, write letters, see Gregory tonight.

"Shall I help you undress?" Brad repeated.

"Where's Hollis?"

"She isn't here. C'mon, Marianne, you're not fit for anything but bed right now."

"It does look—good." It would be nice to crawl between the cool sheets. Spend the rest of her life snoozing, no worries, no problems, just dreamless sleep.

"Point me in the right direction." She struggled to get to her feet, hands gripping the armrests. But it was no go. She couldn't. She flopped helplessly back on the cushions.

"Give me a minute," she whispered.

He knelt and removed her shoes. Then he raised her skirt and tugged gently at the waistband of her pantyhose.

"Brad—I don't think . . . *What* are you doing?"

"Lift," he ordered.

She did as he said, grasping the arms of the chair, raising her hips slightly, and the hose rolled out from under her. A draft of cool air across her legs from the air conditioner made her shiver.

"You're not going to take my clothes off!"

"Somebody has to."

A hot blush rose to her face. He was stripping her. She could undress for Gregory or have him undress her, throw her clothes off in a kind of nutty frenzy, but naked before Brad? It didn't seem right.

He brought her up. "Raise your arms, sweetie." Her dress went, her slip.

"I want to take a shower," she said in a childlike voice she barely recognized as her own. "I feel—gummy."

"All right. But I'm going to have to give it to you."

"No. I can do it."

"My dear, you don't look as though you could stand up for the five minutes it would take. I don't want you keeling over in the tub."

Her mind was too clouded to think about what was happening—Brad undressing her, giving her a shower. Did he do it for other women? Sabrina? She didn't feel embarrassed anymore. She felt sexless, as if she had regressed to childhood, the year five, when Aunt Em shampooed her hair in the big claw-legged tub in the dark bathroom in the house in Passaic. The warm water, the comfort of ministering hands was the same as it had been then, a touch like magic that drew a secure circle around her, shielding her against whatever might threaten in the outside world.

"Don't fall asleep on me," Brad said, wrapping a towel around her sopping head. Taking another towel, he buffed her back, arms, torso, legs.

"You're so good to me, Brad. I don't deserve it."

"I know you don't. Come along."

He tucked her in bed, bringing the sheet up to her chin.

"I love you, Brad," she said, her heavy lids fluttering to keep open.

He kissed her forehead. "I love you, too, sweetie."

Slipping down into the darkness of sleep, with the last glimmer of her conscious mind she thought she saw Brad's tear-bright hazel eyes gazing down at her. Was he going to cry? Because she was sick? Funny, lovable Brad.

Looking at her sleeping face, pale as the pillow beneath it, tendrils of damp hair curling at her earlobes, he thought, why did I have to fall in love with her? There are plenty of attractive, intelligent, sexy women around, one of whom might easily love me. Why *her*, damn it?

When Marianne had cabled about her plans to come to China he had looked forward to her arrival with the kind of foolish, youthful excitement he hadn't felt in years. He had hoped that in a foreign setting he might get Marianne to see him in a different light. He had planned dinners, strolls along the riverbank and in the parks where they could be alone, where he might, like some clever seducer, take her in his arms, kissing her until she exclaimed, "My God! What took you so long?"

Then that asshole Gregory had popped up. Couldn't she see through the handsome facade? The man's ego was monumental; he was nothing more than a clever con man. Couldn't a woman like Marianne, intelligent, on top of her profession, figure it out? But women—and men, himself maybe a case in point—fell in love with a kind of mindlessness that they wouldn't think of allowing in everyday life.

When he thought of her sleeping with Gregory, he wanted to kill the man. Murder had never been so close to his heart. He understood crimes of passion now.

In the shower, seeing, touching Marianne's beautiful body, the firm breasts, the curve of her hips, he had to fight the urge to lift her, thrown her on the bed, and take her.

She stirred in her sleep, moving her lips. He smoothed a wisp of hair from her forehead, bent and kissed her. Her skin still felt clammy. Arsenic, the doctor at the hospital had said. In another half hour she would have been dead.

That had given him a jolt. Thinking of it now as he continued to gaze at her, he realized how much time they'd already wasted. He was thirty-six and tired of waiting for the right moment. He'd just come flat out with it, tell Marianne he loved her. Take it or leave it.

Marianne was resilient. Twenty-four hours after her tussle with food poisoning she was back on her feet. Hollis, taking dictation for a letter to Oscar at Casey, apologized.

"I had to go all over town for those stupid cigarettes," she said for the third or fourth time. "If I had known . . . I should have been here. My God, when I think of it."

She riffled the pages of the steno pad resting on her lap with long, nervous fingers. Window light behind her chair brought out the gray in her hair. "If Mr. Young hadn't come at the right time . . ."

"I could have died. Maybe." Marianne chuckled. "I'm tough. It takes more than a stomachache to kill me."

"The one time I go out this had to happen."

Marianne was beginning to find Hollis's repetitive apologies agonizing. "Please don't blame yourself, Hollis. You're my secretary, for God's sake, not my keeper. You haven't had very much time to do the things *you* want to do. I don't expect you to be on call every minute. It's over, done. I'm okay. That's what's important now, isn't it?" Marianne smiled, trying to feel more warmly toward Hollis.

"Did you ever get your cigarettes?" Marianne asked.

"What?"

"Your cigarettes. The Winstons."

"Yes, finally. In the Friendship Store." She patted her blouse pocket. "What do you think it was that you ate?"

"Dunno. We both had the same breakfast. Nobody else in the hotel, as far as the management could discover, had food poisoning. I must have picked it up from the sweet bun I bought from a cart."

"I'd never trust street food in a foreign country, especially here," Hollis said.

Hollis thought people who found China exciting had rocks in their head. Dirty, noisy, and smelly, what was so wonderful about it? She hated the crush of people, the jabber of foreign tongues, the scarcity of even the simplest luxuries. She missed her home, her privacy. But what did it matter in the long run? She had a job to do and the job was in Canton.

"Nice of Gregory to send flowers, don't you think?" Marianne remarked.

"They're lovely." Gregory had sent them immediately after Marianne related her near brush with death. Sprays of creamy cymbidiums with delicate salmon throats filled three vases in the connecting room and a water glass in one of the bathrooms, where a single green stalk leaned its burden of blossoms against the mirror.

"Gregory thinks China is bad luck for me," Marianne said. "Nearly done in by a spinning wheel and then a sweet bun."

"He isn't suggesting you leave?"

"He wouldn't dare."

As soon as she had felt able Marianne asked Jimmy Kwong to come to the suite.

"What gives?" she asked. "It's been four days now and CHINATEX hasn't contacted me. Are they souring on the deal? A deal, I might add, that hasn't even been discussed."

"If they had decided they didn't want to do business, they would have told you. They're busy taking your competition through the hoops."

"How much competition could I have?"

"Hard to say. China's supply of silk isn't limitless. Naturally, they want to get the highest price."

"Naturally."

"Also, with this so-called modernization—or limited capitalism—program, there are city and privately owned companies. How many are into silk I don't know."

"Well, we're dealing with CHINATEX. I don't want to switch."

"I just mentioned it in case this fell through."

"I hope not. I'm pressed for time, Jimmy. I can't afford to go through the lengthy preliminaries again."

Kwong removed his glasses and polished them with a corner of his handkerchief. "For what it's worth, I saw the CHINATEX people—Lu, Wei, and a couple of other guys I didn't recognize—with your friend, Mr. Windham, at the fair yesterday."

"Oh?" She said nonchalantly, but inside she was feeling somewhat betrayed. In their telephone conversation the evening before Gregory had made no mention of it.

"Doesn't surprise me. He's after silk, cotton as well. However, I would think they'd give us different teams," she brooded.

"Only makes the bidding sharper."

"That's okay. I know Windham Mills has more financial clout than Casey, but I also know that I'm going to get that contract. At a fair price. You can bet on that," she added fiercely.

That evening Marianne and Gregory dined at the White Swan. A Western meal. Continental cuisine, it was called. Chateaubriand, little new potatoes rolled in parsley, a salad of fresh lettuce, tomatoes, and cucumbers.

"Where do they get this food?" Marianne asked. "I'm sure these potatoes don't grow in China. And I haven't seen any meat on the hoof."

"Hong Kong, some of it. Beef from Australia."

After dinner they strolled the mezzanine, peering into the display windows of the shops. Gregory wanted to buy Marianne a jade necklace.

"You gave the diamond one back, if you remember," he said. "I'm hoping you'll be more receptive to the jade."

"Yes, but really, Gregory—"

"I'll buy it when you're not around to argue," he said, cutting her off. "A *fait accompli*."

She laughed as he kissed her softly at the temple. "China is the place to buy jade. And thanks to Sung, I now know a little bit about it. He taught me to distinguish between the excellent and the average. Which is all to your good, my sweet."

"Shall we go upstairs?"

Barely moving her lips, she said, "All right."

It was like the first time she had gone to bed with Gregory. She didn't really know why. Maybe it was because she'd been so perilously close to death. But she hadn't died. She was alive! *Alive,* her nerves tingling, her blood racing with excitement, her skin shivering with anticipation.

Gregory did that to her, made her glad to be alive. Touching every part of her body, his hard mouth on her flesh tantalized breasts and nipples, shooting spasms of pleasure through her veins. How Gregory knew her! He was adoring and passionately savage by turns. They moved together, their bodies attuned in erotic give and take, revolving slowly, Gregory on top, then Marianne.

Soon desire became unbearable. "Yes—yes," matching the cadence of her voice to his hard, punishing thrusts.

Clinging to Gregory as if he were the last man alive in a decimated universe, she climaxed, her body convulsing under his gasping shudder.

"Beautiful," he murmured, pressing his damp forehead to her cheek. "Beautiful, beautiful."

A few minutes later they lay side by side, propped up on the pillows. Marianne sipped a glass of mineral water, relaxed, happy, but back to earth. Suddenly, a disturbing thought crossed her mind.

"Kwong said he saw you the other day at the fair," Marianne said. "Seems you have the same negotiating team from CHINATEX as I do."

"Do I? Yes, I suppose so."

Marianne let a silence fall between them for a minute or two. "Noncommittal, aren't you?"

His head turned. "What is there to be committal about? I don't like to mix business with pleasure."

"Oh, come off it, Greg. Who's talking business?"

"CHINATEX is business. I don't mind discussing jade or Burma or the labor market potential in Sri Lanka. But CHINATEX is in process and I'd rather not talk about it."

"All right. But one question. I'm your competition, isn't that right?" Impatient because he did not answer, she repeated, "Isn't that right?"

"Yes. But Marianne, could I be frank?" He kissed her bare shoulder.

"Of course you can."

"Proceed."

"I won't insult your intelligence by telling you it's a competitive world. But what you don't seem to realize is the more responsibility you take on in the corporate system, the bloodier it becomes. Lying and conniving is adolescent compared to the just-this-side-of-legal and sometimes not-so-legal conspiracies that go on. You don't belong in that kind of jungle. You're too ethical. You haven't a dishonest bone in your body.''

"Are you telling me I have to be a crook to succeed?"

"A little larceny helps."

Her laughter came easily. "You mean that?"

"Marianne, you don't know what it's like."

"You think Casey was handed to me on a platter?"

"Not exactly. But you had Carol Olmstead behind you."

It was the same thing Horace Blake had said. "Everything I got I earned," she defended. "Do all men believe that a woman's success is based on luck or pull or sex?"

"Oh, c'mon, Marianne. Carol *was* behind you. Twelve, thirteen, fourteen years in the corporation and they give you a subsidiary? Guys have had to fight thirty years for what you already have. Unless Papa is chairman of the board."

"Maybe, just maybe, I'm a little brighter. Maybe I have more go, more determination than those 'guys.' *Hmmm?* But you should talk about platters and papas who are chairmen of the board! Didn't you inherit Windham Mills?"

"Yes, but . . . aw, hell." He threw back the sheet and started to get out of bed.

Marianne put a restraining hand on his arm. "Wait, Gregory. Yes, but *what*? You did get the mills from your father, didn't you?"

"You might say so. But I already owned Windham when he died."

"How's that?"

"There are those who'd say that's where the larceny comes in."

"You stole the company?"

"My father thought so."

"Tell me about it. I won't lecture or judge. I swear."

"I'm not so sure . . ."

"Please, Gregory, I promise. I'll just listen."

"All right." He smiled at her. "Why not?" He slid back into bed, settling back on the pillow, putting an arm around Marianne's shoulder. "Where shall I begin? With my father?" He threw his head back and contemplated the ceiling for a few moments. "Yes, that's as good a place as any. I was never my father's favorite, even as a kid. But things got really bad during my college days. My father and I had some terrible fights. He was such a moralistic, bible-thumping jackass." Bitterness twisted his mouth.

"When I got my degree," Gregory continued, "it was understood I'd step into the sales manager slot. But Dad found out I'd knocked up some girl. She got an abortion, but somebody told Dad and he hit the roof."

Gregory fell silent, staring into space.

"What did he say?" Marianne prodded gently.

"Say? He yelled, 'You're a no-good loser, a spineless, godless parasite! If you want a job at Windham, you can sweep the floors and carry out the trash. That's all you're good for. You'll never get the mills. I'm changing my will and giving the company to your cousin Burt.

"I was twenty-two, Marianne. It felt like I'd been condemned to man the galley oars. Locked out of the captain's cabin . Forever. But I was smart and I had fight. I made some clever moves, some that wouldn't get me a recommendation for sainthood. That's where the larceny comes in." He chucked Marianne under the chin.

Marianne recalled her own anger at the Hansfords and how shocked Uncle Bob was when she swore that never again would she allow herself to be demeaned. She could understand Gregory's feelings of rage, his resolution to make his father regret his cold, unkind treatment.

"I won't bore you with the details, Marianne. Some of them aren't pretty. And I want you to like me."

"You know I do," she said, nudging him playfully. "Tell me what happened."

"Well, the abbreviated version is that I came up through the ranks—floor manager, sales, vice-president, finally easing the old man out to retirement before he knew what had hit him.''

"And the will?"

"He tore it up—at my request."

"You put pressure on him."

"A little."

"I can imagine." She had the suspicion that his self-portrait of a rough, tough operator was exaggerated, part of his need to appear the strong power player. "You won't tell me what kind of pressure?"

"Nope." He settled himself more comfortably on the pillows.

"And you think I can't get to the Billings boardroom?"

"I don't think, I know."

"You're wrong. I'm not going to destroy anyone else to get there, but I'll get there all the same."

"Shall we drink to that?" he asked.

"You don't believe me." Her eyes flashed up at him.

"I'm trying," he said soberly.

"That's better. But Gregory, I'm giving you fair warning. I'm not as soft as you think I am."

"You couldn't prove that tonight," he said, drawing her on top of him in a dizzying embrace.

CHAPTER XX

O N FRIDAY, TWO WEEKS AFTER THEY HAD ARRIVED IN
Canton, the Casey people were finally ushered into the
privacy of an office at the Trade Fair.

"We hear you have been ill," Mr. Lu said. "So sorry."

How had he heard? Through the grapevine? From
Gregory, or Kwong, or a CHINATEX person who had
seen her escorted from elevator to taxi? But it didn't
matter. It was no secret, just an embarrassment.

"I'm feeling much better."

"Good."

Fully recovered physically, there still lingered a faint
uncertainty like an afterthought on the edge of her conscious awareness. There was something about her illness that she ought to remember but couldn't.

"Did you read in the newspaper about the typhoon
coming in the South China Sea?" Mr. Lu asked. "We
hope she misses Canton."

They discussed past typhoons, the weather in general,
and a new Shanghai-made movie now showing at the
Golden Voice Cinema.

After a brief pause, Mr. Wei, who had so far only spoken in Chinese, said in an excellent though accented English, "What do you think of our silk display, Miss Oliver?"

Marianne turned to Jerry. "I think Mr. Cooper can give you a more educated opinion than I."

Jerry nodded. "Nicely representative, Mr. Wei. The Canton crepe and crepe de chine and the brocade are first class."

Jerry's response reassured Marianne. She was never certain about his reaction, although by now she should be. Jerry liked to play salty cynic, sometimes the buffoon, but when it came to his field of specialization, he could turn into the serious professional.

"We'd like to look at more samples of raw silk," Jerry was saying. "What about derniers?" This was the yarn count based on a system of weight.

"Thirteen-fifteen is standard," Mr. Lu said.

"Agreed. But do you carry the heavier derniers?"

Mr. Wei leaned forward, his hands on his knees. "We have that." He turned his head, addressing one of the men in Chinese, a new member of the team who had been introduced as Mr. Fong. He rose now and left the room.

Tea was served by a Chinese girl dressed in the neat white blouse and blue-skirted uniform of fair attendants. Though she wore no makeup, she had not abandoned feminine vanity. Her lustrous black hair had been permanented, wide waves and little curls peeking discreetly from behind her ears.

Jerry continued. "Miss Oliver's also considering spun silk." The short lengths of inferior silk obtained from filaments of waste material, pierced or double cocoons and known as "spun" was less expensive than the raw. It went into the manufacture of shantung and pile fabrics, which Marianne hoped to promote for a moderate-priced line of summer wear.

"How much silk were you interested in buying?"

Marianne answered Lu with a question. "What is the weight of your average bale?"

"In pounds? One hundred and forty-five."

"I see. Jerry?"

Jerry removed a small notebook from his coat pocket. "That's the figure we used in our estimates. We might start with three, maybe four thousand bales."

Marianne, who had been forewarned to impress upon the Chinese that her interest involved a long-term understanding, said, "Mr. Cooper is referring to our hope that this consignment will be the first of a continuing flow."

At this Mr. Lu and Mr. Wei brightened visibly. When the interpreter explained to the others, they (including Mr. Bao, who had sat stonily unmoved throughout the meeting) smiled and nodded.

"That sounds satisfactory," Mr. Lu said.

Marianne waited for him to quote a price. But he went on to say, "Perhaps we should meet again. Day after tomorrow? By then Mr. Fong will be able to present the samples you requested."

Having lunch at the hotel with the Casey people, Marianne remained optimistic. "I just know it won't be long before we can get down to the nitty-gritty of the actual contract."

"Don't bet on it," Jerry remarked caustically. "First they're probably checking Casey out, fine print and all. Billings, too. They're going to make certain you're good for the money. Second, they've got other customers lined up and they're giving them the same song and dance."

"Maybe I ought to make an offer," Marianne suggested.

"Don't," Jerry advised. "The Chinese have to make the first move."

"I know. I'd just like to get a jump on the competition."

"Wouldn't we all? You better believe those boys are trying their damnedest to do the same to you."

They were. Windham Mills especially.

Until now Gregory had done very little direct business with China. Synthetic fibers were his mainstay, DuPont his chief source. The expensive sheeting one of his mills specialized in used Sea Island and pima cotton. Another, Murdock in South Carolina, produced cotton wash-and-wear as well as silk blends. In the past he had purchased silk from Japan and Brazil, but with the opening of the Chinese market he had decided to switch. Sung had always taken care of his Far Eastern transactions, acting as an intermediary. But Sung, tipped off that the People's Republic was taking over Hong Kong after their lease expired in 1997, was getting out. Currently involved in a highly complex series of deals, he was unable to help his friend. Gregory, who had wanted to look over the prospects of contracting Chinese labor, had decided to kill two birds with one stone by handling the textile negotiations himself.

Like Marianne, Gregory had received a thorough briefing before leaving for Canton. His China team consisted of a good lawyer experienced in international trade agreements, an excellent interpreter, and two other men, one who acted as his secretary and the other as his accountant. But Gregory preferred to negotiate informally. The protracted "getting to know you" process of the Chinese put him on a short fuse. He balked at the round of banquets and tours through communes and factories. Questions concerning Windham Mills' operations, production machinery, labor costs, and annual profit annoyed him. He realized that this was a necessary preliminary and tried whenever he could to let Gus, his accountant, answer, afraid that his own irritation would show.

When asked how long Windham had been in the family and if his father still participated in the running of the mills, he nearly lost his control. What damned business was it of theirs? He knew that family relationships were important to the Chinese, but they had touched a wound. He didn't like to talk about his father. In fact, he couldn't understand why he'd revealed his estrangement from the old man to Marianne.

What Marianne didn't know was that the son-of-a-bitch had been suing him to get the mills back when he died in an automobile accident.

For a short time Gregory had been under a cloud because his father and he had quarreled only a few hours before the accident. An inquiry had been made the next day. Gregory's lack of shock or grief, his failure to shed a tear or show distress, increased the suspicion. But he had quickly been cleared when the autopsy had shown the elder Windham had actually died of a heart attack at the wheel.

I *could* have killed him, Gregory had thought afterward. God knows I've wanted to more than once. Even now, over twenty years later, an acid taste rose to his tongue when he recalled Windham, Senior. He was never any kind of father to me, Gregory thought bitterly. A goddamned bastard, a toe-the-line-dictator, a sanctimonious ass. If Grandpa hadn't been around when I was growing up, I'd have taken to the road. Grandpa. There was a real man. He could be a mean fighter if crossed, but he had more affection in his little finger than Dad could muster in his whole body.

Gregory felt he resembled his grandfather. Like him, he got a thrill out of playing the game—victory for victory's sake—and the prize that came with it—the power and the money—just sweetened the deal.

He knew that China imposed a quota on their cotton exports in order to have enough at home to clothe their teeming population. But China's need for hard foreign currency had forced her to sell a percentage of the cotton production, and Gregory was going after a big piece of it. Silk was another matter. Too dear for Chinese consumption, silk, in various stages, was sold on the open market. The problem was that long-time customers had first choice and what remained was offered to new buyers like Gregory and Marianne. He was determined to get his contract from CHINATEX. As for Marianne . . . poor, lovable sweetheart. If she wanted to play with the boys, she'd just have to learn the hard way.

"So heppy to meet the professor. You are teaching met-a-metics?"

Brad, invited by Sarah months earlier, was visiting one of her classes. A chair had been brought in for him by a young male student eager to practice his English.

"Physics, mostly."

"Ah, good subject."

Brad sat in the back of the room. He admired Sarah's poise, her fluency, her ability to interpret an alien subject such as English literature to her Chinese students. Some forty-odd young men and women were in attendance, their black heads bent over pencils and notebooks. Every now and then when Sarah made a point they would lift their eyes to gaze attentively at her. There was little of the whispering, the rustle of pages, the coughing, the scraping of feet that made up the busy undertone one found in an American classroom. When he had first started teaching in Canton Brad had found this heightened silence, this intense concentration a little unnerving. He had measured his words carefully, conscious of his poor grasp of the Chinese language, afraid to make an embarrassing mistake, knowing that if he did no one would laugh or correct him. What made the language even more difficult were the four different tones used in pronunciation. The pitch of one's voice could change the meaning of a word, sometimes radically. But as time went on and Brad got to know his students well enough to insist they point out his mistakes, he relaxed, and their breathless attention became less intimidating.

After the class had been dismissed, Brad and Sarah talked at her desk.

"Marianne called me last week," Sarah told Brad. "Said she had been ill."

"Food poisoning. Arsenic, actually."

"Oh my! My! Was it serious?"

"According to the doctor, yes."

"That's terrible!" She put a veined hand to her mouth. "Where did she pick it up?"

"She attributes it to a bun she bought from a street cart."

"Well—it's conceivable that such food might have been prepared in a place that had rat poison, but not likely. Vermin here have been brought under fairly good control. I'm not too sure arsenic is that easy to come by either. It seems rather strange.''

"Yes." He thought the whole incident a little strange. The afternoon Marianne took sick the switchboard had received instructions not to ring her room. Both Marianne and Hollis did not remember making such a request. Fortunately through some bungle Brad's call was allowed to go through. Had the telephone operators been mistaken about such an order in the first place? Possibly. Trained hotel workers knowledgeable in English were in short supply during Fair time.

On the other hand supposing that telephone order actually had been given. Maybe someone had been making sure she wouldn't be reached in time. But who?

Sarah was saying, "I wish I could have known sooner. Is she all right now?"

"Fine."

"I don't see much of her," Sarah said.

"Nor do I." He resisted the urge to tell Sarah about Gregory.

"You're very fond of her, aren't you?"

The question surprised Brad. This was the first time she had touched on his personal feelings. Their conversation had mostly been about politics, Chinese history, Brad's education, his teaching experience.

"Yes. I am." He hesitated, then plunged. "I'm in love with her."

"Oh." The strained look on her face smoothed out for a moment. "And she with you? Forgive me," Sarah went on when he didn't answer immediately. "Perhaps I'm being too forward. But it's the matchmaker in me. The mother. You would make a good husband, a good son-in-law."

Brad smiled. "I'm afraid that's not to be. Marianne is fond of me, but she looks on me as a brother. Nothing more."

"She knows you love her?"

His eyes went past her to the blackboard. "She seems

not to," he said. "I think she must, deep down, but she doesn't want to acknowledge it. She would rather have me as a friend. Not a lover."

"Why can't she have you as both?"

What could he say? Explain biology, sexual chemistry? Sarah seemed so far beyond sex herself. It wasn't that the Chinese, from whom Sarah had adopted many of her cultural attitudes, were necessarily Puritans, but sex was seen in the context of marriage in this country. A time and a place for everything.

"She ought to marry again while she's still young and can have more children," Sarah was saying.

"She says she *is* married—to her career."

"But—again—why can't she have both?"

Brad shrugged, then laughed. "You'll have to ask Marianne."

"I find it hard to talk to Marianne."

She says the same about you, Brad thought. But not wanting to hurt this fragile woman, he kept silent. Brad had sensed a world of torment locked up inside Sarah.

"She resents me," Sarah sighed. "With good reason, of course."

"But that's all in the past," Brad tried to reassure her.

"Some carry the past to their graves."

"I wouldn't give up. If you and Marianne could spend time together, you'd work it out." He sounded like a pop psychologist. But what could he do? He wanted to help these two people to come closer, to touch, yet he didn't know if it *was* too late.

"Yes—well . . :" The folded hands on the desk suddenly gripped tightly together, the white knuckles standing out on the knobby fingers. "When—Karen—comes," she said, slowly spacing her words, "maybe we can—share—a common interest. I—look—forward to seeing her."

A spasm contorted her face for a brief moment. "Bradford—I wonder . . . It's late."

"You're tired." He got to his feet. "Thanks for having me. You're an excellent teacher and I've picked up a few useful pointers.'' He curbed the impulse to stoop and kiss her cheek. "We must have a meal, the four of us, when Karen gets here.''

"That will be nice.''

He was at the door when he heard Sarah gasp. Turning, he saw her groping in her handbag, her face the color of old wax, her lips blue. From where he stood he could hear her desperate, ragged breathing.

"What is it?" He was at her side in a few long strides.

"My . . .'' A vial of pills trembled in her hand.

"Do you need water?''

She shook her head, placing a disk under her tongue.

"Should you lie down?''

Again she shook her head.

Noticing a Thermos on the windowsill, Brad brought it to the desk. He poured some tea into the cap and set it in front of Sarah.

"Thank you,'' she whispered. "It has to dissolve. Glycerin.''

"Heart?''

She nodded.

"How long?''

"Oh—a few years.''

Somewhere outside a bus beeped, a bicycle bell tinkled. Footsteps and voices passed the door. Faint color came creeping back into Sarah's face, the lips losing their ghastly blue tinge. She sipped some tea.

"I don't want you to tell Marianne,'' she cautioned.

"She's your daughter. She has a right to know.'' And it would make a difference, he thought. Knowing her mother was so ill would bring understanding.

"No,'' Sarah said. "No. I want you to promise, to *swear* you won't tell her. Or anyone.''

"Why not?'' He didn't want to argue or further upset her, but he found her stubbornness baffling.

"Because she'll feel sorry for me. She'll insist on my going to the States with her because the doctors there are better. Oh—I don't know.'' She touched her hair, tweaking a strand into place with nervous fingers. "She's very bossy. I simply can't cope with that now. Don't tell her, I beg of you. You *mustn't*."

As Sarah's agitation grew, Brad, feeling he had no business pressing her, finally agreed. "I promise. Please, Sarah, calm yourself."

She sighed heavily, leaning back in her chair, her eyes closed.

"You can trust me, Sarah."

"I know I can." She opened her eyes and smiled. "I feel very close to you, Bradford."

The light was fading. A single feeble ray of sun angling in from a high window caught a thin silver shaft of dust motes.

"There is so much to do yet," Sarah said. "So much. If only they had not forsaken Mao and his principles. This new premier means well, but he is giving the communes back to the farmers, breaking the factories away from the state, letting people open their own shops. Soon there will be rich and poor again."

"No system is perfect, Sarah. The leadership is trying to strike a balance between socialism and capitalism. They want to modernize China, to give their people a standard of living on a par with that of the western world."

"And with the western world's problems, too. A rising crime rate, divorce, social diseases, vandalism. I don't like to sound pessimistic, but that's the way it is, isn't it? Oh, well. We'll survive, I suppose. The Chinese are like bamboo, bending with the storm, standing upright again in calmer weather."

Brad noticed how "they" and "we" were interchangeable.

"I sometimes wonder what made you such a staunch supporter of the Chairman," he said. "You did come from a fairly conservative background, didn't you?"

"Yes. But both William and I loved the Chinese, the common folk, and we saw early on that their lot wouldn't be improved by anything except cataclysmic change.

You see, there had to be a complete sweeping away of the old to make room for the new. William and I felt strongly about that."

She paused, looking past Brad, her eyes remembering. Then Sarah, usually so sparing with words, began to talk on and on, her voice level and without emotion. She spoke of politics and her own life, going back through the years to Liberation, telling Brad things about herself he was certain no Westerner and few Chinese had heard before. He did not interrupt, but let her speak, confounded by this unexpected outpouring. Why have you chosen me as a confidant, he wanted to ask. Because I'm sympathetic? A substitute for your daughter? Or had the accumulation of years, events, catastrophes, triumphs, held in for so long suddenly become too much? Maybe her attack, the heart abruptly grown to an enormous pumping monster in her chest, threatening to stop after each painful hammer, had reminded her once again of her tenuous hold on life.

This was a confession of sorts, the making of a will, the tidying up. He felt a great empathy for Sarah and an anger, too, at her blind adherence to an ideology that left no margin for error.

The room had grown dim and Sarah still spoke, pausing to wet her lips with tea every now and then. She was nearing exhaustion, her upright posture having slackened to rounded shoulders, her voice cracking.

"I must ask you once again," she said, "not to speak of this to anyone."

The keeper of secrets. Good ol' Brad. "Don't you think if you told Marianne—"

"No!" She cut him off sharply. "Her least of all. Your word of honor, Bradford."

Word of honor. He wanted to laugh. That stale, now meaningless phrase had gone out with fourteenth-century knights in rusting armor. Perhaps Sarah wasn't so much a Maoist as she was a holdover from the age of chivalry—King Arthur and his Camelot.

"Word of honor," he promised.

*   *   *

One evening Brad and Marianne were taking a stroll along the streets of Sha Mian Island not far from the White Swan. It was late afternoon and he had just come from the University, with several hours until his evening class would convene.

"I was hoping you could have a late dinner with me after I'm through," he said.

Marianne linked her arm in his. "I'd love to, Brad. Can't. Not tonight."

"Otherwise engaged, is that it?" A discordant note crept into his voice as he continued. "Don't tell me, let me guess. Gregory Windham."

"Brad," she chided. "Just because you don't like him doesn't mean *I* have to feel the same."

"Seems to me you did at one time."

She waved her hand. "He's changed, Brad. He really has. His son died last year and it hit him hard. It mellowed him. He's—well—more thoughtful."

"A man like Gregory Windham doesn't change."

"You're wrong," she said earnestly. "People have the capacity to see their own mistakes, to grow. Things happen—a tragic death, a first, heartfelt love—and suddenly they see things differently." She smiled up at him. "I'm giving Gregory a chance. I believe he's sincere in wanting to shrug off the old skin."

"You're wrong, Marianne!"

"That's my funeral, isn't it?" Marianne said lightly, sidestepping an argument. "Let's not talk about Gregory. Tell me about Sha Mian, this island of the Pearl. The guidebook says it was once restricted to foreigners."

"Yes. Gates closed at night. No Chinese allowed after dark. Another humiliating put-down among many similar ones that the Chinese haven't forgotten. The island is also a reminder of the forced introduction of opium into China by British merchants. Even though it was against Chinese law, these English speculators funneled opium into China from India and made a bundle from the addicts they created. You can see why the Chinese distrusted outsiders for so long, why they now insist on establishing mutual trust and respect in business deals."

"Yes. And Sha Mian, as well as the rest of China, is theirs now."

"Not quite. There's Hong Kong, which is practically in the bag. And Taiwan."

"The Chinese are sensitive about Taiwan, aren't they?"

"Wouldn't we be if a bunch of crooked politicians, swindlers, and tax evaders grabbed the Florida Keys and set up their own republic, then said the rest of the country rightfully belonged to them? Formosa, as Taiwan was once called, has been part of China since the end of the seventeenth century."

They had turned the corner on Central Avenue and stopped in front of a small building with stained glass windows reminiscent of a church.

"We're now in a neighborhood that was known as the French concession," Brad explained. "And this was their Catholic church. I believe it was built in the 1880s. It's a printing factory now."

They walked on, coming out on the river embankment.

"After the second Opium War," Brad said, "the foreign merchants who had their warehouses and factories burned in the city exacted an indemnity from the Chinese. With part of it they built Sha Mian from a river sand bank. You can still see the old villas, the gardens, the tennis courts."

Under the dappled shade of banyan trees the river breeze cooled them pleasantly. They paused in front of a rusting spiked iron fence. Marianne, looking past it, saw what had once been a magnificent house built in the style of a French country château, the paint now peeling, the masonry crumbling. A cinder driveway lined with ragged palms skirted the neglected expanse of lawn, its weeds a lush, poisonous green. It was easy to imagine how the drive once crunched under the tires of stylish phaetons or high-fendered motorcars, the bustled, hatted, and gloved women sitting stiffly next to their men in heavy worsted and tight collars. Riding out with their wives to tea, to a reception or fashionable supper, these traders and entrepreneurs must have been a proud if not arrogant breed, secure in their roles as bearers of the white man's burden. They saw themselves as bringing light to a pagan nation, forgetting that these so-called heathens had already created a refined civilization when their own ancestors were still clouting each other with clubs. Poor deluded devils. They were gone now. The high windows catching the milky sun, haunted by ghostly faces from a colonial past, looked out on a far different world.

But the villa was not deserted. Even as Marianne watched, a young Chinese woman followed by a troop of children emerged from the heavy front door. Two by two they marched in orderly file to the center of the lawn. The young woman spoke to the children and they arranged themselves in a double line, some turning to stare at their observers. The little girls with huge hair bows pinned to the backs of their heads, the little boys with their caps and colorful jackets and mismatched pants never failed to intrigue Marianne. She continued to watch as the young woman snapped her fingers, bringing the group to attention. Then to her example the children began the flowing, stylized motions of *tai chi*.

"Warm-ups," Brad said. "Good for toning the body. You ought to try it."

"Yes," Marianne agreed. "I should get into some kind of exercise program. Swimming, if nothing else. 'When' is the big question."

"Gregory keep you that busy?"

She removed her arm from his. "Gregory is not on our list of approved topics, Brad."

"Sorry. I have nothing against the man. In fact, we have a few things in common. Taste in women, for example. We both found Sabrina rather appealing, at least for a time."

The shaft found its mark. Marianne didn't like to be reminded of Gregory's former lovers. Talk about his ex-wife, the mother of his children, didn't bother her. Ruth belonged to the distant past. But Lily and Sabrina were recent history, women Gregory had been intimate with since he had met her.

"I never realized," she said, her voice sweet as syrup, "you could be such a pleasant son-of-a-bitch."

CHAPTER XXI

KAREN ARRIVED IN CANTON ON A SATURDAY MORNING wearing a rumpled T-shirt and tight jeans that outlined her slim, boyish hips like a second skin. To her mother, waiting beyond the customs barrier, Karen looked child-like, hardly self-sufficient enough to have traveled the far distance from New York alone. However, surging forward to take her into an eager embrace, feeling her daughter's pointed breasts against her chest, Marianne was suddenly and uncomfortably reminded that Karen was now fifteen, a young woman. She held her tightly, telling herself that all children grow up, that it was all right, that she still had years ahead to enjoy with Karen, that . . ."

"Moms!" Karen protested, "you're smothering me!" Disengaging herself from Marianne's arms, she went into Brad's bear hug.

"Shall we pick up the rest of your luggage?" Brad asked, eyeing Karen's electric blue duffel bag.

"There isn't any. That's all I brought."

"But darling," Marianne said, recovering from her

lapse into sentimental regret, "didn't you pack at least one dress?"

"No."

"Well—no big problem. If you need clothes, the hotel shops carry everything from soup to nuts."

"Why would I need clothes?"

Marianne ignored the grumpy, rather aggressive tone. It had been a long flight.

On the way to the White Swan Karen sat between Brad and Marianne. Karen's face wore a self-absorbed expression. She barely glanced at the passing scene.

"Did you have any trouble getting the extra time off?" Marianne asked. They had decided that Karen would spend at least ten days in China rather than one week.

"No." She turned, looking squarely at Marianne, a sudden defiance glinting in her eyes. "I told Miss Rexford I wanted to quit and was coming over here to get your permission."

Marianne went stiff with shock. "You what?"

"I want to quit. School is a big zero. What am I supposed to do with stuff like ratios and right angles and hypotenuses or the case function of nouns? How will that stuff help me in real life?"

"I see." Marianne paused as if to give this pronouncement serious thought. "Then what do you propose to do with yourself?"

"I'm going to join The Blessed Angels of Christ."

Marianne looked over at Brad in bewilderment. His eyes, sparking with amusement, turned instantly sober.

"You can't be serious," Marianne said.

"Oh, yes," Karen assured her.

How could a child change so in just a few weeks, a perplexed Marianne wondered. Karen had seemed fine when—after her disappointment with Frankie—she had decided to room with Tilly. She had assured her mother that everything was going to be all right. This sudden defiance was not like Karen at all.

The taxi had arrived. Brad handed Karen's bag to her mother.

"Aren't you staying?" Marianne asked.

"I have a meeting. See you later."

Marianne sensed that Brad was exiting because he anticipated a mother and daughter argument and didn't want to take sides.

After giving Karen ample time to unpack and relax a bit, Marianne decided it was time to talk.

"Now," Marianne said with what she felt was an understanding smile, "tell me all about it. What is this Blessed Angels of Christ?"

"I wish you wouldn't say 'this' in that tone of voice." Again the aggressive edge.

"I'm sorry. I want to know. Really."

"All right. Remember I told you I was going to their church?" Karen took a deep breath. "They're wonderful. It's hard to describe how wonderful. If you could only meet them, you couldn't help seeing what I mean. They're so much more than a religious denomination. They're super-friendly. And affectionate. Before services everyone hugs the person on either side. And it isn't faked. They mean it. You can just feel the vibes of love."

"What sort of doctrine do they have?"

"Well, they've taken the best of several faiths— Christian, Buddhist, Taoist, Mohammedan—and combined them into one. They believe in the brotherhood of man."

"That seems a lofty ideal."

"They're mostly spiritual, Moms. There's meditation and finding yourself. Seeing the inner light. They own this big place in Maine; it's called Christhaven, a farm where the disciples work."

"A religious commune. I thought those went out with the sixties."

"This isn't anything like that. We're structured. And we have our faith to keep us together. We believe." The earnestness in Karen's shiny young face chilled Marianne.

"Faith in what?"

"God the Almighty. Our Redeemer."

"You can get that in church. You don't have to quit school and live in a commune to believe."

"You don't understand, Moms," she said impatiently, getting to her feet. "How can I explain? Mother Ruth, Father Jacob, Cousin Isaiah, Esther, Paul, Jeremiah . . ." She waved her hand. "We're *family*. We have ties to one another that are stronger than blood. We *care*."

God's children. Blessed Angels with biblical names. It sounded like a Sunday School pageant. But the child was serious, dead serious.

"Who are these people you mentioned?" Marianne asked. "Have I met them?"

"No. But you'd love them. They're decent, sincere, and really into helping others."

"And you find them appealing. You want to go and live with them. May I ask how long you've been thinking of Christhaven? I mean, you didn't just decide on the spur of the moment, or did you?"

"You don't have to be sarcastic about it."

"What do you expect? I was under the impression that after that blowup with Frankie things were working out at school. And suddenly you hit me with this. People I've never seen, don't know anything about, and you want to go live with them. I suppose you have to give them money?"

"Only what I can afford."

Marianne, like Brad, had the sudden impulse to laugh. She had prided herself on raising a daughter who had escaped the pitfalls of a modern teenager. Karen hadn't taken to drugs, shoplifting, booze, or promiscuous sex. How lucky I am, Marianne had often thought, how fortunate. When she read about student marijuana busts, when friends complained about their rotten kids who stole cars or got pregnant, she felt almost smug. It had never occurred to her that Karen would become a born-again Christian, wanting to run off and live with a bunch of religious fanatics. Blessed Angels, Mother Ruth, Father Jacob. What solid, established denomination would go in for such pretentiousness?

"I went up to see them last weekend," Karen said. "They were putting in a vegetable garden, good organic stuff. No chemical sprays. And they have this wonderful dorm, one wing for the women, one for the men. And the chapel! You ought to see it. But the main house is where everyone meets in the evening. After supper they sit around the fire and sing. And their faces . . . they are all so *caring*." Karen's eyes shone. "Moms, I want to live there. It's the best place in the world. You just can't say no."

Her pleas reminded Marianne of how earnestly Karen had begged for a puppy. But this was no puppy. This was a colony of vegetarian campfire gurus who were trying to persuade a girl of fifteen to quit school and join them. The only reason they hadn't already roped Karen into their club was that they knew Marianne would have the authorities on their doorstep before the kid had unpacked her bags.

"Let's think it over," Marianne hedged, deciding that tactfulness was the best approach. "Maybe you could visit Christhaven for a week or two this summer and see how you like it."

"No." Karen took a deep breath. "I already signed up."

"Without asking me?"

"I was sure you'd say okay."

"What gave you such a crazy idea?"

"It's not crazy. I thought you'd be glad to have"— she shrugged—"to have me off your hands."

Marianne felt her stomach freeze. She stared at Karen, the coldness fanning up to her chest. "What?" The word came out hoarsely, and she tried again. "What in God's name are you talking about?"

"You shouldn't use the Lord's name in vain," Karen said with a smug piety that gave Marianne the urge to slap her.

"Never mind the preaching. You just made a statement. Have I ever—*ever*—given you the impression I wanted you 'off my hands'? Have I? Well, answer me!"

Karen lifted her chin and the spark of defiance was back, but stronger now as she faced her mother.

"Yes! When were you ever around? How many times did you come to see me in a play, a recital, a soccer game? Remember *Madama Butterfly*? Mrs. Eddlestone came, not you. Other mothers visited homeroom in parents' week. Not you. You dropped in once. *Just once!*"

"Karen, I thought—"

"What? You thought what? Other mothers *did* things with their kids. Frankie's mother went ice skating with her, taught her to play tennis. You got me a pro. Big deal! How many outings and vacations and camping trips were we supposed to go on next week, next month, next year and never did? You gave me Sparky and took him away. You took my friends away, too, sent me to that crappy school because I would be a nuisance in New York. I hated that school then and I hate it now!"

She was close to tears, and Marianne stood up, feeling helpless, hands at her sides, her stomach churning. All that resentment coming out, all the remembered slights, the small betrayals, the hatred, thrown at her like barbed missiles, an artillery of bitter recrimination. The worst of it was that she was right. *Time passing.*

"I did the best I could," Marianne said, wounded, her heart aching, but still refusing to go down under this adolescent barrage. "I sent you to that school because I thought you'd be happy there. If you were unhappy, you should have told me."

"I did. A lot you cared."

"But I do care, darling." Marianne sank down on her knees beside Karen's chair. Her daughter stiffened and would not let Marianne touch her. Marianne got to her feet feeling as though a fist had lodged in her chest. She took a deep breath.

"I care very much," she repeated, making her voice level. "I fought to keep you when you were a baby. If I hadn't given a damn I'd have let you go to the Hansfords. You know about that."

"Yes," she said in a tone that meant "so what?"

"You mentioned it once. Uncle Brad told me the whole

thing. *He* cares. But he's—well, he's Uncle Brad. These people, Mother Ruth and the rest, they *love* me. They're a family, they make me feel that I *belong*. Can't you get that through your head?"

And I believed I had a happy, fairly well-adjusted daughter, Marianne thought ironically. But no. It's all coming back like hens to roost, all the postponements, all the broken promises. Brad warned me.

"At Christhaven I'm going to have a mother, father, sisters, brothers, and God. One family," Karen said. "I'll know who I am and where I belong."

"Sure you will. You give yourself to them body and soul—plus a heathy financial donation—and they'll keep the evil world at bay. You won't have to think about it. You won't have to have a single thought in your head they don't put there."

Karen stared at her mother defiantly. "Right. What's wrong with that?"

She wanted to say, "The Angels will make a slave of you, a robot, just like those poor people who committed suicide at Jonestown." But she couldn't. More criticism would only drive the wedge deeper.

"Nothing. If that's what you really want. If you want to have someone tell you what to do, to make all your decisions for you, it's great."

"It's *not* like that."

The telephone rang, breaking the mounting tension between them. It was Gregory wanting to have dinner with Karen and Marianne.

"Why don't you go without me?" Karen sulked. "Wouldn't you rather?"

"Of course not. I won't go unless you do."

"Okay, okay. I'm going to take a shower."

Marianne followed her into the bathroom, picking up the clothes Karen had dropped.

"Your Grandmother Oliver is dying to meet you."

"She's a communist, isn't she?"

Bent over, turning on the shower, her sharp shoulder blades offered a tender vulnerability. How thin she looks, Marianne thought with a twist of the heart. Vegetarian food. Probably fasts, too. She's just a kid, unformed, rebelling against parental authority, looking to find herself, just like any teenager. Karen's anger isn't personal. It's just being fifteen.

At dinner that night Karen went into a lengthy explanation of the Blessed Angels to Gregory. "Father Jacob, our founder, has a Ph.D. in Sanskrit from the University of Toronto. Mother Ruth was a philosophy major. Half the people are college-educated. So you can't say the Blessed are a bunch of dumb hippies. People like that have put a lot of thought into the colony."

"Blessed Angels," Gregory mused. "Isn't that the outfit that's being sued by some folks over in Scranton? They're charging the Angels with brainwashing their son."

"Oh, *that*. A couple of failed parents trying to get back control of their son through publicity."

"Uh-huh. That's what the Angels say. What I want to know is what's in this religious scam for them?"

"It's *not* a scam, Gregory. Does there always have to be something 'in it'?" Karen's tone was much milder than it had been when she had argued with Marianne. She liked Gregory. He had a way with young people.

"Everybody has an angle," Gregory said.

"Their angle is their belief in the spirit, the soul, in a higher Being Who will guide us to a place of contentment if we only let Him," Karen assured him.

"Meanwhile, as His earthly representatives, this Father Jacob and Mother Ruth do the guiding?"

"He speaks through them."

They were having an early dinner and the dining room was still fairly empty. Marianne had persuaded Karen to buy a dress (her bag held only a nightgown, a few T-shirts, and an extra pair of jeans)—a summery white linen with toasty brown Mondrian stripes across the shoulder and hem. It was a good fit. Despite her thinness Karen looked grown up and quite pretty, her dark hair and eyes contrasting with the white dress. Looking at her, Marianne felt proud. This lovely creature was an extension of herself, no matter what strange ideas were clamoring in her head.

"God has always spoken through His prophets," Karen said, answering Gregory's question.

"That's standard dogma. But no one has ever been able to prove it."

"You don't *prove*. You have to accept some things on faith. We all accept Einstein's word about relativity, don't we? You and I can't prove it."

"You've heard of the Reverend Moon?" Gregory asked. "He's made millions out of that kind of faith. Lives in a mansion, owns no one knows how many more houses. Drives nothing but Rollses and Caddies. Is into dozens of businesses. Was even convicted of income tax evasion. Where did he get that kind of loot? From poor suckers he conned into believing he had a private pipeline to God."

"We're *not* like the Moonies. Or the Hari Krishnas. We don't solicit on street corners and at airports. We don't intimidate people into joining."

"But the Angels ask you for money, don't they?"

"How else can they run Christhaven?"

"On faith," Gregory said, smiling broadly. Marianne tried not to laugh. Karen's body turned rigid.

"You're making fun because you don't know anything about Christhaven."

"I know enough to have a healthy suspicion about their income."

Karen, her face flushed, pushed her chair back. "Excuse me," she said, tossing her napkin on the table.

"Karen—" Marianne began.

"I'm not hungry."

Gregory, watching her go, shook his head. "Guess I put my foot in it."

"She takes this very seriously," Marianne said, wanting to run through the dining room after Karen. "She's very sensitive about the Blessed Angels right now."

"Hell. She'll get over it."

In the morning Karen asked Marianne again for permission to quit school and join the sect.

"I hate to play the heavy, but you're under age and until you're eighteen I will not approve my only child becoming a cult dropout."

"I'll go on strike. I won't crack a book. They'll have to expel me."

"You want that? All right. If that's your pleasure, go right ahead, but there's no way you can move in at Christhaven."

"What difference does it make to you?" Karen's aggrieved voice grated.

"All the difference in the world."

"Bullshit."

"And watch your language."

It was a Sunday morning and no meetings had been scheduled with CHINATEX. Marianne had made arrangements to bring Karen to Dr. Chen's, where they had been invited to lunch.

"Get dressed," Marianne said. "Your grandmother is expecting us at eleven o'clock. Jeans are all right."

Karen disappeared into the bedroom and came out some minutes later wearing the dress Marianne had bought her. She carried white pumps, also a recent purchase, in her hand.

"Is this too much?"

"No. You look terrific." Marianne found Karen's abrupt change to amiable compliance an encouraging sign. "Nervous?"

"How did you guess?" She slipped into her shoes.

"I was nervous, too. The first time. Grandmother is really very nice. Nothing to be anxious about."

"What shall I call her?"

"Just Grandmother would be fine."

Sarah was waiting for them in the central room, sitting on a wicker chair. Voices could be heard in the inner courtyard. Marianne was pleasantly surprised when Sarah rose and kissed Karen's cheek.

"My," she said, with more animation than she had shown to Marianne, "but you are a grown young lady! I didn't expect . . . well, sit down, sit down! Could I get you some tea?"

"No, Grandmother. Thank you."

"My, my!" Sarah repeated and fell silent.

"Karen will be here for ten days," Marianne interjected. "Maybe you could show her some of the sights."

"But, Moms, I thought you said you would have time—"

"Yes, I know. I will have time. But it would be a fine opportunity for you and Grandmother to get acquainted while I'm at meetings."

"Meetings," Karen echoed.

Marianne refused to feel guilty.

"I shall be happy to take Karen around," Sarah said. "Is there anything in particular you'd like to see?"

"Yes," she challenged. "I'd like to know what kind of churches you have here in Canton and if people are allowed to worship."

"Indeed they are," Sarah said mildly, a faint glimmer in her eyes. Pride? Marianne wondered. Amusement? "Perhaps the Huaisheng Mosque would be of interest. We also have a Roman Catholic Cathedral, and I believe I heard some talk of the Baptists, but I'm not sure. We can also arrange a trip to Buddha Hill."

"What religion are you?" Karen asked in a provocative tone.

"I don't have a religion," Sarah said equably, "in the sense you mean. I don't feel the need."

"You're an atheist?"

"Perhaps. But I do have faith. I believe in the perfectability of man. Wasn't that one of Christ's messages? I believe that we all will have a just society here on earth one day."

"But that's not a faith."

Sarah smiled. "Read the *South China News*. It's filled with stories of war, murder, terrorist bombs—considering the mess we've made of things, the idea that the human race can be perfected requires an enormous amount of faith, wouldn't you say?"

Karen looked at her grandmother, whose eyes in their bony sockets reflected friendliness, and grinned.

Sarah asked if they would like to watch her and young Zelie, Dr. Chen's daughter-in-law, fix lunch.

Crossing the small courtyard, where some purple flowers had come into bloom since Marianne's last visit, Marianne began to feel good about Sarah and Karen. She had anticipated a clash, Karen's missionary zeal facing off against Sarah's unyielding ideology. She had prepared herself to hear angry words, maybe have Karen flounce out of the house as she had done at dinner with Gregory. This acceptance, tenuous as it was, the smiles exchanged, seemed almost miraculous. Who would have thought it possible? And Sarah actually showing affection! More than she ever did for me. I've been by-passed, Marianne mused. But what of it? If Sarah is loving toward Karen, some of it should rub off on me.

"Can't you talk some sense into her?" Marianne asked Brad.

It was two days later. That morning Marianne had attended a twenty-minute meeting with CHINATEX at which nothing had been accomplished. John Summerfield, the China watcher, was right when he said the negotiations with the Chinese moved at the speed of continental drift. And on top of that, Oscar had called from Casey informing her that one of their long-time customers, Walter's, was pulling out. She felt tied in knots. Dealing with Karen hadn't helped.

"No more than I could ever talk any sense into you," Brad said.

"Are you saying she's like me? I can't see it. I never went off half-cocked about some self-appointed psuedo-zealots."

"*Hmmm.*"

"You know I didn't. Why do you say '*hmm*'? That's so irritating."

Hollis appeared in the bedroom doorway. "Miss Oliver, I hate to interrupt"—she had materialized so silently that Marianne hadn't heard her—"but you said it was important this letter go right away. I thought if you signed it I could take it downstairs and put it in the mail."

"Yes, yes. Of course."

When Hollis had gone, Marianne turned again to Brad. "Karen will just have to be unhappy for a while."

"You're letting her go back to school alone?" He handed her a cold, foaming beer.

"What else can I do?"

"Keep her here. She's bent on this thing, Marianne. Send her back and she might run away."

"Oh, I don't think so."

"How can you be sure?"

Marianne contemplated Brad sitting across from her. His white, short-sleeved shirt exposed his brawny arms, giving him a strong, solid look. "I'm not, really. But I'm not going to let myself think the worst."

"Because it might distract you from the business at hand?"

"That's one of the reasons."

He wiped the dampness from the bottom of his glass with the palm of his hand and carefully set the glass down on the coffee table. "She *is* like you. Single-minded. Latching on to something she wants, going for it—no matter what the price."

"I resent that." She twisted the ring on her finger. It was a jade one to match the necklace Gregory had given her.

"Trouble with you," Brad went on implacably, "is that you don't see the obvious parallel between your relationship with your mother and Karen's with you. You're still blaming Sarah Oliver for neglecting you. But it was done out of expediency, just as you have neglected—"

"*Don't say it!* I've never neglected my daughter." Brad had touched another raw nerve. He was becoming expert at it.

"Perhaps 'neglected' was a bit strong. How about 'left to her own devices'?"

"We've been through this all before, Brad, and I

don't much like it. You nag. It's a habit you have. You nag me about Karen, you nag me about Gregory.''

"Why not Gregory? He's *your* half-baked zealot."

Marianne, torn between anger and the sudden desire to laugh, said maliciously, "You're jealous of Gregory, aren't you? Come on, confess. Just plain jealous." And as a faint blush rose to his face she went on. "Why, Brad! I do believe you're in love with me yourself."

Brad rose from his chair, took his empty beer glass and went to the bar. He opened the little refrigerator under it and brought out another bottle of beer. Then he stood there, leaning on his hands, looking down at it.

"You haven't denied it," Marianne probed, still smarting from his remark about neglecting Karen.

He turned so suddenly the bottle fell over on its side and bounced to the floor with a ringing thud. He ignored it.

"Do you need to ask?" His voice was low, pitched to a cold intensity, his eyes blazing with a resentment Marianne had never seen before. "Don't tell me you didn't know."

"No—no. I didn't," she replied, astonished, uncomfortable with this sudden turn of events.

"C'mon, Marianne, after all' these years? Good ol' Brad—always to the rescue. Always at your side. And you never once suspected that I loved you—the way a man loves a woman? You didn't guess?''

His voice was trembling now with an anger barely held in check. "Damn it, how self-absorbed can one woman be?"

A small flicker of fear formed a cold place under her heart. Brad had become someone else. A man she had sensed was there, but had no wish to acknowledge.

"I was teasing . . ."

"Sure, teasing. All these years, teasing. Good old fusty bachelor Brad. And I would have given my right arm for you to look at me *once*, just once, the way you look at that asshole Gregory."

"I never knew," she murmured.

"It figures, Marianne," he said, picking up his coat

from the chair. He stood over her, bending so that she could see the black pupils of his eyes. Enraged tiger eyes, fighting mad. "You're so goddamned self-centered you wouldn't know an honest feeling if it came up and hit you like a fist in the gut."

He strode to the door and turned to her angrily. "I hope like hell you lose that contract, Marianne. A little failure now and then might make you more human!"

Listening to the echo of the slammed door, Marianne knew he meant it.

CHAPTER XXII

The Chinese had finally quoted a price, one that was higher than Marianne wanted to pay. She asked to think it over.

Jerry had warned her, "Hong Kong businessmen—and I'm talking Hong Kong Chinese—bargain like bazaar rug merchants, their asking bid so out of sight it's laughable. They expect you to hammer it down—a lot of yelling, hair-pulling, and moaning about how you're gonna ruin them if they take a penny less. But the Chinese over here don't give you that kind of comedy. They quote you a price, they mean it."

Now Marianne had to come up with a counterproposal, one not so low as to make her seem unreasonable or so high as to cut her own throat.

To complicate matters, Jimmy Kwong had learned through his own particular sources that the price of raw silk might be going up shortly. Maybe to fifteen, sixteen dollars a pound, he said. How much truth Marianne could credit to that rumor was uncertain. Kwong's information had been gleaned from an overheard conversation in a teahouse and the half-tipsy assurance of an "old boy," an overseas Chinese trader. If the rumor was correct, she was under more pressure to make a deal as soon as possible. If. There was more guesswork to these negotiations than Marianne cared for. She liked to throw dollars and cents—so many bales at such and such a cost—into the computer and get an answer she could work with. But the economic scene was so volatile in China these days—changing, sometimes drastically, from day to day—she had to stay flexible, if not loose.

Kwong, who at the beginning had been a great help, was seriously in love with his Chinese girlfriend; his heart and mind were no longer dedicated solely to Casey. Pursuing his courtship relentlessly, he had managed to meet his Chinese sweetheart's family—father, mother, sister, and a brother (another brother was in the People's Army). Liyan, like all Chinese, was closely attached to her family. The only way she would consent to marrying Kwong was if her relatives could come to the United States, too. Kwong, not quite prepared to take on the Lin clan, offered a compromise: residence for him and Liyan in Hong Kong, a place from which Liyan could make frequent visits to Canton.

But complications developed there, too. Liyan's mother, changeable as the weather, suddenly decided she didn't want her daughter to marry at all. Liyan's salary was needed at home. Though Kwong offered to contribute the same amount to the communal income, the mother still hesitated. Then, doing another turnabout, she told Jimmy that she had wished for a Chinese son-in-law, not one who, except for his features, was American.

Kwong remained cheerful in spite of Mama's blowing hot and cold. He could have gladly strangled the old dumpling, but love restrained him, and he made a great effort to treat her with the respect a future mother-in-law would demand. He did not dare to think ahead to the legal intricacies of the marriage, the hassle with Chinese emigration authorities and the U.S. Department of Immigration.

Marianne, fed a step-by-step, half-jocular account of Kwong's suit, sensed the young man's frustration.

"It will come out all right in the end. You'll marry your Liyan, go back to New York with her, and raise a dozen children."

Though romantically preoccupied, Kwong managed to maintain his competence as an interpreter. But he had little time now to hang around the Fair and overhear gossip. Marianne would have given anything to know what her competitors were bidding. As closely as she could ascertain, there were two companies besides Windham Mills: a Filipino firm and Pantex of Rhode Island. She had seen the Filipinos, a trio of saucer-faced, smartly suited men, talking to Mr. Lu in the lobby. Jerry had told her about Pantex.

"It's an outfit run as a hobby, more or less—mostly more—by Dan Hopper. He's a sixty-year-old billionaire who likes to keep his hand in. He's shrewd, has done business with the Chinese before, and is what they call an 'old friend.' "

"In other words," Marianne said, "if he offers them the same price as I do, they'll take him and leave me out."

"I wouldn't say for a fact. Maybe they'll sell to both of you. Depends. Depends on inventory and up-to-date production. One way around it is to allow you to buy fewer bales than you want."

"That won't do. If I don't get a certain minimum then it's not worth my while to manufacture a silk fabric. And I can't wait until next season, next year. I've got to try to get things rolling at Casey as soon as possible. Maybe I ought to quote a price and let the chips fall where they may."

"You might have to do that anyway. But for now I'd say cool it. Who knows? You might get lucky."

Kwong, having an hour to kill before Liyan got off work, ran into Jerry at the Bai Yun bar, where he had stopped for a beer. As a rule, on off-hours Jerry had his little Candy-cane with him. Today he was alone and—

judging from the uncoordinated way he manipulated his bushy brows—not altogether sober.

"Kwong! Hiya! Where's the China doll?"

Jimmy explained.

"Candy's shopping," Jerry said. "Oh, how that girl loves to shop! It's going to take a cargo jet to haul what she's bought home."

Kwong sipped at his beer. Jerry ordered another scotch. "Only one little thing," Jerry said. "She's got expensive tastes. In jewelry. She loves good jewelry, not the plastic stuff, but the real article. And she can tell the difference."

Jerry finished his scotch. "Terrible booze. They must distill it from bok choy. Brrrh! What were we talking about?"

"Candy."

Jerry smiled. "Yeah, Candy. There's a pearl necklace she's got her heart set on. Beautiful piece of oyster work. Trouble is, they won't take a check."

"What about a credit card? Most of the government-run Friendship Stores take Visa or Master Charge."

"Not this one."

"Well, listen, if you're in a bind I could lend you some cash."

"Say, could you? That's great! I hate to ask our boss lady for an advance. Doesn't look good for business. Is a thousand too much?"

"I don't have that kind of loose cash on me right now. If you could wait, my folks are sending me—"

"How about five hundred? I'll pay you back the minute we hit the States."

"No problem. Be glad to do it, Jerry."

Marianne had not heard from Brad since his outburst. Imagine holding those feelings inside all these years, then letting go in one shocking explosion, she reflected. Canton's climate seems conducive to bitter accusations and confessions. Karen and now Bradford.

She missed him. She missed the daily phone calls, the walks they took in the early evening along the banks of the Pearl River. She missed being able to discuss her meetings with the Chinese team, the funny way Boa sniffed, Hsu's doodles with a green felt pen, Mr. Lu's laugh that came at unexpected moments. She missed talking about Karen and Sarah, the friendship that was growing up between them. But she'd be damned if she was going to be the first to say "I'm sorry." Sorry for what? It wasn't fair to be castigated because you couldn't return a man's love.

Brad did call her on Friday afternoon. No mention was made of their quarrel, but his voice was cool.

"I thought I ought to let you know that the Hansfords are in Canton."

There was a long silence. "You're kidding."

"No. I saw them at the Chinese opera last night. Ed's lost a lot of weight, which makes him look more dour than ever. Dorothy's aged, but she manages to disguise it under tons of makeup. They're staying at the White Swan."

"What are they doing in China?" Marianne's hand took a firmer grip on the phone. "Do they know I'm here?"

"Apparently touring the People's Republic happens to be the 'in' thing among the 'Town and Country' set this year," Brad said. "And yes, they know you're here."

"Oh, Brad, you didn't tell them, did you?"

"They asked about you and I didn't see why I should make a secret of it."

"And I suppose you let them know Karen was here, too."

"I didn't volunteer the information. They just assumed she was and I didn't contradict."

"Shit! Thanks, thanks for nothing. I don't want to have anything to do with those people. You know that."

"Change your hotel, then," Brad said, still in the same maddeningly cool voice.

"Like hell. We've settled in here quite nicely, thanks. They're not going to drive us away. Is there anything else I should know?"

"Nothing that you don't already. I see no point in going over the same argument. If you want to stay mad and vindictive toward the Hansfords, go ahead, indulge yourself."

"Indulge myself! That's quite a twist. I'm not like you. St. Bradford, the all-knowing, all-forgiving. Except when it comes to me. That uncalled-for blast you gave me was not only unfair, it was downright malicious."

"Is that the way you see it? Well, just put me down on the top of your enemies list. One name more or less among the many won't matter."

He hung up, and the dead phone stared at her like the slammed door had the afternoon he had stormed out of her room.

After she had calmed down and given herself more time to think, her mind returned to the Hansfords. Okay, she told herself, they're here. So what? Why panic? The hotel had twelve hundred rooms, and her chances for bumping into them were slim. If they called, she could always put them off. More than likely they'd only be in Canton for a few days and, if she was lucky, she wouldn't hear from them at all.

But she wasn't lucky.

She had just returned from a conference with Stan Golch, the lawyer Carol had sent over, and was walking through the lobby when she saw the Hansfords picking up their messages at the desk. She was hoping to sneak by to the elevator, but as she passed, Dorothy turned. Marianne's first impulse was to look through her ex-mother-in-law as though she wasn't there. But when Dorothy's face lit up in recognition, Marianne heard herself say, "Hello, Mrs. Hansford."

"Why, Marianne!" Dorothy exclaimed.

Ed hung back, bleakly noncommittal as usual.

"What a pleasant surprise!" Dorothy's voice, in perfect *grande dame* pitch, rose to the awkward occasion. Marianne might have been a dear acquaintance who had just stepped into her Long Island living room.

Marianne, finding the situation neither pleasant nor surprising, mentally kicked herself for having acknowledged Dorothy Hansford in the first place.

"Bradford must have told you we were in Canton. A

Sinbad tour. I wouldn't recommend it. The hotels in some of the towns were unbelievable. But the scenery made up for it. Picture postcard on the River Li. We took—"

"Mrs. Hansford, I really must—"

"This is our last city. We've been all over. Wuxi, Shanghai, Suzhou, Peking—or Beijing, as they call it— the Summer Palace, the Temple of Heaven. We saw the Wall, of course. I couldn't get past the first station—you know, those enclosures where the soldiers used to shoot their arrows? I didn't expect the steep climb. Have you been there?"

"No, I—"

"You shouldn't miss it. And Xian—those life-sized terra cotta statues. Warriors with topknots, mustaches, funny hats—"

"Mrs. Hansford—"

"Thousands of years old, still standing there, guarding that Emperor's tomb. I forgot which one. Ed, do you remember?"

"Mrs. Hansford—"

"And the Grand Canal. Polluted, muddy. People actually living on those boats, washing their clothes in that water—"

"Mrs. Hansford, *please*!"

Dorothy, her mouth half-open, paused.

"I really must run," Marianne said.

"Yes, yes, of course." Her smile trembled at the corners. "So nice to have seen you." She extended her hand, and when Marianne took it Mrs. Hansford did an extraordinary thing. She burst into tears.

It was so unexpected that Marianne, still holding Mrs. Hansford's limp hand, could only stare at her.

Ed put his arm around his wife's shoulders, a look of tender compassion on his face. This look, too, was something that astonished Marianne. She had never expected to witness Ed Hansford giving way to a human emotion. To see his granite features relax into gentleness was like watching the Sphinx suddenly break into a smile.

"It's all right, Dot." Ed gave his wife a handkerchief and she let go of Marianne's hand.

"Such a scene." Dorothy, burying her face in the handkerchief, spoke in a muffled, tear-choked voice. "I'm so sorry!"

She looked up at Marianne, her makeup in ruins, smeared eyeliner and mascara like streaks of soot under her eyes. "I realize you have every reason to despise us, Marianne, but could you—could we talk? Just ten, fifteen minutes? I won't ask for more of your time."

Marianne, feeling uncomfortable rather than hostile, wanted to refuse. Dorothy's tears embarrassed her.

Ed spoke. "It would help." For him this was a tremendous unbending, a plea.

"All right," Marianne agreed. Brad is right, she thought. I can't go on holding a grudge forever.

The Hansfords' room was just that, a standard hotel room, not the kind of accommodations Marianne would have associated with this couple who had always traveled first class. No river view here. The gauze-curtained windows looked out on a dull street scene, the tops of distant buildings, and a chimney belching smoke. An upholstered chair had a cigarette hole in it and the carpet near the bathroom was marred by a dark, ugly stain. The suitcase open on the luggage rack, like Ed's sport coat, was a good one, but worn. The seedy atmosphere was definitely not up to Hansford standards. Had they come down in the world? Or was it simply, as Dorothy had indicated, their tour's inferior choice?

"I hate to go all to pieces like that," Dorothy apologized, the gracious hostess again. "Please sit. Could we fix you a drink?"

"No, thank you."

Dorothy went to the mirror, grimaced at it, reached for a Kleenex, and patted her cheeks, wiping the mascara smudges from under her eyes. "What a sight!"

She came back and seated herself primly on one of the twin beds, facing Marianne.

"Ed, must you stand?"

"I'm all right." Stationed near the window, hands in

pockets, he rocked on his heels. His face, harsher than it had been in the lobby, looked thin, the pouches under his eyes baggy and dark.

Dorothy sighed. "Now, Marianne, you must understand that I've waited a long time to have this talk. I've wanted for ages to tell you how—how sorry we were." She paused, giving Marianne a small, meaningless smile. "I—this isn't easy for me. 'Sorry' doesn't begin to convey our regret. We were so wrong. From the very first, when Toby brought you home."

Marianne felt more and more uncomfortable. She didn't like to see this kind of self-abasement. Apologies should be dignified, not a form of *mea culpa* breast-beating that put the one who was being asked to forgive and forget on the hot seat. What am I supposed to say, Marianne wondered—that I'm sorry she's sorry?

"We—we should never have gone to court over Karen." Dorothy sniffed and dabbed at her nose. "Never. I know now what an awful thing it is to separate a mother from a daughter." Dorothy's voice trembled. She touched the Kleenex to moist eyes. "I . . ." She swallowed.

From his stance at the window, Ed begged, "Dot, please. Don't upset yourself."

She shook her head. "No. It's better to talk about it. Have it out. Better. Marianne—our—our Hazel died. Three months ago. Cancer."

"How terrible! I'm *so* sorry." She was genuinely shocked. Hazel was such a decent person. Five years older than Toby, she would have been forty-one now. And with so much to live for—a husband, three children, a whole future to look forward to. It didn't seem right.

"Dennis kept the children, of course," Dorothy said, giving Marianne a pained look. "We weren't about to make the same mistake twice. The two boys are at Oxford. The girl is at boarding school. We don't get to see them much. It's"—she twisted her mouth—"lonely. I suppose that's what you have to expect when you get older."

Marianne could see now what Dorothy was leading up to. Karen. Gripped again by the memory of past humiliation, she had the wild desire to shout *"No!"*

"You have a husband who seems fond of you," Marianne couldn't help saying, an edge of bitterness to her voice.

"Thank God for that."

Ed came and sat down beside her. Dorothy reached over and took his hand. "Without him, I don't know what I would have done. I give the impression that I let things roll off my back, that I don't care. It's not so. I'm not strong like you, Marianne. I fell apart when I lost Hazel." She clung to Ed's hand. "And Toby's death affected me the same way. You must remember, he was my child, too."

It had been easy for Marianne to forget Dorothy's relationship with Toby. Dorothy's coldness, her snobbish denial of Marianne, had made her seem like an antagonist, not like a mother bereaved by a son's death. "People have different ways of dealing with loss," Brad had once said. "Refusal to accept it is one."

"You can see so many things differently in hindsight," Dorothy said. "I can't go back and do it all over again. I can only hope to make up for it now."

Marianne remained silent. She tried to look at Dorothy objectively, to consider her as she would a slight acquaintance, a woman whose son and daughter had died, whose only claim to mortality was three grown grandchildren in England whom she rarely saw and another granddaughter whom she was not allowed to see. I ought to feel sorry for her, Marianne thought again. And in a way I do. But Dorothy hasn't really changed. I don't doubt her regret over the way she handled me in the past, but I'm sure that regret is based on pure self-interest rather than on a sudden affection for me. Dorothy wants to see her granddaughter.

"I was hoping," Dorothy went on, "that we could come together on a new footing. Be friends." The smile on her ravaged face looked forced.

"Possibly." This cautious promise was all Marianne could give.

Ed had not as yet spoken to Marianne. At least *he's* kept in character, Marianne thought.

"I'm on a tight schedule," Marianne continued. "I'm here to negotiate a contract with the Chinese."

"Yes. Bradford filled us in. You're president of a company called—Casey, is it?"

Had Brad left anything out? "Yes." She got to her feet. "If I'm free in the next day or two I'll give you a call. How long are you staying?"

Dorothy looked at Ed. "A few days. But we could extend it."

"Not on my account, surely." Marianne smiled.

"Why not? Mending fences is more important than sightseeing."

When the door closed, Ed said, "Did you have to toady up to her like that?"

"If I ever want to see Karen again, yes. I'd give anything to have her on weekends, for summer vacations. Anything."

"They have laws now where grandparents have visitation rights. We could go to court."

"Karen might resent it. Besides, it's too messy."

"If that's the way you want it," Ed said, shrugging. He rose and removed his sport coat, went to the closet, and hung it up. Dorothy watched him with contemplative eyes.

"I'm glad we came, Ed. Bumping into Marianne that way made the whole trip worthwhile. Did I ever tell you that I saw Karen when she was about six? Someone told me that Marianne had an apartment on Amsterdam Avenue, so I drove there and parked the car across from the apartment and waited."

"Oh, Dot."

"I recognized Karen the minute she came out: Toby's dark, curly hair, the long arms, the tilt of her head. It was Toby, Ed. My heart turned right over. If Karen had been alone I'd have walked over and introduced myself.

But she was with someone. I—I just didn't have the nerve."

"What did you do?"

"What could I do? I drove back to Long Island, crying all the way."

He put his arm around her shoulders and held her for a few moments. "And you never told me? God, I hate that woman."

"Oh, Ed."

"So we wanted custody. What was wrong with that? Marianne didn't have two nickels to rub together, still going to school, no family to back her up. Father and mother living in a commie country. We could have given Karen everything, everything."

"I know. But we went about it in the wrong way. I just wish . . ." She broke off, her eyes filling with tears.

"Don't cry, Dottie."

"I won't." She swallowed a sniffle, touching the balled-up Kleenex to her nose. "I must say Marianne's come up in the world. President of a company."

"Yes. I read about her in *Business Woman.* The 'New Star in Textiles.' Made out as if she's really some kind of genius. She slept her way to the top. It's that simple. Don't fret, darling. I'll see to it that you and Karen get together. If Marianne doesn't come through, I swear she'll regret it. I have connections, I can make trouble . . ."

"Don't be hasty, Ed."

"Hasty, hell. We've waited too long as it is."

Marianne couldn't decide what to tell Karen about the Hansfords. It was difficult to change overnight from despising her former in-laws, hard to make a turnaround. However Dorothy wept and apologized, the Hansfords had scarred her too deeply for Marianne to change overnight from despising to accepting them. But she also realized she couldn't keep them from Karen indefinitely. Sooner or later they would meet. Even now Karen might learn of their presence at the White Swan and ask embarrassing questions. Marianne didn't want Karen to accuse her of deliberately perpetuating a hostile estrangement. To Karen, in her present state of Blessed Angel grace, such an unforgiving attitude would further damn her mother as un-Christian.

But a postponement—or reprieve—was handed to Marianne when Karen, returning from lunch at the university with Sarah, asked if she could go to Nanjing, a city on the Yangtze River. One of Sarah's colleagues, Zhang Anyi, a woman professor who taught sociology, had become interested in the recent resurgence of Christianity in China. Anyi was planning to visit Bishop Ding Guanghxun, principal of the Nanjing Theological Seminary, and had invited Karen to go along. Sarah, when consulted, thought the religion part would be harmless. She had been working on Karen, as Marianne knew, with her own version of utopia. Sarah, of course, felt it was a more powerful medicine than any mild-manner Anglican priest could offer. Marianne didn't argue the point. She knew from Karen's remarks that Sarah's propaganda was received by her daughter with the same kind of indulgence with which she accepted chopsticks instead of forks. To Karen, Sarah's Maoism was simply a cultural aberration. Marianne did agree, however, that this trip was a good opportunity for Karen to see a little more of China.

Marianne packed Karen off with a sense of relief. Her daughter temporarily taken care of, she could put thoughts of the Hansfords aside and concentrate on the negotiations. At the moment they were going well. Marianne had made her counter-offer and the Chinese were now deliberating among themselves. Jerry said they might take a day, a week, or a month. No one could guess.

Gregory, subject to the same kind of Chinese procrastination, was growing testy. He could leave Canton, as he told Marianne, and relinquish authority to his second in command, who knew as much about Windham Mills as he did. But by now the contract had become a personal matter, a duel between him and the "wily Chinee." Aside from remarks concerning his impatience and the ineptness of CHINATEX, Gregory never discussed his dealings with them. But his grim-jawed determination came through. In an odd way his attitude only served to strengthen Marianne's own resolve.

She and Brad were still on cool terms. He had not called back since the afternoon he had given her the news about the Hansfords. Their estrangement bothered her. She told herself that Brad would get over his anger in time. But she knew they wouldn't be able to take up where they had left off. Undeclared, Brad's love had never been a threat. Now out in the open, Brad's feelings put their relationship on an embarrassing plane. How could she talk to him now without wondering if he imagined her lying in his arms, or underneath him, her naked legs folded about his moving hips. Love tinged with sexual overtones prohibited a platonic friendship.

The night after Karen had left with Anyi, Marianne had a strange dream. She dreamt that Brad was standing over her, his teeth drawn back in a grimace, half smile, half snarl.

"You've been baiting me, you bitch!"

"No, Brad, it's not true."

"Liar!" His eyes glowed like orange agates in the darkness. There was an object in the hand he held at his side, something she could not see but sensed was lethal.

"Leading me on. Playing cat and mouse with me while you were fucking Gregory."

"Brad, no!"

"Why do you keep saying no? You don't deserve to live!"

He raised his arm and she could see what it was he held in his hand now. A knife. At least a foot long, it gleamed menacingly, silvery sharp.

"Brad—no!"

The knife's terrifying descent in slow motion filled her with black horror. Her scream woke her.

The light clicked on. A white-faced Hollis, standing at the switch, said, "Are you having a nightmare? You scared me."

Brad's hand with the glinting weapon still clouded her mind. "Have I . . ." She swallowed. "Have I been talking in my sleep?"

"Screaming," Hollis said.

"Screaming? *Brr*." She shook her head. "Just a bad dream. I'm okay now. Sorry I woke you."

Hollis seemed to be waiting for her to go on. But Marianne, disinclined to explain, said, "I'll be all right, Hollis. Thank you for your concern. You can turn the light off."

Marianne lay in the darkness for a long time trying to analyze her dream. Why should her subconscious mind picture Brad as wanting to kill her? Even if he was angry it didn't make sense. A man doesn't murder a woman because she doesn't love him. Not even in a dream.

CHAPTER XXIII

AT THE BEGINNING OF THE FOURTH WEEK, GREGORY, after a short, irritating and unproductive meeting with CHINATEX, opened the door of his suite to find Lily Sung sitting, legs crossed to display her elegant calves, on an easy chair.

"Hello, Greg." Her almond-shaped eyes smiled seductively. "I thought I'd give you a little surprise."

"Christ!" Greg let out his breath. "A coronary is more like it." The dumb bitch was following him!

"Aren't you glad to see me?"

"Hell, no!" Through the bedroom door he caught a glimpse of her Vuitton luggage standing at the foot of the bed. "How the hell did you know I was here? Don't answer, Sung."

"That's right. But don't be afraid. He thinks I've come to Canton to visit my Auntie May."

"I'm not your Auntie May." He crossed the room and yanked Lily to her feet. She was surprisingly unresistant, supple; her skin under his hot, angry hands was cool. "Listen, you little bitch, I want you out! Out!"

She swayed toward him, still smiling. "I love it when you're brutal."

She smelled of gardenia. The fragrance, mingling with the afterglow of the double martini he'd had for lunch, took him back to the time he first went to bed with her. The storm of passion he had aroused in this woman had overcome whatever scruples he might have had about making love to Sung's wife. They had indulged themselves in a night of sensual pleasure. Satiny limbs, golden globed breasts, sensitive hands, and pouting mouth, moving, questing, she had offered herself in ways that elevated sex to a new and highly erotic plane. But that was then and this was now. Stripped of allure by the cold, hard fact of her unwelcome intrusion, the memory quickly faded. Whorish and demanding, her voluptuous curves, packed into a slim, golden body, spelled nothing but trouble.

"I mean it, Lily. Why did you come? What do you want?"

"You." She put her fingers to his lips.

He shrank back. "It's over. Get yourself another playmate."

"I want *you*." She moved closer, lifting her chin. "Scared?"

There were tiny lines at the corners of her eyes that he had never noticed before. Lily was how old? It was hard to figure with Orientals, and she would never tell him.

"Scared shitless," he mocked.

She took hold of his belt, both hands trying to work it loose.

"Let go, Lily."

Her hands fluttered free. She was wearing an aqua sheath with an off-the-shoulder neckline revealing a fair portion of those golden breasts.

"Would you like a feel?" she asked, capturing his hand, putting it inside her dress. The firm mound with its little button nipple sent a small shock through his body.

"No! Damn you!" He pulled his hand away as if she had thrust it into a fire.

"Then let me have one." Quickly as she spoke she unzipped his pants, manipulating him under her quick warm fingers. He felt himself rising and hated her, hated himself. He pushed her so violently she stumbled back.

"You whore!" He had never come so close to hitting a woman.

"You used to like it."

"I told you it's over. Now get the hell out of here. If not, I'll—"

"You'll tell Sung."

"I mean it, Lily. . . ."

Her eyes narrowed. "Oh? He's served his usefulness, is that it? Going out of business in Hong Kong and not much help to you anymore. Poor Sung, thrown on the garbage heap—like Lily, his wife."

"I'm tired of this soap opera, Lily. Tired of arguing with you, tired of being blackmailed. It would be a relief to have Sung know." He went to the telephone. "I'll call him now. Isn't that what you want?"

"Wait."

He knew his bluff would work. Sung would believe him before he'd believe Lily. He wasn't going to be manipulated by a whore like her.

"Forget Sung," she said. "I've got a better idea. You still running after that bloodless guppie—Oliver, isn't it? Yes, Marianne Oliver, and she's staying at the White Swan. Maybe we should call her."

"Leave Ms. Oliver out of this."

"Why? No, I think she ought to be included. A little person-to-person chat would be nice."

"She wouldn't believe anything you had to say. She knows how you pulled the same stunt at the Mandarin."

"Does she? You sure she doesn't have a little lingering suspicion? And when I call, won't that suspicion be more than a little one? I'll do a good job. I'll describe your suite, beige wallpaper with a blue diamond design, a chip in the dresser's glass top, the bed"—she craned her neck to see—"a beige spread with blue stripes. Is that where you and she screw? She'll know it."

He wanted to kill her. Instead he calmly picked up the phone. "Give me Miss Oliver at the White Swan, please."

Lily shrugged, moving over to the chair. She fished a pack of cigarettes from her purse.

"Yes, I'll wait," Gregory said, watching Lily. "Line's busy. Have you decided what your story's going to be? That I sent for you, begged you to come? Better make it foolproof. Marianne's a smart woman."

She lit her cigarette, blowing twin plumes from her cameo-carved nostrils. Cool. But then, she always was.

"Very well, Gregory, have it your way," she said, shrugging. "For now."

He said nothing, slowly placing the phone back in its cradle.

"I'm patient, I can wait. You'll be back." Her almond-shaped eyes slid provocatively over him. "You and I, we're two of a kind, you know. It took you a day before you got over your tantrum and came barreling up to the Peak the last time. We did it on the bathroom floor with Sung in the next room, remember?"

Gregory knew he had to get her out, and fast. "There's a plane to Hong Kong at three-thirty." He looked at his watch. "Be on it."

He called the desk to send someone up to collect her bags.

"Aren't you going to take me to the airport, Gregory, sweet?"

"No. I'll put you in a cab."

He settled her in and gave instructions to the driver. She rolled down the window, calling to him.

"What is it?"

"You haven't said goodbye." Before he could answer, she reached up and—putting a stranglehold around his neck—brought his head down, kissing him savagely on the mouth.

When Gregory finally managed to untangle himself, he turned away in disgust only to find Hollis Albek staring at him from the entrance of the hotel. She had seen it all, he was sure—the luggage and the kiss. Christ. What rotten luck.

"Hello, Miss Albek," he said affably, giving her his best smile. "Seeing an old friend off. Have time for a drink?"

Settled in a booth over gin and tonics, Gregory explained earnestly. "Mrs. Cheng, the lady you saw, is a business acquaintance." The lie came smoothly, easily. "She inherited a shirt factory from her husband and is doing very well. She came over from Hong Kong to discuss an order she wants me to put in for her."

"Attractive woman," Hollis commented.

"Yes—well . . . I wonder if you'd do me a favor?"

"If I can, certainly."

"It's like this. . . ." He smiled again, a smile that intimated a friendly conspiracy between them. "I'd rather you wouldn't mention anything to Miss Oliver about Mrs. Cheng."

Her eyes remained expressionless. No surprise, no doubt or curiosity, just a gray blank.

"My relationship with Mrs. Cheng is strictly business," he continued, "and since Miss Oliver and I unfortunately"—a wry twist of the lips—"are competitors, I would like Mrs. Cheng's visit here kept a secret. Her order combined with mine puts me in a good bargaining position with CHINATEX."

"I understand."

He would have given his eyeteeth to know what she was thinking. Was she buying his story? He'd have to take his chances. She'd never believe the truth, and neither would Marianne.

"I know you're loyal to Miss Oliver," he continued. "She thinks the world of you, and I wouldn't hold it against you if you decided to tell her about Mrs. Cheng. Far be it from me to pressure you."

Even if she did go back and talk it could do no more than mystify Marianne. He hoped.

"I see no reason to report it." She gave him a wry smile. "I don't believe it would make a difference. Miss Oliver has so much on her mind right now."

"Yes, I know what you mean. I'm afraid her daughter's visit has been quite upsetting."

"Miss Oliver is very upset," Hollis agreed. "And then there's this news from home that isn't the best. Customers leaving Casey . . . Oh—am I speaking out of turn? I thought you and she shared—"

"Of course. I know all about it," he lied. What gives with this woman? he asked himself. If Hollis knew anything about competitive bidding she'd have realized she was giving away a company secret. Marianne wouldn't "share" that kind of information with him or anyone.

"We have very few secrets from one another," he said, wincing inwardly at his sanctimonious tone.

"Except Mrs. Cheng."

Smart. Real smart. This woman was playing some kind of game. What did she want? Money? "Tell me, Miss Albek, are you happy with your job?" Nothing like direct confrontation.

"Yes. Why do you ask?"

"I thought you might be looking for advancement. Many good executive secretaries go into middle management."

"And you have an opening?"

"I could arrange it." He gave her his best smile again.

"In exchange for what?"

Gregory let the question hang. It wasn't that he was above hiring a spy. Everyone did it, from the small electronics plants in Silicon Valley to big ITT. But Hollis was a dark horse, hard to gauge.

"No strings attached," he finally said. "I'm looking for qualified people. Think it over. Feel free to discuss my offer with Miss Oliver," he added. "It's all aboveboard." Hollis would tell Marianne if she wasn't interested. Instinct told him she was. Instinct also told him that though she probably earned a good salary, more was better.

"Here's my card."

Hollis took it, studying it for a long moment. "Thank you for the drink," she said, tucking it in her handbag.

* * *

For once the connection between New York and Canton was clear.

"Marianne, don't worry too much about Walter's," Carol Olmstead was saying. "New buyers are coming into the market every day. You've got a hotshot sales manager. One of the best. He's hustling right now."

"It's the meanwhile I'm worried about," Marianne said. "The Chinese are more finicky about selling to companies that can't show a good balance sheet than I had anticipated. Unless I doctor Casey's, we won't stand up under hard scrutiny."

"Not to worry," Carol said. "Jim has promised to back you at the next board meeting."

"Back me? But I thought Billings had already decided to do that."

"Well—yes. But one or two are having second thoughts."

"Who? Felton Knox?"

"Well, you know Felton."

"I know Felton. And it's no comfort."

"They said they'd give you a chance, and Jim is going to hold them to it. As soon as he can he'll see that the treasurer forwards a financial statement of the corporation plus a covering letter to let the Chinese know we're responsible for Casey. You'll get those papers if I have to forge them myself."

"Oh, Carol, how can I ever . . ."

"Win, Marianne! Win a favorable contract. The only way we can prove that you've got the know-how is to swing an important deal."

Karen had returned from Nanjing steamed up not only about the Bishop but about the Blessed Angels as well, her decision to join them reaffirmed. The worst of it was that she now had Sarah on her side. Marianne couldn't quite fathom that mystery. Atheist, Maoist, Sarah Oliver saying maybe it would be a good thing if Karen spent time at Christhaven?

"She'll get a taste of communal living," Sarah said simply.

It was Sunday. The three of them were at the Orchid Gardens. Sarah and Marianne were sitting on the veranda of the teahouse while Karen was leaning over the rail a few feet away, throwing bread crumbs to a crowd of golden carp in the lotus-padded pond below.

"She'll get more than that," Marianne said. "She'll get a strong dose of distorted values. I read one of the tracts Karen brought over. 'Forsake all those who are not blessed and holy. Cleave to your real brethren and sisters. Your true mother is not always one of the same flesh and blood, but one of the spirit.' That kind of brainwash."

Sarah, gazing thoughtfully at her granddaughter, said, "Karen's too smart to be taken in by such nonsense. It will fall away. Her lesson will be in getting along with people, pulling together, learning to subordinate her personal wishes for the good of the group."

"Mother, you don't believe that Christhaven is anything like one of your communes?"

"I think it is, very much so."

Why are you doing this? Marianne wanted to ask. Why are you deliberately turning my daughter against me?

"Don't you think Karen ought to listen to her mother? It seems to me that the Chinese lay great stress on filial respect and obedience."

"They certainly do. I'm not advising Karen to go against your wishes. I'm only hoping you can bring yourself to see her point of view."

"But that's so unrealistic." She had wanted to say "insane." "You haven't any idea what these cults are like. And no matter how you or Karen twist the argument, I can't see Karen quitting school and running off with the Blessed Angels."

A flush stained Sarah's cheeks. "The last thing I wanted was for Karen to run off. We always seem to be at cross purposes, don't we?"

"I try not to argue with you, Mother. We don't agree on politics. Okay. That's understood. But when it comes to my child, I think I should have the last word."

"But you do. I'm merely pointing out—"

"I know, I know," Marianne interrupted impatiently.

Sarah looked away, her mouth set firmly.

Karen turned from the veranda rail. "Are you two fighting?"

"We're not fighting," Marianne said defensively. "Just a difference of opinion."

She shouldn't let Sarah anger her. Her mother was entitled to speak her mind. What difference did it make what she said? In a week she and Karen would be gone. She might never see Sarah again.

Karen cocked her head. "It's too nice a day to argue."

For once the sky was cloudless, a pale, washed-out blue. It was cooler, too. The wide-branched trees protecting the veranda from the sun threw pleasant shadows over them.

"I love their roofs, don't you?" Karen said, raising her eyes to the green arched roof.

They remained in silence for a minute or two, then Sarah said, "You'll be having a birthday in ten days, won't you, Marianne?"

"Yes." She remembers, Marianne thought with surprise and a rush of sudden warmth. I didn't think she would. All these years and she hasn't forgotten. Will I ever understand this woman?

"Thirty-six," Sarah mused.

Sarah pushed back a thin lock of hair that had sprung loose from the braided coil at the nape of her neck. In the leaf-speckled light her face, scored with wrinkles, looked old and sad. Marianne's heart constricted. Was Brad right? she wondered. Have I become hard, unforgiving? Sometimes I feel—as I do now—compassion for my mother that comes very close to love, and at other times I get so damn mad and resentful I can hardly contain myself. All those years growing up I had Sarah in my head as a sweet and loving soul who'd open her heart and arms to me and embrace me with tears of joy. But that was a childish fantasy. Poor Mother. It isn't her fault she didn't turn out to match the dream.

Karen, moving from the rail, put her arm around her grandmother. "She's my pal. Aren't you, Grandma?"

"I hope so." An upward glance—a look of love.

The look triggered something in Marianne she would have preferred not to acknowledge. Her feelings toward Sarah were complicated enough without having to deal with jealousy, too. Yet she was jealous of the relationship between her mother and daughter, jealous of their easy camaraderie, the looks they exchanged, the smiles. It was ridiculous. A grown woman jealous of her own daughter.

"Shall we go?" Marianne asked. She was expecting another overseas call from Carol Olmstead. "Or, if you wish, you two can stay."

Karen said, "Grandma was going to show me a Buddhist temple, Luirong Si. Did I pronounce it right?"

"You did fine. Do we have your permission, Marianne?"

"Certainly. How about taxi fare, Karen?"

Sarah tucked her lips in. "There's no need for that. I can well afford to treat my granddaughter."

At four-fifteen Marianne, still waiting for her overseas call, answered the ringing phone to hear a quavery-voiced Sarah at the other end.

"What is it?" Her heart turned over. Sarah did not make a habit of calling.

"It's Karen. No—no, she's all right. She had a fall, broke her arm, but the doctor is putting it in a cast. She'll be all right. I just thought I'd let you know."

"Where are you? The Foreign Clinic? I'll come right over."

"It's all right, Marianne." Sarah's voice had a firmer ring to it now. "I'll bring Karen to the hotel. No need for you to be here. We'll be ready to go in a few minutes."

Marianne hung up, wondering what next. God, how she wished this whole business was finished and she could go home.

A half hour later Sarah and Karen arrived. Karen,

pale, her eyes haunted with recent pain, had her arm in a cast.

"I fell," she said. "Somebody pushed me and I fell down the stairs. It was the weirdest feeling, all those little golden Buddhas in their niches flashing by. Lucky I didn't go to the bottom."

"What do you mean somebody pushed you?" Marianne asked anxiously, remembering her own near miss at the textile factory. "Not on purpose, I hope."

Sarah explained. "There was a crowd of sightseers. We were at Hua Ta, the temple pagoda. Karen wanted to climb the inner staircase. I waited—nine stories is too much for me. And she was starting down, and those people in back of her, I suppose, were impatient."

"I guess I lost my balance," Karen said.

Shaking the frightening picture of a falling Karen from her mind, Marianne moved to where Karen sat and gently took her face in her hands. "I'm so glad you're all right."

Turning to Sarah, Marianne said, "Mother, why don't you stay? Can I get you something, a piece of fruit?"

"No, thank you. I must be getting back." She looked uncomfortable, her dark blue skirt and blouse shabby in contrast to the elegant furnishings. Marianne had brought her a tan and cream pantsuit and another of lime green as gifts from home. Thus far Marianne had seen her in neither.

"I'll go down with you," Marianne offered. "And get you a taxi."

"It isn't necessary," her mother said primly. "I've ridden in elevators before."

There was that impenetrable pride again.

"Goodbye, child," Sarah said to Karen. "Take care of yourself."

Karen threw her grandmother a kiss as she went out the door.

Karen got up from her chair, walked around the sofa, then flopped down on it, holding her plaster-coated arm stiffly in front of her. "That ties it! A broken arm."

"You'll have to stay," Marianne said. "I can't let you go back to school in that condition."

"Why not? What can you do here to make it heal faster? Doctor said six weeks. Might as well be six years."

"Do you mind staying on here in Canton all that much?"

Karen plucked at her cast meditatively. "I dunno." Her mouth twitched. "Actually, I guess not."

"You seem to be enjoying yourself. A side trip to Nanjing. You and Grandmother trotting around to temples, churches."

"Yeah. You'd be surprised how many places there are like that just in Canton. Could you beat it? In a socialist country, too. Shows you can't do without religion, though Grandma disagrees."

"But you like her. You find a lot to talk about."

"Oh, yes!" Karen's dark eyes lit up. "She *knows* so much. I can ask her any question about Buddha, Mohammed, or even Christ and she'll give me the answer. She was explaining about the Buddhist monk, let's see if I can get the right name, Bod—Bodhidharma, the founder of Zen."

Again Marianne felt a pang of envy. Why was it so hard for her and Sarah to find things to talk about? What have I done to earn this silence, this wall between us, she wondered bitterly. But it's easier for grandparents to get along with their grandchildren, skipping a generation, she reminded herself once more. Grandmothers, freed of responsibility, the daily irritations of child raising, come to the relationship without heavy baggage. They can talk, laugh, enjoy, have fun.

Marianne got up to place a pillow behind Karen's back and the phone rang.

Again it wasn't Carol, but Dorothy Hansford.

"Hello, Marianne. It's Dot, Dot Hansford. I hope you haven't forgotten us. . . ."

Marianne had. Completely.

"I know how busy you are. But we heard that Karen is here with you now, and we were wondering if you're both free this evening. We could all have dinner down-stairs."

"Dinner won't be possible, Mrs. Hansford," Marianne said. "I'm expecting an overseas call and Karen's broken her arm."

Karen, raising her voice, said, "Who is it, Moms? Did you say Hansford?"

"We'll have to make it some other time," Marianne went on. "My schedule is very tight—"

"Who is it, Moms? Somebody with the same name as me?"

"Just a minute." Marianne put her hand over the mouthpiece. The moment of truth had come. There was no easy way she could lie about it. Dorothy couldn't be put off. She'd only call again.

"It's Dorothy Hansford."

"Who?"

"Dorothy Hansford."

"My dad's mother? Here in Canton?"

It grated to have Karen refer to Dorothy with such eager curiosity. "She and her husband are touring China."

"Well, I'll be. . . . Do we get to see her, or are you still mad?"

"We are speaking, but barely."

"Let's have dinner, then."

"Not dinner." The thought of sitting through a lengthy meal with Dorothy and Ed Hansford was more than Marianne could contemplate. Dorothy would chatter endlessly while Ed would look on, silent and morose.

"Please, Moms?" Karen wasn't about to give up.

Marianne acquiesced. "Suppose we just limit it to a cup of tea for now. I really can't be too far from a telephone."

Dorothy fluttered and fretted over her newly discovered granddaughter in a sustained flow of words, wanting to know how the accident had happened, if the Chinese doctor could be trusted, if he knew anything about proper casts, about X-rays.

Ed did not speak but kept staring at Karen. Marianne

noticed that for a few moments his eyes grew suspiciously moist. She could guess why. Looking at Karen he saw Toby. As she grew older Karen's resemblance to her father became more pronounced. She had the same dark, curling hair, the same shape to her nose and mouth. Even the intent way she listened, head cocked to one side, was so like Toby. And for a few moments while Dorothy rattled on, Marianne thought of her dead husband with a sudden poignant sadness she hadn't felt in years. What a pity he couldn't be here to see Karen now. If he had lived, would their lives have been different? Would she have taken a different road, been less career-minded, less assertive, less driven? Toby had wanted her to have a profession, had encouraged her to finish her education. Would he have resented her career later? She would never know. They had been so young then, so unformed, united lovingly in a short marriage that never had a chance to prove itself.

"And what are you planning to major in at college, Karen, dear?" Dorothy asked. Before Marianne could intervene, Karen explained that she was forgoing college and launched into a detailed account of life with the Blessed Angels.

She described the cult, the biblically named hierarchy, the devotees, the dogma, the rituals, the "hugging and good fellowship"; Christhaven, with its unsprayed radishes and lettuces; the chapel, with its hand-hewn pews; the mess hall; the after-dinner songfests.

For once, an habitually effusive Dorothy had nothing to say.

CHAPTER XXIV

GREGORY WAS IN AN UNUSUALLY MELLOW MOOD.

"Something good must have happened today," Marianne said. "You're so agreeable."

"I'm always agreeable."

They were sitting on the beige sofa in Gregory's suite. Gregory, his feet propped up on the coffee table, was sipping Hennessey cognac.

"How's my Blessed Angel?" Gregory quipped, acknowledging Karen's accident.

"She overdid it today. Went to bed early. I gave her a pain pill so she'll be sure to have a decent rest. She needs it. But I can't stay long."

"Oh, Christ."

"I don't like leaving her with that arm."

"She's got Hollis. And a telephone, if she really needs you."

"Yes, I suppose. But still . . ."

"Relax." He ruffled her hair.

She sighed heavily. "I should. But I can't seem to."

"Sure you can." He put his arm around her shoulders

and drew her around, his mouth prodding hers open, the hot tongue darting in, finding hers, probing and tasting.

"*Mmm.*"

She loved that growl deep in his throat. Lifting his feet from the coffee table, he moved, shifting Marianne under him, kissing her again and again with increasing fervor. The length of his body, heavy on hers, his seeking tongue and mouth stopped the breath in her lungs and she groaned. He rolled to the floor, bringing her with him so that she lay on top. His mouth clung to hers, not letting go. Molding her to his body, he pressed her buttocks into his swollen erection. How quickly he could take over her senses, make her forget, even only momentarily, the present. How swiftly he could bring her to yearning desire, to passion.

"'Hey!'" He reached under her dress, tugging at her undergarments. He staggered a little as he lifted her in his arms.

"Too many *dim sum*," he muttered, nuzzling her breasts. He took a nipple in his mouth, giving it a little nip.

Carrying her to the bed, he stumbled, dropping Marianne on the coverlet, where she gave a little bound. She started to laugh, but he was on her, smothering the sound, his mouth claiming hers in a long, hungry kiss.

"I love you," he said, lifting his head, kissing each breast in turn. His mouth trailed downward and she closed her eyes, letting herself float along in sheer sensual pleasure. His mouth, touching and testing, took her further and further away from the irksome day-to-day world. She didn't have to think, only to feel. And as he made love her excitement increased and she could hear herself panting, a husky, breathless sound. When he sought and found the core of her femininity, a sheer animalism gripped her. She clung to him, clutching his hair, passion mounting inside her, rising on a tidal wave of pure sensation. The crash, when it came, shook her with an uncontrollable series of spasms, racing through her in shuddering ecstasy.

He mounted her, thrusting into her iron-hard, the erotic

friction tossing her on that rising wave again. Kneading his heaving back, she muffled a scream as she climaxed again two beats before he gave a gasp, exploding in one final burst.

He lay sprawled over her, murmuring, "I love you."

Why did she doubt him? Why were there always lingering suspicions, thoughts of Lily Sung?

Gregory rolled away and pulled her close. His skin was warm, the muscles under her cheek hard and reassuring.

"You're having a birthday next week, aren't you, sweet?" he asked after a brief silence. "What is it, twenty-nine?"

"Naturally."

"We'll celebrate. A banquet at the Ban Xi—how's that?"

"Sounds like fun. I've never had a Chinese birthday party."

"I'll let you do the inviting."

"I'll invite my mother, of course. Karen, Hollis. And I think I ought to invite Brad."

"Why him?"

"He's a long-time friend," she said. "He'd be hurt if I excluded him."

"All right, it's your birthday. Who else?"

"I'd like to ask three members of the CHINATEX team."

Gregory rose on an elbow. "What the hell for? Haven't you seen enough of that crowd?"

"This is a social occasion."

He flopped back on the pillow. "I get it. Trying to get the jump on me, huh?"

"Nothing of the sort. I like them. Mr. Lu is charming—interesting, too. Mr. Boa knows the family of the girl Jimmy Kwong wants to marry and says he'll put in a good word. And Mr. Wei was once a student of my mother's. All three of them have been with the CHINATEX committee from the start, and after four weeks they seem like old friends. But if you object—"

"Hell, no. It's your birthday. Invite the whole gang. Genghis Khan, if that tickles your fancy."

Marianne leaned against the headboard and tilted her chin to have a better look at Gregory's face.

"It won't spoil things for you?"

"Why should it?" He smiled, chucking her under the chin. "No, honestly, I think it's great. It's your party, whatever you say."

"I suppose I should have Jerry and his wife. Golch, too. Kwong will beg off. He's too busy with Liyan these days. I can't think of anyone else. Give me a day or two and I'll let you know definitely." She swung her legs over the side of the bed.

"Where you going?"

"I've got to get back. There's Karen, you know. And I'm still waiting for a call from New York, plus I have some paperwork to do. I have an early meeting tomorrow morning with the team."

He slid over to where Marianne sat, circling her chest with his arms, fondling her breasts. "Another ten minutes?"

"No. I really must go."

She rose and went into the other room, where her clothes lay strewn about the floor. She began gathering hose, shoes, slip, dress.

"You really want that contract, don't you?" Gregory called to her from his bed, annoyed that she had other things on her mind besides him.

"Haven't you asked me that question before?"

"I don't remember."

"Yes. I do want it. Very much."

She headed toward the bathroom. He followed. "Do you think you'll get it?"

"I'm certain I will." She started to close the door. He put his hand out and held it.

"It won't be the end of the world if you don't, you know."

"I don't care about the end of the world. All I know is that when I go home I'm going with a piece of paper in my hand that says Casey has bought a load of silk from China."

"Winning isn't everything, Marianne."

"It's the only thing, Gregory Windham! I learned that from you." She pushed his hand away and shut the door.

*   *   *

As soon as she came into the room where CHINATEX
was holding their meeting, Marianne could sense a change
in the atmosphere. There was a stiff formality, a distance that hadn't been there since their first encounter.
Everyone was sober-faced, including Mr. Lu, who until
now had never been without a smile.

After the preliminary cups of tea and an exchange of
polite inquiries, Mr. Lu cleared his throat.

"We have had long discussion about your offer, Miss
Oliver, which we appreciate was made in good faith.
So sorry, but we find it too low."

Marianne fought to keep her voice calm and businesslike. "How much too low?"

"A dollar fifty."

"All right. I'll raise it a dollar. But that's my top and
final price."

"I'm so sorry, Miss Oliver. It is still too low."

"I see," she said.

"I will be honest with you," Mr. Lu said. "I believe
your competitor would be willing to outbid you no matter what figure you gave us. He's very anxious to get
our product."

"May I ask who this anxious competitor is?" She had
a feeling she already knew.

"I don't think that would be proper."

Jerry spoke. "This competitor can't be serious."

"Maybe, yes. We have not come to a concluding
agreement yet. But we are wanting to get the best price."

"Naturally," Marianne said. "But I can't imagine how
anyone, even producing in volume, could pay such a
high price for raw material that must go through several
costly operations before it becomes a salable fabric."

Mr. Lu folded his hands. "That, of course, is the
bidder's problem."

Would Gregory lose money just to outwit her? Ridiculous. He was too much of a businessman for that.

"So you say it's not final?" Marianne asked. It was
obvious that one of her competitors had known in advance what her highest bid would be. It was too precise

to be chance. Someone in her own group must have leaked the information.

"Not final." If Mr. Lu's smile was meant to be reassuring his next words were not. "But we have questions about Casey." He conferred with his colleagues in Chinese. Kwong scribbled a hasty note and shoved it across the table to Marianne.

They're worried about the company's ability to pay. There's a rumor you're losing customers. Someone's put a bug in their ear.

Marianne wrote back. *That's no bug. That's inside info.*

Mr. Lu turned to Marianne. "We would like more specifics on tax returns, the latest profit and loss data?"

"Billings is sending a more detailed report," Marianne said. "They will reaffirm financial backing for Casey."

Mr. Lu was silent while the CHINATEX interpreter relayed the message to the others.

"You must understand," Mr. Lu said, "that this recent happening has nothing to do with you—ah—personally." He smiled again, a small dimple pulsing at the corner of his finely drawn mouth. "We find dealing with you a pleasure."

"Thank you. The pleasure operates both ways. You are not only hospitable but most kind. It's been an enjoyable experience and I'm still hoping it will end on a mutually satisfying note."

"We all hope."

Later at the White Swan Marianne held a meeting of her own. "There's been a leak." She looked around at the faces. Though no one came out and denied it, they looked surprised.

"They're guessing," Jerry said. "The Chinese are canny, sharp as dog's teeth. Why shouldn't they be, when they've been trading with foreigners for over thirty-five hundred years? It's in their blood."

Golch spoke. "I have a suggestion." An older man

with a white, bushy mustache, he was neat-appearing, always in a three-piecer even in the worst heat. "Perhaps we could all take lie detector tests."

Marianne let Golch's sarcasm pass.

After the meeting, Marianne had Hollis send another telex to Carol at Billings requesting a hurry-up on the financial report. Then she called Gregory, inviting herself over for a late afternoon drink. She was going to quit pussyfooting around, have it out with him. It angered her to think someone might be getting a blow-by-blow account of her group's private deliberations.

Gregory was in an expansive mood when Marianne arrived. His hearty greeting aroused her suspicions.

He fixed them both a drink, the soda still fizzing as he handed one to Marianne. "Over the phone you sounded like you had something serious on your mind."

"I do. I want to talk about my little exercise here in Canton."

He raised his brows in mock surprise. "Ah—let me guess. You regret going to bed with a heel like me. You don't love me, never have—"

"Oh, stop it, Gregory. Be sensible. I'm talking about CHINATEX."

His face smoothed out into lines of sobriety. "You know my rule, Marianne. Never mix business with—"

"Pleasure. Well, your rule isn't mine. I'm mixing. And I won't keep you in suspense. Somebody is outbidding me, somebody who is aware of my highest figure."

"Are you sure?"

"Pretty sure. What's more, this person—whoever—is also aware of Casey's financial difficulties and is hinting we're insolvent."

"I warned you this wasn't a tennis match."

"I want a straight answer, Gregory. Was it you?"

He got up, hands in his pockets, and looked down at her. "Want another drink?"

"Was it you?"

"It wasn't me," he said, taking a handful of peanuts from the bowl on the coffee table.

"I wish I could believe you."

He paused, a peanut between thumb and forefinger. He sat down beside her. "We're not going to fight about this, are we? You see what I meant when I said we should leave business out? Out." He popped the peanut into his mouth.

"I know how much you want this contract, and I have the sneaking feeling you want to beat me out of it just to teach me a lesson."

"Marianne, you've been seeing too many movies."

"Have I?"

He rubbed his jaw. "I hate this. You're accusing me of stealing company secrets without one shred of evidence. You don't need inside information to guess at a rival's bid. As for Casey's solvency, I'm sure you had to give CHINATEX some kind of guarantee. They could figure it out for themselves."

"Maybe. But my hunch—"

"Hunch! Are you talking about feminine intuition?"

"And what's wrong with that?"

"Look, Marianne, let's get this whole thing straight. I love you. There's no question about *that*, I hope? Okay. I love you. But once you step out as my competitor in the business world, I'm not going to treat you and Casey any differently than another firm who's bidding against me."

"I didn't expect you to. I just don't want to be fighting against odds that are rigged."

"I'm not rigging your odds, Marianne. However, that doesn't mean others aren't or won't. You seem to forget that there are more than two of us trying for that contract. Dan Hopper of Pantex, for instance. When he zeroes in on a deal he doesn't stand politely at the gate and say 'After you, ladies.' It's not me, Marianne."

She didn't know what to believe now. Gregory seemed so sincere. But sincerity was part of his stock in trade. "I fooled him," he had told her, speaking of his father. He had fooled Sung, too, sleeping with his wife for how many years?

"Marianne," he chided, "get that awful look off your face." He put his arm around her and kissed her ten-

derly on the lips, on the cheek, pushing back her hair,
trailing kisses across her forehead. "I love you. I want
to marry you. Come on, smile for me."

Marianne smiled, though she had the urge to weep.
Nothing had been resolved. The doubts and suspicions
still lingered, faint, like cobwebbed shadows on the edge
of her mind.

Marianne needed to talk to someone. She couldn't
discuss her problem with anyone in her group. One of
them might be leaking information to the opposition.
Consulting with Carol long distance on a static-filled
international phone line was too frustrating.

Brad was her only candidate. She knew he disliked
Gregory, but she also knew he could be highly rational,
putting his personal feelings aside long enough to give
her some perspective on the situation.

He was guarded when she telephoned him. She ignored his cautious hello and plunged in.

"I'd like to see you, Brad. Frankly, I'm in a bind here
and need some advice. I can't explain over the phone.
Could we take one of our walks this evening?"

"All right," he agreed, after a slight hesitation.

The days were lengthening, the overcast May sky
holding gray light well past six, subtly darkening into a
black night. The lamps on the riverboats were beginning
to go on, glimmering yellow in the gathering murkiness.
As Brad and Marianne walked a fishing sampan, its
two-man crew mending a huge butterflylike net, bobbed
near the shore.

"So you see," Marianne said, finishing her story,
"one of my competitors has an inside track. There's got
to be a leak."

"Who do you suspect?"

"On my team? I can't imagine. When I first knew
Jerry I sized him up as someone I could trust implicitly.
I would never have thought that he would risk his professional reputation by playing the spy. He's a cynic, a
jokester, doesn't like the Chinese, but from what I heard
he would always try to work out a deal to benefit his

client. But now I'm not too sure. He's having financial problems. His wife is on a spending spree. I saw her yesterday wearing a recent purchase around her neck, a string of matched pink pearls, the very expensive kind that practically glow in the dark. I've already given Jerry an advance on his fee. He's borrowed from Kwong and from Golch. If anyone is open to accepting a little extra under the table, Jerry is."

"But no actual proof. Just a suspicion."

"Right. Then there's Hollis. She came highly recommended for honesty and loyalty. I have a feeling she'd like to get ahead, so I don't think she'd risk her future by getting mixed up with a payoff. She's pretty sensible. She may not be my closest friend, but I believe she's solid. Kwong? I feel the same about him. The lawyer, Golch? A man of his standing in the international legal hierarchy? No way. Of course, there is—or was—Art Schultz. Poor Art, I don't think he had it in him."

"A monetary bribe, if it's high enough, can be very tempting."

"But we're not dealing with gold or diamonds. Just raw silk. How much would anyone pay for information where a textile is concerned?"

"Hard to say. Could your suite have been bugged?"

"We looked. If it was, the apparatus has since been removed or is in such an unlikely place we'll never find it."

"Then maybe that's your possibility. Let's assume for argument's sake it was or is bugged. An employee of the hotel could have paid to let someone in to set up a listening device."

"The hotel staff is very carefully screened. But you may be right."

"Okay. Let's assume we are. Then the next question is who's got his ear to the keyhole? My bet is Gregory Windham."

"Because you don't like him."

"Because he's just the type who would. He's known as a determined, if not ruthless, fighter. Do you question that?"

"No. But so is Dan Hopper of Pantex. And I wouldn't put Philippine Silk above ruthless, either."

Brad grunted.

"I've asked Gregory," Marianne said. "He denies passing any information about me to CHINATEX."

Brad looked at her, his eyes widening. "You didn't expect him to admit it?"

No, she thought, I didn't. But to Brad she said, "I expected him to tell me the truth."

"Suppose it was Gregory," Brad said. "Could you go on defending him, knowing that he was trying to freeze you out any way he could?"

"It wasn't Gregory," she said firmly. But how could she be sure after what he'd said to her—"Once you step out as my competitor, I'm not going to treat you any different than the others."

"You haven't answered my question," Brad said.

"I don't answer hypothetical questions." She was in too deep with Gregory, her emotions were too entangled, a web of feelings rooted in Gregory in a way she'd never thought possible.

"Shall we sit?" Brad indicated a bench at the river's edge. They crossed the street. "I never understood what you see in Windham," Brad said.

Marianne wiped the damp sheen from the bench's wooden slats with a Kleenex and they settled themselves side by side, studying the river in meditative silence. On the opposite bank lights appeared, glowing like pinpointed stars in the purple evening. A river junk with a high laddered sail swept grandly by, the voice of the crew coming to them on the breeze.

Marianne's thoughts gravitated to Gregory. What *did* she see in him? The very things that had attracted her to him, made her doubt him now. Gregory Windham was a doer, audacious, bold. To Marianne in her early years at Billings, still bucking sexual prejudice and working hard to make herself known, these qualities seemed admirable. She had been attracted by Gregory's masculine vigor, by his self-assurance, by his firm belief in himself.

No weak hesitations, no uncertainties for him. "Ruthlessness" had meant courageous risk taking then.

And later, after Hong Kong and Lily, after she had thought she was finished with him, she rediscovered the tender side of Gregory. The night he had opened up about Charlie, the outpouring of his grief had bridged her mistrust.

Why did she have it now? He had sworn that he had had nothing to do with furnishing Casey information to the Chinese. She wanted to believe him, just as she wanted to believe he really loved her.

"You have a birthday next week," Brad said.

"Yes. Gregory is giving me a banquet. I was hoping you'd come."

"I don't see why my being there should matter. With Gregory—"

"Please, Brad," Marianne implored wearily. "For old time's sake."

"Old time's sake. How appropriate. I'll be there."

"Good. The Ban Xi. On Wednesday. At six."

It didn't dawn on Marianne until she got back to her suite at the White Swan that Brad knew everything there was to know about the game plan for the CHINATEX contract. He knew about Casey, too—its shaky foundation, her presidency contingent upon pulling it out of the red. He knew much too much for a man who was not eager for her to come away the victor.

Was there anyone in Canton she could really trust?

CHAPTER XXV

MARIANNE WAS EXAMINING A RACK OF SILK KIMONOS IN the hotel's boutique when she saw a woman resembling Lily peering through the glass show window. It was only a brief glance, for as soon as the woman's eyes—blazing with hostility—met Marianne's, she withdrew. Curious, Marianne went to the door to look, but the woman had already disappeared among the stream of shoppers.

She chided herself for harboring feelings of jealousy and suspicion about Lily. The woman wasn't worth that much emotional attention. Marianne had more important things on her mind.

But despite her earnest intent to dismiss Lily from her thoughts, Gregory's former mistress continued to intrude. That night Marianne could have sworn Lily was following her.

She and Stan Golch had been discussing the procedure for establishing letters of credit for Casey with the Bank of China. Their talk had taken place at Golch's hotel and had lasted past midnight. Marianne was returning by taxi and was within a few blocks of the White Swan when the vehicle broke down. Impatient, anxious to get to bed, she paid the driver off and proceeded on foot. The street was intermittently and dimly lit, the arcade shops boarded up for the night. Except for an occasional silent cyclist, the roadway and sidewalk were deserted. After the hordes that moved, thronged, and jostled in a never-ending stream during the day, the city seemed like a ghost town evacuated by a sudden mass exodus. The silence, the absence of pedestrians seemed eerie, but Marianne had no fear of walking alone. Though statistics cited the crime rate in China as increasing, muggings and robberies—against foreigners in particular—were still rare.

Nevertheless, Marianne had only gone a short distance when she had the uneasy feeling that she was being followed. It was the same escalating fear she had experienced that night in Oak Park. She tried to tell herself that she was tired, that her imagination was working overtime.

A car with only its parking lights on (in compliance with an ordinance which forbade bright headlights at night) swished by, chasing shadows in and out between the arcade posts. Marianne had the crazy impulse to call after it as darkness swallowed its red taillights. There wasn't even a bicycle rider now, just herself and the following presence, the click-click tapping of heeled shoes.

She went on, thinking that maybe the footsteps she was hearing were simply an echo. But the insidious sounds weren't an echo. They were footsteps. Ahead of her a shaft of light escaping from a shuttered window shone like a small beacon. She passed through it, hearing voices in Cantonese within, a strange babble that heightened her feeling of moving through a hostile world. Were the footsteps getting closer? She slowed her walk so the person behind could overtake her and go by. Whoever it was seemed to do the same. Marianne thought of what she could possibly use as a weapon. Her purse? Not heavy enough. Her eyes swiveled to the left and right searching for a heavy piece of wood or a brick. But darkness and her hurrying pace limited her vision. She felt panic then, a feeling of utter helplessness and terror. She fought the urge to run. Turning quickly at the next corner, she slipped behind an empty high-sided cart that had been pulled up on the sidewalk.

A woman appeared. Dressed in slacks and a dark ankle-length hooded cape. She paused at the curb under the streetlight, staring intently across to the opposite pavement. Then, turning in profile to look up and down the arcade, she drew back the hood.

It was Lily.

"I saw her. She's here in Canton."

"What am I supposed to say? She and Sung come to Canton frequently. I have nothing to do with her, haven't for years. I swear it." Gregory was annoyed. It was one-thirty A.M. and Marianne's call had roused him from a sound sleep.

"She was following me!" Marianne's voice rose.

"Are you sure?"

"I saw her twice. Once this morning outside the boutique downstairs, then tonight when I was on the street."

"Look, there must be dozens of Chinese women who resemble Lily." Damn Lily! he cursed silently. I should have put her on that plane myself. "And even if it was Lily, why should she be following you?"

"I thought *you* could tell *me*."

"Oh, Christ, Marianne. First it was someone spying on your team, now Lily Sung's following you. Be reasonable."

"I am being very reasonable," Marianne said.

The next morning Gregory called Sung. They discussed the recent meeting between British diplomats and Hong Kong businessmen.

"Don't know any more about the conditions of relinquishing the lease than you do, Gregory. Just wait and see."

"How's Lily?" Gregory asked casually.

"Fine. She's in Canton this week. Went to visit an aunt. I thought you might have seen her."

Was there a subtle message in that last statement? Did Sung know? It wasn't the first time Gregory had asked himself that question. But even if he knew, he'd never confront Gregory. Admitting his wife was having an affair would mean losing face.

"Well, give her my love," Gregory said.

"Will do."

Gregory tried to think of a way he could trace Lily. She had followed him once before—to Delhi, where he had gone to attend a textile trade conference. She had registered at another hotel under the name of Anna Bing, a woman who had owned a whorehouse in Kowloon and who had befriended Lily in her early days.

He began dialing the hotels and could hardly believe it when on the second try he found Lily at the Sheng Li.

"Gregory, darling! I'm so glad—"

"Cut the shit, Lily. I know what you're up to. And don't try to blackmail me. I've told you before, I don't give a damn if Sung knows or not. I think he does. As for Marianne—I've told her everything. If I hear you've been following her again, I'll come over there and drag you all the way back to Hong Kong by the heels."

"Go to hell," Lily said, and hung up.

Marianne was getting anxious. She hadn't heard from Carol since their last conversation. Hadn't received the Billings papers. Hadn't received a plausible explanation from Gregory about Lily.

Gregory had been so cagey. He had called back the morning after her scary episode on the way to her hotel through deserted streets and said that Lily was at home in Hong Kong. But Marianne had the feeling that he was trying to hide something.

"Moms!" Karen called, interrupting her thoughts. They were in the suite, Marianne on the sofa with an unread *Wall Street Journal* on her lap, Karen on the phone. "It's Brad. He's coming to the hotel to lend me a book he wants me to read. He'd like both of us to have dinner with him. I said okay. Is it?"

"Well, I'm—"

"Expecting a phone call. Hollis will get it and have you paged."

"Well, I don't know."

"What's the matter, Moms? Are you mad at Uncle Brad about something?"

"Of course not. I'll be glad to have dinner."

In the afternoon Karen went out shopping for paper cutouts and chops (seals) to take back with her. At six she called Marianne to say she was waiting to have names carved on the chops she had bought, and would Marianne go on and meet Brad without her?

"I'll get there as soon as I can, Moms. Save me a place."

At present Karen seemed the safest subject. In the past there wasn't anything she and Brad couldn't talk about, but now she shied away from mentioning Lily, Gregory, Sarah, or her dealings with CHINATEX for fear of treading on dangerous ground.

Marianne also mentioned she had bumped into the Hansfords. They too had become a safe topic. "You'll be pleased to know that I had a long talk with Dorothy. In fact, she invited me up to their room, and I went."

Brad's eyes registered approval. "That's good news, Marianne. I hope you'll let them see Karen."

"I already have. We had tea with them in the Terrace Room."

"Really? Great! What brought about this change?"

"Oh, I don't know. Dorothy broke into tears in the lobby. She seemed so pathetic."

"I had the same impression. I felt sorry for them both."

"I did, too, at first. But Dorothy, even in sorrow, has a way of manipulating people. I don't trust her."

"She can't do much harm now when you hold the trump card—namely, Karen." Glancing past her shoulder, his face suddenly brightened. "Speak of the little devil, here she is."

Karen, somewhat breathless, carrying a tote bag filled with packages in her good hand, slid into the booth next to Brad. "Sorry, but they told me it wouldn't take long, and it just did."

She fished in the bag and held up a chop, a small stone seal the Chinese use to stamp their names on letters and documents. "I got three of them—one for Father Jacob, one for Mother Ruth, and one for myself."

"They make nice souvenirs," Brad commented.

They went on to talk about the best places to shop in Canton, Karen maintaining the real bargains were to be had in the local stores on Beijing Road.

It was a pleasant meal, almost like old times on Amsterdam Avenue, Marianne felt. They were eating dessert when Dorothy and Ed walked into the restaurant. Dorothy saw them at once. With Ed trailing behind, she came up to their table.

"Hello, Marianne!—Brad!—Karen! Imagine, here you all are! What a coincidence! We're not barging in, are we? How's the arm, Karen? I was just asking Ed why he thought we hadn't heard from you again, Marianne. We had such a lovely chat the other day, and it seemed to me—"

"Won't you sit down?" Brad invited. "We're almost finished, but you could join us for a cup of coffee."

The invitation annoyed Marianne. Not only was she anxious to get back upstairs, but another session with the Hansfords so soon after the last was depleting her small store of goodwill toward them.

They didn't refuse. They sat and talked, or rather Dorothy and Karen talked. Marianne had never known Karen to be so gabby. She had always been somewhat reticent among adults, but now it was as though she had suddenly found her voice. Canton seemed to have put her on a kind of high. She had scads to say to Sarah, to Brad, and now to Dorothy Hansford. Was it the missionary zeal of the Blessed Angels that had loosened her tongue? Or was Karen simply growing up and away from her?

"Why don't you two come to our banquet?" Marianne heard Karen say to Dorothy. "It's Moms's birthday at the Ban Xi and will be a real bash."

Marianne could have strangled her. The Hansfords were the last people she would ever invite to a personal celebration.

Dorothy latched on to the invitation with a gushing

enthusiasm that irritated Marianne all the more. "I wouldn't miss it for the world! Imagine! What an occasion! It will be like old times."

What old times? Marianne wanted to ask.

Sarah had been planning a little birthday celebration of her own for Marianne and was disappointed when she heard that a birthday banquet was being given by Gregory Windham, the American tycoon who was courting her daughter. She did not know if she wanted to go to the Ban Xi. They would dine in one of the rooms reserved for wealthy American tourists and she would feel awkward, out of place. How much pleasanter it would have been if they could have had their birthday meal in cozier surroundings with good people. The food might have been humbler—diced vegetables and fish rather than suckling pig—but just as tasty. However, she supposed that her daughter preferred a banquet. She hadn't met Gregory Windham. She understood from Brad he was a wealthy capitalist, one of those who had made enormous sums of money by exploiting the poor. Was Marianne going to marry him?

"I'd be hurt if you didn't come," Marianne had said.

Marianne hadn't the slightest idea how difficult it would be for her mother to sit through a formal dinner with strangers. But Sarah couldn't see how she could gracefully refuse.

On the morning of Marianne's birthday Karen came down with a slight fever. The doctor prescribed some white pills and advised her to curb her activities for a day or two.

"I'll call the banquet off," Marianne said, recalling only too vividly the time in Chicago when Karen's cold had developed into pneumonia. "You can't go in your condition."

"But Moms," Karen protested, "everyone's been invited. And the cook's probably got the pig half roasted. It's your birthday."

"I know."

"So what are we going to do?" Karen was stretched

out on the sofa, her plaster-casted arm resting on a pillow. "The two of us mope around together?"

"We could play cards."

"Gee—that sounds like great fun," Karen said sarcastically. "Really, Moms. Don't cancel your party. The Chinese and Uncle Brad and Grandma and everybody else will be disappointed."

"No they won't. Karen—"

"They will. Look, it's okay. I'll be all right. I'll watch television. Just bring me a doggie bag."

"Karen—are you sure?"

"Yes. But I'll feel even worse if I spoil your party. So please go and have a good time. I'm not a kid anymore. I can be by myself for a couple of hours."

Though Marianne had invited her entire team, Hollis, Jerry, and Candy were the only ones who came. Golch was also laid up with a respiratory infection (had his germs been passed on to Karen or vice versa?), and Kwong had been asked to attend a meeting of the Lin clan.

There were twelve at the table: Sarah, Hollis, Brad, the Coopers, the Hansfords, the three Chinese, Gregory, and herself. She missed Karen. Karen would have enjoyed chatting with Brad and Sarah and meeting the Chinese. She would have gotten a kick out of the sight of the suckling pig being carried ceremoniously and triumphantly in from the kitchen on a huge platter.

To Marianne, however, the drawn-out banquet was an anxious ordeal. She couldn't pry her mind away from the notion that someone here was playing the informant, feeding CHINATEX facts—and God knew what lies—about Casey. But who?

Marianne couldn't remember having had a stranger birthday party. What an odd assortment of guests. Nevertheless, she had to concede that—aside from a few unexpected rude remarks about the food from Hollis, Ed Hansford's sour face, and Sarah's clammed-up silence—the party had hung together pretty well. The conversation—admittedly fueled by *mao tai*—hadn't lagged, and no one had started an unpleasant argument.

While the pastries for which the Ban Xi was famous were being served, a young man in the red-jacketed uniform of the restaurant approached and discreetly handed her an envelope. Holding it under table level, she opened it and saw that the folded sheet was a telex from Carol. She couldn't imagine why it was being delivered here at the Ban Xi unless the message was urgent. Had something happened? Had the Billings board decided not to back Casey after all? Marianne unfolded the telex and read it:

HOLLIS LATE HORACE BLAKE MISTRESS. ALBEK NOT REAL NAME BUT ANAGRAM OF BLAKE. HER CREDENTIALS FORGED. SOMETHING FISHY. WATCH YOURSELF.

Marianne stared at the words, fighting shock and disbelief. She struggled to maintain her composure and not let the others see how stunned she was. They mustn't know, least of all Hollis.

"Anything wrong?" Brad asked.

"No." She tried to smile, though her face felt as if it had been masked in hard putty. "Just birthday wishes from Carol Olmstead."

She'd been expecting some kind of revelation all along, but not this. Her suspicions had been just that, part speculation, part fantasy, not the cold, hard type of a telex. SOMETHING FISHY. WATCH YOURSELF. She tucked the printed message into her purse, where it seemed to rest among the lipsticks and loose change like a ticking bomb.

It was true that enigmatic Hollis had never stepped out of her role as "good secretary," had never become friendly. But she was cold to everyone. It was her manner. Was there something behind that chill facade, something that Marianne had missed? Ambition? Hatred? Both?

I'll call Carol later, Marianne told herself. Straighten out the whole thing.

Gregory, bending politely toward Sarah, his hand on the pastry plate, said, "Would you like another cookie? Or whatever they're called."

"No—thank—you. I—" The "I" came out in a sudden loud gasp.

Startled, Marianne looked across at her mother. Her face had turned a ghastly white, her mouth blue. She gasped again and a horrible grimace of pain drew her lips back.

"Mother!" Marianne cried.

"Oh, God!" Sarah exclaimed. Slumping sideways, she would have fallen to the floor if Gregory hadn't caught her. The next ten minutes were chaos.

"What happened? What happened? What happ—"

"She's fainted."

"Passed out."

"Get a doctor! There must be a doctor around."

"Better an ambulance. Someone call an ambulance."

"Only for accidents in the street," Mr. Lu advised.

"Is she breathing? Here, give her room."

Gregory summoned a taxi. Brad carried Sarah to it with Marianne at his heels.

At the hospital Marianne sat at Sarah's bedside. It had been two hours since Sarah's attack and she was resting now, asleep. She had suffered a stroke, which had affected her speech and her left side. Marianne had sent Gregory back to the Garden. His restless pacing outside the ward, his loud demand for a private room had unnerved Marianne.

The doctor had informed Marianne that Sarah must have had several small strokes prior to the present one.

"But I never knew she was ill,' Marianne whispered. She turned to Brad. "Did you?"

He gave her a pained look.

"You knew! She told you and not me. I don't understand. Why?"

"She didn't want you to know."

"Why?" she demanded angrily. "I'm her daughter. Did she have to deny me daughterly concern?"

"She didn't see it that way, Marianne. She thought she was sparing you unnecessary worry. Look, there's nothing you can do. Why don't you let me take you back to the hotel. If there's any change, I'll call you."

"No. I don't want to go."

"Okay. Let me see if I can find something to drink. Hot tea would taste good."

Marianne sat watching as a tremor flitted across Sarah's face. The yellowed eyelids fluttered but remained closed. A stroke. How could keeping her illness a secret be an act of kindness? It was just one more way of shutting me out of her life, Marianne thought. She felt numb. Too much has happened tonight, the overlong banquet, the Hansfords, the condemning telex, Mother's collapse. Now Brad tells me that he knew she was ill while I didn't.

"Will—yum," Sarah said, the name emerging thickly. "Will—yum." She muttered something in Chinese. "Where did you get—that fishhh? Is it plaish? Lovely fishhh for dinner. We'll have a feasht. No, shtay on that shair where I can look at you while I clean it. Darling Willyum. Don't go away." A tear slid out from a closed eye and slowly made its way down Sarah's waxen cheek. She opened both eyes briefly, glancing blankly at Marianne before she closed them again.

The bitterness Marianne had thought she had anesthetized welled up in her, a surge of pain. Rawness scraped at her throat, smarted her eyes. It hurt so much she wanted to cry out. Sarah was reliving her life with William, her husband, but the child sitting there waiting patiently for a word, a small sign, did not exist.

"Willyum, my love, jusht hold my hand. Willyum . . ."

Unable to bear the ache of unshed tears, Marianne drifted out into the cheerless corridor. Brad, carrying a Thermos of tea in one hand and two cups in the other, emerged from the stairs and was shocked at Marianne's pale, forlorn expression.

"How's Sarah doing?"

"She's delirious. Talking in her sleep. She doesn't know me." Marianne smiled wryly. "I guess she never has."

"Sit down, Marianne." Brad's chin indicated a backless bench against the whitewashed wall. "Sit down. I think there's something you ought to know. Your mother made me promise I would never tell you this. I had to swear to it in two languages. But I'm going to break that promise."

"Are you sure you want to? I can't imagine what it could be. Let me guess. I'm not really Sarah's daughter but Aunt Em's illegitimate child raised as a niece—"

"Stop it."

"I can't help it, Brad." There was this horrible pressure behind her eyeballs and an acid taste in her mouth.

"Sarah is very ill, she might not come through," he said in a more kindly voice. "I want you to forgive her while she's still alive. For your own peace of mind."

"But I have forgiven her. I've accepted Sarah as she is and I've accepted the place I've had in her life."

"You haven't forgiven her. . . . Here, drink your tea."

It was unsugared, strong, but hot and somehow bracing.

"Do you know why your mother hadn't written to you for twenty-eight years?"

"She forgot." Oh, if I could only crawl into some quiet dark place and cry and cry.

"Marianne, please. Are you listening? Your mother didn't write because she was in prison."

"*What?*"

"In prison."

Marianne stared blankly. "But why?" she asked, dumbfounded. "How? She never said—"

"She didn't like to talk about it."

"But—but she told *you*."

"Yes. I was visiting her class one afternoon and she had an attack. Afterward she started to talk. It's a long story. She and William were first arrested in 1951 simply on the charge that they were Americans."

"But that was a short time after I was sent away."

"Yes. The Korean War had broken out and anti-American feeling ran high. They spent seven years at Quan Cha and when released came back to Canton. They hadn't been at the University long when the Chens, whom they were living with, were detained for some minor infraction. A neighborhood cadre chief had turned them in. Your parents stood up for their friends and protested. For their trouble they were also tried and sent to jail.

"When they returned again to Canton it was just in time for the upheaval of the Cultural Revolution. William was killed, as Sarah told you, and she was incarcerated. She didn't tell me much about those years. She only said that the last stretch was the worst. During previous confinements she had been allowed books, a privilege denied her at Qin Cheng. She was freed in 1977 after Mao died."

"And she never said a word, never hinted, never gave me the slightest clue. Prison!" Marianne was aghast. "Twenty-eight years. My God! She's been in jail nearly half her life!"

Horror mingling with sorrow and a sense of guilt engulfed Marianne. She thought of her mother shut off from the world for all those years, living on short rations, probably put to hard labor, unable to communicate with her loved ones. It would have killed a lesser person.

"But why didn't she tell me? Why didn't she say something?"

"She couldn't. Despite her long imprisonment she still feels loyal to Mao, she still believes in the revolution."

"But that's fantastic, idiotic!"

"It's not an uncommon feeling among the intellectuals who were persecuted. They were all dedicated to the same goal but differed in their ideas about how to attain it. Sarah said she was sent to prison by persons who were jealous of her and her husband and who had misguided concepts of what Mao wanted from his followers. Now, of course, she is quite upset because Deng is changing China's course. She feels the current premier is trashing the Great Helmsman's Liberation."

It was a martyrdom for her, Marianne thought, like Job's in the Bible, put to test after test and still holding tenaciously to his faith in God. What could possibly motivate such sacrifice? Were people like Sarah, whether Maoist or Christian idealists, motivated by an honest wish to enlighten the world, to make it a better place?

But that didn't matter. The stunning realization that

her mother's long silence had been due to imprisonment, not indifference, was all that mattered. Even if Sarah had tried to correspond with a daughter living in the United States, the letter never would have reached her.

If she had only told me, Marianne thought miserably, it would have made a difference. The barriers would have come down. But pride made her mute. Damn stubborn, willful pride. How can I forgive her? A Sarah who really loved her daughter would have explained, would have put thoughts of Mao aside, would have tried *anything* to bring them together.

A doctor emerged from the ward, the same one who had admitted Sarah.

Marianne rose. "How is she?"

"Not good." He spoke English with a French accent. An older Chinese, he had been educated in Paris, he had told Brad, and to Marianne his French training gave him an air of competence that was reassuring. "She's weak and undernourished," the doctor continued. "She's had a hard life. I'm not sure she'll make it."

Brad took Marianne's arm. "Want me to go in with you?"

"Come in a few minutes. I—I'd like to be alone with her first."

Marianne entered the ward distractedly. It was very late and the patients were in their austere iron beds, arranged in military rows that ran the length of the room. Some sleeping, some muttering, some snoring, others stretched out, hands folded on chests as if already prepared for burial.

Marianne sat down in the same chair. Sarah's eyes were closed. Marianne bent forward and whispered, "Mother? Mother, can you hear me? I know why you didn't write. Mother?" Marianne searched her mind for something that would link her to this frail woman. "Do you remember the little pink bonnet I wore as a baby? Aunt Em said I came all the way from China in it. She said you had made it. Do you remember?"

Her mother's lips trembled. Marianne moved closer to her. Sarah was humming—no, singing—in a low, barely audible, broken voice: "Shleep, baby, shleep . . . father washes . . . thy . . . mother is shaking . . . dreamland turee . . . down falsh a li'l dream on thee . . ."

But that had been Aunt Em's song, Aunt Em's lullaby! Was it possible, Marianne wondered, that a child retained the song but not the source? Was it *my* mother holding me in her arms, the squeak of *her* rocker, *her* low, sweet voice that I carried in my memory? Not Emma, but Sarah?

"Mother . . ."

Sarah's eyes opened, but the uncomprehending look was still there. After a few moments, however, the eyes began to clear, the blue deepening around the dark pupils.

"Marianne," she articulated, her tongue working around the "r" with difficulty. "Oh, Marianne." And she smiled in recognition, a smile of such infinite sweetness and love it illuminated her face, transformed it, and—for a fraction of time—made it young again.

Marianne took her mother's hand, tears brimming, washing down her cheeks. "Oh, Mother, I'm so sorry. Don't go. There's so much . . ." She put her right hand over her mouth to stifle the sobs. Behind her stood Brad. Her concentration on Sarah had been so keen, she hadn't heard him come in from the corridor.

"Mother . . ."

Brad put his hands on her shoulders to steady her. "Mother, I . . . I forgive you."

But Sarah was past that now. She had lapsed into unconsciousness. An hour later she died.

CHAPTER XXVI

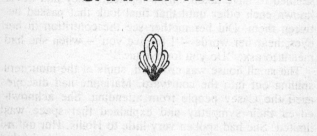

S ARAH WAS CREMATED AS SHE HAD WISHED, WITHOUT fanfare. There were no wreaths of white paper flowers, no burning of joss sticks, no firecrackers, no spirit tablets, and no cortege marching solemnly to the beat of drums. That was the way of old China. And though these customs were slowly reviving, Sarah wanted no part of such costly arrangements. Her instructions had been to treat her death as she had lived—simply, minus theology or ritual. The Chens did hold what could be construed as a memorial service, where Dr. Chen spoke of Sarah's life and dedication to China. Sarah's colleagues and students also gave short eulogies. "She was loved," Brad translated for Marianne. "She was our sister."

Karen, recovered from her fever, sat at her mother's side, holding her hand, weeping silently. Next to her was Gregory, perched on the edge of his chair, his face composed except for an occasional twitch of the jaw.

Marianne remained tearless. Her eyes ached and her mouth quivered, but the tears did not come. I'll cry

351

later, when I'm alone, she told herself. Grief gnawed at her heart. She had come to her mother too late. Years of waiting, weeks of searching for an understanding of the woman who was her mother, the attempts to breach barriers—all had ended abruptly. Finding and losing Sarah seemed to have taken only a moment. They had never known each other until that final look that passed between them. Did her mother see the contrition in her eyes, hear her words—"I forgive you"—when she had meant to ask, "Do you forgive me?"

The small house was crowded, some of the mourners spilling out into the courtyard. Marianne had discouraged the Casey people from attending. She acknowledged their sympathy and explained that space was limited. She had spoken very little to Hollis. Her unfinished business with her secretary was put aside in the face of her grief for Sarah.

"She's in heaven now," Karen said in the taxi on the way back to the hotel. "Whether Grandma felt there was a heaven or not, she's there. I think she really did believe—in heaven and God, too."

"Maybe," Marianne said, remembering how some buried impulse had made Sarah cry out His name when she was stricken at the Ban Xi.

"Moms"—Karen laid her head on Marianne's shoulder—"can't we go home?"

"Not yet." Unfinished business. The contract, which seemed to have slipped from her grasp, and Hollis. So many things to be decided, to be done. There was Gregory pressing her for a marriage, a Gregory she was no longer sure of. And Brad, whose friendship had turned into an unexpected and disturbing love.

"Canton isn't the same without Grandma," Karen said. "It's too sad. I'd like to leave."

"Soon." More unfinished business. There was Karen still to be persuaded that joining the Blessed Angels was like going into a nunnery, still to be convinced that she was too young to give up the outer, mundane world for a cloistered life with a dubious cult.

Karen, sighing heavily, lifted her head from her mother's shoulder and looked out the window. "Guess it must have rained."

The leaves on the banyan trees still glistened with raindrops, the damp beneath them, wet patches on the drying sidewalk. The sun, suddenly coming out from a bank of lowering clouds, bathed the puddled streets in a milky white light that hurt the eyes. Marianne found her sunglasses and put them on. Karen turned to her mother.

"Moms, are you going to marry Gregory?"

"I'm not sure. Would you mind?"

"Should I?"

It was an answer that told Marianne Karen would mind very much.

Marianne locked the outer door of the suite and slid the chain into its groove. She was alone, having sent Hollis on an errand to Golch and Karen to the park. What she had to do wouldn't take long.

Crossing the carpet, she entered Hollis's room. Hollis had offered to move out, as she had done earlier when Karen had returned from Nanjing, but Marianne had assured her it wasn't necessary. She and Karen didn't mind doubling up. Now Marianne was glad Hollis had remained in the suite. It would make her task easier.

Marianne stood looking around, observing the neatly made bed, a pair of bamboo armchairs, the side tables and lamps—a replica of her own room on the other side of the connecting living room. Hollis's dresser top, however, was far less cluttered, bare except for a can of Avon lilac talcum, a comb and hairbrush, and a lipstick, also Avon. The desk top held a portable typewriter, a tape recorder, a leather pad with hotel stationery, and telex blanks.

Marianne moved quickly to the desk and eased the drawer open. She found more stationery, a Guangzhou telephone directory, a room service menu, and a steno pad whose hieroglyphics she could not read.

Next she went through the dresser drawers. They revealed nothing but underclothes, surprisingly exotic for someone like Hollis: black lace bikini panties, peach teddies, and lacy slips and bras.

The closet was hung with more sober apparel, dresses and pantsuits of the conservative fashion Marianne was accustomed to seeing on Hollis. Shoes were lined up on the floor underneath: sensible walking shoes, a pair of black Amalfi pumps, and blue bedroom slippers. Two suitcases, utilitarian Samsonites, were on a shelf above. Marianne got them down. Except for some crumpled tissue paper, a few stray gray bobby pins, and a lilac sachet, they were empty.

Marianne stood thoughtfully surveying the contents of the closet again. Then, crouching, she pushed aside the hanging clothes. There at the back of the closet she saw a black attaché case. Lifting it out, she discovered it was locked. Marianne rose and went back across the noiseless carpet into her own room for her ring of keys. Two were small, one fitted her own attaché case. She couldn't remember what the other opened.

Returning to Hollis's room, she tried the second key. It went into the lock but wouldn't turn. She forced it, and the lock popped with a sound that startled her. She opened the case. In a buff folder on top were the balance sheets and tax returns from Billings she had so anxiously been waiting for. Beneath were several telexes from Carol that Marianne had never seen:

DON'T GO ABOVE AGREED FOURTEEN-FIFTY. SALES MANAGER PICKED UP TWO NEW CUSTOMERS FOR CASEY. GOOD ONES. THINGS LOOKING MUCH BETTER.

Marianne, squatting over the case, her fingers gripping the lid, felt sweat breaking out on her forehead. FOUR-TEEN-FIFTY. NEW CUSTOMERS. Facts deliberately withheld. Here was her evidence. All she needed to know. She was horrified—furious. Evidently Hollis had been giving Marianne enough of the incoming messages from Carol to keep her from becoming suspicious when she spoke to Carol on the phone, always a garbled and unsatisfactory mode of communication. The only reason

Marianne had received the urgent warning at the Ban Xi was that Hollis had not been at the hotel to intercept it.

Why hadn't Hollis destroyed the incriminating papers, the withheld messages? Ego, a monumental self-assurance. She thought she was safe, invincible. She could dispose of them at her leisure. The sheer arrogance, the deceit, the hypocrisy of this woman who pretended to be a devoted secretary infuriated Marianne. She wanted to strangle her; she could almost feel the sallow throat under her hands. But Marianne couldn't allow herself anger. She needed a clear head. She hadn't been able to contact Carol for further information and must rely on herself and the contents of the case to trap Hollis into a confession. Almost certainly Hollis would deny everything, explaining the report and telex messages in a rational way that Marianne must refute.

Marianne closed the attaché case and took it into the connecting room, where she and Hollis had set up their office on a table near the window. Glancing through the curtains, she noticed it had started to rain, a heavy downpour beating against the glass. That meant Karen would be returning shortly from the park and Marianne preferred not to have her present during what could be a stormy confrontation. She went to the phone and tried to get Brad. She wanted him to meet Karen downstairs in the lobby and keep her occupied. But Brad was teaching a class and couldn't be reached. She left a message but had little hope that he would receive it in time to intercept Karen. She had dismissed Gregory as an alternative when a key was inserted in the lock and the opening door was caught by the chain.

"Miss Oliver?"

"Just a moment, Hollis." Another tape recorder was on the work table. Marianne got it, switched it on, and shoved it under the sofa. Then she went to the door and let Hollis in.

"It's raining," Hollis said, removing her plastic scarf, shaking drops of water from it. "Golch says if nothing develops in the next few days he may have to go back to the States."

"He's not going back. Our arrangement was that he would stay until things were settled one way or another."

Hollis shrugged and started for her room.

"Wait!" Marianne's voice was harsher than she meant it to be. "There's something we have to discuss."

Marianne moved back to the table and, facing Hollis, put her hand on the case.

"Is that mine?" Hollis asked.

"It is."

"But why . . ."

"I think you know," she challenged.

"I don't. That's my personal case. It should be of no interest to you—or to anyone." There was no resentment in her voice, only a firm assertiveness.

"It's of great interest to me, Hollis." Marianne flipped the lid open. "Would you consider this report from Billings—the one that is so important to my negotiations—your personal property?"

"Oh, that," Hollis said airily. "I put it there for safekeeping until your mother's funeral was over. I know how upset—"

"Is that why you withheld Mrs. Olmstead's telex dated April 29th?" Marianne interrupted harshly. "My mother was alive then."

"You were out when it came," Hollis said. "I guess I forgot."

"It's not like you to forget—*anything*, Hollis. In fact, you have a very long memory."

"Everybody forgets. I'm not perfect. Look, Ms. Oliver, I don't believe you have any reason to give me a dressing down."

"There's a lot more I'd like to give you. You've been leaking information to our competitors."

"That's ridiculous."

Marianne decided to bluff. "Mr. Windham as much as told me so."

A faint flush appeared on Hollis's pallid cheeks. "He's lying."

"Sit down," Marianne said. "This is going to take longer than I thought."

Hollis sat in a straight-backed chair, upright, shoulders squared, her hands folded in her lap. "I don't see why you're putting me through this, Miss Oliver. I think I've proven my worth." Her voice was steady, unapologetic, without a trace of self-reproach. It was the voice of a woman who knows she has done a good job and has nothing to be ashamed of.

But Marianne wasn't buying it. "Why did you come to me with a false name and forged credentials?"

"I don't know what you're talking about."

"Albek isn't your real name."

"It most certainly is. Would you like to see my birth certificate—my passport?"

"Birth certificates and passports can be altered."

"They can be, but mine are genuine."

How cool she is, Marianne thought. What a marvelous defendant she'd make in a criminal trial, clinging to her story, unshaken by cross-examination even though she's guilty as hell.

"I have some very interesting information about you, Hollis. Your last name is not Albek, which happens to be an anagram of Blake. You and Horace Blake were lovers."

"That's ridiculous!" She gave Marianne a patronizing smile. "I've never known a Horace Blake."

"For some reason," Marianne went on calmly, "you seem to think I was responsible for Horace Blake's suicide." This too was a bluff, but a logical one. "Horace was an embezzler, no better than a common thief, isn't that so?"

Hollis blinked an eye. "I seem to have heard a few gossipy rumors about the man—an accountant, wasn't he? Accused of some petty malfeasance."

"Two million dollars is hardly petty. Blake stole two million dollars that wasn't his, got caught, and panicked. And since he was such a fundamentally weak and cowardly man, he took the easy way out."

Except for a slight, almost imperceptible hardening of the eyes, Hollis's expression did not change. "Don't you think that's putting it rather simplistically?"

"Not at all. Blake was selfish to the end, he didn't care how his actions would affect his children—his wife didn't matter—or the woman he professed to love. I'd say he was a pretty damned gutless bastard."

Hollis, her eyes blazing, sprang to her feet. "Shut up!"

"What else would you call a man who—"

"Goddamn you, you bitch! Don't you dare call Horace a gutless bastard. You and the rest of that Billings gang weren't good enough to shine his shoes. You—*you* could have saved him, but no, you sat by while they destroyed him so you could advance your own career."

Marianne, surprised that Hollis had unraveled so quickly, remained silent.

"Fucking bitch!" Hollis's voice bubbled with hate. "I suppose you have a tape recorder taking this all down. Where is it?" She looked wildly about. Then, dropping to her knees, she fished it out from under the sofa. Marianne made no move to wrest it from her.

"Thought you'd trap me, did you?" Hollis flung the tape recorder at the mirror on the opposite wall, shattering the glass. The noise registered in Marianne's head with a terrifying jolt, and for a few moments Marianne was afraid Hollis might attack her. Her knees were trembling, but she did not move. She kept standing at the table, one hand on the attaché case. Outwardly calm, her nerves honed to the sharp edge of fear, Marianne waited.

Hollis was breathing heavily. Suddenly, she sank back into her chair. "I don't give a damn. Not a damn." She covered her face with her hands. When she looked up she went on calmly. "Yes, I forged my credentials. They were going to send Betty Furlow over to you, but I paid her to let me come instead."

"What did you plan to do once you were my secretary?" Marianne asked.

"Kill you," Hollis said in a voice barely audible above the pounding rain. "I wish to God I had."

Marianne's palms went damp thinking of the near accident at the silk factory and that rat poisoning she had almost died from.

"I . . . I don't understand why you—"

"Shit, you can't understand *anything*," Hollis screamed. "You've had everything you've ever wanted handed to you. Beautiful face, brains, someone to sponsor you, everything you need in this world to get ahead. Plus two men falling all over you." She leaned forward, the marble eyes brimming with tears. "Do you know what it is to be poor—and plain? Do you know how it hurts? Horace was the only good thing that ever happened to me. His marriage was a farce. He knew his wife wouldn't give him a divorce unless he paid her price. That's the only reason he took the money. And then *you* had to blow the whistle on him. Damn you!"

Marianne, shaken but in control, said, "The dream I had, that nightmare . . . You were there so fast when I screamed. Did you intend to knife me?"

"Maybe."

"The near accident at the silk factory, the rat poison in my food . . ."

"Well what of it?"

"There's more, isn't there? Karen's fall, you managed that, too. Well, *answer me!* Didn't you?"

Hollis's lips twisted with hate. "Suppose I did."

"God! God!" Marianne, her restraint suddenly wiped out in a tidal wave of black rage, had to fight the urge to bash Hollis's complacent face. "You're a cold-blooded monster! A . . . child! How could you?" She swallowed, waiting a moment before she could find her voice.

"What puzzles me," she went on, her tone tight with suppressed anger, "is why you didn't try to kill me long before this. Not enough nerve?"

"Hell, no. From the moment Horace died I wanted to kill you. You were in Chicago. I hired a professional mugger and the fool bungled it."

"What a disappointment!" Marianne said, irony and distaste edging her voice. "Failed in every one of your clumsy attempts. But in the meanwhile you worked to see I didn't get my contract."

"Why shouldn't I? I know how much it means to you. You *used* Horace. He was the pivot on which your career turned. Why should it be crowned with success?"

"So you gave or sold information—to whom?"

"Your lover, Gregory Windham." She sneered. "All the time he's been screwing you, he's really been *screwing* you. He knew your top price. I gave him the latest Casey fact sheets and he doctored them, then slipped them to CHINATEX to make you look even worse. A prince of a guy, isn't he?"

The cold sickness Marianne had felt throughout this confrontation settled like a hard ball in the pit of her stomach. I've suspected Gregory, even confronted him, she thought. Why should I be surprised? Because I didn't want to believe the man I loved—the man who swore he loved me—was guilty. Now I have no choice. Gregory—who did not care to mix business with pleasure—has played me for a fool. The pain was so bad she wanted to cry out. But resolute will again kept her from showing any emotion. She wouldn't give Hollis the satisfaction.

"What's more," Hollis went on, her voice warped with rancor, "he's been fucking some Chinese woman on the side. I saw him kissing her outside the hotel."

"Get out!" Marianne ordered in a cold, brittle voice. She would despair later. But she had to get rid of this woman first, this horrible creature. "I don't care where you go, what you do, but get out."

When Hollis didn't move, Marianne strode into Hollis's bedroom and tumbled her suitcases from the shelf. Then she began to tear dresses from their hangers.

Hollis came up behind her and grabbed her by the shoulders, flinging her aside. Marianne lost her balance and hit the edge of the dresser. Pain shot up from her hip, a red geyser that climbed swiftly to the top of her skull.

"You bitch!" Hollis exclaimed. "You're not going to treat me like you did Horace. I'm not the pussycat he was. I'll kill you first."

She ran to the bed and withdrew a knife from under the pillow, a long, slender knife, the knife of Marianne's nightmare.

"You're mad," Marianne said.

"Angry, yes, but not insane. I've never been saner in my life."

Suddenly, curiously, Marianne felt no fear. Her mind

was lucid, uncluttered as if the painful shock of her bruised hip had dulled fright and heightened perception. She didn't think about the danger, about this out-of-control woman who threatened murder. She only thought of the necessity to outwit her, of how to get the lethal weapon from her hand.

"Give me the knife," Marianne demanded, her back to the dresser.

"Like hell."

"You won't get away with it." Reaching behind her, Marianne's fingers closed on a heavy bottle of perfume.

"Maybe not, but I'd die happy knowing that pretty face of yours was carved up."

As Hollis took a step toward her the outer door rattled.

"Moms! Open up!" Karen called. "Forgot my key! Brad's with me."

Hollis's body went taut.

"Marianne?" Brad called.

Hollis's knife hand trembled. Marianne took advantage of the moment and threw the bottle of perfume square in Hollis's face. The knife fell with a dull thud. In a flash Marianne had Hollis's arms pinned behind her as Hollis screamed in pain and dropped to her knees. The outer door crashed open.

"Marianne!" Brad called.

Hollis crumpled like a paper bag, covering her face with her hands, sobbing.

An hour later Hollis was put on a plane by the Chinese security police. She would be met in Hong Kong by a member of the local constabulary and replaned to New York with instructions to have the authorities waiting for her there.

"It's the best we can do," Brad said.

He was sitting on the sofa beside Marianne. They had barely spoken to one another other than to send Karen to the other room when the police arrived. Marianne had been shaken to her very core.

"The Chinese don't have any jurisdiction over Americans who attack Americans," Brad said. "The U.S. legation might have known how to handle her, but you said you didn't want to wait."

"No. I wanted her far, far away." Marianne fell silent again as she remembered Hollis's malevolent smile.

"Hollis was selling information to Gregory," she said suddenly.

"I'm really sorry, Marianne."

Marianne's eyes filled with tears. "If I had been smarter I would have seen it coming. I would have believed you. God, what an idiot!"

"Don't be so hard on yourself, Marianne. You're human, that means you make mistakes along the way."

He put his arm around her, the old, familiar Brad, her comforter, her confessor.

"What . . . what . . ." She swallowed past the ache in her throat. "What I can't understand is why I ever thought I loved him. I pretended his ruthlessness was vitality, ambition, a drive that I could relate to. Christ."

Brad was silent. She was too wrought up to wonder what he was thinking. If he had said "I told you so" she would have turned on him, but he sat quietly, holding her, listening.

"I knew he had faults—machismo, arrogance, a tendency to manipulate—but it seemed that he had mellowed after his son died." She lifted her tear-stained face to Brad. "I think he loved—loves me. But it's twisted. . . ."

"Could be that's the only way he knows how to love."

Marianne got up and went to the table, took a Kleenex from the box, and wiped her eyes. She heaved a deep sigh and squared her shoulders. A determined look shone on her face. "I can play dirty, too. I'll get in touch with Lu. We'll have a little talk. I won't mention any names, but he'll know he was given the wrong Casey fact sheets. I'll hint at the way some competitors wanted to deal me out of the negotiations. I'll allude to how some mill owners can't be trusted—shifty business arrangements, reneging on their contracts, things like that. Again, no names. But Lu won't be able to mistake my meaning. He'll know I'm talking about Gregory Windham."

"No holds barred, is that it?"

"You bet!"

CHAPTER XXVII

MARIANNE DREADED SEEING GREGORY FOR WHAT WAS certain to be an unpleasant meeting. But she wasn't going to slam the door on him and refuse to talk as she had seven years earlier in Hong Kong. She needed to confront him face to face.

"Why see him at all?" Brad asked incredulously when she told him her plan. "Why are you always putting yourself through hoops? In many ways you're starting to remind me of Sarah—she'd never take the easier out if there was the slightest chance she might be compromising her principles."

"It's not principle," Marianne had defended. "Gregory loved me, or imagined he did."

"Even while he was carrying on with Lily?"

"Yes. I'm not making excuses for him. I have to square things away. I'm really quite selfish, Brad. You see, it will make *me* feel better."

But it was an ordeal just the same. Gregory was not one to easily give up anything—or anyone—he felt belonged to him.

363

Gregory had laughed at first, but now he was outraged. "Hollis is crazy. She made the whole thing up. Lies."

"Why should she lie?" Marianne asked innocently. She had gone to his suite at the Garden where she could time her own entrance and exit, thus giving her the illusion of control.

"She lied because she was jealous," Gregory said. "Damn it, couldn't you see how much she resented your looks, your brains, your having me? She wanted to hurt you—didn't she say that? What better way than by making me out a Judas."

"She leaked information to *someone*."

"You'll believe her before you'll believe me?" he asked incredulously.

Was Gregory right? Had Hollis named him out of spite?

"Yes, I believe her." She wasn't going to allow Gregory to sell himself to her again. He'd betrayed her. In more ways than she cared to count.

"You're making a serious mistake, Marianne," he said sadly. He tried to embrace her.

She shrugged away. "Greg—please. Don't." It angered Marianne to think that he felt he only had to touch her to bring her to heel. A kiss and a hug and she'd fall into his lap. What conceit! "Do you think I could ever trust you, be happy with you—after this?"

"After what? You were happy enough with me before Hollis's cockeyed story."

"Do you remember telling me that you wouldn't treat me any differently than other competitors? 'Just this side of legal and not-so-legal conspiracies,' to quote you. You never wanted me to have that contract, did you? You wanted me as a well-tamed, domesticated lesser half because you love me, or so you said."

Marianne wanted to weep when she thought how much of her emotional self she had invested in this man. The thought that it might have been worse, that she might have married him, that other women had gone the same road did little to ease the pain. Yes, she could understand why she thought she had fallen in love with him

Gregory Windham, an achiever, a real charmer, a man who could be generous and loving and tender. But she saw now, as from a distance, that the price was too high. Gregory gave only when he got in return.

"I want to give the jade necklace back," she said, "and the ring—"

"Oh, Christ! *Again?* Keep the damn stuff. I don't want it." He was hurt and angry, and for a moment she felt sorry for him. But only for a moment.

"You know, Marianne," he said, his voice calmer, underlined with a steely resonance, "I could break Casey as easily as I could break a toothpick." He lifted one large hand and made a fist. "I told you before you didn't belong in the corporate world."

"I know. And you wanted to make sure I failed in it."

"For your own good. You will anyway."

"Is that a promise or a threat?"

He didn't answer.

"You really don't give a damn about me, do you? You want that contract and you don't care how you get it, even if it means stepping on or over me." She took a long, hard look at him, then stood up.

"Goodbye, Gregory."

She didn't look back as she went out.

"Moms," Karen said, "Grandma and Grandpa Hansford called while you were out. They'd like to take me to see the Seven Star Crags. We'd stay overnight at Zhouqing. Can I go?"

The eager plea in Karen's voice went through Marianne like a knife. Her daughter was fraternizing with the enemy as effortlessly as if the Hansfords had never caused Marianne a moment's distress. She knew what she wanted to say. She wanted to sit Karen down and tell her the whole sordid story. She would like to explain how Dorothy and Ed had opposed her marriage to Toby, how they had made things tough, how they had tried to get their granddaughter away and then denied the child the money that was her inheritance. Details that Marianne thought she had forgotten—the grotesque wig Toby had worn in his coffin, the black grosgrained ribbon on Dorothy's hat at the trial—came back to her now, painfully vivid. But looking down at Karen's upturned, expectant face, she knew what she must say.

"Yes. You may go."

"You're sure it's okay? You're not mad at them anymore? I know they wanted to adopt me when I was little and that you stopped talking to them because of it. Was there something else?"

"Right now it doesn't seem important. Go ahead, baby. Have fun."

"Thank you, Moms." Karen put her arms around her mother and laid her cheek next to hers. "You're terrific!"

"Haven't I always been?" Marianne asked lightly. Then, unable to let go, she held her daughter closer, a sudden tightness constricting her chest. "Did I ever tell you how much I love you?"

"Not lately," Karen said, untangling herself, kissing Marianne again.

"Will you be able to manage with that arm?" Marianne asked, afraid that in another moment she would melt into sentimental tears.

"Haven't I so far?"

"I'll help you pack."

Stuffing a pair of jeans into her duffel bag, Karen said, "You know, Moms, I'm not all that sure about the Blessed Angels anymore."

"Oh?" Take it in stride, Marianne told herself. Don't push it. "Why is that?"

"I dunno. Now that I think about it some of the people seem a little . . . I don't know . . . shallow, I guess. They pretend to know a lot about Buddha and Mohammed and even Christ, but they really don't."

Can this be? Marianne thought, trying hard not to show her elation. Am I hearing right?

"Grandma *knew* so much," Karen went on. "History and philosophy and religion, things like that. She could recite whole pieces from the Dhammapda, the Way of the Law. And poems from Tao."

"She was a scholar."

"She read *so* much."

She had time, Marianne wanted to add, years of time. During those early prison terms when she had been allowed books she must have spent hours poring over the writings of the great thinkers of the world. Or had the authorities censored what she could read? Was she permitted access to Buber and the Veda and the words of Confucious along with Mao's *Little Red Book*? Marianne didn't want to think about the tortured life her mother had endured, the suffering. Don't grieve, Brad had told her. She wouldn't want you to grieve. She loved you, I saw it on her face before she died.

If only time could be pushed back. If only she had understood.

"You look so sad," Karen said. "Do you miss Grandma Oliver?"

"Yes. Yes, I do. Very much."

"I heard something interesting at the Taiping," Jimmy Kwong said to Marianne. "Old Windham blew up at this last meeting with CHINATEX. Accused them of intentionally stalling."

"Is that good?" Marianne was still trying to get an appointment with Mr. Lu.

"I'd say yes. The rumor is that he did more. He called some of the samples they showed him shoddy. Said he was going to be giving them a huge order and wanted everything first class. That kind of act makes a lousy impression. The Chinese don't like customers who throw their weight around. They're sensitive."

"I don't blame them." She hoped the rumor was true. It sounded like something Gregory would do. "He should have left those negotiations to a China expert."

Marianne tried reaching Mr. Lu again. When she finally got him on the phone he said that he couldn't schedule a meeting for another three days. "Thursday afternoon at five. Yes?"

The fair's offices closed at five-thirty. What could they possibly accomplish in a half hour except for CHINATEX to give her a final thumbs down?

*   *   *

At Marianne's request, Brad had gone over to the Chens' to pick up a few effects Sarah had left for her daughter. It was a pitifully small bundle wrapped in blue China silk. Marianne, undoing it, felt the pathos of Sarah's poverty. A lifetime: childhood, school, marriage, motherhood, a young woman caught in the ferment of revolution, a prisoner of it, and death. This sad little packet was all there was to show, the sum total of Sarah's existence. She was sixty-three when she died, Dr. Chen told Marianne, although her mother would never admit it to Marianne. Had keeping her age a secret been her one vanity?

Brad said, "Where's Karen?"

"She's gone with the Hansfords to the Seven Star Crags. They plan to stay until tomorrow afternoon."

"Oh? Does it bother you to have Karen spending time with the Hansfords?"

"Yes and no. I'll never get to like those two. As for Karen, she'll have to decide on her own how she feels about her grandparents."

"That's very noble of you."

"I don't feel noble. Just trapped. By circumstances."

"Karen seems to like them."

"She likes most everybody. Lately, even me."

"Oh, come on, Marianne. She's always loved you."

"You wouldn't have thought so if you had heard her go on about the terrible, uncaring mother I've been when I tried to dissuade her from joining the Blessed Angels."

"All teenagers go through a period when they defy their parents, no matter what the reason."

"Well, it's a real shock when it all starts coming out." She shrugged. "I suppose they have to get that stuff off their chests. It's better. Maybe if I'd been that way with Sarah—gotten my resentments out in the open—we might have come to terms. I'll never know."

"But you and Karen seem to be getting along fine now."

"We are. She's even giving up the Blessed Angels. . . . My mother's doing, it seems."

"You probably had a lot more to do with it than you think."

"Perhaps."

Marianne looked down at the opened bundle. "Look—a ring." She held up a heavy signet ring with the initials "W.O." carved on the onyx. "My father's, I'm sure. I wonder how that survived the Red Guards."

In the small heap Marianne found an enameled comb and a silk-fringed shawl, finery Marianne couldn't imagine her mother ever having worn. There was also one of Mao's early publications, an odd bequest to make to a capitalist daughter.

"Dr. Chen said Sarah left her clothes, including the pantsuits and the coat you bought her here, to be divided among the daughters and daughter-in-law," Brad told Marianne. "He hoped you didn't mind."

"Of course not." Marianne had donated the jade jewelry Gregory had given her to the hospital where Sarah had died. They would put it toward an ambulance.

She returned to her mother's things. Unwrapping a creamy, translucent dish painted with peonies, she held it to the light. "What do you suppose it is?" Marianne asked Brad. "Ming?"

"I can't say for sure. It may very well be."

There was a thin leather-bound text of poetry written by William's father; a Swiss-made wristwatch stopped at two-twenty, its crystal smashed; and, at the bottom of the small heap, a lumpy packet done up in brittle red tissue. Marianne carefully pulled the paper aside. She saw a hank of pink wool yarn, two crochet hooks, and a pair of pink bootees that went with the pink bonnet Marianne had worn as an infant. Apparently they had been left behind in the haste to get baby Marianne to safety.

Marianne, her eyes suddenly veiled in tears, stared at the bootees, touching them with trembling fingers. She remembered the lullaby her mother had sung to her as a child. She saw her mother on her deathbed, and fought desperately for control. Damn, damn, I'm not going to cry, she told herself. It's all so foolish. What are a few strands of wool?

The paper tore as she tried to refold it. She couldn't see. A swollen lump constricted her throat, tears crowded her lids, her lashes. She impatiently brushed the tears away. It was stupid to cry. It had all happened so long ago. A lullaby, pink bootees. My God! How sentimental could you get? It didn't mean anything. There were so many terrible things to cry about: old men and women dying alone in musty rooms, people filled with hate killing one another, children starving to death in Africa, ignorance, disease, tragedies wherever you looked. But it didn't help to think about that. This pair of crocheted shoes was in some obscure way a tragedy, too. Sarah's and hers. She mustn't cry. She must be rational, mature. But the dam inside holding back so much intense feeling continued to crumble, and a moment later she found herself sobbing. Regret, grief, a sense of unutterable sadness, and, above all, guilt washed over her in a torrent of weeping she could not control.

Brad took her in his arms and she pressed her face against the solid comfort of his body.

"Let it all out, darling," he soothed. "Let it all out."

She could never let it all out—the years of waiting and wanting, the misunderstandings, the failure to communicate. The chance to make amends, to set things right, was irretrievably lost. Words left unsaid would never be spoken. How could she ever forgive herself? Why hadn't she been able to sense her mother's illness? Sarah's unhealthy waxen complexion, her shortness of breath should have given her a clue. But she had been blind, wrapped up in her own affairs, only wanting her mother to fit into a preconceived image. And now Sarah was dead and there was no way to reach her.

Gradually, Brad's tender stroking of her hair, the reassuring support of his arms, the murmured words of understanding gave her some sense of consolation.

"Poor Sarah. God, such a wasted life," Marianne sobbed.

"It wasn't wasted, Marianne. She was a woman with a purpose, just as you are."

"It was those last minutes, knowing why she hadn't sent for me or written, seeing her smile. Oh, Brad—that smile! You saw it. I loved her too late. I don't think she knew."

"Of course she did."

He led her to the sofa and drew her onto his knees, where she nestled, curled up against his chest like a child.

"It's all right, cry," Brad repeated, pressing his lips to her hair. He tilted her chin and kissed her wet eyelids, her damp forehead, her tear-smeared cheeks, her hair again.

She never knew at what point the tears suddenly ceased to flow, at what point Brad's kisses changed and became erotic and searching, nor when she began to respond with her own mouth, slowly at first, then eagerly. That he could kiss so thoroughly, so passionately astounded her. His kisses had always been so filial, a peck on the cheek, on the brow. Never like this. His hot mouth searing hers brought a feverish flush to her face. Was this really Brad, the Brad she had talked, laughed, and joshed with through the years? She pushed him away so that she could look up into his eyes as if to be certain. She saw the passion—the man—she had never seen before, the tiger eyes on fire.

"Brad?" A question, half fear, half wonder.

He pulled her back, his mouth crushing hers, hard and insistent. The arms holding her were trembling with excitement; she could hear the thud of his heart. He loved her, he wanted her, he had always loved and wanted her. Again she found herself returning his fervid kisses, all wonder and questions now lost in a tumult of sensations, lost in a river of fire that ran through her veins, burning her flesh, igniting a sharp, sweet yearning in her loins.

Naked in bed, he covered her aroused body with a frenzy of kisses, pausing, whispering hoarsely, "Marianne, Marianne, Marianne," as if her name had been unfamiliar until this moment of miracle.

She ran her hand through his hair, the tough, springy auburn that had been his trademark to her for so many years, always dear, different now, yet the same.

"I never imagined . . ." she murmured, her thought unfinished, broken by his questing hands, words lost in a sudden tremor, the thrill of astonished pleasure. The feel of his skin, the long, tough body, hard as a rock and smooth, his erection pressed against her thighs, electrified her. How could Brad's maleness have escaped her in the past?

Raising himself on his elbows, he looked down at her with eyes so full of love she wanted to weep again. She wrapped her arms about his neck and drew him close, listening to the heightened beat of the pulse in her own throat, where his lips rested.

"Some days I thought I'd go mad," Brad murmured. "Wanting you."

"Brad, I—"

"No. Don't talk. There's only now, just now . . ."

Touching, stroking, kissing, the sensual minutes expanded, became a world of time for her and Brad to discover each other, the selves they had known but not really known until this moment. Under Brad's avid mouth and exploring tongue Marianne's flesh melted into his, a union she never thought possible between two people. This was the Brad who had always been by her side, the Brad she had been fashioned for.

He knew instinctively where and how to touch, how to place lips and tongue and hands to bring out sensation after mounting sensation as if he had studied her body long before and memorized breasts and belly and her moist, pulsing sweetness. She came, one orgasm leaping into another as he moved himself up and entered her, his hazel eyes consuming her. She closed her own eyes against his devouring glance, her pelvis twisting and rising to meet each downward thrust, wrapping her legs about his hips, wanting him deeper and deeper, until a sudden shudder racked his body and a moment later she joined him in that ultimate shared ecstasy.

"Brad," she whispered, holding him tightly, not wanting to let go. "Oh, Brad, I do love you!" She felt the undiluted intensity of pure joy. Delight, tenderness, gratitude, wonder, bliss. Was this love? It had to be.

"Brad, I've been thinking," Marianne said over the breakfast table that had been wheeled into the connecting room of the suite.

"Thinking what?" Brad was happy, happier than he had ever been in his life. And she looked radiant, like a girl of sixteen. Or did he imagine it? No. She had enjoyed every moment of their night together. Her cry of astonishment when she had come told him how wonderful it had been for her, too. Glorious, precious, she had been his at last, a gift he had thought he would never receive. Even now he felt euphoric, a little drunk, seeing every object bathed in a benign light. If he died now he would be content, having lived a full life, loved by Marianne.

"What have you been thinking, love?" Love, not fraternal, but the warm, joyous, sexual and spiritual bonding between a man and a woman.

"CHINATEX, my contract."

"Contract. You ought to have dozens of contracts." Her hair was still tousled, the curve of her breasts barely veiled by the filmy negligee she wore. Delicious, fabulous.

"When I see the Chinese again," she went on, buttering a muffin, "I'm going to be firm in my price, open and frank about Casey. I'll correct the doctored sheets, of course, but I'm not going to lie about the company's financial status."

"No, no. You shouldn't lie, never lie." He could look at her and look at her and never have his fill. Marianne, a dream he had dreamt for so many years, come true. No longer a friend, no longer somebody else's wife or lover, but *his* love, *his* woman now.

"I'm going to try and make CHINATEX understand

Casey's potential," Marianne was saying. "How our success will eventually increase my purchases from them. Brad? Brad! Are you listening?"

"Of course. I hear every word. Why shouldn't I be listening?"

"You have a funny look on your face."

"Morning after." He grinned sheepishly. Had he ever been angry at her? She was such an angel. "Go on, I'm listening."

"I'm not going to mention competitors, nothing against Gregory, implied or otherwise. No dirty tricks."

"Absolutely not." She was finally his, not Gregory's or Toby's or anyone else's. She said she loved him. He knew she did.

"I'll just do my damndest to convince CHINATEX that Billings stands behind me, that any commitment I make will be honored. Sound okay? *Brad!*"

"Pardon? Yes, yes, of course."

"Oh, you!" She threw her napkin at him. "You *haven't* been listening."

"I love you, Marianne." He grasped her hand across the table.

She smiled at him. "Did I happen to mention that I love you, too?"

"I don't remember." He got to his feet and drew her from her chair. "Refresh my memory," he said, drawing her into his arms, feeling her soft curves against his body and marveling again how miracles really do happen.

CHAPTER XXVIII

MARIANNE GOT THE CONTRACT. THE SHORT SESSION with CHINATEX she had feared would be a rejection proved quite the opposite. They'd accepted Casey's bid.

The Casey team celebrated their victory at Jimmy Kwong's wedding feast. Marianne was radiant in an elegant backless gown, the top sequined in glittering blues and greens, the skirt a watered blue-green silk that flared at the ankles in a bowed ruffle. Kashmir blue sapphires dangled from her ears.

"Too ostentatious?" she asked Brad.

"The bride better beware," Brad teased.

"I'll change."

"No, you won't. You're absolutely stunning. Where's Karen?"

It was a riotous affair, combining old Chinese customs with a few touches of Americana. Kwong had hired a hall at the Sha He and had it decorated with golden-colored papier-mâché lanterns and scarlet candles. A small orchestra composed of horns, cymbals, flutes, drums, and a *yün lo* (ten gongs on a wooden frame) positioned at one end of the restaurant made up in noise for what it lacked in size. Between Chinese sets a stereo blared out the beat of Prince and Boy George while conversation and laughter strove to rise above it. The lovely bride, smooth of cheek and bright of eye, wearing a dress of traditional red (one of Marianne's wedding gifts), went from table to table to receive the toasts of her guests. Sometime during the meal several firecrackers went off, the bang-bang, pop-pop silencing the crowd for a few moments. The culprits responsible—three young boy cousins—were reprimanded by an officious-looking Chinese grandfather who came running into the room.

Balloons were released, confetti was thrown. The bride was urged to sing. She obliged with a Chinese ballad rendered in an atonal nasal voice describing two lovers— according to Brad—who were standing in the rain, weeping as they said goodbye to one another. For an encore Liyan sang "Clementine," all seven verses in English, which she had learned by rote from watching television. The Americans found the performance not only charming but hilarious and gave the pretty bride a thunderous ovation.

Karen, cheeks aglow, her hair dotted with confetti, loved the crashing cymbals and brassy horns, the bride's singing, the Mao-capped male relatives who paid serious attention to their food, the doll-faced little girls who clapped in time to rocking Prince. She admired the bride's glossy black hair, the bridegroom's owlish happiness, the bride's mother, dressed in plum silk, who sat regally in her chair beaming at everyone. Happily seated next to Golch's grandson, Rory, a young man who had just concluded a trek through Australia's outback, Karen seemed suddenly older, more mature. And Marianne noted that the couple was exchanging addresses, Rory writing his on Karen's plaster-casted arm. The cast grown dirty in the last ten days was covered with autographs of people Karen had mostly forgotten. From the way she smiled at Rory, it did not appear she would forget his. A late bloomer, Marianne thought. She's finally reached the boy stage.

Marianne and Brad said their goodbyes and left the celebration early while Karen stayed on. Rory had promised to escort Karen back safely to the hotel once the festivities were over.

"Rory seems like a nice kid," Brad remarked as they descended the stairs past rooms thronged with noisy Chinese diners.

"Very."

Standing outside in the shadows while Brad phoned for a taxi, Marianne watched one pull up to the curb. She was about to come forward to hail it when Gregory got out, followed by Lily. Smiling smugly, Lily stood by while Gregory, a disgruntled look on his face, paid the driver. He did not see Marianne. Watching Lily as she captured Gregory's arm, clinging to it possessively, Marianne experienced a fleeting sense of humiliation. Was this the role she herself had once played?

Brad, coming out to where she stood, interrupted her thoughts. "I saw your friend Gregory. Was that Lily with him?"

"Yes."

"Feel funny about seeing them?"

"You know something? I'm actually relieved. Like there but for the grace of God go I. . . ."

At the hotel Marianne busied herself at the bar fixing them both a creme de menthe on the rocks.

"I've been playing around with the idea of Casey expanding into ready-made clothing, women's wear," Marianne said, pouring the green liqueur from jigger to glass. "But I've decided not to use cheap Hong Kong or Mainland labor. I'm interested in a quality line. Do you realize how silk fabrics have revived in popularity? There are polo shirts, raincoats, blouses, dresses, lingerie. Even men's suits made of silk. Silk blends, too. It could be very exciting. I could hire a first-class designer, create a distinctive line of clothes the sophisticated woman feels she can afford. Get a good ad campaign going. Twist the Board's arm for the money—TV, department store promotions, direct mail, newspaper and magazine ads, the works."

"Sounds challenging," Brad said. "But before you venture into tomorrow, I'd like you to come right here." He motioned, opening his arms wide.

"Just imagine," she said, snuggling in his embrace, her mood suddenly changing. "Silk. All those centuries of romance and intrigue behind a fabric that starts with a little worm feeding on mulberry leaves. Caravans of ancient Romans and Persians trekking over deserts and mountains just to trade for that precious cloth. China silk! And here I am—admittedly by a much easier and open route—on the same quest."

"So in spite of everything that's happened, you're still glad you came to China?" Brad questioned.

Marianne smiled in answer, her eyes glowing. Happy eyes at last, bright with tears. The eyes of a woman who had been on a long, lonely, tortuous journey all her life, and who now, at last, had come home.

All Futura Books are available at your bookshop or
newsagent, or can be ordered from the following address:
Futura Books, Cash Sales Department,
P.O. Box 11, Falmouth, Cornwall TR10 9EN.

Please send cheque or postal order (no currency), and
allow 60p for postage and packing for the first book
plus 25p for the second book and 15p for each additional
book ordered up to a maximum charge of £1.90 in U.K.

B.F.P.O. customers please allow 60p for
the first book, 25p for the second book plus 15p per
copy for the next 7 books, thereafter 9p per book

Overseas customers, including Eire, please allow £1.25
for postage and packing for the first book, 75p for the
second book and 28p for each subsequent title ordered.